CONSEQUENCES

BY THE SAME AUTHOR

FICTION

The Photograph
Making It Up
Spiderweb
Heat Wave
Cleopatra's Sister
City of the Mind
Passing On
Moon Tiger
Pack of Cards and Other Stories
According to Mark
Corruption
Perfect Happiness
Next to Nature, Art
Judgement Day
Treasures of Time
The Road to Lichfield

AUTOBIOGRAPHY

A House Unlocked
Oleander, Jacaranda: A Childhood Perceived

PENELOPE LIVELY

CONSEQUENCES

VIKING

VIKING
Published by the Penguin Group
Penguin Group (USA) Inc., 375 Hudson Street, New York, New York 10014, U.S.A.
Penguin Group (Canada), 90 Eglinton Avenue East, Suite 700, Toronto, Ontario, Canada M4P 2Y3 (a division of Pearson Penguin Canada Inc.)
Penguin Books Ltd, 80 Strand, London WC2R 0RL, England
Penguin Ireland, 25 St Stephen's Green, Dublin 2, Ireland (a division of Penguin Books Ltd)
Penguin Books Australia Ltd, 250 Camberwell Road, Camberwell, Victoria 3124, Australia (a division of Pearson Australia Group Pty Ltd)
Penguin Books India Pvt Ltd, 11 Community Centre, Panchsheel Park, New Delhi – 110 017, India
Penguin Group (NZ), 67 Apollo Drive, Mairangi Bay, Auckland 1311, New Zealand (a division of Pearson New Zealand Ltd)
Penguin Books (South Africa) (Pty) Ltd, 24 Sturdee Avenue, Rosebank, Johannesburg 2196, South Africa

Penguin Books Ltd, Registered Offices: 80 Strand, London WC2R 0RL, England

First published in 2007 by Viking Penguin, a member of Penguin Group (USA) Inc.

ISBN-13: 978-0-7394-9048-8

Printed in the United States of America

TO JEAN

CONSEQUENCES

Part 1

THEY MET ON A BENCH in St. James's Park; it was the sixth of June 1935. Lorna was crying because she had had a violent argument with her mother; Matt was feeding the wildfowl in order to draw them. He sat with his sketch pad on his lap, one hand in perpetual motion, the other chucking an occasional morsel in order to keep the birds attentive. He drew; the ducks shoved one another and commented; Lorna stopped crying and watched, increasingly entranced. When eventually Matt became aware of her, he looked sideways, and was done for.

Some while later, they went to a tea shop. By now, Lorna had learned that the duck-sketching exercise was in the service of a commission to illustrate a book on estuaries and waterways. Matt was an artist, primarily a wood engraver. He learned—or rather, came to understand, since she spoke of none of this—that Lorna was a girl somehow at odds with her circumstances. They sat for several hours over a pot of tea and a plate of cakes, and then they wandered the streets, impervious to time. By the end of the day, both realized that their lives had altered course. Lorna went home to Brunswick Gardens to a further outburst of disapproval from her mother. Matt knew only that he must see her again, and forever.

In due course, she brought him to the house and presented him to her parents, who were initially gracious, if a touch cool. When subsequently Lorna's father discovered that wood engraving was not a hobby but Matt's livelihood, the condescending interest turned to *froideur.* He told Lorna that this artist chappie was a nice enough young man but it wouldn't do to let things go any further, d'you see? Lorna replied that things already had: she and Matt were engaged. She was wearing on her finger a little Victorian ring that they had bought in the Portobello Market the previous week for ten and sixpence. Matt had pawned an easel in order to pay for it.

Gerald Bradley shouted; Lorna sat in mutinous silence. Marian Bradley came in, wrung her hands, and joined in the shouting, at a ladylike level. When the scene had run its course, Lorna got on a 73 bus to Islington, where she found that Matt had just taken the first proof print of the duck engraving. There was the swirl of ducks in the foreground, their plumage intricately textured; beyond was the sparkle of water and the patterned fall of willows, leading the eye somehow deep into the picture, so that it became three dimensional, an intricate and calculated reflection of the backdrop to their meeting; she saw that place, but saw also now this artifact that was the brilliant expression of his hand and eye. And to one side, framed by ducks, was a small distant figure seated on a bench, a girl—dark hair, white curve of a dress. "That's you," he said.

They were married at Finsbury Town Hall. The witnesses were Matt's friend Lucas Talbot and Lorna's old school friend Elaine, who was in a lather of excited anxiety and kept repeating, "I don't know *what* your parents are going to say." After the deed was done, the four of them had an awkward lunch at a Lyons Corner house, Elaine still twittering, and clearly not much taken with long lank Lucas, who ran a small printing press in Fulham. Then Lorna and Matt went to Brunswick Gardens to face up to the Bradleys.

In years to come, they would recount that her father had actually said, "Never darken my doors again." This was poetic license, but the message ran along those lines. There was a short, cold exchange in the drawing room, where the two couples sat on sofas, confronting one another across a great bowl of lilies whose scent filled the room. From elsewhere in the house came the loud assertive voices of Lorna's two older brothers, joshing one another. At one point the parlor maid knocked to ask if tea would be required. Lorna's mother replied that it would not. There was no shouting on this occasion; Marian Bradley was aggrieved and petulant, her husband had withdrawn into a mood of disgruntled dismissal. A great gulf opened, into which the lilies sweetly fumed. Everything that might be said hung in the air, until none of them could stand it any longer, and Lorna went up to her room to gather up a suitcase of clothes, while Matt waited in the hall. Downstairs, Gerald had a stiff whiskey and Marian rang for the maid: perhaps tea wasn't such a bad idea after all.

"What was so appalling about an artist?" Lorna would wonder, much later. "There was art on their walls. They bought pictures. Daddy had William Nicholson paint Mummy's portrait."

And Matt would laugh. "Exactly. Tradesmen. Not the sort of people you want marrying your daughter. Irregular habits, erratic income. He was quite right."

Relations were resumed within a few months, of a kind. Letters and Christmas cards were exchanged. By that time, Lorna had become someone else, perhaps the person that she was always meant to be. Her mother wrote breezy little missives about social events and the boys' sporting fixtures; for Lorna's birthday she sent a silk purse from Harrods. Opening this at the kitchen table in Somerset, Lorna felt as through she were in receipt of goods from another planet; her previous life seemed now like a myth, somewhere she had dreamed away her early years.

Matt knew only that he was entirely happy, wholly in love, and that years of this rolled ahead, waiting for him.

When she was a child, Lorna did not understand that London is a huge city. Oh, it went quite a way, she realized that—she had been on the bus right from Kensington to Piccadilly Circus. And the park was immense, a great green expanse reaching from the homely familiar base of the Round Pond and Kensington Gardens to distant Park Lane. But that was the extent of it. Beyond that. . . . Well, she really had not much idea if there was anything beyond that, except that there were outposts to which she had been taken, like Buckingham Palace, and that other park alongside, and Trafalgar Square with the lions, and the great wide glitter of the river. It was not until much later, years later, in time of war, when the bombs were falling, that she heard of Poplar and

Stepney and Lambeth and somewhere called the City of London. But by then she was far away, amid the Somerset hills, alone, a child on her knee, anxiously tuning the wireless for the six o'clock news each evening. The world was in flames, and London with it, both the London she had known and that other London of which she had been entirely ignorant. At those moments, it seemed to her that time and space compacted; she dipped back into that other place, where they knew nothing of what was to come, and felt some strange kind of compassion.

She spent her childhood in Brunswick Gardens, in a big white stucco house flanked by other big white stucco houses from which emerged each day men much like her father, wearing dark suits and bowler hats, carrying furled umbrellas, and women much like her mother, in silks and furs, and children much like herself, who trotted beside nannies pushing high shiny prams. When she was small her day revolved around the afternoon walk to the Round Pond, and drawing-room tea later with her mother, if her mother was at home. This was a timeless period from which there floated up occasional images: the jewel-green feathers of a preening duck, a golden cavern in the coals of the nursery fireplace, the treasure trove of gleaming brown conkers in long wet grass. Later, when she was older, there were morning lessons with other little girls and a governess in a neighbor's house, and later still she went to the Academy for Young Ladies on the farther side of Kensington High Street, where she did French and piano and some history and poetry and elocution, until she was seventeen and it was felt, supposedly, that she had learned enough by now.

Her brothers, two years and four years older than she was, had long since been hived off into an exclusive male world; they had vanished into boarding schools, and had come back in long trousers, with hoarse voices, talking in code. Then they disappeared again, to Oxford, and returned occasionally to treat her with kindly patronage. She did not much like them, and felt bad about this. They were lords of creation: the Boys. Her father smiled upon them with gruff indulgence; her mother fluttered around them, proudly attentive to their needs. They brought their Oxford friends to the house, who seemed to Lorna like a set of brother-replicas—the same robust confident voices, the same jokes, the same aura of some exclusive fraternity. She was eighteen, and would shortly embark upon the extended initiation ceremony that was obligatory for girls of her class and background. She would have to spend the next couple of years going to cocktail parties and balls and weekend parties, at which she would meet more and more young men. She presumed that most of these would be like her brothers and their friends. If by the end of this period she had not signed up for marriage, she would have deeply disappointed her mother and would be seen as a failure. The whole prospect filled her with gloom.

She knew that she was not like other girls of her kind. She got on well enough with them, she had friends, but she could not share their compliance with the expected routines of shopping excursions, dress fittings, social visits alongside mothers. She did not know what it was that she wanted, only that it should not be this. From time to time she had caught glimpses of alien interesting worlds. She came across paintings, furnishings, clothes that were exotically different from those favored by her parents and their circle; she became aware of people who lived quite differently, who turned their backs on the mandatory life structure centered upon a good income and a handsome house, who lived in a hand-to-mouth kind of way, like poor people did, in lodgings or cottages and houseboats, who did not have jobs, who painted or wrote books. Such folk were the butt of jokes in the copies of *Punch* that lay on the drawing-room table at Brunswick Gardens—sandal-wearing vegetarians in smocks—but Lorna did not find *Punch* particularly funny. She was more interested in this proof that there was another way of living, out there in the grown-up world, a way that did not require shopping in Knightsbridge, and dressmakers, and enrollment in the lineup as wife material. She thought it quite possible that she might want to get married, one day, but she flinched at the idea of a life spent with one of her brothers' friends.

She heard of girls who went to university, and raised this with her parents, who were aghast. Her mother told her that no man liked a bluestocking; her father said the varsity wasn't appropriate for a girl, but she could do a domestic science course if she so wished.

She had been quite good at drawing when she was at the Academy for Young Ladies. She made a bid for art college, and was laughed out of court. Her mother said she would be mixing with the most unsuitable types; her father didn't say anything, merely raised his eyebrows.

She went underground. She joined Kensington Public Library, and began to read—serendipitously, eclectically. She read novels and poetry and travel books and thus escaped—briefly—from the Brunswick Gardens regime, in which she was soon caught up as a fully fledged junior adult. She must now help her mother to arrange flowers, she must do local errands, she must walk the dog. In the afternoons she must shop with her mother, or pay visits, or go to the Hurlingham Club and play a game of tennis with old school friends. In the evenings—well, in the evenings there began now the considered process of her display in the marketplace. In the evenings she must wear a pretty frock—smile, dance, be pleasing.

In the books that she read nobody did this kind of thing. She recognized in Jane Austen a mirror world, of a sort, but elsewhere she found conduct and assumptions that were a revelation. She read *Ann Veronica* and *The Constant Nymph,* with gathering interest. She read about love, and became increasingly convinced that it was not to be found in drawing rooms and at country house parties. But love, in a sense, was neither here nor there. She was not in any desperate hurry for love; more, she wanted confirmation that the system into which she had been born was not necessarily inevitable, that there were alternatives and that they were fine, they were neither laughable as proposed by those *Punch* cartoons nor disreputable as implied by her mother's bland rejection of all practices that did not conform with her own. Her mother—and everyone that her mother knew—operated according to a set of rigid requirements, which dictated how you should dress, down to the precise width of a lapel and set of a hat, which told you how to furnish your home, how to behave in specific social circumstances, how to speak, breathe, live. Those who failed to conform were seen, quite simply, as misfits: they were not one of us.

In her surreptitious, underground explorations, Lorna began to find not just proposals of an alternative world but also of an alternative self. She discovered unsuspected tastes and enthusiasms. She bought bright posters from art galleries which she stuck up in her bedroom: Matisse, Dufy, Klee. She saved up her allowance and achieved some clothes of her own choice—lighter, brighter, different—and wore them when she dared, in defiance of her mother's cries of outrage: "But it's such a horrid color, darling. You look like a gypsy. Go and put on the new tussore silk."

She and her mother clashed more and more. Lorna was branded difficult. She heard the word through half-closed doors, her mother in complaint to her father: "She is being so wretchedly difficult these days."

Lorna looked at the rest of the family and thought that she was like a changeling in fairy stories. Her brothers were tall, fair, rawboned. She was small, dark, and neat. She sat at her dressing table and stared at her triangular face, framed in a short dark bob, and could find nothing of her father's large florid countenance, but there was a little fold of skin at the corner of her eye that was a betrayal—he too had that. And her nose was her mother's—narrow, slightly uptilted. I am theirs all right, she thought, there was not some unfortunate mistake in that expensive nursing home where I was born. But something got left out when I was assembled—whatever it is that makes you comfortable with what you have been given.

She knew that she was privileged. She had only to look about her. As a child, she had taken for granted all that visible evidence that there were two kinds of people in England—those who had and those who had not. Or rather, gradations of having, from those like her parents and their friends, who had everything, through others who had perhaps an adequate sufficiency, to those who apparently had nothing much at all, who drove the rag and bone cart, hawked matches, begged on street corners, smelled not very nice, and should be given a wide berth. She grew up with instinctive awareness of social status, attuned like everyone else to nuances of speech and behavior, with an eye that could place a person at once by the clothes they wore, by what they were doing. You did not think much about it, you simply knew. Unconsidered, the world just seemed conveniently defined, with different categories of existence, rather like the big nursery jigsaw puzzle, with its horses and cows and sheep and pigs and hens and geese.

But a time came when other responses crept in. Embarrassment; sympathy; curiosity. She saw herself through the eyes of others, and did not much care for what she saw. She looked at the rotted teeth and rickety legs of the old woman who begged at the tube station, and winced.

When they drove out into the country in her father's Rover, she eyed the street upon street of little houses in which other lives happened, of which she knew nothing, and she wondered. So she was privileged, she was among those who were to be envied. But she could not feel enviable or grateful; some part of her protested, was critical and hostile and . . . difficult. It was as though she had some alter ego who told her she did not belong here. But she had never known anywhere else, and where else could there be?

She began to question the most sacred assumptions. Why must some people be poor? Why do I have to wear stockings, and gloves? Why are men's and women's lives different? Why must I go to the Langfords' dance tonight? Her mother sighed and shook her head. Her father folded his newspaper, stared at her, and said he hoped she wasn't becoming a silly little socialist. Her brothers laughed and patted her on the head and went about their business.

Lorna and her mother were permanently at odds. Lorna sat sullenly in a corner throughout a debutant tea party; her mother said that she was ashamed of her, she had let everyone down. She declined a dinner invitation from a red-faced young man who had pawed her in a taxi, and who talked of nothing but horse racing; her mother observed that the young man's father owned a thousand acres in Gloucestershire. She was silent and rebellious at dress fittings; she read a book when cousins were visiting; she went off on her own and did not tell her mother where she was going. There were heated exchanges; doors were slammed.

And thus it was that on an exquisite June morning Lorna sat weeping on a bench in St. James's Park, with the willows cascading into the lake, and a cohort of bright-feathered ducks eddying about at her feet. She became aware that she was not alone on this seat, looked sideways, stopped crying, and the rest of her life began.

When Matt was young he did not know where London was. The word was familiar; you heard it on the wireless or in conversation, that thumping sound—London. It meant Big Ben and the Houses of Parliament, and solders in red coats and crazy black hats; the King and Queen lived there; its people talked Cockney. His parents had never been to London, nor indeed had anyone he knew. The place was an irrelevance, for those living in a small market town close to the Welsh border. Matt's father was a local government official; his interests were sternly focused and his horizons parochial. He had been born in the town and had never seen any reason to stray farther than Chester, for an annual dinner from which he returned with a sigh of relief. Matt's mother came from a village three miles from the town, to which she had moved when she was a girl to work at the Town Hall, where David Faraday was a junior functionary. The family joke was that they had courted beside the tea urn, which accounted for Mary's addiction to tea.

When Matt was sixteen he learned where London was. By the time he was seventeen he knew that he had to go there, not on a visit but for a long time. This knowledge sprang from several years of communion with Mr. Lavery, the art master at the grammar school, who was his mentor and friend. The words "art college" fell from Mr. Lavery's lips when the two of them were standing before Matt's pen and wash drawing of a landscape beyond the town, a piece of work that even Matt—a modest lad—could see was pretty good. "What is an art college?" he asked.

Mr. Lavery told him, and the seeds were sown.

A year later, he said to Mr. Lavery, "What is a wood engraving? How is it done?" He had in his hand a book that he had bought for a shilling in the secondhand bookshop on the High Street: *Erewhon* by Samuel Butler, with wood engravings by Robert Gibbings.

It was not the text that had appealed to him, but the illustrations, at which he had gazed with fascination.

Mr. Lavery explained. Matt said that he wished he could have a go himself. Mr. Lavery explained further: wood engraving is a sophisticated and highly technical form of graphic art, dependent on an expensive material—boxwood—and alas, not really appropriate for the curriculum of a school art department. He talked further about art colleges.

Bryony, Matt's elder sister, was going to be a teacher. She, too, had achieved grammar school, the girls' institution on the other side of town, and had excelled. She was the pride of her parents, and was spoken of approvingly among the neighbours; education was highly regarded in those parts and at that time. Bryony would go to teacher training college in Chester; her mother worried about the evils of metropolitan life but felt that Bryony had the strength of character to cope. She was a serious and rather taciturn girl; she and Matt found less and less to say to each other as they grew older, and cohabited in a kind of amiable boredom.

Art had stolen up upon Matt. It fingered him when he was quite young, he later realized, remembering an infant passion for pencils and paper, and later endeavors with sticks and stones and leaves and seeds and berries that could be turned into intricate sculptural arrangements upon the garden path. He had always wanted to make things. Not the mechanical constructions of model airplanes or meccano but things that demanded original materials, flair, and ingenuity. He had found a seam of clay in a field beyond the town and made little sculptures, which he tried to fire in his mother's oven, to her distress. He discovered the possibilities of papier-mâché, using glue and newspaper, and created an elaborate bas-relief of Theseus and the Minotaur, inspired by the primary school's *Book of Myths and Legends*. He requested crayons and paints for Christmas and birthday presents, and scrounged paper from rubbish bins and local shops. And then when he arrived at the grammar school there was that fertile ground of the Art Room, and the heady encouragement of Mr. Lavery. He borrowed books on art from the town library and pored over the Italian Renaissance, French classicism, Rembrandt, Turner, Constable, the Impressionists. He was long familiar with the town's small art gallery, which held the work of several local nineteenth-century painters and not much else; now he was amazed by these revelations of exalted practice. So this was what art could do.

He became Mr. Lavery's special project, with license to haunt the Art Room in free periods and after school. Mr. Lavery wore a corduroy jacket with leather-patched elbows, smoked Woodbines, and lived alone in a terrace cottage on the edge of town. A small exhibition of his work at the school had caused some consternation among parents, who had been anticipating a few peaceable watercolors. Mr. Lavery was into Vorticism. The parents toured the exhibition, tight-lipped, and hoped to one another that he was not teaching the boys this sort of thing.

They need not have worried. By and large, their sons were not remotely concerned with art; art periods were regarded as intervals of light relief, when you let off steam. Mr. Lavery was prepared for this; he maintained a kind of order by way of laconic wit at the boys' expense. They recognized him as a maverick form of adult, whose opinions and behavior hinted at worlds with which they were unfamiliar, and were accordingly wary or contemptuous, depending on temperament. Either way, they did not care to provoke his ironic comments, and tempered their behavior; mostly, they just made it clear by their halfhearted application that they had better things to do than mess about with this sort of stuff.

Except for Matt. He realized early on that if he was going to persist with his unorthodox commitment he would have to learn to ride out the derision of his peers. The few boys in the school with a serious commitment to music had the same problem. The esteemed activities here were cricket, rugby, and athletics. Matt was fortunate in that he was robustly built. Those inclined to torment him as an arty-farty came to recognize someone who did not care much about what others said in any case, and who was likely to give as good as he got if it came to a dustup. In time, Matt was allowed to go his own way, somewhat solitary but not unpopular, seen simply as an eccentric, but a person to be reckoned with.

Mr. Lavery was astute enough not to pay too much overt attention to Matt. Matt's work was in a class of its own; he knew this, and Matt knew that he knew it, and to make too much of that would have done Matt no good. His tutorship of Matt became a personal matter, pursued in the privacy of the Art Room out of hours. Here, he kept Matt supplied with materials, suggested new directions, criticized and encouraged, and when Matt was seventeen Mr. Lavery began to speak of art colleges.

At first, David and Mary Faraday were dubious. They appreciated that Matt had evident talent—were proud, indeed—but the notion of formal training in this area was foreign to them. His father could not see what it would lead to, and wondered about work prospects. His mother shied violently at the notion of London.

"But why would you have to go *there?*"

"Because that's where the best colleges are. Mr. Lavery says so. He says Liverpool or Chester wouldn't do. Mr. Lavery says it's the Grosvenor School of Modern Art I should aim for, in London."

The image of London presented itself, as the family sat around the supper table. Bryony saw the King and Queen receiving her brother on the balcony of Buckingham Palace, and was irritated. Matt saw an immense light-filled studio in which students stood before easels, and an elevated version of Mr. Lavery cruised among them. His mother saw streets lined with women of ill-repute, and blanched.

His father saw expense, and said so.

"Mr. Lavery says I could get a scholarship. He says he'll write letters for me. He wants to talk it over with you."

And thus Mr. Lavery's cautiously floated proposal took shape, blossomed, generated much correspondence, the selection of a portfolio of Matt's work and, eventually, a trip to London for Matt, his portfolio under his arm and many instructions from his parents and Mr. Lavery in an envelope in his pocket.

He was amazed by the place—by its size, its dirt, its streaming impervious crowds of people—but he was too fraught about the task in hand to pay more than superficial attention. He must now expose his work to people who were accustomed only to the best. To do so felt both presumptuous and exhilarating; at one moment he was unbearably diffident, at another excitingly assured. "Just be yourself," his parents had said, won over at last by Mr. Lavery and the contemplation of

Matt's evident promise. But who was he? A schoolboy from the sticks? An aspiring artist? Both. And also a person whom he sensed but still hardly recognized—a maturing self who had conviction and opinions and boundless determination. He would get this scholarship; he would go to London, he would be an artist, come what may.

When the letter from the Grosvenor School came, and he read it out to the family, his mother sat stricken and speechless; the women of ill-repute were right there in the room now, leering. Matt's father said, "Well done, son." Bryony, impressed despite herself, looked at her schoolboy brother and decided that this was perhaps a person of some account. She recognized that art has a certain cachet, and realized with private chagrin that those drawings and paintings that Matt had from time to time allowed the family to see must, after all, be the real thing, or, at least, some eery accessory to the real thing. She gave Matt a kindly cuff on the shoulder, and said she hoped he wasn't going to get all uppity now. His mother rallied, faced down those lurking women, and began to talk anxiously of clothes, equipment, and sheltered accommodation.

Matt was by nature buoyant, but he now experienced a wild exhilaration, a sense that he had not before known, soaring above the exigencies of daily life. He could hardly believe his good fortune. And yet at the same time he knew that he had been right in that kernel of self-belief he had always had, that Mr. Lavery had been right in his support, and that he could join his peers in that imagined studio, knowing that he was as good as they were, and perhaps better than some. But, beyond and above all that, he savored the knowledge that, miraculously, his life was now on course. He was licensed to do exactly that which he wanted to do, for the next three years at least. After that—well, after that would be up to him, but for the foreseeable future he could spend each and every day doing what he liked best: he could draw, he could paint, he would learn wood engraving.

All this came to pass, not as he had imagined it, partly because reality never conforms to expectations but also because he himself became a subtly different being. The London at which he had gawped in amazement on that first visit became a familiar element through which he moved with ease; he learned how to manipulate the city, how to live cheap, how to use it. And the art college itself, at first a bewildering experience of alien attitudes and assumptions, of astonishing license, of people who spoke differently, dressed differently, lived differently, became within months a natural habitat, and he a distant older relative of the boy who had arrived there, and had placed himself nervously before an easel on that first morning.

Matt grew up. He shot through several years in each of the first months, or so it seemed. He felt as though he was some hatching insect, the dragonfly bursting free. He had friends, he had a mattress on the floor of a much-occupied attic, above all he had uninhibited access to a studio and to practicing artists who encouraged and criticized. He worked in pubs and bars to pay for paints and materials—the art college supplied only a certain amount. He sold some work shown in a student exhibition. And, above all, he became an engraver.

From the moment that he first placed a block on the sandbag and made the initial tentative lines with the graver, he knew that that intuition had been right: this was his medium. He could not have said exactly why; it had to do with the complexity of the process, the way in which what you first saw and drew—that image of a real scene—must be passed from one material to another, from the sketch pad to the tracing paper to the block and thence eventually to its final form, the subtle and delicate arrangement of black and white that was the finished print. But it had to do also with the way in which the fortuitous shapes and patterns of the physical world—trees, water, sky, buildings—were transformed by hand and eye into something that reflected what you saw but had now become a creation in its own right: the engraving was a dazzling black-and-white complement to the world of color.

Wood engraving thrived right now. He pored over the work of his eminent older contemporaries—Eric Gill, Robert Gibbings, Edward Wadsworth, Gertrude Hermes, Blair Hughes-Stanton—and sat at the feet of his own distinguished teacher, Iain Macnab. He learned the possibilities of the form, the potential; he saw how each artist makes of it something different, something new. He thought: I can do this.

And the time was ripe. There was a demand for the work of a

promising engraver. At a party after the college's annual student show, in his last year there, Matt met Lucas Talbot, a man a few years older than himself who earned a tenuous living as a fine press publisher. The Heron Press operated from Lucas's dilapidated Victorian house in Fulham; he invited Matt to visit, and acquaintance blossomed into friendship. Lucas was, in a sense, everything that Matt was not; he was awkward, shy, socially inept, alarmed by women. Matt had been at the hub of student activity at the college, talked easily to anyone, was sexually confident. They liked one another immensely. Lucas knew that Matt was already a fine engraver, and that he would soar. Matt admired Lucas's ferocious dedication to the creation of handsome editions. Within weeks Lucas had commissioned Matt to work on a series that he planned on English topography.

"W-w-which do you fancy?" he asked—the stammer always surfacing at moments of diffidence or excitement, "Moors and mountains or estuaries and waterways?"

Matt hesitated, unaware that the rest of his life hung in the balance. "Um . . . I don't really mind, either sounds good . . . Oh, let's say estuaries and waterways."

"Done," said Lucas. "Would thirty guineas for the twelve prints be all right? I'm afraid I can't manage any more."

Matt, for whom this would be comparative riches, said that this would be fine. Between them, they began to plan the structure of the book and the subject matter of Matt's engravings.

In the interests of which, on that June morning, he selected a bench in St. James's Park, put his sketch pad on his knee, took some stale bread from his pocket, and thus invited the fates to smile upon him.

The cottage stood beside a lane. At the front, it looked out over the high hedge bank of its garden, across the lane and the sloping field beyond to a wooded valley that reached up into the Brendon hills. Behind, fields and copses rolled away down to the Bristol channel coastline; there was a long thin slice of pewter sea and, on a clear day, the distant shore of Wales. Square and squat, cob and thatch, dug solid into the red Somerset earth, the small building had seen out generations of farm laborers. People had been born here, died here, had heard rumors of wars, had achieved the vote, had sweated over the same patch of landscape and stared at the same sky. Now, the place stood empty, bar the mice and the black beetles and the spiders. Empty, and two pounds a month.

Matt and Lorna stepped gingerly inside. The place smelled of damp, and two centuries of wood smoke, and a faint suggestion of the dead jackdaw that had fallen down the chimney and lay on the hearth, a brittle carcass. Matt picked it up and carried it out. He threw it into the hedge and stood for a moment, noting the view of the hills. He saw the roof of a house in the valley, with smoke curling up from a chimney; he saw stooked corn in a field: he saw the distant dotted shapes of sheep. He saw pattern and structure; pictures began to form in his head.

He went back into the cottage and joined Lorna on a tour of inspection. There was one main room on the ground floor, into which the front door opened directly; an open fireplace with a blackened kitchen range, a stone sink. Another, smaller room led off this, with a window that looked out onto the long triangular garden. Shaggy grass, gooseberry bushes, apple trees, and a plot that remembered vegetable gardening, with some stumps of cabbage and a tangle of long-rotted beans.

"It's the Marie-Celeste," said Matt. "Where did everybody go?" There was a built-in dresser in the main room, empty but for a cracked cup, a child's rusted tin top, a moth-eaten tea cosy.

A wooden staircase led to the upper floor. Two rooms and a landing. They stood at the window of the largest room and looked down toward the coast. A small ship perched on the silver streak of the sea. The fields were pale bleached stubble, or rich red plough; the hedges and woodland were darkest green.

Lorna said, "This is our bedroom."

"Are you sure? This place means oil lamps, and candles, and water from the tap outside. You have never lived like that."

"Have you?"

"Not quite."

"Then maybe it's time we did."

Outside, there were two sheds. The smaller one, at the end of a short path from the back door, housed the privy. The other had a concrete floor, a window, and a long workbench all along one side.

"Aha . . ." said Matt.

There was a standpipe beside the door. Matt tried the tap: water gushed. "It's from the stream, I suppose. We'll need jugs, basins, a tin bath."

Beside the larger shed, a lean-to sheltered the remains of a log pile. Matt picked up chunks of wood, stacked them one upon another. "And a saw, and an axe, and a wedge. The village is over a mile away, do you realize?"

"Bikes," she said. "And one day, when you're rich and famous, a little car."

"It is not always going to be a sunny afternoon in September. In the winter things will be very different."

"I didn't know you had this pessimistic streak. What else am I going to discover today?"

He put his arm around her shoulders. "I don't want you to be under any illusion about what it may be like here, that's all. And what will you do all the time?"

"Do?" she cried, "Do?" She flung out her hand. "When there's all that out there? Explore. I've never seen the countryside except through the windows of Daddy's car. And dig this garden. And clean up that range and learn how to cook."

And make a home, she wanted to say, but thought it mawkish. The first home that will be the way I want it, and a million miles from Brunswick Gardens.

"We might find something in the village with running water and electricity."

"Not for two pounds a month. Not with a view of half Somerset."

They had arrived here by chance, luck, by a series of unconsidered movements. They had traveled, somehow, from the bench in the park to this implacable little building. Lorna thought: it has been waiting for us. Matt thought about tools, and a spade and a fork, and furniture, and, one day, a printing press.

After the wedding, they had left London. A friend of Matt's had offered a month's use of his rooms in Marlborough while he was away in France. There, they had learned one another. They had learned every inch of one another's bodies; they had learned every look, every tone, every inflection of the voice; they had learned one another's tastes, thoughts, responses. Lorna had thought that this was the first time in her life that she had known another person, known them as though they were a facet of herself. Matt thought only: so this is love.

They walked for miles in that expansive landscape. They rode country buses to Stonehenge, to Dorchester. Matt sketched and painted. Lorna discovered for the first time in her life what food costs; she scoured the town for the cheapest eggs, for cut-price broken biscuits, for herrings and haddock. The little money that they had must last for as long as possible. Matt had finished the engravings for the book on estuaries and waterways; that payment was their small capital, when that was exhausted he must get another commission, or sell some of his work that was banked now with Lucas Talbot in London. Lorna had a Post Office savings account in which she had hoarded birthday money from godparents and most of the allowance from her mother that was supposed to be spent on toiletries, gloves, fripperies. She had nearly fifty pounds, and thought that she must always have known, with some secret intuition, that she would one day need this, that it would be a lifeline. Matt refused to let her draw on it: "I am not going to become a kept man." She laughed, and knew that the money would be there, the ultimate resource.

When the month was up and they had to leave Marlborough, they simply drifted west. It was high summer, languid August days, and the thought of London was abhorrent. Matt had given up his garret room, and they would have to look for somewhere else if they went back, and in both of their minds was the thought: why go back? Why London, anymore? They stayed a week or two near Bath, with a farmer's wife who rented out a caravan, and moved from there to rooms above a grocer's shop in the little Somerset town of Williton, simply because they had got off a bus there, had been struck by this rich corner of West Somerset—its hills, its deep lanes, its sudden startling vistas—and saw the TO LET notice in a window. And it was there, after a few weeks, that they had heard about the cottage, had hired bicycles, and had come upon it, tucked down beside the lane, on this afternoon of sun-struck red ploughlands fingered by the long shadows of trees.

"It won't always be like this," Matt repeated. "Think of rain. Snow." But he was already wandering back to that shed with the inviting workbench. He brushed away cobwebs and opened the window. Light flooded in.

Lorna was beside him. "In summer, you'd work here. In winter, inside—by the kitchen range."

They made their way through long grass around the garden. Matt found some raspberry canes. The hedge was covered with brambles, the blackberries ripe.

"How do you grow things?" Lorna said. "I have no idea. I shall find out."

"We are all peasants at heart. In search of Arcadia."

"I don't know what that means. I just want to plant things and see them grow."

He turned her face toward him, and kissed her. "You are the most unexpected girl. Have I ever mentioned that I love you?"

"From time to time."

From somewhere out of sight beyond the fields, nearer to the sea, there came a distant whistle. Smoke fumed up beyond a clump of woodland. They remembered the train, the branch line to Minehead.

Lorna said, "A train seems all wrong here. Bustling through the place."

"This is the twentieth century, and you're not allowed to forget it."

"When it's the twenty-first, there won't be trains. People will just get onto conveyor belts. I read that somewhere. I'm glad we shan't be around."

The train whistled again, farther away. The smoke diffused.

They went in search of the farmer who was renting out the cottage.

His wife came to the door of the farmhouse in the nearby hamlet and said that he was up on the hill, checking stock. If they walked up the lane, they would probably meet him.

He was a small dark man, riding a chunky pony. He stopped, dismounted, and they stood talking while the pony clinked the bit and its skin twitched against the flies.

The deal was struck. Ten shillings a week, and he would throw in a supply of firewood. "It's quite a run-down old place. Not much modern comforts. Sure it's what you want?"

He was puzzled by them, they could see; their youth, their accents, which were not that of people who propose to live in decaying cottages.

They assured him that it would be fine. "My husband is an artist," said Lorna. "He'll be able to work there."

The farmer was evidently unimpressed by this news, but appeared gruffly entertained, perhaps at her tone of pride. His wife would give the place a clean-out, he said. When did they want to move their things in?

They explained that they had, as yet, no things. They would need to look for some cheap furniture. Their new landlord made some suggestions about possible sources. Lorna thought of the great cargo of possessions at Brunswick Gardens, the freight of chairs and sofas and tables and mirrors and ornaments, of mahogany and rosewood and oak, of velvet and silk and chintz; the cottage would carry the opposite of that, it would travel light. She saw a scrubbed table, kitchen chairs, a bed. Maybe a couch for visitors to sleep on. Lucas must come—shy, lanky Lucas, Matt's friend; she liked Lucas. Yes, a couch—and a jug and basin for their bedroom, and a little chest. Crockery for that dresser in the main room—bright, sturdy plates and cups, the antithesis of the ornate porcelain at Brunswick Gardens. Pots and pans. Rugs. She furnished the place in her head, as they stood there, Matt and the farmer now talking about local sites of interest: the slate quarry in the woods across the valley, the ruined Cistercian abbey down the lane, the old railway—the mineral line—that once carried iron ore down from the hills for shipping over to Wales. The farmer's forebears came from Wales as miners in the last century: that dark, Celtic look was explained.

Matt thought of them going to these places, the two of them. He saw his sketchbook filling; he saw his tools lined up on the bench in that shed, a block on the sandbag waiting for him to start work. The press; a stack of paper. He felt primed with energy, as though the landscape around him—the contours of the hills, the intimacies of tree and leaf and gate—were rushing into his head and reforming into shapes and lines. He would hone his style; he would sharpen his technique. He would accumulate enough work for an exhibition; he would hunt out more book commissions. There was Lorna to look after now; he no longer had only himself to think of.

They moved into the cottage three weeks later, having spent much of their small capital, and some of Lorna's nest egg, on essential furnishings and equipment. They had two armchairs with sagging springs, a deal table, kitchen chairs, a bed, a couch, an array of unmatching crockery, some worn floor coverings. A primus stove, a slop pail, a chamber pot. Two packing cases to double as tables and storage areas. Hurricane lamps. They felt rich. Lorna was amazed to discover in herself some proprietorial instinct. She had never cared tuppence about the trappings of her room at Brunswick Gardens; now, she cherished each of these unassuming effects. She loved the rag rugs they had found in a jumble sale, the patchwork bedcover from a flea market, the Victorian jug and basin that had cost a sinful five shillings in an antique shop. She had a chipped brown pitcher which she filled with great sprays of scarlet hips and haws from the hedgerows; she wrestled with the old range, and produced her first triumphant meals; she washed their clothes in the big copper that was in the shed and pinned them to the line. When they pushed their bikes up the hill from the village and she saw the solid little outline of the cottage ahead, she thought: home.

October sank into November, and home showed its claws. Damp stained the walls; the cold must be fought with a paraffin stove and a mountain of firewood; when the wind was the wrong way, the chimney smoked. Matt eyed her thoughtfully, on one mean gray day: "When you've had enough, say so."

He was sitting at the kitchen table, the block in front of him. It was too cold now to work in the shed. The tools were laid out in a neat row to his right, the different sizes and shapes—the graver, the square graver, the spit sticker, the oilstone for sharpening. He had just finished tracing a completed drawing onto the block and was ready to engrave—always a heady moment. Soon, the farmyard along the lane would start to bloom from the boxwood, translated into an intricate creation of lines and curves, of light and dark.

Lorna was at the draining board beside the sink, cleaning a chicken. She had already plucked it; now came the tricky part. The farmer's wife had shown her how, and she was hoping that she would remember which bits of that slippery rainbow interior she must go for. The chicken was a treat, a handsome gift from the farm, where she and Matt seemed to be regarded as slightly feckless children, to be indulged with the occasional bag of potatoes, half a dozen eggs, this fowl. At Brunswick Gardens, she had occasionally gone to the kitchen with some message from her mother and seen the cook doing just this, and had turned away fastidiously. Now, she wanted to say to Brunswick Gardens: look at me, look what I can do, look at the person I have become.

She ignored Matt; the chicken required all her attention. When she had finished, she slid it into the basin to wash it out, and put the entrails on a sheet of newspaper. The newspaper was a week old—she picked up discarded copies from the village shop—and the black print chattered of far off things: Hitler, the Rhineland, questions in Parliament. She stared down for a moment, reading, before she wrapped the entrails; it was as though for a moment there were some ugly intruder in the room. Then she rinsed her hands along with the chicken, wiped them dry, and turned to Matt.

"I was going to boil it, but if I can get the oven hot enough I think I'll try roasting. I've got some dripping."

"I wasn't talking about the chicken."

"I know you weren't. I was politely ignoring you, because what you said wasn't worth answering."

He laughed. "So we're bedding down here, are we?"

"It looks like it." And she smiled at him, that sudden smile that seemed to light up a room, that had other people smiling back, willy-nilly. She had smiled thus on the bench in the park and he was lost.

"You are a total distraction," he said. "Don't look at me like that. Go and do something useful."

She came around behind him and rested her cheek against his. "How long will you work?"

"Did you have something else in mind?"

Sometimes they made love when the moment seized them, when they couldn't resist it, going upstairs to the iron bedstead whose springs squeaked and groaned, but what did it matter, there was no one to hear.

"Well, maybe . . . But I was thinking of the paintings. I want more."

They had whitewashed the damp, stained walls of the cottage, top to bottom, and now in spare moments Matt was decorating some of them with frescos. In the small room that led off the kitchen he was creating a frieze of waterfowl, which commemorated their meeting. A troop of mallard, shelduck, graylag geese circled the room, just below the ceiling; in each corner, willows poured down; there was rippling stylized water. This room was grandly termed the parlor, by the farmer's wife. There, Lorna and Matt kept the bed for visitors, which doubled as a sofa; there were packing-case tables, and a shelf for books they had picked up from the secondhand bookshop in Minehead. They called it the snug; there was no fireplace but it could be made modestly warm with the oil stove.

"I'll do another half hour or so," he said. "Then I'll paint, before the light goes. You could get the ladder in, and the paints."

She smiled. There was something about her, something heightened, charged; he could sense it, with that intimate awareness of her that he now had. He put down the graver and stared at her.

"What is it? What's up?"

"Well . . ." She twisted her hands. "It's just that—I'd better tell you. I've not had a visitor this month."

She had not meant to come out with it, not just yet. And now she was blushing—because she hadn't been able to stop herself using her mother's coy euphemism.

"I wondered . . ." he said. "I'd noticed. Did you think I hadn't? So . . ." And now he felt a sudden rush of euphoria. He had never thought about having a child, children were neither here nor there, but confronted with this, with her standing there with that look on her face, he knew all at once that of course he wanted a child, a child was the natural and obvious outcome. And anyway . . .

"Anyway, we can hardly be surprised." He grinned at her.

"That thing . . ." she said. "That thing was supposed to . . ."

"Well, that thing evidently didn't work."

Lorna had never thought about happiness in her earlier life, perhaps because she had not previously been conscious of being happy. Oh, she had known the fire of well-being, of exulting in a particular moment—a spring morning, being swirled around in a dance, the exuberance of her own mind and body. But she knew now that there is another condition, of a different quality, a state of being that lifts you above ordinary existence, that pervades every moment, that confers immunity. It turned the discomforts of the cottage into an atmospheric backdrop that would always refer her now to this particular transcendence. It made chapped fingers and frozen feet not so much irrelevant as an accompanying theme song; it sidelined the carrying of buckets from the tap; the scamper to the privy on a cold, wet morning; the scrubbing; and the tussles with the range and the oil stove. All of this was real, and sharp, and she was often cold, often tired, but everything was overlaid with this sublime content: pushing the bike up the hill after a foray to the village shop, in the knowledge that in a few moments she would see Matt; thinking about the night to come as she peeled potatoes or wrung out a shirt, that she would be lying beside him again. And again, and again.

"So there'll be three of us," he said. "What's that going to be like?"

"Is a baby a person?"

"They become people."

"It'll be half you, and half me," she said. "It won't entirely feel like someone else."

She loved his gaiety, his seriousness, his energy, his capacity for concentration; she loved the way he frowned when he was working, and the mole on his left shoulder, and the smell of him and his thick, springy brown hair. She had had no idea, none at all, that you could feel thus for another person; it was as though you acquired a sixth sense. She had loved her parents, in some quite other way, when she was a child; she still felt residual stirrings of that affection. But what she knew with Matt was a thing apart—it was like stepping into some other, brighter world.

Matt had had few dealings with women before he went to the Grosvenor, beyond the occasional flirtatious exchange with local schoolgirls back home. Plunged into the heady atmosphere of the art rooms, he had at once fallen into various liaisons, mostly transitory and superficial, but occasionally more intense. An episode with one fellow student lasted several months, and was his sexual initiation. The sex had been a revelation at first, and then became a slightly guilty indulgence because he knew that he was not in love with the girl; in due course she detected this, grew indignant, and went off with someone else. Matt settled back to passing encounters, with a certain relief, though he missed the regular sex. He had standards of his own, and thought it wrong to try to get every possibly compliant girl into bed, though most in his circle would have thought that entirely understandable behavior. They were young, they were modern young, they saw themselves as in apposition to the assumptions and attitudes of conventional society.

He did not make love to Lorna until they were married. During their first times together in his garret room after their meeting, he had to force himself away from her at moments when he thought he could bear it no longer. He would go and sit on the single wooden chair while she sat on the bed. He set about painting her, to keep himself six feet away from her, and occupied, while still able to look at her constantly. That portrait hung now in the snug at the cottage.

They ate the chicken for supper that night, with some cider from The Valiant Soldier in the village; it was a feast. A late autumn gale was buffeting the cottage, but it was warm within, with the fire built up and the heat from the range; the room was full of flickering shadows made by the hurricane lamps. Lorna nibbled the flesh off the wishbone and held it out across the table. They hooked fingers around it and pulled; when it broke she held the larger piece.

"I don't know what to wish for. I seem to have got everything I want."

"We could do with an Austen 7. Or a couple of brand new Raleighs, if we're going to be more modest. Who is it that grants the wishes, anyway?"

"God?"

"No, no. Someone pagan and primitive. We'd probably stand more chance there."

They had agreed their disbelief, early on. Where I grew up, Matt told her, God was a pillar of society—the ultimate pillar of society. He was the squirearchy, and the Chief Constable, and my headmaster, all rolled into one. He was the final authority and you crossed him at your peril, but at the same time he allowed the world to carry on as it does. I thought: if that's his line, then no thanks.

Lorna had considered her own religious experience in this light and saw that—yes, the Church as she had known it was a backdrop to Brunswick Gardens' requirements and practices: weddings and christening parties for which you must be correctly dressed, to the last button and stocking seam, Christmas carol services and her father pushing a crackly note into the collection bag. Did she believe in God—a god? Had she ever done so? Well, no.

"You shouldn't wish for *things,* anyway," she said. "You wish for abstracts. That you'll be nicer, or cleverer, or better at something. Or that something will or won't happen. Maybe I should wish Hitler would drop dead."

"I doubt if half a chicken bone is going to sort Hitler out."

"Then I wish this baby will be healthy . . ."

". . . wealthy and wise?"

"We'll leave out wealthy. Wise might be quite a good idea."

"Unlike her parents." He grinned.

"Her?"

"I have a hunch."

Lorna could not imagine this baby. The world is full of babies, but she had never much noticed them. In nine months' time—no, less—there would be a baby that was of immediate personal relevance. Her baby; their baby. And she could not grasp the fact, she could not conjure up any baby. Her body was in a state of disorder: no monthly bleeding, swollen and tender nipples, she began to feel nausea. It was as though she had been taken over by an alien force, and was now headed in some unimaginable direction, programmed to bring this about, come what may.

And she was perfectly content. So be it. They had not meant this to happen, not just yet, but no matter. Already, her condition was coming to seem just another facet of this new life. She thought: a year ago I would never have dreamed that there could be Matt, that we could be here, like this, that I would feel as I do, that I could have become a new person. And in another year everything will be different yet again. It is always like that, and always will be; you are forever standing on the brink, in a place where you cannot see ahead; there is nothing of which to be certain except what lies behind. This should be terrifying, but somehow it is not.

He said, "You're not to come upstairs today. At all. I'm working in the bedroom."

She stared. "Why in the bedroom?"

Matt grinned. "You'll see."

He was there from morning till dusk. She heard the boards creak as he moved around. In the middle of the day he came down and ate bread and cheese at the kitchen table, hurriedly, looking abstracted.

"What are you *doing* up there?"

"Wait. Patience."

When the light was draining, outside, he called her. "Now you can come."

The room. Their bedroom. It was peopled, populous; it was full of color, and life, and action. The walls were dancing, figures spun across them, holding hands, man and woman, naked, vibrant, joyous. They whirled from corner to corner, arms outstretched to one another—this pair, that pair, these, those, the same all around the room, dipping down, flinging up toward the roof, a continuous sinuous wave of movement.

Lorna put her hand to her mouth. "Is it us?" She saw the curves of breasts, of buttocks, graceful heads that had no features. Man and woman. Woman and man.

He shrugged. "Maybe. What do you think?"

"I think it's lovely. I think it's us. But . . ." She gazed around the room.

"But what?"

"What would the farm people say?"

"They're not going to see them, are they? And if we leave I'll put a coat of distemper over it all."

He walked over to the bed. "Come here."

They undressed, face-to-face, both smiling, on the edge of laughter. The window was open; beyond, the wind in the oak tree, and tumultuous birds.

Lorna said, "I'm cold."

He pulled her down onto him. "You won't be. Just you wait."

They walked up the hill, the three of them—Matt, Lorna, and Lucas—and sat in a field that overlooked the Luxborough valley. Matt had brought a picnic in the rucksack—cheese sandwiches, apples, cider. It was Easter time, and unseasonably warm. The men were in shirtsleeves, Lorna had bare legs and wore a cotton smock that she had made herself, which billowed above her pregnancy. They lay on a grassy ridge, with piled cumulus clouds above and munching sheep all around.

"Down in there," said Matt, pointing into the dark woodland that lined the valley, "is something called the Druid's Grave—except that it is not. A Bronze Age burial site, in fact. And up over to the left, where you can't see, are the old mine workings—the wheelhouse and so forth. I'll take you there. You can use Lorna's bike."

They knew this landscape intimately now, had walked every lane, track, and field within range of the cottage, had cycled miles until Lorna's condition made this more difficult. And now the winter was packed away and the sun was out and the place had sprung into growth—the trees in leaf, cliffs of primroses at the sides of the deep lanes.

"Yes, please," said Lucas. He was in a state of rich content. He was with the two people he liked better than anyone, pitched into their bright company from the exacting daily routine of the Heron Press—playing hooky in order to see how Matt's work was getting on, and to bring the good news that three of his prints had sold, placed in an exhibition by Lucas. He had arrived at Washford station with the welcome cash in hand, to be met by Matt and Lorna for the two-mile walk up to the cottage. From the moment he got onto the branch line train at Taunton, he had felt as though transported from one element to another, relishing the emphatic divide between city and country. London dissolved behind him as the country train made its way across fields and between steep hills, a shadow trail of the engine smoke traveling alongside. It stopped frequently, at stations with alluring names: Norton Fitzwarren, Bishops Lydeard, Crowcombe, Stogumber. Schoolchildren got off, and women with shopping baskets. When they reached Washford, he was almost the only passenger—and there were Matt and Lorna on the little platform, waving.

It was good to have Lucas at the cottage, thought Matt, good to be out here in the sunshine, indeed everything was good at this moment. Three prints sold, and he had a book commission from the Curwen Press, and Lucas was talking about a new project—an edition of *Lamb's Tales* from Shakespeare, with engravings by Matt. Months of work. And money coming in; not princely sums, but enough to keep them going.

He stared up into a sculptural pile of cumulus, gleaming white against a hard blue sky, and saw a Wedgwood design, or puffy cherubim on a ceiling frieze. The mind is cluttered with images, he thought—everything we see refers us to something else. Perhaps only children see with absolute purity of vision; they see things for what they are and nothing else. The rest of us see signals from elsewhere, and always have done, ever since people began to think. First they see gods and ghosts and symbols and portents. And then they are battered with the images of everywhere and every time and all that they see is invaded from elsewhere. Eighteenth-century potteries float in the twentieth-century spring sky; cherubim are trumpeting Handel high above Somerset.

We don't see plain anymore, he thought. I am an artist, and I don't see plain. I see what it has been suggested that I see. I look at a tree and I see it as Dürer saw trees, as Samuel Palmer did, as Cézanne did. Who has ever seen plain?

Lorna felt the baby move. A flutter; a curious little local independence within your belly. It had only just begun to do this, and the sensation fascinated her. She sat cross-legged, watching blue butterflies on clover heads; the men lay on either side, hands locked behind their heads. Lucas appeared to be asleep. Matt, she saw, had gone into one of those thoughtful trances from which he would surface with a surge of energy.

Her own head was full of seeds: lurking mind-pictures of the different flower and vegetable seeds that she had been sowing these last couple of weeks—seeds that were like fluff, or grains of sand, or tiny balls, or fine brown dust. She saw the potatoes that she had laid out yesterday, each one with its potent sprigs of growth. She sat there feeling the sun on her skin, seeing the mist of green over the woodland down below, the sharp little blades of new grass under her feet—everything growing, rushing into life. And me, she thought, I'm adding to it—we are, Matt and I. Clever us. Except that it isn't really clever at all, it just happens, and we're only doing what is always done, seeing to it that things go on, that someone will come after us, that there is a future.

Matt jumped to his feet. "I'm ravenous. Time for the grub." He delved into the rucksack. "Wake up, Lucas. Here—the village shop's best mousetrap, and the pick of last year's apple harvest."

Lucas opened his eyes. "I wasn't asleep. Just relishing happenstance. That I happened to get chatting to Matt that evening at the Grosvenor. That you two happened upon each other." He took a bite of sandwich. "Very decent mousetrap, if I may say so. You know, you've stepped out of a game of Consequences: you two. Matt met Lorna—on a bench in St. James's Park. He said to her: 'Let me rescue you from your ivory tower.' She said to him: 'There's a ladder in the basement, and my parents are out this evening'—The World said: 'They'll never get away with it'—and the consequence was. . . . Well, we shall have to wait till August to find out what the consequence was."

Lorna laughed. She turned to Matt. "What did you really say? Oh, I know—the ducks. You told me what the ducks were called."

And that afternoon floats into this one, conjured up in their two heads, the London park superimposed upon the Somerset hills. Matt sees her white dress, the little green bag she carried that lay beside her on the bench; he sees again for the first time the shape of her mouth, the set of her nose, her eyes. Lorna sees his hand moving to and fro across his sketch pad; she sees the glint of the sun on his hair, she sees his lips pursed in concentration. Each hears the other's voice. They hear, too, the sharp cries of waterfowl, they see the dark green water of the lake that is ribbed and dimpled with light; each cruising bird trails a silvery V-shaped wake.

He turns his head; he notices her.

She smiles, uncertain.

So does he.

Both look away, disconcerted, and focus upon the throng of birds around them.

"There are so many different *kinds,*" Lorna says.

"That is a tufted duck," says Matt, pointing with his pencil. "And that's a pochard. Those fellows are graylag geese. A shelduck there. Mallard, of course. You probably know all that."

"No," she says. "None of them. Except the mallard." There are mallard on the Round Pond in Kensington Gardens; she has grown up with mallard. "What's the big brown one?"

"Ruddy shelduck. And here comes a pelican. I don't really want him—he'll bully the others out of the way."

She becomes bolder. "May I look?"

He turns the sketch pad toward her. "This is just a preliminary. Note taking, as it were."

She says, "It's lovely. Duck portraits." She gazes, fascinated. She looks at him, and he at her; both return to the ducks, after rather longer.

He tells her about wood engraving. He tells her about the Grosvenor School of Art, where he was a student under Iain Macnab. She has never heard of Iain Macnab, but she nods wisely. She tells him that she likes Matisse and Braque, that she goes to the Bond Street galleries sometimes but not all that often because . . . well, because it's a bit difficult. She does not tell him very much because she feels that this young man would have little time for the life that she must lead.

Later, in days to come, she would do so. When she came to realize that he wanted her for herself, and that it was neither here nor there to him whence she came.

"He made me feel reasonable," she told Lucas. "He made me feel as though how I wanted to be was perfectly normal. Nobody had ever done that before."

"What she means," said Matt. "Is that I had no objection to milk poured straight from the bottle and I didn't tell her what to wear. The poor girl just needed a spot of license."

"That room of his in Islington seemed like paradise," said Lorna.

"Ah, that room. The original garret—starving artists, for the use of."

"He had painted the walls different colors. The bookshelves were made out of planks and upturned flower pots. The table was an old rabbit hutch. I ate fish and chips for the first time."

"Such deprivation," said Matt. "You poor love. It doesn't bear thinking of. Never mind, you've made up for it since. The cottage is fish and chips on a grand scale. Or rather, bread and dripping and rabbit stew. Do you know, Lucas, she can skin a rabbit?"

"Congratulations," said Lucas. "I'm most impressed."

Lorna beamed at him. "I'll show you how. You never know when it might come in useful."

"I'd appreciate that." Lucas thought Lorna the most appealing and attractive girl he had ever met. It did not occur to him to envy Matt because patently a girl like Lorna was not for the likes of Lucas—she was destined for some charismatic being, for Matt indeed, and ever had been. It seemed to Lucas entirely inevitable that Lorna and Matt should have found one another, and he felt content—privileged—to have a place at the edges of this charmed alliance. He was a diffident man rather than a humble one, conscious that a gawky body, extreme myopia, and a stammer could make him off-putting. Resigned to a degree of social isolation, he compensated for this with tenacious fostering of the Heron Press—his concept, his creation. All he wanted in life was to design and produce superlative examples of the bookmaker's craft. In the basement of the ramshackle house in Fulham he labored at the press, setting type, printing, packaging, while in the office upstairs Miss Kelly, a middle-aged lady of stern demeanor but the requisite energy and efficiency, dealt with most of the paperwork and helped out generally when the pressure was on.

Today, on the Somerset hillside, Miss Kelly and the Heron Press were relegated. He felt marvelously conscious of the moment, of here and now, of this day. Of his companions. One will always remember this, he thought: probably when I'm a hoary old chap in . . . Christ, in nineteen-eighty-something . . . I'll still see today. The valley, and Matt's blue checked shirt, and her in that pink frock. And I'll hear their voices.

But all he said was, "Q-quite a place, this. I'm game for another mousetrap sandwich, if that's in order."

After Molly's birth, Lorna lay on her side and gazed at the baby, and Molly stared back with wide-open eyes and the strange unearthly look of the newborn, as though, Lorna thought, she had arrived from some mysterious place. But when Lorna got out of bed and crept over to the chest to get a glass of water, she glanced at herself in the mirror and saw that she too had that look, she was not the person that she had been yesterday, she had changed her skin. The district nurse clattered up the stairs and scolded her for moving about. Lorna got back into bed and resumed her silent communion with this small being who was no longer a part of her but a wonderful extension. The preceding hours fell away, that timeless tunnel of pain, and she simply lay there, sore, exhausted, and heard the cadenced exchanges of wood pigeons outside and the voice of the district nurse downstairs talking to Matt. She lay still, and around her on the walls the figures of Matt's fresco danced—in celebration, it seemed. Presently Matt came up with a cup of tea and said, "I have this feeling that she is called Molly." He put his finger on the baby's cheek: "Molly?" Then he went over to the window, opened it, and more bird sounds floated in, with the smell of grass after a shower, and the faraway whistle of the train. Lorna said, "Molly will do nicely." And then she went to sleep, plunging at once into blissful unconsciousness, while Matt sat on the bed holding her hand.

By that second winter at the cottage, they were hardened, braced for the tussles with the oil stove, the icy trips to the privy, Matt's labor of log splitting, Lorna's daily servitude at the washing copper. In wet weather, Molly's nappies fumed alongside the kitchen range. On one dark January day, she developed croup; this awful harsh barking noise came from her crib, and Matt in a panic cycled down to the farm to ask them to telephone for help. The district nurse came, brisk and reassuring, summing up the situation at once; she was used to very young mothers, and croupy babies were two-a-penny. She sat on the couch in the snug, Molly propped over one shoulder, and gave instructions. "You're learning all the time, with your first," she said kindly to Lorna. "Most girls have their mum breathing down their neck, telling them what to do."

Lorna doubted that her mother had ever confronted a nappy, let alone croup. She said, "My mother's rather a long way away," and the nurse nodded tactfully, scenting some dark disorder, some unspoken drama. They were not your run-of-the-mill young couple, this pair.

She said, "I used to come here to the Turners. Four children—bit of a madhouse, it was. You've perked the place up no end." Her eye fell on Matt's frescos. "The duck paintings are nice. More to my taste than those you've got up in the bedroom, I have to say."

In the interests of salvaging his reputation, Matt displayed the engraving of a local farmyard scene. "Now that I like," said the nurse. "Never mind it being rather modern style—you can still see what's what. You carry on with that kind of thing." She got up, and gave Molly to

Lorna. "There you are, dear. She'll be fine. Steam inhalations if she has another bout, like I said."

"Thank you. I feel so relieved."

"All in the day's work."

They stood at the door and watched the nurse wheel her bicycle out into the lane. Matt said, "Someone like that—someone *useful*—gives me a crisis of confidence. Art is of no use to anyone."

"You don't really believe that."

Molly whimpered. They went inside.

He was working steadily. The book commission from the Curwen Press had been followed by another; there was Lucas's Shakespeare project. From time to time, he would return to the series of original engravings inspired by local places which would form the core of an exhibition one day: the old wheelhouse of the mineral line, the quarry in the woods, a churchyard. Some days he was out in the landscape with his sketch pad. Mostly he was in the shed, or at one end of the kitchen table, the block in front of him, the tools lined up alongside, while Lorna fed Molly at the other end, or prepared vegetables, or simply watched for a few minutes.

Today, he was at the last stage of an engraving of a scene nearby—a cottage with geese in the foreground, trees, a wall, a figure against the curve of the lane. Lorna could see the ghost of his drawing now on the block, lurking on the black surface that turned silver as it was tilted. There were roughly gouged areas where the ginger-brown boxwood showed—the shapes of the geese, of the cottage—and silver planes of meticulous fret and pattern. Sky was a shower of black and silver lines, the solidity of a wall was a pile of little silver brick boxes. There were tiny scraped lines of thatch, silver scribbles that were leaves, the sharp stitching of grass fronds, the curve of a tree trunk—silver/black on one side, an intricate medley of lines on the other. The light changed each time the block was shifted, from black to silver, and you saw that somehow Matt's drawing had floated onto the wood, and out of the block shone this new transformation of that scene: it was that place, but it was now something else entirely—it was an artifact, a flight of fancy, an interpretation.

Lorna said, "Those geese hiss at me when I go past on the way to the village."

"Of course. You're on their territory. Take a stick with you."

"I know how to say boo to a goose." She came around and stood behind him. "This is going to be one of your best. How many have you done now since we came here?"

"No idea. A fortune in boxwood, that's all I know. I should be getting back to Shakespeare—Lucas is chivvying. You may have to pose for Titania, in your nightie."

"I saw her once, at the open air theater in Regent's Park. About a hundred years ago, it seems. Puck came leaping out of bushes."

Matt put down the graver in surprise. "Really? I saw that. You could stand at the back for one and six. You'd have been the toffs with deck chairs. Maybe we were there at the same time. Titania takes on a new significance."

"Maybe we walked past each other. Not knowing."

"Oh, no," he said. "I'd have known."

She hugged him. "I'm disturbing you." She sat down again, picked up a letter. "My mother says they want to come and see us. In the spring. And to meet Molly."

"Of course." He looked across at her. "We can cope with this, can't we?"

Matt's parents had visited not long after Molly's birth, with Bryony, making the ponderous journey by road from the Welsh borders in the Austin 7. They had contained their dismay at the primitive condition of the cottage with much determined comment about what a lovely spot this was, and had been rapturous over Molly—even Bryony, who was now established in her first job, and every inch the career teacher. She held the baby in a gingerly grasp, as though she might attempt to escape, and said to Matt, "Well done, you." The three of them stayed at a local bed and breakfast; they explored the area, walked on the moor, and made long daily calls at the cottage. Lorna cooked rabbit stew, a chicken from the farm, and baked cakes. Matt's mother took him aside to tell him that she was a lovely girl: "We thought it was all a bit hasty, at the time. We felt you'd rushed into it, both of you. Now I know her, I can understand, more."

Lorna had felt awkward with them at first, and then, gradually, had relaxed. Removed from the requirements and expectations of her own parents' world, she had discovered that she was now more capable than she had ever realized of being at ease with people—with any sort of person. She no longer felt herself so glaringly defined, an unwilling specimen of a particular world.

Now, she said to Matt, "We'll manage. It won't be like your parents, but we'll manage."

Matt went to London. He had finished the set of engravings for Lucas's edition of *Lamb's Tales;* the blocks had to be safely delivered to Fulham. It was the first time that he and Lorna had been apart in nearly two years.

"You'll be all right? *Sure?*"

"Of course. *Go.* Enjoy it. See friends. You've been cooped up here long enough."

"So have you."

"I've never been less cooped. I do what I want, every day, don't I?"

All the way to London, in the train, she was in his head. He saw her face, riding above the fields and hills, the little towns, the station platforms. Arriving at Paddington, he felt battered by the crowds, by this accelerated world. In his student days, he had found the perpetual movement of the city stimulating, challenging; now, as he made his way to Fulham, he wondered if he could ever feel like that again.

"I seem to be a country bumpkin," he told Lucas. "Take me to some rowdy pub, so that I can find my feet."

Over a pint, he acclimatized. Places like this had been his habitat, time was. "That's better. I'm learning the language again."

Lucas was distressed. He had just heard that an acquaintance of his had been badly wounded in Spain, fighting with the International Brigade. "They'd never let me loose with a gun, not with my bloody eyesight, but there must be something I could do. One should go." He pulled himself up. "N-not you. Me."

"Why not me?"

"Because you've got Lorna. And Molly. It's different."

"Whereas you're expendable?"

Lucas shrugged.

"Don't be so idiotic," said Matt. "No one's expendable, wife and baggage or not. But I know what you mean. Trouble is, I simply can't imagine myself shooting people, however strongly I felt. Can you?"

"If the Fascists aren't stopped in Spain, it'll be France next, eventually us. Spain is the confrontation. How can one stand back?"

"You're not answering my question. Maybe you're lucky that your glasses let you off the hook, in the last resort."

Lucas looked away. "All right, we're not soldier material. True enough. But when push comes to shove . . ."

Matt said, "That is something we may find out in due course, if the pessimists are to be believed."

They fell silent. Matt got up to go to the bar. "Enough of that. I'm under instructions to enjoy myself. Let's celebrate this book. Pint?"

Some while later, slightly drunk, Lucas reverted to his mood of gloom. "All I want is to make books. That's all I think about. You're an artist. . . . We're private people. But there's the world snarling away, Hammond getting his leg blown off in Spain, and you can't stay private. It's . . . it's intolerable."

"People have had to put up with it since forever. Nobody's exempt from history. If our turn comes . . . well, it was ever thus. Anyway, it may not. Hitler's a loudmouth. I prefer to think he'll back off, like some people are saying."

The pub was a warm, convivial haven, full of talk, bursts of laughter, hazy with cigarette smoke. Do I miss this sort of thing? thought Matt. But right now it was Lorna he missed. He imagined her in the cottage, lighting the lamps, getting something for supper. A couple of days, and he'd be back there.

Lorna's parents visited, in early summer, when Molly was going on for two years old. Marian Bradley picked her way cautiously over the threshold of the cottage and stared around: "Oh, my dear . . ." she said, after a few moments. Lorna and Matt saw her gaze drift across the open range, the dresser with its assorted crockery, the scrubbed table, the stone sink. They all moved through into the next room, which seemed at once a size smaller, overwhelmed by Gerald Bradley's bulk and his wife's force field of unease. Marian sat on the sagging couch, and looked around some more. "Well, it's cozy," she said gamely. "Quite original, painting pictures on the walls like that, I must say." She noticed the window, and the green reach of Somerset beyond: "Lovely view, anyway."

They accepted cups of tea, and slices of cake. Molly was displayed, and worked a certain magic. Marian took her jacket off and lit a cigarette. Gerald spoke at some length about a man he'd been at school with who lived now at Something Manor, a couple of miles away. Had Matt and Lorna come across him? They had not.

During the next couple of hours Lorna knew that she had traveled a long way since last she saw her parents. She was reborn, it seemed, and while they were not strangers—by no means—they had acquired a strangeness. She felt sad about this, but also quite accepting. Her childhood seemed to be shut away behind glass, filled with these familiar figures, her mother and father and brothers, who were now distanced—known, and yet also unreachable. Her parents sat there in the cottage, talking hectically; she felt as though they were acquaintances. She wondered if they felt the same.

Her father talked about the boys. Roddy had finished at Sandhurst, with flying colors. Martin was in chambers with a leading barrister: "One of the very top men, I understand." And Roddy was engaged to someone called Sally.

"Such a sweet girl," said Marian. "One of the Nesbits. You went to dancing class with them, Lorna."

Matt was quiet, courteous, attentive. He listened, with apparent interest, as the names of friends and relatives he did not know were paraded by the Bradleys. From time to time Marian would remember his ignorance and offer some quick benign enlightenment. Later, Matt realized that they had never once asked him a personal question, that in fact they knew little or nothing of his own background.

"I suppose we should meet his people," Marian had said, with stiff resignation. This was on the last occasion that Lorna had seen her alone, a few days after she and Matt were married, when she returned for the last time to Brunswick Gardens to collect the rest of her things.

"I don't think there's really any point," Lorna had replied.

She could not imagine the conjunction of those two sets of parents. She had visited Matt's family soon after they were married; the Faradays had been surprised but welcoming. In her mind's eye, she saw her mother and father receiving the Faradays in the Brunswick Gardens drawing room, and shuddered.

The small room in the cottage began to feel more and more constricted, as the visit progressed. Lorna suggested a stroll along the lane. Her father looked relieved, and rose with alacrity. Outside, they moved in a cohort between the hedge banks, Marian quickstepping on high heels, Matt with Molly astride his hip. Lorna pointed out wildflowers, and recited names. "I never knew anything about all this," she said. "Now I can't stop hunting for things I haven't yet found. I've got a book."

Marian peered at toadflax, bush vetch, red campion. "So pretty . . ." She was a townsperson to the hilt; the country, to her, was a pleasing backdrop seen from a train or through car windows. Family holidays had been spent at Biarritz or Torquay or some southern French resort.

Gerald had been on shooting parties and could put up a passable show of rural interest. He wondered which hunt operated in these parts. Matt and Lorna did not know. Gerald talked knowledgeably about pheasant drives. "Do you shoot at all?" he asked Matt.

Matt laughed. It was the first spontaneous and assertive sound that had come from him that afternoon, and the Bradleys both looked startled. They were gathered in a gateway at that moment, contemplating the sweep of landscape before them—the fields tipping down to the distant gray sea, which reached away to the coastline of Wales, with the darker smears of Steepholm and Flatholm perched on the horizon.

"I'm afraid I can't imagine myself with a gun in my hand," said Matt.

Gerald appeared perplexed. "Really? Oh, well . . ."

"You know, it's beginning to feel a tiny bit chilly," said Marian. "Perhaps we should go back." A thought struck her. "And we haven't seen any of Matt's drawings."

They returned to the cottage. "You needn't, you know," Lorna said to Matt, quietly, as they went in. "We can make an excuse."

He shrugged, and squeezed her arm. "Don't worry—it's all right."

Marian clapped her hands. "Do let's see, Matt."

He brought out some recent work from the series of engravings inspired by local scenes, and spread the prints on the kitchen table.

"Awfully good," said Gerald. He seemed genuinely surprised.

Marian inspected, with little exclamations. "*So* clever . . . the way you've done the roof of that barn."

"I can't be doing with this abstract stuff you see around nowadays," said Gerald. "You steer clear of that, Matt."

Marian took his arm. She looked at him, eager. "Darling, I've had a thought. I want us to buy one!" She turned to Matt. "*May* we?"

"Good idea," said Gerald.

Matt smiled. "Which one would you like? But it's a present. My pleasure."

"Oh, but how sweet of you. Really, you shouldn't . . . I can't decide . . ." Marian's hand hovered. "This one, I think. I can just see it in the small spare bedroom by the window." She had chosen the study of the farmyard by the lane, with the geese.

I don't want that in the spare room at Brunswick Gardens, thought Lorna. Like an extra bit of wallpaper. None of this has any place there—here, where I live now, and the way we live, and Matt's work. None of it has anything to do with Brunswick Gardens or that world. Molly began to grumble; Lorna gave her a rusk and stood by, trying to look pleased while the engraving was packaged and her mother gave more little cries of satisfaction.

And then began the process of departure, oiled by the sense of relief all round. Much was made of Molly: "I'm going to send some little smocks from Woollands," said Marian. Gerald busied himself with the car, checking oil and water. He pecked Lorna on both cheeks, shook Matt by the hand. Marian embraced Lorna: "You must bring Molly to see us in London." They got into the car; Marian settled a rug over her knees. As the car turned into the lane her hand fluttered at the window. In spirit, she would now be back at Brunswick Gardens, Lorna knew, a task completed, an awkward day now shelved. She wondered if her mother still loved her, or if her dereliction had effectively stemmed what mothers are supposed to feel. "You have been an utter disappointment," Marian had said, during that last disastrous confrontation. Lorna thought that nothing that Molly did could ever change what she felt about her, nothing.

She said to Matt, "You didn't have to give them the engraving. You should have let them pay for it."

"Even penniless artists are entitled to the occasional lavish gesture. I enjoyed it. Momentary sense of power."

"I love you."

"God knows why."

The sun had come out; light chased across the hills. A buzzard floated straight ahead, high above. They stood at the garden gate and watched. "Look," Lorna said to Molly. "Look up there." The baby stared at her, and broke into a seraphic smile. There was a smell of crushed grass, and wood smoke.

From somewhere, there came a rumble. It rose to a low roar, died away; like distant thunder, like gunfire. Lorna found herself shuddering. "What on earth was that?"

"They must be blasting, in the quarry." He put his arm around her shoulders. "Could there be a cup of tea, do you think?"

They went inside, restored to privacy, to intimacy.

Matt was acquiring a reputation—some capricious process whereby his name traveled, and left ripples in the arcane world of those concerned with wood engraving: the galleries, the presses, the collectors. Lucas had placed the rest of the prints left with him in exhibitions, and all were sold. He began to talk of a one-man show, up in London. Finish your Somerset series, he urged, this could be a big thing, this could put you in the front rank. Evangelical fervor smoked up from his letters—that eager commitment to Matt's talent. Matt wrote back, teasing Lucas for being an entrepreneur, but was secretly touched, and worked harder than ever, putting in long hours, day after day.

And thus, in due course, Lorna found herself on the train to London, heading for Lucas's house, and the opening view of the exhibition. Matt had gone ahead with the engravings, to supervize framing and hanging. When she arrived at Paddington, with Molly in the pushchair, he was there to meet her—exuberant, excited by the effect of the exhibition: "The room is perfect—white walls, bare floor. It sets them off. I still can't quite believe it. When we'd finished the hang, I just looked, and thought: crikey, did I really do all that?"

Lorna hugged him.

She was bemused by the opening view: all those strangers, chatting in groups, cruising the room, scrutinizing the engravings. People came up and told her how proud of Matt she must be. She overheard snatches of comment: ". . . really a remarkable style, quite individual, extraordinary sense of volume," ". . . look at that use of white," ". . . his silvery grays are most effective." Red stickers appeared all over the place. Matt was wanted everywhere; she watched him across the room, and glowed with pleasure. She was wearing a dress from Brunswick Gardens days, blue chiffon, that had lain in the chest at the cottage for three years. She disliked resurrecting it, but had nothing else suitable for the occasion. Each time she caught sight of herself, reflected in a mirrored door, she was startled, as though at a glimpse of the past itself: but that's not me, that person is gone.

They stayed several days at Lucas's house. Lorna took Molly to see her parents, determinedly. Her brother and his wife now had a baby, a boy. "We're all so thrilled," said Marian Bradley. "Daddy is pleased as punch. What he wanted, of course."

They went to art exhibitions, Matt met up with old friends. Lorna said, "Shouldn't you have more of this? Maybe we should leave the cottage."

"Is that what you want?"

She shook her head.

"Well, then. Me neither."

Molly ceased to be a baby and became a child. She ran about; she spoke. Matt looked at her and saw this amazing fusion of Lorna and himself, who was also someone entirely unique and unpredictable. Lorna thought that she could no longer conceive of a time when Molly had not been there; oh, she could remember a world without Molly, but it was also an impossibility, an anachronism. Molly was so emphatically present, so undisputedly there—how could she ever not have been? She ran in and out of the cottage; she brought small offerings from the garden—a twig, a berry; she pointed—"Bird!"; she listened—"Train!" Her discovery of the physical world became a rediscovery for Matt and Lorna; they too gazed at spider webs, at the tapestry of a butterfly wing, at the red spires of lords and ladies in the hedgerow. Matt, seeing suddenly with Molly's intimate close-up attention, began a new series of engravings in which small things became intimate structures, studies in form and pattern: shells, leaves, the firework display of dried cow parsley heads.

Mrs. Mason in the village shop said, "I don't care to look at the papers anymore, myself. All this war talk. It just depresses me. Sure you want *The Times,* dear? I just stick to the *Western Gazette* these days. Local news is good enough for me. Sugar, flour, bread, marg., tea, a quarter pound of bacon—is that all? My brother's joined the ARP in Williton. Trust him—he always did enjoy bossing people about. I told him: you're going to be really disappointed if it all comes to nothing, aren't you? No swanning around in a fancy helmet. Well, we'll see. Personally, I don't want to think about it."

Lucas wrote: "Matt's star remains in the ascendant. Three of the exhibition engravings sold out the entire edition; high demand for the rest. I am the complacent middleman, stashing away the shekels. How do I remit to you? Check? Or are you still keeping money in an old sock? There has been a run on *Lamb's Tales,* too—much packaging and posting. It has been a question of all hands to the mill, Miss Kelly and I shoulder to shoulder. I am wondering about an *Arabian Nights.* Does that attract you, Matt? Or are you committing further infidelities with the Curwen lot—or, heaven forbid, Golden Cockerel? Now that you are the man of the hour, I must become a humble supplicant. Well, think about it. Or, if the oriental theme doesn't inspire you, what about Gilbert White of Selborne? Or *The Compleat Angler*? More appropriate, perhaps, given your back-to-nature way of life.

"Have gas masks reached deepest Somerset? I received mine without enthusiasm. Pictures in the paper of responsible citizens filling sandbags for the protection of key points, with much jollity. It is all surreal, is it not?

"How does your garden grow? And Molly? Lorna, I have not yet skinned a rabbit, but I have my eye on the deer in Richmond Park, if the worst happens."

"Now that this wretched war scare is over, we are off to Menton for a fortnight," wrote Marian Bradley. "Heaven. The Med should still be warm enough for swimming, and Daddy will get some golf. Roddy and Sally join us there, leaving little Peter with Nanny."

Whenever a parcel arrived from Lawrence's in London, with fresh blocks, Molly was allowed the brown-paper wrapping as drawing material. Lorna would cut the sheets up into small pieces, and the little girl would sit at the kitchen table, the tip of her tongue stuck out in concentration, and scribble with her crayons. She was being Matt, Lorna knew, and her creations must be treated with respect, given cardboard frames, placed in a cardboard portfolio and tied with tape.

That fourth winter in the cottage, they were veterans—not impervious to cold and damp, but resourceful. Lorna had the measure of recalcitrant oil lamps and the sullen kitchen range; Matt kept the log pile stacked high from the wood dumped periodically at their gate by the farmer. They were established local figures now, in a sparsely occupied landscape where everyone was known to everyone else within a radius of several miles, where information traveled as though on the wind, where every chance encounter required a ritual exchange. Matt, out sketching, would be greeted and sized up by farm laborers, by boys out rabbiting, by landowners, by postmen, by the driver of the milk lorry.

"I am the local oddity," he said to Lorna. "Fiddling away while others work. Grasshopper and the ants. Sitting around drawing things is pure self-indulgence—that's the view, though people are too polite to say so."

"How do they think you earn a living?"

"I'm a man of substance, presumably."

"But living here, like this?" She laughed.

Time was, she had not thought much about how people earn a living. At Brunswick Gardens, you did not talk about money—that was vulgar. Patently, money underpinned the life that was lived in that house; her father's departure every morning to the place known vaguely as The Office had some eerie connection with money, but that was not a matter for discussion. Occasionally, others were referred to as "not well off," in lowered tones, as though perhaps they suffered from some chronic ailment.

Nowadays, she knew all about money. She knew the price of everything in the village shop, she knew how to budget, calculate, scrimp, save. She was a connoisseur of jumble sales and thrift stalls. She enjoyed the triumphant discovery of a pair of old curtains that could be cut up and made into a skirt for herself, a dress for Molly. Money had become interesting: a challenge. In these parts, people talked much about money; vulgarity was not an issue. They talked about the price of hay, of rents and rates, of wages and leaseholds. The local paper was full of fatstock prices over which Lorna pored in fascination, and could then see the populated fields as money on the hoof. This fractured vision became intriguing—a flock of sheep as part and parcel of the landscape, its living expression, white shapes against the green slope of a hillside, but also a sober statement of rural economy—someone's income, someone else's meal.

The farmer's wife had given her an old chicken coop and some pullets which, in the fullness of time, began to lay. Now, they had a few eggs. There was a daily hunt in the hedge, which the hens preferred as a nest site. They had their own vegetables, too, in season. Lorna found all of this intensely satisfying.

"Before, I had never in my life done anything useful," she told Matt. "Now there is a point to everything."

"Spring at last," wrote Lucas. "I suppose you have primroses and lambs and all that. Here, we have our urban version, but it's hard to feel uplifted, isn't it, with all the papers all gloom and doom. I heard Herr Hitler on the wireless, last September, ranting. A beastly sound—it keeps coming back to me now. And we thought we were spared. Oh, well—one feels oddly resigned, this time around. On a happier note, sales of *Lamb's Tales* continue on their steady way. And I hear the gallery is just about sold out of engravings now. I saw the Curwen Press book, and I have to admit—through gritted teeth—that it is pretty nice. I was much taken with the new Spiderweb print, Matt. Marvellous. One of a series, you say—nature studies. Basis of a new exhibition, maybe, in a year or two? If the world holds still."

"If there's a war," Matt said. "I shall have to go."

"I know."

"You couldn't stay here alone."

"I could," she said. "If I have to. And I'm not alone. There's Molly."

"Your parents . . . or mine."

"*No.* Don't talk about it. Not till we have to. *If* we have to."

On Molly's third birthday, they cycled down to the coast, the little girl in the pillion seat that Matt had made. On the beach, she pottered among the rock pools while they sat and watched. She came to them with small trophies—a ribbon of seaweed, a brightly banded pebble. She was intent, serious, busy—bustling to and fro, wearing cotton knickers and a sunbonnet.

"I want to know what she will be like when she's twenty," said Matt. "I want a sudden quick glimpse into the future."

"I don't."

"Why not?"

"It would be appalling to know the future. You couldn't live, knowing the future."

"I don't want the entire narrative. Just a few interesting snapshots. Molly in some other incarnation. What will she be? What will she do?"

"We'll find out, won't we? We'll be watching."

"Middle-aged fogies," said Matt. "Making noises of disapproval, just like our own parents."

"Only if she wants to live in Kensington, and play bridge. Which she won't."

"Perhaps that will be her form of rebellion. Each generation kicks out at the one before. Artists always do that. It's obligatory."

"Do you?"

"Engravers are a law unto themselves. We all think we're innovators. Doing it differently."

The tide was out. The sea seemed to be retreating to the distant coast of Wales, leaving a great expanse of glittering Bristol Channel muddy sand, fingered by long slicks of water. Behind them, the cliffs were veined with pink and gray; rock falls had brought down chunks of the alabaster. Matt picked up a large pink piece. "This is going to be a Henry Moore maquette—one of those earth mother figures."

Lorna had brought a cake, and three candles. They found a flat rock at the foot of the cliff, and she set out the birthday tea. The candles guttered in the breeze, and had to be relit before at last Molly blew them out. Then she became intent once more upon beachcombing, while Matt and Lorna sat looking out at the far-off sea, at the white glimmer of the Welsh coast, at a skittering dog, at a row of gulls lining the rock pools. There were scarves of cirrus cloud against a clear blue sky; the late afternoon sun was warm on their faces.

"Actually," said Lorna, "I am not remotely interested in the future at this moment. I want to stay here, like this, as we are, forever. I want it to be now, always."

Molly comes staggering over the pebbles toward them, holding a shell. "More cake?" she inquires. "Blow the candles again?"

Marjorie Sanders, from Roadwater, leaned her bike against the wall of the cottage, and stepped inside. "Thank you, Lorna—cup of tea would be nice, after the hill. In fact, I'm not me today, I'm the billeting officer. Ever so important, I am. Power of life and death. If I say so, you get an East End mother and four children. In your case, I doubt it. Now, you've got just the two rooms up and this—is that right? And you've not got running water or electric? I'm going to be putting you on the reserve list. We know how many billets we've got to find, for Williton rural district, and we won't need to scrape the barrel, far as I can see. I'm not being rude, you've made this place a nice home, but you'd be hard put to it to squeeze any extra in. So I'll just tick you off, and be on my way, when that kettle's boiled. Heaven knows how they're going to settle in, when they come. If they come. I mean, town people are different, aren't they?"

"It's going to happen, isn't it?" said Lorna. "The war."

"I suppose so."

They were in the shed. Matt was taking the first print from a newly engraved block. He eased the back of a spoon to and fro over the paper, back and forth, across and across, picked the paper off and there was the proof print: an intimate scrutiny of dandelion clocks, which made them into something startling, unique.

He stared at the print: "It makes me wonder what the hell I'm doing, fossicking away."

"Don't," she said. "Don't wonder. You wouldn't have, before. It's just that everything's gone wrong. Look—I found the first ripe blackberries."

When it came, it came in the form of tea urns, the train, and crying children. They cycled down to Roadwater, alerted to the need for helpers at the village hall, leaving Molly with the farmer's wife. Eight hundred women and children from London were anticipated at Washford, who would have been waiting, and traveling, for many hours, all of whom must be allocated billets before nightfall. Matt joined those helping to escort and identify the evacuees; Lorna was put onto the distribution of tea and sandwiches. First, there was the bustle of expectation, instructions, queries, the assembling of trestle tables, chairs—an almost festive atmosphere. Then suddenly they were here, and the place was full, lines of people spilling out into the road, ranks of drab, tired women clutching babies, toddlers. The hall became hot, smoky, ripe with the smell of sweat, and children. Lorna gave tea to a richly pregnant girl, and found her a chair. The voices all around were those of strangers, alien, not the soft Somerset voices to which she had grown accustomed; these people came from a London that she never knew existed. "I'm a Londoner too," she said, trying to make contact, and the women stared at her with skepticism. There were so many of them, and the rumor was that there would be more trainloads tomorrow and Monday. Suddenly, the cruel black print of newspapers, from which you shied away, was turned into an awful reality, in which the certainties of the world that you knew were swept aside; it was like being plunged into the irrationalities of dream, of nightmare. This bemused mass of women and children, who should not be here, who did not want to be here. What was it that was expected? What annihilation? What Armageddon?

There were many blackberries that year, wortleberries up on the hill, mushrooms, hazelnuts. The hedges glowed with hips and haws. The sunshine reached far into October, the leaves turned, the first frosts came, and an autumn gale or two. The oak tree beside the cottage rattled acorns onto the roof and shed a small branch.

Everything had happened, but also nothing. London was not burning; nor Liverpool, nor Birmingham, nor Manchester. Things went on as they had before, except that they were different. You must obey remote, draconian regulations: comply with the blackout requirements, stick sheets of cardboard over the cottage windows, eat what you were told to eat, go to Williton to register for a ration book. People grumbled and complied, laughed and negotiated. In a trickle, then a stream, the London women got on the trains and went back; they were homesick, they couldn't be doing with the food, the quiet, this foreign land.

You stood at the gate and watched for the postman, holding Molly's hand. What did he have in his bag today? He had taken on a new significance, and he knew it—now he was half apologetic, half portentous. "Just a letter for you—nothing for him. Young Ted Moult had his papers, though. They're taking the boys first. They always do that, don't they? Your husband'll be in the clear for a while. Maybe they won't want him at all, the way things are going."

When the winter arrived, it bit sharp. On New Year's day the frost was deep into the ground, the ploughlands ice hard, the trees stiffly white. The tap had to be unwrapped from a cocoon of sacking each morning before they could get water. The privy was a test of endurance. It was February when at last the thaw came, and then the spring was one of tranquil beauty; days as warm as summer, everything rushing into growth, birds nesting in March.

At first, this time seemed simply like an extension of life before, though infected by all the dictates of the day—the restrictions, the regulations. Matt bought a wireless; it crouched on the kitchen dresser, an alien presence that became insistent each night, as they turned on the nine o'clock news and that clipped voice filled the room. And Matt himself began to change; he was often silent, he found it hard to work, his state of unrest was grimly apparent. When March came, he offered himself to the farmer, and helped out with lambing and other jobs. "I have to be up and about," he told Lorna. "If I sit here, working, I feel . . . pent up." Many of the local young men were now gone, those not in reserved occupations, and Lorna knew what was in his mind, though they did not talk of it—that he would volunteer before his call-up papers came.

When at last Germany moved, and the wireless talked every night of Norway, she knew that it was only a matter of time. In the event, his papers came on the day that German forces invaded Belgium, and she realized when she saw him holding the brown envelope that he was relieved.

He said, "Well, this is it. I'm to go for a soldier."

"Right away?"

"Yes."

"Oh . . ."

"We knew." He put his arms around her. "It'll be all right. It's you I'm worried for. It'll be hard here. I think you should . . ."

"*No,*" she said. "I'm staying. If it's too hard—well, I'll think of something."

It was high spring. The hedges and woods were full of warblers; there were creamy rivers of may blossom. That night, he made love to her with a kind of desperate passion.

"We are being broken in," Matt wrote. "It is a tedious process. Much marching about and being shouted at. I hold a gun, for the first time in my life, and believe I understand how the thing works. Then we march about some more, and do physical jerks, and different men shout at us. Initially, we are culled. I had not realized that there are so many people in this country unable to read or write. An illiterate soldier is no good to the army. They whipped them out and took them away; apparently they will come back in due course, miraculously enlightened. I am told that I should apply to be an officer. I don't see myself as a leader of men, but they say the food is better.

"Oh, my darling—if I could tell you how I miss you. It has been forty-seven days, and it feels like a thousand years."

Every night, she listened to the news, alone, Molly upstairs asleep, and the catalog of distress and disaster was spelled out in those crisp tones—unemphatic, unemotional. She found herself going more and more into the village, to sit on a bench in the recreation ground, while Molly played with other children, and to be with other women whose men had gone. In early June, two boys who had been at Dunkirk came home to the village on leave, and their stories ran like wildfire from mouth to mouth. She saw that what you heard each night, that measured account, bleached of everything except facts and figures, was a hollow mockery of what was really happening. Once, she went with the farmer's wife to Minehead and saw a newsreel: long lines of exhausted, unshaven men, some with bandaged limbs or heads. "And you can be sure they're not showing us the half of it," said her companion.

In August, she watched the skies, as did everyone. From time to time, planes went over, high above, anonymous, and people wondered if they were theirs or ours. But the daily fights of which they heard each night, this terrible maelstrom up above, were far away, over Hampshire and Sussex and the Channel. Except, she thought, that that is not so very far away, not far away at all. And then, in September, everything changed again, and now it was London of which they heard, night after night. The London women and children were back, hundreds of them, scattered all over the landscape, their voices always startling in shops, or on buses, or in school playgrounds.

Lorna puts the leaflet on the dresser, behind the cherished Victorian teapot from a Bring and Buy sale. STAY WHERE YOU ARE, it says. The government is instructing her what to do in the event of invasion. She must not take flight, as people had done in France, Holland, and Belgium, thus preventing soldiers from getting at the enemy, and inviting use as a human shield. If she does this, the enemy may machine-gun her from the air. Her and Molly. She looks out into the lane and sees it filled with people from the village, from the farms around, people she knows, carrying suitcases, pulling carts with mattresses and blankets, and from somewhere above Croydon Hill, the enemy planes are coming, swooping down across the fields, their guns primed.

So she must stay put. She must stay where she is. And anyway, where would I go? she wonders. They will ring the church bells if the invasion comes. People are quite brisk and matter-of-fact about it; the Invasion Committees have everything in hand, they say. There is a deal of defiant talk. But she suspects that there are others who have that knot of fear in the stomach.

She walked the lanes and the fields in the late summer heat. Everything seemed sharper than ever before, more arresting, as though she saw with heightened vision. The hedgerows hinted at autumn: there were tawny hips and haws, red and green blackberries. But there was growth still: the sharp green of young ferns springing up in the wake of the hedge trimmer, canary-yellow flights of toadflax, and the pink flush of young oak leaves—reminders of spring, as though time now and time to come coincided, coexisted, as though the future were subsumed into the present.

The news came from the farmer, stopping by on his pony, his usually dour face lit up: "Telephone message for you. He's got three days' leave. Washford station at half-past two tomorrow."

She rode down on the bike, Molly in the seat behind her. Standing on the platform, you could hear the train coming, minutes before, the warning whistle, then you saw a plume of steam, then at last there was the busy sound of its approach, and she thought it the most thrilling thing she had ever known, the most exquisite anticipation. And then it was there, hissing alongside the platform, and a door opened and he got out, this khaki-clad figure, infinitely familiar but now also oddly strange.

They had been apart for nearly four months. All the way back to the cottage they talked, as though each day of separation must be charted. When Molly got tired, Matt carried her on his shoulders, her legs hooked around his neck. Back home, they talked on, wandering the garden path, between the vegetable beds, while Molly ran to and fro.

Lorna said, "I can't believe you're here." She had to keep touching him, looking at him.

"Nor me. I've lain awake at night, imagining this."

"Before, we just took everything for granted."

"Yes. One won't make that mistake again."

He had changed out of uniform into his own clothes. "That's better," she said. "You looked somehow—older—before. Different, anyway."

"The army is a determined leveler. That's what uniforms are for. Except that of course some are more level than others."

"Is it awful?"

"Some of it. The worst is being away from you. But another side surprises me—the sense of purpose, expectation. The feeling that a great machine is grinding into action, and you are part of it."

He was about to go on an officers' training course. She heard this with relief. "That means you won't be sent overseas then—not yet?"

"Not yet. Eventually, I suppose."

The hours leaked away. Matt hauled logs from the deposit at the gate, and chopped a great mound of firewood.

"I do that now, you know," she said. "I've got quite good at it."

"Not while I'm here, you don't." He fixed a broken window latch, dug a trench and emptied the privy, trimmed the oil lamps.

She found him reading the STAY WHERE YOU ARE leaflet. "Christ," he said. "They don't believe in looking on the bright side, do they?"

Lorna said, "People make jokes about it. Mrs. Mason says she's going to defend the Post Office with her father's Boer War blunderbuss." She looked at him. "Will it happen?"

"If it does, that's why I'm in the army, me and all the other blokes."

He read a goodnight story to Molly. "Which one do you want? Red Riding Hood? Goldilocks?"

Molly turned the pages, pointed. "That one? The Three Little Pigs?" said Matt.

Lorna went downstairs. From the kitchen she could hear his voice: "'I'll huff and I'll puff and I'll blow your house down . . .'" She did not like that story, tried to steer Molly away from it, which was perhaps why it had been chosen.

The nights were an ecstasy, as though they were the first, as though they had never made love before. They did not want to sleep, to lose a moment of this rationed time.

Lorna said, "After the war, shall we have another baby?"

"Half a dozen, if you like."

"We'll have to find a bigger place."

"That could be done. I'll have plenty of work. People will be crying out for art, and the good things of life. Wait and see."

"Do you miss it—work?"

"Don't have time to, on the whole. I do some sketching, when I get a chance. Try to bank a few images. You'd be surprised what you can do to a machine gun. Let alone tanks on Salisbury Plain. A far cry from spiderwebs and chestnut leaves. My postwar exhibition will have a rather different flavor."

They walked up the hill. There was a concrete pillbox up there now, squat and stern, staring down toward the Bristol Channel. Molly was entranced: "A little house!" She went inside, and reported empty cigarette packets and a beer bottle. Matt and Lorna sat outside it; the harvested fields were bleached golden, tractors crept to and fro, unfurling the red Somerset earth.

Matt said, "My parents want you to go to them, if it gets too difficult here."

"It's kind, but I'd rather stay."

The Bradleys had fled Brunswick Gardens and were living in a hotel in Cheltenham. Marian had sent a card: "We are quite comfortable, but I miss my own things desperately. One can only pray the house does not get hit." Matt had smiled: "I don't see your parents as evacuees, but no doubt it is being done in style."

"Actually," said Lorna, "I sometimes imagine staying here forever."

"That's fine by me. Forever has a good sound to it, right now."

Time ran out. Suddenly he was putting his uniform on again. He had been offered a lift to the station in the farm truck. They waited at the gate, Molly now bewildered: "Why does he come, and then go away again. Why doesn't he stay here?"

And then he was gone. The truck rattled away down the lane and everything became very quiet, and still. And empty.

Lucas wrote: "Well, I am in action at last, if you can call it that. The bombers turned their attention to our patch of London last week—we have had incendiaries, several direct hits, and a couple of UXBs—unexploded bomb to you. We Wardens are rushed off our feet, and I am thankful for it. I can't exactly look the armed forces in the eye, but at least I am doing *something,* and thank goodness that myopia and astigmatism don't keep you out of the ARP. Any old crock can be a Warden, and plenty are. There's one chap at my Post who's only got one arm; he copped it last time around, in Flanders. The Posts are a melting pot, you meet all sorts, it's an eye-opener, frankly. Classy girls, and old lags—all in it together. If this war does nothing else, it's given us a good shake-up. Makes you pull out all your own stops, too. As you'll be aware, I'm not exactly a figure of authority, but there are points when you damn well have to pull rank: put out that light! Get into that shelter! You'd be surprised at me. But by and large it's a question of running hither and thither, and taking each crisis as it comes. A girl started to have a baby in one of my shelters last week—we got an ambulance just in time, but it was a near thing. I'm a dab hand with incendiaries now, if they're on the ground—it's the roofs that scare me, they can be smoldering away and you can't see. And I don't like land mines; they float down like great black coffins, and you can't hear them, but you've got to see where they fall, and dash to get people into action. I go through bike tires like nobody's business, and spend half my time off mending punctures.

"Has Matt finished learning how to be an officer yet? I've had a couple of laconic postcards—he seems to be absorbing the style. And you? It must be rough on your own, Lorna. I think of you."

"I am still not convinced that leadership is my calling," wrote Matt, "but I'm damn sure I can do it as well as the public school types here, and better than many. The company is not to my taste, on the whole—indeed, I think of my time in the ranks with nostalgia, at points—but I've found a few kindred spirits. One thing about war, it brings you face-to-face with other people in a new way. I have a hunch that this is going to do funny things to the world as we know it. I don't think that after the war—and there'll be an after, I'm sure of that—people will put up with the way things have been. Men aren't going to go home, eventually, after what they'll have been through, and knuckle down again to doing without, while others are doing nicely, thank you. I'm on the side of the masses, of course, and rubbing shoulders here with the ruling class has made me even more so, but at the same time I feel rather semi-detached—artists are a class unto themselves, I suppose, and confused about their own role. No wonder they're a bolshie lot, by tradition.

"Rumor has it that there will be Christmas leave. And also that we'll go back to our units, and be posted elsewhere soon after. Kiss Molly for me, many times. I love you. Take care of yourself—take care of both of you."

At night, she heard the planes. She would lie and listen to that purposeful drone, right overhead, a throbbing sound, menacing because you had been told what it was. Once, she got up, went down and outside into the darkness, and looked up, but there was nothing to be seen, just black sky full of sound. They were heading for the Welsh coast, for Swansea and the steelworks farther east, and when they had dropped their bombs they would head back, and you would hear them again. There were local incidents: a stick of incendiaries on some farm buildings not far away, bombs that fell on the moor. Load shedding, people said, or maybe the pilot saw a light.

Christmas dinner was a pheasant, slipped to Lorna in the village shop, with a nod and a wink. Matt had forty-eight hours only. He was shortly to rejoin his regiment. After that . . . well, after that was anyone's guess.

"I don't relish the idea of the Far East. That is on the cards, they say."

"Nor do I," said Lorna. "I don't relish that at all." The map of the world hung in her head: great oceans, unthinkable distances.

"I've always felt untraveled. Abroad is a closed book. A couple of student sprees to Paris, and that's about it. I've rather hankered after seeing more of the world. Now that it's about to be on offer, free, courtesy of His Majesty's Government, one feels a bit differently. All the same . . ."

She looked at him, across the ruins of the pheasant, the sprouts and potatoes from the vegetable patch. "All the same . . . You're up for it?"

"Given that there's no choice, one had better be."

The next day, he left again, and the place fell silent once more, and empty. Except for Molly's chatter, her pattering steps. Except for the postman's knock, the sound of the farmer's tractor, his brisk greeting, his wife's more expansive exchanges, the women who gathered by the swings on the village recreation ground, Mrs. Mason in the Post Office, all those you met in the lanes . . . Oh, there were people on every side; the void was within, not without.

She bought a map of the world, and hung it against the kitchen wall. Now those great seas and spaces were a reality, as well as in her head. The wireless cited places of which she had never heard: Tobruk, Benghazi, Salonika, Rangoon. She located them on the map, and realized that she knew nothing, nothing. What were those countries? Who lived there? Why must they be fought over? Geography lessons at the

Academy in Kensington had been volcanoes and deserts and icebergs: history was the six wives of Henry VIII. But Matt knew about all sorts of things. She had wondered at this, in those months when they were first together, had been amazed to realize that much of what he knew came from his school days. She saw that there is another kind of education, which had passed her by.

But she had always liked to read. At the cottage, she read: books that they found in the Minehead secondhand shop, books from the mobile library that stopped at the gate on the second Monday of each month. Even now, the library continued to come, and she scoured the shelves in search of enlightenment. She read books about art, for Matt, and history, for herself, and books about travel, and biographies of famous people. Sometimes she returned these after a cursory nibble, feeling guilty, but at least now she had heard of Cromwell, or Gladstone, or Samuel Johnson. But none of this was of any help when she confronted the enormity of the map, with its myriad names and places, its proposal of mysterious diversity. And there was England, up at the top, an insignificant little place.

In the village shop, you learned much; you heard that the evacuee family with the Sproxtons had upped and gone, that there was measles at Park farm, that there would be a delivery of corned beef on Thursday. You heard who had been fingered by the map: "Charlie Sanders has been posted overseas," says Mrs. Mason. "He can't say where, but his dad thinks it's Malaya. And Bob Lake's in the Middle East somewhere."

The next time, the embarkation leave time, he did not manage to telephone the farm. He simply appeared. The cottage door opened, and in he walked. Lorna turned around from the sink and thought for an instant that she would faint. The whole room rocked; she gasped. Molly said, "Daddy's come!" in an astonished voice. And then he had his arms around her, around them both, the room steadied, he was here, truly here, and she was wild with joy. And with foreboding.

It was February. Catkins, snowdrops, the first flush of green. Later, she would reach back for that time, and it was a blur, out of which floated a few concrete moments.

She wakes to find herself tucked against his body, his breath on her neck, his hand on her breast; she lies there, at peace.

He sits at the kitchen table, his face puckered. He is drawing a picture for Molly. She wants a cat. "I can't remember how cats go," he says. "How many whiskers do they have?"

He is bringing in an armful of firewood. He pauses outside the door and stamps his feet to get the dirt off his boots—one, two. The latch clicks, the door opens, he pitches the wood into the basket. A sequence of sounds that she has heard for the last five years, and will hear forever: stamp, stamp; click; thump.

He says, "I've told the gallery to send you the money if they sell any engravings."

He says, "If we had not met, that day, I think I would have imagined you, somehow."

He says, "Molly has your eyes."

He says, "I've got all these ideas in my head, for work. When I get back."

He says, "Yes. We embark on Thursday."

They went together to the station. She propped the bike against the fence alongside the platform, and they stood there until the train came.

And then she stood again as it left, holding Molly's hand. She watched the train get smaller and smaller and then vanish, leaving only a trail of smoke. That night, when she heard the familiar whistle, the sound was different: menacing, inexorable.

In March there were gales; a branch fell and blocked the lane. Old Mr. Timms died, up at Croydon. A fox got one of the hens. Molly had whooping cough. The wireless talked of Yugoslavia now; Lorna stared at the map.

"We are at sea," Matt wrote, "and that is about as much as I can say, or the censor will adorn this with black splodges. Apparently, we call in somewhere before long, and mail will be taken off. I have seen dolphins, and I am playing a lot of whist—an activity new to me—and there is even the chance to sketch a bit. If I were more famous and had more clout, maybe I could have been one of these war artists—now there's a thought. As it is, I get the pad out, and am considered an eccentric, but harmless—it is rather like being back at school. You must look forward to my postwar studies of lifeboats, rope coils, and capstans.

"Write, my darling. Letters reach us eventually, and are a salvation."

Lucas had sprained his ankle while on ARP duty: "Casualty of the blackout—my war wound, in a very small way." Marian Bradley was finding Cheltenham a little tedious: "One does miss one's friends, and there is nothing by way of theaters, and of course the shops so empty." Lorna's brothers were both in London, with desk jobs at the War Office: "Nice and safe, thank God." The Faradays were concerned about how Lorna was managing on her own, and pressed her to come to them whenever she wanted to. Bryony was now a senior mistress at her own old school, and sent her love.

These snatches of information seemed like messages from another time. Lorna could hardly remember what her brothers looked like. Moving from day to day, from task to task, she felt as though she had never known anywhere but these familiar hills, as though this were the only reality, and everything beyond a construct of the imagination, some old fantasy of hers.

She sought out proofs of Matt's engravings—prints not good enough for sale—and put them on the walls. She began to teach Molly to read.

In April there was a late snowstorm; she built Molly a snowman, and put Matt's scarf around his neck. The farmer's daughter had twins, up at Wheddon Cross. The frost got the apple blossom. Molly gashed her leg on a gatepost; the nurse did three stitches. It was all Greece now on the wireless; the Germans in Greece.

People talked of the war as though it were a condition: a chronic condition. There was before the war, that other era, and there was after the war, the promised land. And for now there was just an interminable present. The word had its own resonance, as though it had lifted clear of meaning, had become simply a sound. It infiltrated the language of children. "It is because of the war?" asked Molly, when the hens got fowl-pest.

But the primroses came and spring sunshine that flowed across the hills. Lorna planted seeds; she dug a trench for the potatoes. For her twenty-seventh birthday, her mother sent some handkerchiefs and a bottle of cologne; she wondered if Lorna would like to bring Molly to see them at Cheltenham: "We could put you up at the hotel for a few days." In the village hall, the women gathered to make jam and to knit things for sailors. There was a searchlight battery at Luxborough; the darkness hummed and was striped with light, when the planes went over.

When Matt's letters arrived, they were already several weeks old. Lorna read of yesterday, and wondered about today. And she, too, wrote into the future; it was as though they existed now in different dimensions of time.

In May, the ferns in the hedge banks were tongues of green flame; swallows nested in the eaves of the cottage. Lorna took Molly down to the coast to play on the fossil beach; there were concrete blocks, rolls of barbed wire, a pillbox on the cliff top. She told Molly; "We came here once for your birthday. Do you remember?" The little girl nodded: "There were pink candles. That was a long time ago." "Yes," said Lorna. "It was a very long time ago."

Lucas came. He had written: "I need a breath of air. May I impose myself?" He was hours late, having missed the connection in Taunton. Trains were packed, he said—delayed, infrequent, the whole country seemed to be on the move. "And if you're not in uniform, you get those looks. Not quite the same as a white feather, but not far off."

"You can't help it," she said.

"No, but try telling that to gimlet-eyed matrons from the home counties."

There was an awkwardness; Matt's absence hung over them as though they both kept looking for the third person who should be there.

"When Himself comes back," said Lucas, "will you go on living here, do you imagine?"

She shrugged. "Maybe. I can't . . . look ahead."

"He's getting quite a name as an engraver, you know. He's in the top flight now."

She smiled, delighted.

"I hope he won't get too grand for the Heron Press."

"Don't be an idiot, Lucas."

Suddenly, they were at ease. Lucas told stories of his blitz experiences; he played snap with Molly, read her a story. When she had been put to bed, Lorna turned the wireless on. The news was all about Crete; German parachute landings. She looked up at the map, and then flushed.

"I didn't know where any of these places are. I felt a fool."

"A crash course in geography," said Lucas. "Good idea. Do you know where he is?"

"Egypt—the last letter. He could say as much as that, apparently. Not where, exactly."

"Well, it's one way to see the world. Very inspirational—no doubt he'll make good use of it."

"Yes," she said. "Yes, of course he will."

In June, the start of June, she is outside the door, filling the bucket from the tap, when she hears the gate whine on its hinges. She turns, and there is the postman, so she smiles, and waves.

But the postman is neither smiling nor waving. He has a new look on his face, a look she does not recognize.

The man is beyond apology; he is felled by what he has to do, made speechless. He simply holds out the telegram, avoiding Lorna's eye. He has seen these before. He knows. And his knowledge leaps to Lorna. She knows, too, at once. She stands there in the sunshine, knowing, and takes the envelope, and the postman gives a sort of shake of the head, and turns away, and goes. A thrush sings piercingly, nearby.

The farmer's wife came, alerted by the postman. She put her arms around Lorna, a thing unheard of, and her eyes were red. "My dear," she kept saying. "My dear." She was there, and then others were there, stepping diffidently into the cottage, and Molly stood wide eyed, and Lorna sat at the kitchen table, a cup of tea in front of her that someone filled and refilled, and the day seemed to go on forever, the hours stalking by, while she waited for this to have been a mistake, some monstrous error, a dream.

And then night came, and the people went, and everything was still the same. She gave Molly her supper, and put her to bed, and read her a story, and then she came down and sat in the armchair, and she began to cry. She cried in a way that she had never known, would not have thought possible, so that she was gasping; she shook; her tears were relentless; she felt that grief was scouring her, draining her empty. She sat there hour by hour, sometimes rigid, staring at the walls, at the ducks and the willows, sometimes crying, unstoppably crying. And then at last she crept up the stairs and into bed, and lay there, wide eyed, as dawn came into the room.

After a few days, a week, she did not know how long, she went to the farm, and told them she had to go. She asked to use the telephone. Then she returned to the cottage and began to dismantle it. She packed away Matt's tools, and his blocks, and any prints and sketches that were left. She took his clothes to the village hall, and asked them to give them to the Red Cross. She packed up the china from the dresser, the teapot, the Victorian jug and basin, the patchwork bedcover, the books, Matt's portrait of her, and her own clothes and Molly's. Everything else she left, including an old box under some sacking in the shed, which she had not noticed, and a chunk of pink alabaster from the beach, carved into a figure, that had rolled under the bench.

She wrote to Lucas: "Matt was killed in action in Crete, perhaps on the day that you visited. I do not seem able to stay here. I am going to Matt's parents."

She took a brush and a tin of distemper up to the bedroom and painted over the dancing nudes. The other frescos she left untouched—the ducks and the willows. On the last night, she sat gazing at these, looking and looking.

And thus they went, she and Molly, and the cottage sat empty, but filled with the legacies of their occupancy: the painted walls, and the table and chairs and bed and couch, the pots and pans, the axe, the oil lamps. The farmer's wife came and took what she could use, as requested, and presently another family moved in, a man who worked on the farm, with his wife and children, and they made their own adjustments, left their own mark, as did others, year by year, decade by decade, passing through. The only permanence was the building itself, the cob of the walls, the slate of the roof. From time to time, some remedial work was done—a coat of limewash, a roof repair. Piped water arrived, within, and electricity. The frescos downstairs flaked and faded, but were left as they were, because people quite liked them, the place was a tenancy anyway and it was said that the farm wouldn't want them done away with, for some reason. The shed became a depository for animal feed, fertilizer, bikes, garden tools, discarded children's toys. The oak tree grew a few more feet, an ash sprang up from nowhere, someone planted a quince. The century moved on, taking the cottage with it.

Part 2

FOR THE FIRST YEAR in the Welsh border town Lorna did not care where she was, or what she did. The Faradays were kind, concerned, and themselves paralyzed by grief. She took a job behind the counter at a local shop in order to be able to pay her way. Molly started school; in that muted household, her bright presence was the only solace.

Eventually, Lorna began to look around her and realized that she could not stay here, like this, forever. She must make a home for Molly, somehow she must be independent, she must earn a living. Mrs. Faraday had suggested a secretarial course; Lorna took afternoons off from the shop and learned how to type and do shorthand, whose strange hieroglyphics helped with the process of anesthetization, which was all that she sought. She moved from day to day, her head full of hooks and dots, and the lettering of the keyboard, and the face of the cash register in the shop. In the evenings, she was too tired to do anything but see to Molly, eat, sleep. She had no interest in the future but saw that there had to be one, for Molly, if not for herself. If it were to be here, well and good, but she must live otherwise, find somewhere of her own, different work.

Marian Bradley had written, suggesting that Lorna join them: "Daddy and I could move out of the hotel, and rent a little house, where there would be room for you and Molly." Lorna had known that this would never do, but was touched by the gesture; she was gently evasive.

Lucas wrote: "No news of you for quite a while. I trust things go as well as they can do. Here at the Heron Press, there is great disarray. The splendid Miss Kelly has abandoned me—retiring, if you please. I must advertize for a successor, and shrink at the thought of some supercilious young woman who will run rings around me."

Lorna replied by return of post. She said: "Please may I apply for Miss Kelly's job?"

The house in Fulham had three floors and a basement. The Press occupied the basement, with the office and packing room on the ground floor, alongside the kitchen. Lucas himself lived untidily on the floors above but insisted now on making over the top floor to Lorna and Molly. They would have a bedroom, a sitting room, and share the bathroom with him. He was apologetic: "You should have a place of your own, but it would be quite impossible to find anywhere." It was 1943; London was battered, bloody, brought to its knees. There was rubble, darkness, an exhausted populace. The Faradays had been dismayed by Lorna's decision: "There could be bombing again." She had known only that Lucas's letter had seemed like a beacon, that it offered a haven of some kind, an association with Matt's world. The Press. Lucas.

The Press was far from being in full production. The paper shortage meant that Lucas had to curtail operations, and limit himself to small editions. With little money coming in, he had taken on work proofreading for various journals; he would sit hunched over the kitchen table, in his out-at-elbow sweater, muttering and exclaiming: "Oh my goodness . . . Look at this . . . Illiterate fellows . . ."

Lorna took Molly to school in the mornings, and after that would set about reestablishing order in the Heron Press office, which was awash with unanswered letters and unpaid invoices. By his own admission, Lucas was hopeless at paperwork; Miss Kelly had been an essential feature of the business. Initially, Lorna was daunted. Then she thought: if I can learn how to clean a chicken, and grow stuff, and trim oil lamps, and mend a puncture, then I can find out how to deal with all this. She mastered Miss Kelly's typewriter and the filing system; she worked out what money was owed, from where and to whom. In the basement, Lucas set type; she would hear the grind and clunk as the press rolled.

Grief was muted now, a continuous dull pain, as though she had some incurable illness. She still wept; at unwary moments, the realization of what had happened would come surging up and knock everything else aside, so that she was dazed, unable to function.

But she took satisfaction in what she had achieved: a home of sorts for Molly, occupation for herself, a small income—for Lucas insisted on paying her for the office work. And from time to time she would experience a frisson of pleasure—at something Molly said or did, at the sight of a flower, new green leaves, opalescent clouds above the city.

At the cottage there had been hens that ran if you chased them, but you mustn't, and apples in the grass, with crawly things on them, and the big black kettle that jigged about and hissed when it was getting hot. That was a long time ago; she had pictures in her head. "Do you remember?" Mummy would say, and she would fish for other pictures and sometimes nothing came.

At Grandma's there had been a bath with feet like dogs' feet, and a tablecloth with pink roses on it, and a box thing that played music, and Ovaltine when you went to bed. That was quite a long time ago.

Now there was Lucas's house, which went up and up, and down and down. Right up were their rooms, and right down was the press. Sometimes Lucas let her help him with the press. She had to find letters for him: "Now find me an A. Good. Now an N. Now a D. *Good.* We'll make a printer of you yet." Lucas is a printer, he says. So will she get tall and thin, like Lucas, with a beaky nose, and glasses?

She likes finding letters for Lucas. And at school she likes reading. She can read whole words, whole lines of words, a whole page of words. "Mary runs to her mother. See Mary run. Mary runs to her father."

Father.

When she is seven, quite soon, they are going to go to the zoo. There are no lions and tigers at the zoo now because of the war, but there are other animals, and a place where you can have tea, and there might be a ride on a camel.

There was a life now, at the tall house in Fulham; a determined, stoical, daily kind of life that defied what had happened, what was happening, in the same way that the life of the city itself ignored the gaping windows, the potholes, the sandbags, the blackout, and got on with what had to be done. It was a life without much by way of comforts or consolations: the occasional lucky strike at the butcher, and liver for supper, an extra sweet ration for Molly, a dip into the pub for a beer and a smoke for Lucas. For Lorna, there was just the knowledge that every day you moved on, you moved further from that other day, you moved toward some other time when perhaps you would be whole again, in some way. Getting through time was all that mattered.

Occasionally she felt as though Lucas were avoiding her. They would eat a meal together in the evening, the three of them, but he would quickly make some excuse and vanish up into his own room. If she suggested that he join them for a walk by the river at the weekend, he would be diffident, seem almost unwilling, but then, if he came, he was his old self—an engaging, quirky companion. She wondered if he was regretting the whole arrangement, their presence in the house, and confronted him, one day.

"Lucas, this is just for the moment, isn't it? You mustn't feel you're stuck with us for ever. Sooner or later . . ."

"Sooner or later what?" He looked aghast.

"Well, sooner or later we must move on."

"Where to?"

"I don't know," said Lorna. "Just . . . we can't inflict ourselves on you forever."

He looked away. He took his glasses off and began violently polishing them with a handkerchief, always a sign of agitation. "I know it's not ideal. You should have a proper flat up at the top, with a bathroom and a kitchen, but it's no good, one wouldn't be able to get it done these days for love nor money."

"Lucas," she said. "*We're* all right. It's you I'm worried about. We've invaded you."

He put the glasses back on, blinked a few times, then said rather stiffly: "It is an invasion entirely to be welcomed. My p-privilege."

The matter was not raised again. Molly had her seventh birthday, lost a front tooth, rode a camel at the zoo. The year tipped over into the next. It was 1944; people talked now of after the war as a real possibility, not some improbable nirvana.

At Christmas Lucas's widowed mother came, bringing a turkey. "Don't ask me how," she said briskly. "Someone owed me a favor, that's all." She was taking a short break from intensive WVS duties, back home in Portsmouth: "The blitz may be over, but we seem to be as much in demand as ever." On Christmas evening, Molly in bed, she suggested that Lucas take Lorna out for a drink.

They walked down to a riverside pub, stumbling out of the darkness into the noise and light of the interior—the beer fumes, the cigarette haze, the rank of backs waiting at the bar. Lucas found a table, achieved drinks. "Like an eighteenth-century stew, I always think. Something out of Hogarth. Deeply reassuring, in some way—I love it." There were paper chains and streamers hung from the ceiling, the place was raucous; they had to sit close to hear one another.

Lorna said, "I had never been into a pub until I met Matt."

"Quite right, too—a well brought-up girl."

They were silent for a moment—Matt conjured up by her words. Lucas saw her looking across at a group of servicemen in uniform. She said, "We should have been born at some other time, shouldn't we? Not landed in this."

"Well, that's always true for someone, somewhere. The eighteenth century was no picnic."

"And you're stuck with what you get."

"Quite so," said Lucas. "Unless you believe in reincarnation—an idea that always rather appeals to me. I favor being one of those Indian gods with many arms, next time around. So convenient for operating a press."

"Do you believe in ghosts?"

"I'm afraid not. I'm tediously rational. Perhaps you do?"

She considered. "No. I don't think so. Not as such. But I can't believe people just disappear."

"Well, they don't, do they?" He hesitated, looked away. "Matt is in one's head, isn't he?"

She nodded. Then she reached out and put her hand on his for a moment. "It's getting a bit easier, you know. I sniff the air sometimes. Thanks to you and the Press, in many ways."

He stared intently into his beer, shook his head. "Well good . . . Anything I can . . . Anyway, good."

"Eventually," she said, "I'll have to sort things out. After the war. Goodness, I'm starting to say that now. Like everyone else. After the war, I'll have to think seriously about . . . well, about what I'm going to do, and where to be, and what's best for Molly. Find us somewhere permanent to live. I've wondered about looking for jobs in publishing. Or an art gallery. I thought maybe . . ."

He sat there, gazing at her; what she said floated above the background racket of the pub—the medley of voices, bursts of laughter, "Last orders, please!"

Now? he thought. No, not now. When? Soon? Never? No, no. Soon.

"Time, gentlemen, please . . ."

Give me time. Give me strength.

He unfolded himself from the low seat, held out his hand. "Maybe we should be getting back."

When Molly draws a house, it is high and thin, lined up between similar houses. Many windows; smoke curling from chimneys. Occasionally a different house appears—lower, more squat, attached only to a mirror image on one side. And from time to time there comes a house that stands alone, a little house; this house has a row of chickens in front of it, and a tree alongside. When Molly shows this house to her mother, Lorna goes quiet.

Molly likes to draw. She likes to write, too. In the evenings, after school, she writes in her exercise book. She is writing a story. Lucas says that when this story is finished he will print it, like a real book. But how do you know when a story is finished? Molly's story goes, "And then . . . and then . . . and then." She cannot find a way for it to stop.

She takes this problem to Lucas.

"Perhaps some stories never end," he offers.

"If the person dies it does."

Lucas looks disturbed. "Well—not absolutely. Aren't there other people in your story?"

"Actually," says Molly. "My story isn't about people. It's about cats."

When Lucas comes back to the house at night, if he has dropped into the pub for a quick snifter, or has visited his friend Toby at the art gallery, he sometimes sees a tiny crack of light at the top window. As the Warden, he should come down on this like a ton of bricks, but he does not, and, anyway, everyone is more lax about the blackout these days, and one tends to turn a bit of a blind eye.

He looks for that sliver of light as he gets near, and when he sees it he has the most incredible sense of uplift. In all his life, he has never known this. He did not know that you could feel thus.

Lucas said, "I have loved you since first I saw you. But it was out of the question, then."

She had not at first understood that he was asking her to marry him. When the realization arrived, she was filled at first with astonishment, then with a strange sense of comfort.

She knew that she was not in love with him. She would never be in love again, that was over and done with now, forever. She liked him—oh, she liked him as much as she had ever liked anyone, more than she had ever liked anyone. He was Lucas, he was entirely familiar, he was a part of the landscape of her life. And, when she came to think about it, she knew that she did not at all care for the idea of Lucas with some other girl, with a wife.

She told him. She said, "I can't love you like I loved Matt."

"I know. It doesn't matter."

"And there is Molly."

"I want Molly, too. If she will have me."

So Lorna was married once more in a Register Office. She and Lucas stood before the Registrar, Lucas in a crumpled suit, she in her gray flannel skirt and her only jacket, blue tweed from a village jumble sale long ago. A wartime wedding. But most wartime weddings featured a bridegroom in uniform. Lucas was an oddity, in his awful suit, blinking furiously behind the glasses, which were of course the reason he was a blatant civilian, but the Registrar was probably not aware that Lucas had severe myopia and astigmatism and was useless material so far as the Army was concerned. Both Lucas and Lorna fancied that the Registrar treated him with a certain coolness. He offered perfunctory congratulations, followed by a dismissive look that suggested they should make way for the next couple.

Molly sat in the front row with Lucas's mother, flanked by the witnesses—Toby Shanks from the gallery, and the mother of one of Molly's schoolmates, with whom Lorna had struck up a friendship. That was the full complement of the wedding party. The Bradleys were not present. Lorna had not suggested that they attend. She had written to tell them that she was to marry again. Her mother's evident relief saturated her reply. "I am so glad for you," she said. "Now there will be someone to look after you and Molly."

And your father and I can stop wondering what we could do about you: that was the sub-text. A cheque for £25 was enclosed: "To buy something nice for your new home."

The Faradays sent warm good wishes. Lucas's mother was quietly exultant: "It was high time he settled down. Good for you, Lorna."

This is my mother's wedding, thought Molly. But mothers are not supposed to get married; they already are married. And brides wear long white dresses and veils and carry flowers. Mummy just has a rose in her buttonhole. Now Lucas is my daddy, thought Molly. Except that he is not.

She could remember her father a bit—the look of him and the sound of him, the feel of him and the smell of him. She remembered him drawing a picture of a cat for her, she remembered that he came off the train, wearing soldier clothes. Except that all this was getting fainter, weaker, she had to summon it up.

She liked Lucas. If pressed, Lucas would sing "Old Macdonald had a farm," all through, making the right noises. He could do paper airplanes out of brown paper, that flew across the room. Lucas listened when you told him things.

So this is my mother's wedding, thought Molly. Afterward they were going to have a special lunch in a restaurant; she could choose what she wanted—there might be trifle.

That summer of 1944, the bombs began to fall again. At first they were just a rumor. People were saying . . . Over in Pimlico, something had happened . . . And then they became a truth, an acknowledged new horror, the doodlebugs, these mean little engines that puttered across the sky, and when the sound went dead, your number was up. A new exodus began, the flight from the city. A neighboring family left. There were fewer children around.

Lucas said, "I think you and Molly should go to Matt's parents."

"It's not as bad as the blitz. Is it?"

"It's different. And we don't know if it will get worse."

"The war's almost over. They say."

"Even so."

She was torn, anxious for Molly's safety, but reluctant to abandon a place that was now home, or as close to home as anywhere ever could be again. And Lucas, who was the center of this home. In the end, she took Molly to the Faradays for a few weeks in the summer, and then returned in time for the new school term and, as it turned out, the advent of the V2s—more devastating, more sinister.

"I'm not going back. We can't keep coming and going. It'll be all right. The war could end by Christmas."

This was peacetime. This was after-the-war, that the grown-ups had talked about. There were parties in the streets, with flags everywhere; everything was lit up now, and she had been with Mummy and Lucas to see Buckingham Palace in the night.

It should be more different, Molly felt, this peacetime. She had not thought that everything would go on pretty well exactly as before—had expected transformation, a world that was strange and new, like the glowing landscapes of Heaven, in the Bible storybook at school, peopled with ecstatic figures in robes. But everything was the same, and nobody seemed all that much happier, they still grumbled about rationing, and queues, and you still had to do gym at school in your vest and knickers, and the boys still waited at the corner and tried to bang you with their satchels.

She was going to have a little brother or sister. Now that would be different, she thought, really different. She did not know what she would feel about that, because you cannot know what you feel about something that has not yet happened.

It was not like last time, with Molly. She said to the midwife, "How long has it been now?" and the girl looked away. That look meant: too long. She was very young, younger than Lorna, and new to the district, and frightened: Lorna could see that, through her own fear and pain. And then another contraction came, and another. And now there were no longer minutes, or hours, but one extended roaring present spiced with faces, voices, frozen moments.

Lucas, at the bottom of the stairs, standing aside for the ambulancemen and the stretcher. She saw his anguished face.

The screaming siren of the ambulance. She thought: that is for me. She could still think. She thought: it has all gone wrong, terribly wrong. The midwife was still there, beside her. She was holding Lorna's hand.

A high white room, in which she lay on a high bed; people went to and fro, their footsteps tapping on the lino; a face came swooping down over hers: "Push, please, push now."

She pushed, and the pain swept her up, took her away to some awful private place.

The face came back: "Here's your little boy."

Silence. They have all gone. No, there is a back at the far side of the room; someone in white is doing something at a sink. And she can see a metal cot, and the baby—a small dark head. But she cannot really see; everything has gone gray and misty. And she cannot move; she tries to turn her head, and cannot. She knows that something more is wrong, and she must tell them. But she cannot speak; she tries to tell the person over there at the sink, but nothing comes. And then the person turns around, walks across, leans over her. She hears a bell start to ring.

The room is once more full of people. They seem to crowd around her. Faces; voices. But she is floating now, she is so weak that it is as though she were dissolving, and then she can neither see nor hear, the people ebb away. She is alone.

Lucas sat in the hospital corridor, outside the room with swing doors that sometimes opened or closed as someone hurried in, or out. Nobody looked at him, or spoke to him. Once, he tried to waylay a nurse as she came out: "Can I see my wife?" The girl smiled and was gone.

He sat on, and on. At last a man in a white coat appeared. He had a stethoscope round his neck, and there was a splash of blood at the hem of his coat. Lucas stood up: "C-can I . . ." He wanted to say can I see her now, but the doctor interrupted. "Let's go in here, shall we?"

He led Lucas into an office. "Please sit down. I'm afraid I've got to tell you something."

The baby, thought Lucas. The baby is not all right.

And the doctor told.

"I'm so sorry," he said. "I'm so very sorry." He said some more, about a hemorrhage, and shock, which Lucas did not take in. No, he was crying out—no, no, no. But he did not speak.

The doctor said, "The baby is fine. He has come through well."

Lucas nodded.

They both got up, and the doctor touched his shoulder. "I expect you would like to see her."

She was lying on a trolley, and the baby was beside her in a cot on wheels. Lucas stood looking at her for a long while, and then he put his hand for a moment on the baby's head, which was warm and furry. Then he went.

Presently a hospital porter came across this long lanky fellow sitting on a bench in the car park with his head in his hands and his shoulders shaking. "You all right, mate?" the porter said. "Anything you need? You'd find a cup of tea in the canteen." He was not unused to this sort of thing; that's hospitals for you.

Part 3

THERE WERE THREE OF THEM, in the tall house: Lucas and Molly and Simon. At first Simon did not count, as a person, then gradually he began to do so, acquired personality and language and inclinations. Sometimes, Lucas's mother was there. She would arrive and instantly set about a whirlwind rescue operation, scrubbing and dusting, cleaning out cupboards, filling the washing line in the garden. "Lucas lacks any domestic instinct," she would tell Molly. "But he has a lot on his plate, poor dear." And Molly, sitting at the kitchen table in her school uniform, eating a rather better tea than was usually on offer, would nod. It seemed best to agree all around.

These incursions were something of a relief. Mrs. Talbot would make an assault on every front; Lucas's shirts would acquire buttons once more, Molly would no longer have to keep her school skirt up with string, her knickers would have new elastic, her socks would be darned. Simon would be systematically cleaned and aired, for as long as the visit lasted. Normally, he was in the care of Mrs. Selwood, who came in by day, supervised Simon and did some perfunctory cooking and cleaning. She was fond of reminding Lucas that she had looked after more children than he had had hot dinners, and Simon was devoted to her, but there was no escaping the fact that Mrs. Selwood's methods were slummocky; Simon had dirty ears and was fed on much bread and jam. As Molly got older, and looked at the world beyond, she made comparisons. She revised her own standards and tried to do something about both Simon and the general state of the house, which did not go down well with Mrs. Selwood.

"Madam here doesn't seem to care for my way of doing things," she would say to Lucas, tight-lipped, and Lucas would squirm in distress, and then take Molly aside, imploring her to tread carefully.

Lucas is like a heron, Molly sometimes thought. Is that why the press is the Heron Press? Stalking about the place on his long legs; his thin beaky nose. He was all length and angular movement. Sitting down, he seemed to fold up. On the rare occasions when he put an arm around her, it was an edgy, bony hug. But Lucas was not a hugging and kissing person; his physical awkwardness extended to dealings with the world. His stammer got more pronounced when he had to engage with strangers. He blinked a lot, words rushed out, but disordered and apologetic. With those he knew, he was calmer, quieter, often quite silent. When he was sympathetic, he seemed to twist up into a state of vicarious distress, his legs knotting together. "Oh dear, oh dear," he would say. "What a bother. Oh, *dear* . . ." And then he would busy himself violently with some task.

Much later, her most abiding memory of that time was of being cold. She was cold without and cold within. The internal cold was a great chill void, as though some essential part of her had gone missing. She would come to recognize this as extended grieving; at the time it seemed merely an appropriate complement to the all-pervading external cold—the frigid house in which there was localized warmth only from the kitchen range when it was going, and the little hissing gas fire in the sitting room. In the winters—the brutal winters of 1946 and 1947—she scrambled into her school clothes as fast as she could, washed in cold water, waited shivering for the bus. They all had fingers raw with chilblains; her bare knees, between her long socks and the bottom of her tunic, were permanently blue. The pursuit of fuel dominated their lives, dominated all lives. Lucas acquired a battered old pram from an elderly neighbor; together he and Molly would take this to the emergency depot and heave it back between them, loaded with coal or coke. Then they would do the same for the neighbor, four long treks through the icy streets each time word got around that there was an allocation of fuel. The old lady would reward them with her sweet ration: a treasured Fry's Sandwich Bar for Molly to share with Simon.

This was a disheveled world. A landscape of bomb sites and houses with flapping tarpaulin roofs and boarded windows; households depleted by the war, minus their men. There were plenty of women without husbands, children without fathers—families that were glaringly incomplete.

Like them. Like Lucas, Molly, and Simon. Except that wifelessness, motherlessness were not the norm. They stuck out. They attracted sympathy, expressed with small gestures by way of some discarded toy for Simon, or an invitation to tea for Molly, but they lacked the official status of the war-damaged. Lucas was not an ex-serviceman, he was just another civilian; the circumstances of Lorna's death owed nothing to the war. Theirs was not a historic misfortune—just something that could have happened to anyone, at any time.

Lucas's role as an Air Raid Warden was remembered on the whole only by those with whom he had had words about infringements of the blackout or inappropriate shelter behavior, exchanges that were long held against him. He had relished the job of Warden, had felt that at least he could compensate in some way for his inadequacies as military material. He had been indefatigable, racing from post to post and shelter to shelter during those menacing, noisy nights, doing without sleep, without food, losing track of everything except the requirements of the job. He had known every street of his patch, every house, who lived where, who should be accounted for when the bombs came this way. He had coped with incendiaries, with burst gas mains, with an old man who had a stroke in one of the shelters. He had stood alone and exposed, watching the dark shape of a descending land mine, to know where it would fall and thus whom to alert. He had had to subdue drunks and sort out shelter disputes—the most taxing area of his duties. Bombs were less daunting than recalcitrant people. He lacked authority, and knew it. His uniform gave him formal power, but his natural diffidence was at once apparent to anyone at all combative. "Come along now," he would say, wavering head and shoulders above some beer-sodden fellow causing mayhem in a shelter. "Pull yourself together and stop being a nuisance." And the other shelterers would collapse into laughter, seeing him as a moment of much-needed light relief.

But he had acquired resolve; those weeks and months hardened everyone, so that some discovered an unsuspected capacity for endurance, others became cynical, amoral, concerned only with self-preservation. Lucas found that in the last resort he could face down an argumentative householder, see off a looter, badger the control center for attention to an incident on his territory. This was a bizarre new society in which class barriers were not broken down but subtly eroded; people were cheek by jowl in a way that they had never been before, in the crammed street shelters, in the busy fetid little enclaves of the wardens' posts. You still placed a person by their voice—Lucas was glumly aware that his own inflections nailed him for what he was as soon as he opened his mouth, and might antagonize accordingly—but other things mattered too. Confidence, efficiency, sang-froid, selfishness, greed, shirking. The brisk competence of the WVS somehow excused their resoundingly middle-class tones; the authority and expertise of the firefighters and the rescue workers made them natural leaders, acknowledged by all. Looters prompted universal outrage.

Lucas found a new ease with others. He was never going to be capable of camaraderie; he was always going to have difficulty face-to-face with someone unfamiliar but he discovered that he could join in the desultory chatter at the wardens' post, that he could find a remark to soften a hostile householder, that in a curious way his evident awkwardness would often disarm potential troublemakers. He had become a sort of mascot in some quarters, he realized, seen as an amiable toff who might lack officer qualities but was patently doing a good job.

Equally, his own social assumptions had been brought into question. The prewar world in which he had spent his childhood and youth had things cut and dried: people were clear who they were and where they belonged; everyone assessed everyone else and placed them within or without their own sphere. This was a world divided into us and them, with many subtle and significant subdivisions. From whatever vantage point, people identified kith and kin, and lumped the rest together as that other lot—familiar enough but of a different order.

Speech and dress were the defining factors; you listened, looked, and allocated. To be working class was to recognize your own complex society, with its hierarchies and gradations, and to see the rest as mysterious or offensive, according to inclination. To be middle class was to see yourself as among the chosen, but to be conscious of your own society's treacherous quicksands—the codes and rankings.

Lucas knew himself to be indisputably middle class: father a bank manager, home in a leafy suburb, attendance at a minor public school. Except that he had displayed revisionist tendencies quite early on: he wouldn't join the Cubs, he played rugby and cricket only under duress, he haunted the local public library. As an only child, he received much parental attention. His father was disturbed by what he saw as a bolshie streak; his mother was more tolerant. She was a woman of large energies and no qualifications. In another age, she would have swept to the helm of some organization. As it was, denied the possibility of a job commitment, she became a vigorous worker for local charities. When Lucas's father died of a heart attack at fifty, she was able to make such interests a full-time commitment, disappearing every day to serve the Red Cross, Dr. Barnardo's, the NSPCC.

At Oxford, Lucas fell in with sympathetic spirits. At last, it was all right to be besotted with books, to admire aspiring poets, to wear an open-necked shirt and corduroys, to sit up all night talking about art and literature. He joined the Fabian Society, and began to question the basis of his own circumstances. His father would have had a fit. His mother was more pragmatic; her own exposure to unsuspected areas of misery and distress through her commitment to good works had considerably tempered her outlook. "I'll never vote Socialist," she told Lucas. "But I can see their point."

"Am I a snob?" he asked himself. "Are we snobs?" he had asked his friends, in those late-night sessions, wreathed in cigarette smoke. And they had decided that they were, but that this was not their fault. The case was put that you could be ideologically committed to Fabian beliefs, without being forced into comradeship with people from an alien background. "I'm just not compatible with working-class people," said one young activist. "But I'd die on the barricades in their defense." At the time Lucas had thought this comment unexceptionable but was perhaps slightly dismayed by the knowledge that he felt rather the same himself. His own dealings with those outside his class had been the routine contact with tradesmen, with shop assistants, with all those who serviced the world in which he lived, alongside a more familiar relationship with Joe, who came in to help his mother with the heavy garden work, and Mrs. Carter, who cleaned and did the washing and ironing. But now, at Oxford, he was alongside scholarship men, people his own age and in his own situation, who were doing what he was doing, who were his peers, but who had come from behind the invisible, unmentioned barrier; they spoke with what was called "an accent," they were determined, hardworking, they could be truculent or contemptuous. He struck up a few friendships with such men, and found himself always a touch apologetic, vaguely defensive. He certainly did not feel superior; rather, it was as though he were guilty of some unstated generic offense which was not strictly his doing but for which he must carry the can.

In 1941, in the streets and in the shelters and in the hurly-burly of the wardens' posts he had seldom felt like that. Perhaps it was simply that, for the most part, you were too busy for such refinements of response—your dealings with others were immediate and essential and were concerned with telling them what to do, or being told yourself, or trying to extract information or convey it or argue the toss about who should go where and why. Oh yes, all those subtle signals were still around, but they were muted, they had lost their potency; what mattered were the sirens and the darkness and the great threatening dome of the sky out of which bombs would fall. Set against that, a person's credentials came to seem rather insignificant.

And now that it was "after the war," that yearned-for nirvana, they inhabited this battered place in which the only people not complaining were those too young to remember what it had been like before—that time a handful of years ago which now seemed like another country. Everybody complained about the shortages and the deprivations; women complained about men; the returning warriors went to the pub and complained about everything; the middle class complained about the government.

Lucas did not. This, after all, was what he had hoped for since those idealistic Oxford days. He still sometimes attended Fabian gatherings; he had joined the Labour Party. But he was no longer much interested in theory. Back then, there had been fervent discussion about how best to reconstruct society, about how you could procure the prosperity and happiness of all. Well, the process of reconstruction was now in hand, from the slow assault by bulldozer on the clobbered cities to the majestic creation of the welfare state, and it all felt rather more mundane than euphoric. Lucas was less disgruntled about the lack of comforts and, indeed, of necessities than were most; he had been going without for years and so had most of those whom he knew best. They had all been chronically short of money and were used to making do with what they could afford: a simple diet of eggs and cheese and bread and vegetables and the occasional chop. It was normal to use margarine instead of butter. And fuel was expensive so you put up with being chilly, rather than throw on some more coal or turn up the gas. You seldom bought new clothes but kept an eye out for jumble sales and secondhand stalls in markets. Admittedly, the universal constrictions of today were of a different order; they seemed to depress the entire nation. But even so Lucas could not feel that so far as he personally was concerned things were so very different from before the war. And the same went for Molly, who had spent all her childhood in circumstances of cheerful stringency. The Somerset cottage had been Spartan. Lucas remembered one Christmas he had spent there, the frost thick on the insides of the windows, the candles, and the oil lamps, the daily labor of fetching water from the outside tap, the trips to the privy, Lorna struggling over a load of washing in the big copper; he saw her in the village shop, considering the extravagant purchase of a quarter pound of bacon. But he remembered also, and more vividly, laughter around the kitchen table, a picnic up on the hill, in springtime. And he remembered the merriment with which Matt and Lorna had recounted her parents' first visit to the cottage, and their dismay: "Oh, my dear . . ."

He had not at that point met Marian Bradley, but he knew enough of her, and had seen enough like her, to be able to hear the voice, and when eventually, as Lorna's husband, he did meet her, that long-ago account rang in his head. He and Lorna were received at Brunswick Gardens. He had been acutely conscious of Marian's assessing gaze as he entered the room at Lorna's side; she had looked him over, made her judgment, and turned to her daughter with a practiced smile. "So this is Lucas," she had said. And he had heard that same note of incredulity: "Oh, my dear . . ."

"When I was very young," Lorna had once said, "I pretended I was a changeling. You know, like in fairy stories. I always did feel that I was a misfit. I could never be what Mummy wanted. My hair wouldn't curl and I was hopeless at dancing class. The boys did everything right; I didn't. So I had this fantasy that really I belonged somewhere else and one day the fairy prince would arrive and recognize me and whisk me off."

"I suppose he did," said Lucas. "Matt."

Lorna looked away. They did not much talk of Matt, though Lucas sometimes felt that they should do so more, if only for Molly's sake. Lorna was still distracted by grief—he knew that. Sometimes she would fall silent during a conversation, or freeze in the midst of some task, and he knew that grief had come sneaking up and clutched hold of her again. He knew also that she felt guilty because her feelings for him were not like her feelings for Matt. He had said, "It doesn't matter," and he had meant it; it was enough that he could be with her, always.

"Matt happened, yes," Lorna said, after a moment. "But sooner or later I would have cut loose anyway. I was having awful rows with them, at the time. I wouldn't go to balls and parties and look for a husband, like you were supposed to do. It was because of a row with Mummy that I was sitting on that park bench that day."

"Then your mother is indirectly responsible. We should all be grateful to her."

There was a silence. Matt was a shadowy presense, conjured up by the "we."

"Lucas," said Lorna. "You are the nicest person I know. And I love you."

Soon after that time, Simon was conceived.

A war baby, though the war was in its last dreadful throes by the date of his birth. And now he was a child in this pinched and dingy peacetime, a grubby toddler with Lorna's eyes and a beaky little nose that reflected Lucas's. His deprived status was recognized in every quarter. Neighbors referred to him as "the poor little mite," Lucas's mother descended whenever she could to sort him out. Lorna's parents did not visit but sent parcels of black market goods from time to time—tinned ham and butter and chocolate and scented soap—which seemed like a local version of American relief aid, those benevolent Bundles for Britain. Lucas and Molly received these offerings with interest and a certain cynicism. Molly had had so few dealings with her grandparents that she would not have known them if she met them in the street. She recognized that they were in some unidentifiable way from an alien world, rather as though they were foreigners. Lucas's house was quantifiably different from the Somerset cottage, which she remembered only dimly, but there was a sense in which the same language was spoken in the two places, the codes and the climate were similar. Her grandparents, she sensed, came from elsewhere, a place where things were done differently. She had never questioned Lorna, but she registered the fact that Lorna hardly ever referred to her parents, and took note.

Matt's family, tucked away in the border country, wrote fortnightly letters and made the laborious journey to London every now and then. Molly had been to stay with them in the school holidays, at the neat terrace house in the small gray town from which her father had trekked to London and to art school, clutching his scholarship. They were quiet people, who had first been made anxious by their son's precarious way of earning a living, and now were scarred by sorrow. They hung over Molly protectively, and indeed had suggested that she come to live with them, after Lorna's death. Lucas had put this proposal to her, writhing about in embarrassment and worry: "It's for you to decide. Of course I don't want you to go, but you must think what you would rather do."

She had not needed to think. She knew that it would be out of the question to leave this house. Lucas. Simon.

She said, "I want to stay here."

Lucas reached out and squeezed her shoulder. He took his glasses off and started to polish them. "Well, good. Thank goodness for that."

Part 4

MOLLY WENT TO WORK at the library because someone had left a copy of the *Evening Standard* in the tube. She picked it up, glanced through the pages, arrived at Situations Vacant, and learned that this library, which was in fact called the Literary and Philosophical Institute and hailed from the early nineteenth century, was in need of a library assistant. Why not? she thought. I like books. I am not a trained librarian but I have a shiny new degree, barely used. I can learn. I am rather more than literate, and said to be personable. Better this than dogsbody in an office, or tea maker at the BBC.

She got off the tube at South Kensington, and went home to tell Lucas that she was going to work at the Lit. and Phil.

"How do you know they'll give you the job?"

"Because I shall wear my very nicest smile, and appear to be both efficient and astonishingly well read."

"I'm sure they'll be bowled over," said Lucas. "Mind, books are filthy things. Don't imagine it'll be nice clean work. Especially if they're a hundred years old."

Waiting for the interview, she eyed the competition: two girls in twinsets, tweed skirts, lisle stockings, and brogues, and a youth with acne. It emerged that one of the girls had just finished her librarianship course. Oh dear, thought Molly. She was wearing her new black batwing sweater and a turquoise felt skirt, with a wide elastic belt. Lucas had thought this outfit a touch emphatic: "It's somehow more art gallery than library."

"But I don't have any librarian clothes," said Molly. "They'll have to take me as I come."

Simon said, "Actually, you've got lipstick on your front tooth," and shambled off to school.

She found herself confronted by four people seated behind a baize-covered table in a room lined with floor-to-ceiling bookcases. Unfortunately, she had by now become somewhat infatuated with the library, which reeked of old books, had squashy armchairs and tables littered with magazines—and a warren of rooms, crammed with books in various states of decrepitude, accessible only by imposing mahogany ladders; this interview had begun to matter to her.

There were two middle-aged women in navy suits behind the table, an elderly man, and another man, who sat at one end, slightly apart and evidently in a state of extreme boredom, his eyes on a pile of papers in front of him: a fortyish sort of man, dark, with a rather intense stare on the rare occasions when he looked up.

The elderly man introduced himself as the Chairman of the Trustees and took the lead: questions about her interests, her degree course, her skills. The two women chipped in at points. The job involved rather more than assistance with cataloguing, shelving, and manning the issue desk, it seemed. "We are not just a library, you see," said one of the navy suits. "We are for members a sort of club, a refuge from the daily grind. Things must be welcoming. There are the flowers, and the coffee machine."

Molly said that she was especially fond of flower arranging. Coffee machines were a particular interest.

"Well," said the chairman. "I think perhaps that's all. Thank you, Miss Faraday—we'll let you . . ."

The man at the end stirred, shot a look at Molly, broke in. "May I ask, Miss Faraday, what book is on your bedside table at this moment?"

The chairman drew in his breath, and then cleared his throat. One of the women bounced in her seat.

Molly stared directly at the man. "There are three," she said. "One is the Collected Works of Shakespeare, because my brother is doing *The Merchant of Venice* at school, and I am giving him some help. There is also a Gallimard edition of a novel by François Mauriac; I am finding it quite hard going, but I am keen to improve my French. And there is a novel by Elizabeth Bowen, which I am enjoying."

The man said, "Thank you. May I suggest that Françoise Sagan might appeal more to someone of your generation." He glanced at his watch, and began to line up his papers. The chairman half rose, and indicated the door.

Three days later, Molly heard that she had got the job.

"Well, well," said Lucas. "Clever girl. I advise dungarees and a pair of gardening gloves. Possibly a face mask."

In fact, the library turned out to be far from atrophied. Its core collection did indeed hark back to the early nineteenth century and festered on the shelves, for the most part, but acquisitions were kept bang up to date. There were ranks of new dust jackets in the main reading room, where the membership foregathered for a cup of coffee, a glance at the papers, and their weekly fix of books. There was a waiting list for the latest Graham Greene or Charles Morgan or Vincent Cronin; the new Iris Murdoch flew out of the door. The clientele was the *haute bourgeoisie* of that part of London; membership was a prized commodity. If you were a member of the Lit. and Phil. you were a person of discernment; if you were on its Board of Trustees you were one of the elite.

Molly was acclimatized there within days. Librarianship could be picked up with ease by anyone with their wits about them, she decided. She enjoyed bustling around with an armful of books; she was interested in the intricacies of the card index and the shelving system; she became a deft operative at the issue desk. The members found her courteous, well-informed, and a help if you were stuck for choice: a charming girl, in fact, quite a breath of fresh air.

This last comment was overheard by Miss Clarence, the librarian, and did Molly no good. Miss Clarence had already let it be known that she resented the Trustees' policy of interviewing without her presence: "One is allowed a hand in the short list, and that is that. Not entirely satisfactory." The other library assistant was a woman in her thirties, given to sucking polo mints and in strict fealty to Miss Clarence; she made it clear that she found Molly's arrival an intrusion.

"The two pegs to the right of the washbasin are Miss Clarence's and mine. I suggest the one behind the door for you. You're not library-trained, are you?"

"No," said Molly. "But I've used them." This was a deliberate shaft; Jennifer was not a graduate. Molly did not like being told where to put her coat, and that she should bring her own hand towel for use in the staff cloakroom.

The shaft was ignored; sensibility was not Jennifer's strong point. "One of the other girls on the short list was qualified. Miss Clarence has been told that Mr. Portland spoke strongly for you, and so . . ." Jennifer shrugged.

"Mr. Portland?" said Molly, interested. "The old man?"

Jennifer looked shocked. "The Chairman? No, of course not. Mr. Portland. He's a publisher and—oh, I don't know what else. He's very grand and well off, anyway. Everybody's heard of him."

"I haven't."

Jennifer looked supercilious. "There are some very well-known people among our members."

Miss Clarence evidently felt that Molly was inclined to carry fraternization with the members too far, a response provoked no doubt by the breath of fresh air remark. After a couple of weeks she took her on one side.

"One does, of course, want to be of every service to the members but at the same time it is essential to resist what one has to call time wasting. You were at least twenty minutes with Mr. Trubshaw this morning."

"He'd forgotten his glasses and wanted something light for his wife that she hadn't read before."

Miss Clarence shook her head. "Even so. There was a stack of requests that needed processing. You must learn how to detach yourself—politely, of course."

Without his glasses, Mr. Trubshaw had been unable to spot the tiny hieroglyph at the foot of page thirty-three in any book whereby Mrs. Trubshaw indicated for her own future reference that she had read this work. Molly was impressed by this adroit system and quite ready to help with the trawl of the fiction shelves. It seemed a bad idea to enlarge on this to Miss Clarence, so she nodded and said that she would try swifter detachment, in future. Since many of the members came in for a chat quite as much as for a book, and had to make do with the staff if there was no other member to hand, she thought that it would be hard to comply with this. Especially as many members tended to home in on her, nowadays, perhaps on account of Miss Clarence's more austere outlook.

"I shan't stay there forever," Molly told Lucas, "But it does nicely to be going on with."

When she displayed her first pay packet, Lucas had eyed it with admiration.

"I've never had one of those in my life," he said. "What it is to join the salaried classes."

The Heron Press was in decline. Indeed, it was at its last gasp. A changing climate of book production, the demise of illustration and increased costs were making it more and more difficult for Lucas to produce a book and break even, let alone make enough profit to provide a living.

"This is the twilight of the fine press," he would say. "Oh well, I had a run for my money, I suppose." He now spent most of his time on freelance copyediting and proofreading, working at a disheveled desk in the former Heron Press office, from which would come periodic yelps of dismay and disgust. Occasionally, he would sneak down to the basement to operate the press, in some wistful production of a selection of poetry for private distribution, or an elegant little edition of a favorite essay or story. "Self-indulgence," he said. "Sheer nostalgia. Eventually, it will be just the annual Christmas card. Never mind, we had our day."

The tall house in Fulham was as it had ever been: untidy, grubby, unlike other people's homes. During the years that Molly was away at university she had returned to it each time with a mixture of exasperation and fond relief. If she brought her friends there, they were entranced—by the evidence of an alternative lifestyle, by Lucas's awkward appeal.

"He's not a bit like a *father,*" they would say.

And Molly would reply, "He is an accidental father."

Simon was now interested in football, meccano, and rock and roll. Both football and the music had Lucas on the ropes, as parent. The sound of Simon's gramophone reduced him to a tormented, angular heap, crouched with his hands over his ears, muttering "Oh dear, oh dear, oh dear . . ." In the service of Simon's football, he would sometimes take him up to the park and kick a ball around with him—ventures from which he returned gallantly limping. "That it should come to this," he said to Molly. "I spent my entire boyhood avoiding games if I possibly could."

Molly knew that the time had come to leave the house in Fulham. She was twenty-two, and people of twenty-two do not live with their families, even a family so far removed from the norm as Lucas and Simon. She began surreptitiously to hunt for something to rent, fortified by the pay packet. Eventually she found a room in another girl's flat, with share of kitchen and bathroom.

Lucas was astonished. "But why? You've got a room and share of kitchen and bathroom here."

She tried to explain, skirting the word independence, which was difficult.

Simon looked knowing. "I expect she's got a boyfriend."

"G-good heavens," said Lucas. "Have you?"

"I don't know why you should be so amazed at the possibility. As it happens, I haven't. The girl in the flat is called Glenda and she works at Peter Jones. And listen—I've had a thought. If I'm not here you could have a lodger in my room. Useful income."

Lucas sighed. "I can see you're set on it. Simon and I will go to pot without you, mind. As for a lodger, they'd want cooked breakfast and clean sheets. We'll see."

"I'll only be ten minutes' walk away. I shall come back for lunch on Sundays. And look in often."

"What about my homework?" grumbled Simon.

"We shall have to struggle on as best we can," Lucas told him. "Anyway, my math is improving. You said yourself that we got B+ last week for algebra." He looked at Molly. "You had better take some of Matt's engravings with you to add a touch of class to your new hideout."

The walls of the Fulham house were lined with Matt's work: a farmhouse with geese, a church tucked away among hills, small intimate studies of spiderwebs or blackberries. Shakespeare characters. Ducks, and a lake, and a distant girl in a white dress. Molly had in her bedroom a Victorian jug and basin of flowered china; there was still a dim picture in her head of these objects in another context, which she knew to be the Somerset cottage.

Her parents seemed to her now to be somewhere far away, as though you looked through the wrong end of a telescope. At the same time, they were constant, frozen forever in a particular instant of recollection: her father dressed as a soldier standing in a doorway, her mother in the office here in the Fulham house, her hands on the typewriter, looking up with a smile. Her mother wiping a cut on Molly's leg with cotton wool that becomes bright with blood; her mother pinning washing on a line, and Molly hands her the pegs; her mother standing at a window, here in Fulham, and when she turns around her eyes are shiny with tears.

They are locked into Molly's childhood, her parents. They were somewhere long ago, always there, unchanging. They would never get any older, unlike Lucas, who had gray hair now, and Simon, who was hurtling from childhood into adolescence. She would see them always with her own child's eye, these distant, immortal figures. What she felt for them was a trace of childhood emotion, which seemed to come smoking back, when their images floated into her head. She became for an instant a child again, experiencing them.

Her adult self saw them differently, as simultaneously remote but deeply personal. She saw them also with detachment, as themselves: young people who had not lived for very long. She felt a strange protectiveness toward them, as though she guarded them in her mind, affording them some kind of survival. But at the same time she knew herself to be without them, entirely. To be parentless is to be in some way untethered. For Molly, it was also a recipe for determined self-sufficiency.

"You are such a competent girl," Lucas would say, observing with awe as she negotiated her way through the labyrinthine process of getting a grant to enable her to go to university, as she searched out vacation jobs to eke out the grant, as she emerged with a degree in History and a high zest for whatever lay ahead.

Once, he added, "But so was your mother, in her different way"—shook his head violently and changed the subject. It was at such moments that Molly saw that he grieved still, and presumably forever would.

The trouble with competence was that it landed you with tedious jobs. At college, you ended up as the secretary of societies, or the person who ran the Junior Common Room. At home, she had for years overseen the acquisition and preservation of Simon's school uniform; he would have left the house sockless and capless were it not for her. Lately, she had helped Lucas to wrestle with his income tax forms.

"My income is derisory anyway," he complained. "I am not worth their attention. Are you quite sure they'll send me to prison if I don't do this stuff?" Molly would also take command of the unpaid bills on the kitchen dresser from time to time, and instigate essential household repairs, though this last was a problem since there was never any spare money with which to pay for them.

"You could have a career," said Lucas. "Imagine! You could be something respectable like a civil servant, and hang your hat on a pension. I have never known people like that."

Molly grimaced. "Do you mind?" She was not going to allow competence to edge her into some numbing form of occupation. One had to earn a living, but there was no reason why one should not earn it in some way that also was stimulating, and if possible enjoyable. Both Lucas and her father had been driven by passionate commitment to their respective callings. She knew that she lacked specific talent, so that was not an option, unless she were to discover some unsuspected capacity. As for her mother—well, for her mother things had been rather different. Her mother had stepped out of a moribund world, as Molly understood it, and had reconstructed herself. She was resourceful, thought Molly. Flexible, if you like.

"Don't worry," said Lucas. "I can't really see it happening. You with a briefcase and umbrella. You are indeed dismayingly efficient but there is one mitigating circumstance."

"Mmn?"

"You're also quite pretty. I understate the case so as not to encourage vanity."

Molly did not see how these comments related, but she let the matter pass. Lucas's conversational style had always been opaque.

When she looked at the few existing photographs of her mother, she could not think that she much resembled her. Lorna had been considered beautiful, she knew—delicately built, with that small pointed face. Molly was stockier, with more of her father's build, and his thick brown hair, his stronger features. But perhaps there was indeed something about her eyes, her mouth. . . . Pretty?

Men appeared to find her of interest. She had been in demand, at college. She had lost her virginity, because on the whole everybody did, and it seemed rather staid and unadventurous to be forever saying no. Besides, one had all the natural urges; one wanted to see what it was like. But her considered view was that she had never been in love. Not if the condition was indeed as it was portrayed in literature, on the cinema screen, even in the incoherent confessions of her own contemporaries. Oh, she had been attracted, yes indeed, making the decision to say yes this time not very difficult. But she had not yet known the onslaught, the obsession, the madness. All in good time, she thought. One day.

So she had said yes on several occasions, and in consequence had gone through days of anxiety waiting for her period to come. Everyone did. Girls watched the calendar, quaking; from time to time you heard of someone for whom the worst had happened. Like as not, they disappeared from the college, usually forever.

She had been lucky, but had been affronted by this extraordinarily high price that had to be paid for the most basic human activity. By women, that is. Notoriously, contraceptive devices were unreliable—those horrible rubber things; it seemed astonishing that in the day of penicillin and the atom bomb nobody had successfully addressed this one basic need. Were all scientists men?

Once installed in the flat, Molly felt older. Indeed, during the first week she had a sort of crisis and wanted only to scuttle back to the Fulham house, to the familiar backdrop of her life. Glenda, her flatmate, was a worldly girl who was an assistant buyer at Peter Jones, with her sights set on a serious career in the retail business. She evidently did not reckon much with Molly's present occupation. "What are the prospects? Where do you go from there?"

"Onward and downward, I should think," said Molly.

Glenda shook her head. "I shall be buyer when Mrs. Appleby retires next year. By the way, if you want some new cushions for your room, I can get you a staff discount." She was an amiable girl, with a fund of tales about the private life of a department store to which Molly listened with interest over Nescafe in the shared kitchen, while Glenda painted her nails and girded herself up for the next day's round of creative trading. Gradually, the flat began to feel like an acceptable base; Molly knew that, like the library, it was merely a stepping-stone of some kind, but she was pleased to have set off in this way. I have no idea where I am going, she thought, but I have begun.

Her contemporaries at Oxford differed wildly in their own first moves. Many of the men were disconcertingly positive, pitching at once into jobs in industry, or banks, or chosen safe havens like law and medicine. Others wandered uncertainly into teaching, as did many girls. A few girls simply went home and did some cookery or child minding for friends, openly admitting that they intended only to get married, as early as possible, a position that was held in contempt, by and large. Molly shared this disdain. You only had to look around you to see that women for whom marriage was still the primary goal in life were concentrated at each end of society: the aristocracy and the working class. Everybody else had moved on.

"We are the meritocracy," she told Jennifer, as they unpacked a delivery of new titles.

"Well, speak for yourself," said Jennifer. "And do keep biography separate from history."

"We are where we are because of our own abilities," Molly continued. "That's the point. Of course, you're *much* more able than I am when it comes to librarianship, but at least I'm striving, like a good meritocrat."

Jennifer frowned, unsure if this was a dig. "And Osbert Sitwell is memoir, not biography."

"I know. Pompous old windbag."

"That's not very nice," snapped Jennifer. She did not care for value judgments, where the stock was concerned. A book was a book was a book: a matter of classification and shelf mark.

It sometimes seemed to Molly that the library was a place of silent discord and anarchy, its superficial tranquility concealing a babel of assertion and dispute. Fiction is one strident lie—or rather, many competing lies; history is a long narrative of argument and reassessment; travel shouts of self-promotion; biography is pushing a product. As for autobiography . . . And all this is just fine. That is the function of books: they offer a point of view, they offer many conflicting points of view, they provoke thought, they provoke irritation and admiration and speculation. They take you out of yourself and put you down somewhere else from whence you never entirely return. If the library were to speak, Molly felt, if it were to speak with a thousand tongues, there would be a deep collective growl coming from the core collection up on the high shelves, where the voices of the nineteenth century would be setting precedents, the bleats and cries of new opinion, new fashion, new style. The surface repose of a library is a cynical deception.

Two or three times a year, the Trustees held a meeting in the Johnson Room, an inner sanctum reserved for silent study (or sleep). On these occasions, there was extra expenditure on flower arrangements, and Miss Clarence wore her best coat and skirt.

Molly was detailed to take in a tray of coffee and biscuits half-way through the meeting. The Trustees were familiar faces to her, for the most part—assiduous library users. But this was the first time that she had again set eyes on Mr. Portland, whom she had to think of as her supporter, according to Jennifer. He sat once more at the end of the table, slightly apart, and as she placed a cup in front of him, and offered milk and sugar, he glanced up: a nod, a flicker of a smile. Molly, too, nodded, but forbore to flicker; inappropriate, perhaps.

She was back behind the issue desk when the meeting ended and the Trustees dispersed. She noted Mr. Portland—tallish, tanned face as though fresh from somewhere far away and hot, and that indefinable whiff of expense: something about the cut of his suit, his coat, she thought of pedigree animals, nurtured only on the best. He was heading for the door, but swerved suddenly and arrived in front of her.

"Did you take my advice about Françoise Sagan?"

Molly replied that she had not done so as yet—she intended to get hold of a French edition of *Bonjour Tristesse*. This was not entirely true, though she had in any case given up on François Mauriac.

"And are you enjoying life as a librarian?"

"Very much," said Molly. And beamed. After all, this man had apparently done her a favor; the least one could do was to be agreeable.

Mr. Portland seemed to contemplate her. He stood in silence for a moment, then inclined his head. "Glad to hear it—Molly." The glimmer of a smile, and he was gone.

Jennifer had been pretending to sort request slips, but was evidently provoked by this anodyne exchange. "I thought you said you didn't even know who Mr. Portland was?"

"I still don't."

Jennifer sniffed. "Well, he's not usually like that with the staff."

"Perhaps he's trying to give me confidence," said Molly demurely.

The library consumed her days. In the evenings and at weekends, she consumed London, finding aspects of the city unknown to her during her growing-up years with Lucas. Two or three college friends were around, to serve as company; she made new acquaintances. They haunted cinemas, cheap theater seats, espresso bars. The occasional trip to an Italian restaurant, when they could afford it. But there was little money to spare for such things; by and large, entertainment had to be free or cut-price—a walk in Richmond Park, a ride in the river boat to Greenwich, a bus up to Hampstead Heath.

This was life as a grown-up, ejected from the nursery of student days. You worked, and then you went forth and did whatever you liked—you enjoyed yourself. Work was the enabling factor: it determined how you could live and, indeed, if push came to shove, whether you lived at all. I am now a wage earner, thought Molly—an entirely grown-up situation. She found this rather exhilarating. It was up to you. You had to navigate as best you could. There would be opportunities, and there would be reverses. Rather like Snakes and Ladders, a game to which Simon had been addicted when younger.

A few days after the Trustees' meeting she found a package addressed to her at the library. Within was a copy of a French edition of *Bonjour Tristesse,* along with a novel by Rosamond Lehmann. A handwritten card said simply: With the compliments of James Portland.

Over the kitchen Nescafé that evening, she said to Glenda, "If a man sends you books, what would that suggest? An older man."

"Books! It's normally flowers, or perfume. Books I find definitely odd. How old?"

Molly pondered. "Fortyish, maybe."

"Who is he?"

Molly explained.

"Well, generally speaking, you'd say he could only be after one thing. It's the books that are out of step, as it were."

"Couldn't he just be being kind?"

"I suppose he *could* . . ."

Molly wrote a decorous letter of thanks to the expensive address at the top of the card. And it was several weeks before James Portland appeared in the library again. On this occasion, there was one of the lectures that took place in the main reading room out of opening hours. On such evenings, either Molly or Jennifer was required to attend, in order to arrange and then put away the battalion of folding chairs kept in the storeroom. The lecture was over, and Molly was about to start the process of chair removal, when she noticed him at the door to the room, talking to someone. She stacked chairs, briskly, and then saw him coming toward her.

"May I help?"

"Oh no, please don't. Miss Clarence would be horrified. I mean—thank you so much, but really I can manage perfectly well."

"And was Mademoiselle Sagan to your taste?"

"I liked the way it's written, but I found the emotional part a bit—intense. Perhaps you need to be French."

"Personally," he said, "I didn't care for it at all. I assumed that in my case I was the wrong age and the wrong sex."

"It was very nice of you to send the books."

"Not at all. I am in the trade, so I like to promote reading. Though I suspect you need no encouragement."

Molly said that she had always read quite a lot.

"And are you now all set as a career librarian?"

"Gracious, no." Molly hastily backtracked. "That is—I mean—I haven't been doing it for long enough to be certain."

"Quite so. Well—keep reading. Good-bye."

Later, she said to Glenda, "It's all right. That man. It was sort of in the line of business—the books."

"If you say so."

Glenda had a boyfriend in the accounts department at John Lewis. The courtship proceeded at a leisurely pace because the plan was for eventual marriage when they had saved enough for the deposit on a house, with an engagement staged at the half-way post, whenever that might be. "When we've got about two hundred and fifty quid each," said Glenda. "Around next Easter, with any luck, if we go easy on Christmas. Then we'll get the ring."

It seemed to Molly that passion thus contained by economic expediency was rather sad, but Glenda appeared to be quite content with things as they were. She made lists of eventual requirements by way of furnishings and equipment, which were to be tied in with the wedding-present list: "That'll cover quite a lot of it, bar the big stuff."

Molly thought of her mother's two weddings. The second she could dimly remember; Lucas had spoken once or twice of the first, and she had this pale image of her young parents in a bleak register office—made reckless by love. The antithesis of Glenda's pragmatic approach. In fact, the two experiences seemed unrelated. The difference, she thought, was that her parents had refused to allow their circumstances—her mother's family, their combined lack of money—to dictate what they did, whereas

Glenda and her boyfriend were complying cheerfully with social expectations. They were being good citizens, and not doing anything rash in the name of love. In due course they would have two-point-five children, maintain their mortgage and pension payments, and retire into a tranquil old age.

Well, you cannot know how you will deal with things yourself until they happen. A good deal had happened to Molly in childhood—too much, indeed—but she reckoned that since then she had not met with any major challenges. She had picked her way through the thicket of higher education, but that was more a question of doing things right. So I don't know, she thought, if I am a potential Glenda, or the other sort.

The year flowed from winter to autumn. Suddenly, or so it seemed, Molly had been at the library for nearly twelve months. She was an established figure, an old hand, settled into a state of armed neutrality with Jennifer, and occasional bouts with Miss Clarence, who was appreciative of her efficiency but clearly thought her a potential subversive element: too ready with an opinion, too much a favorite with some of the members. It had been noted that whenever Mr. Portland was in he made a point of having a few words with Molly. It was evident that he took some sort of interest in the girl, and of course it was perfectly proper for him to do so in his capacity as a Trustee of the library, but it did not do for the degree of interest to be—well, overly apparent. Miss Clarence observed, reserving judgment.

Molly had begun to rather like James Portland. He was never other than courteous and friendly, and was given to the occasional sardonic remark that made her smile—some tempered swipe at the library's determined resistance to change, or quick savaging of a vaunted new popular title. He liked esoteric books, recherché authors. Indeed, she began to follow his reading tips, and discovered Henry Green and Ivy Compton-Burnett.

The library was not given to innovation. Certain practices had been followed for decades, and would apparently remain enshrined forever: the magazines in the reading room should include the *Times Literary Supplement, The Spectator, The New Statesman, Punch,* but not *Vogue, Which?* or *Country Life;* new applicants for membership must supply the names of two referees; Trustees served for ten years; the list of proposed acquisitions was scrutinized by a subcommittee of Trustees; a further subcommittee supervised the lecture list.

The lectures. Monthly events for the membership. Mostly, they featured an author talking about his or her latest publication—some biography of an eighteenth-century aristocrat, or travel writer's account of a bold foray into jungle or desert or insightful encounter with a primitive people. Occasionally, local history was the topic; at other times someone had been roped in to talk about ceramics or bookbinding. When on chair duty, Molly would attend the lecture, and was sometimes interested, but mostly rather bored. She felt that the library failed dismally to engage with contemporary issues of any kind. Books were the prompt for many lectures, but they were not allowed to provoke debate or dissension.

Other things struck her as unprogressive or downright impractical. Why allow Trustees to serve for ten years, which meant that you were stuck with people like that garrulous old fellow of whom everyone complained? Equally, why allow a self-perpetuating oligarchy to impose its taste upon the acquisitions list? Why not expand the intake of magazines? Why enforce the referee rule for new members, which implied some sort of social scrutiny, when all you needed to know was whether they were in a position to pay the subscription? From time to time she went so far as to voice these ideas to Miss Clarence and Jennifer, and was rewarded with some coolly dismissive remark. When, occasionally, a radical-minded member would raise one of the same points, she would concur warmly, if unwisely.

It was *Lady Chatterley's Lover* that triggered the crisis. Along with all other up-to-the-minute readers, Molly had bought a copy of the Penguin edition when the outcome of the trial made these available. You couldn't not. The papers had made much of it for weeks; the confrontation between the posse of bright, young, articulate people, some of them academics, who trooped in to give evidence for the defense, and this archaic judge, who apparently thought that people still had servants: "Would you want your family or your servants to read this book?" So she had bought the book, and thought "Gosh!" here and there, and had found it not really to her taste, but that was Lawrence rather than the sex—I mean, the business with the flowers was too fey for words, you could only laugh. And the paperback was still in the holdall that she brought to work, when, one day, Jennifer spotted it. She said nothing, but her sudden frozen posture electrified the cloakroom, where she and Molly were hanging up their coats.

Molly followed her gaze. "Have you read it yet?"

"Certainly not," said Jennifer, scandalized.

Molly smiled sweetly. "You really should. It puts into perspective everything that was said at the trial. And after all that was what the trial was all *about*—that people should be able to read what they want to read and make their own judgments. Actually . . . I've just had a good idea. It would be a brilliant subject for a lecture here—a discussion of the whole issue of book censorship, get that Richard Hoggart or someone to come . . ." She checked herself in the mirror, tidied her hair, and sailed out into the day's work, leaving Jennifer in a condition of speechless outrage.

Subsequently, Molly would wonder what on earth came over her that day. Was it a fit of evangelical highmindedness or—and she had a sneaking feeling that this was the truth—the spirit of sheer mischief? She was a trifle bored at the library, irritated by its stubborn conservatism, increasingly footloose. It was a devil-take-the-consequences moment.

During the lunch hour, she drafted a letter to the chairman of the Lectures Committee. The letter was phrased with careful diffidence, saying how much she personally appreciated the opportunity to hear such interesting speakers, but wondering if the committee had thought of introducing an element of discussion, prompted perhaps by contemporary issues. For instance, the current debate on the legalization of homosexuality and the reform of the abortion laws—both of these matters extremely pertinent to literature, and indeed informing the work of various writers of the twentieth century. And then, of course, there was the recent trial and the publication of *Lady Chatterley's Lover,* a most fruitful subject.

That evening, she wrote out the letter. The following morning, she found the address of the lady in question, and posted it.

The heavens fell the next week. A tight-lipped Miss Clarence handed her a note from the Chairman, summoning her to an interview with himself and representatives of the Trustees.

She had wondered if Mr. Portland would be there. He was not. It was the ladies in navy suits and another man with whom she had occasionally exchanged pleasantries. The atmosphere was pained and somber. The chairman wanted to know if she understood that it was not her place, as an assistant librarian, to volunteer advice on the running of the lecture series. Molly replied that she did, really—she had simply been struck by some thoughts, and had wanted to share them. One of the ladies said regretfully that she understood that Molly had been quite critical recently of various aspects of the library's administrative policies. Molly was unable to deny this, and indeed found that she had no wish to do so. The other lady wondered if Molly felt that this job was quite right for her. The other man observed that the library had certain practices, you know, and did not entirely welcome an element of discord. The exchange between the two sides of the table drifted into a kind of stalemate, until after a few minutes more Molly found that somehow she had given in her notice, and would not be working at the library with effect from Friday week.

She said to Lucas "Well, that's it. Unemployed."

"Was it the turquoise skirt, and those earrings? I always felt you didn't dress the part."

"No, it was *Lady Chatterley's Lover.*" Molly explained.

Lucas sighed. "Well, I suppose you can argue that you fell on your sword for freedom of speech. An interesting entry for the *curriculum vitae.* So where next? *Tribune? The New Statesman?*"

"It'll be back to the Sits Vac pages. I'll find something."

It is her last day at the library. There have been furtive farewells from those members in the know. Miss Clarence and Jennifer have remained coolly neutral.

James Portland comes in. He is in need of a particular book, which Molly helps him to locate. She writes out the issue slip, and he says, "Thank you, Molly. See you next time."

"Actually," says Molly. "I shan't be here, I'm afraid."

"Oh?"

She explains, leaving out a good deal, principally the Lady Chatterley matter. She no longer feels entirely compatible at the library, she says, and they feel the same way about her.

James Portland considers this, impassive. At least, no—not entirely impassive, because there is the impression of a man who is doing some quick thinking. Then he fishes in his wallet for a card, which he hands to her. "Would you like to come and see me at this address on Monday morning? Shall we say ten o'clock?"

"I'm not sure what I'm here for," says Molly.

"I hope that you are about to apply for a job."

She stares at him, startled.

"I am in need of . . . an amanuensis."

"I don't know what that means."

"I need a personal assistant. Someone who will deal with all the day-to-day stuff for which I don't have time. Make phone calls, travel arrangements, book theaters and suchlike. I have a secretary in my office who deals with all business related matters but I prefer to keep private and professional life separate—and my activities spread far beyond publishing. I am a collector and a patron, in a modest way. I have an extensive library here that is in desperate need of arranging and cataloguing—a task for which you are now eminently well equipped. Can you type?"

"Not very well."

"Then you will need to do a crash course, for which I shall pay. Shorthand we won't bother with because I don't like dictating. I'll make the job three days a week to start with, in order to fit in the typing course. Hitherto, I have been getting in someone from an agency, which is unsatisfactory. I would prefer a permanent arrangement. The salary would be what you were getting at the library plus twenty percent—promotion, you note. So what about it?"

The room in which they sat was full of books and pictures: glass-fronted bookcases, paintings each with discreet lighting, so that they glowed against the walls. Over the marble fireplace there hung a large abstract oil painting that seemed in some vague way familiar. There were thick oriental rugs on the floor, a great bowl of roses on the table; the tall window looked out onto a leafy square. It was very quiet. Somewhere else in the house a phone rang, and then stopped. James Portland waited, looking directly at her, smiling.

"I'll apply," said Molly.

There was an Italian couple—Maria and Carlo—who lived in the basement and served as cook and butler. There was Maureen, the daily cleaner. There was George, the chauffeur, who sat outside in the sleek black car until James Portland was ready to go. And now there was Molly, in her small office on the top floor, with her desk, her telephone, and her filing cabinets. Here, she received daily instructions from her employer—call the following people, arrange this, order that—and a sheaf of handwritten letters to be typed up. She was a buffer zone, she came to understand, between James Portland and the world; she kept at bay those to whom he did not wish to speak, she filtered through the more privileged. She negotiated with travel agents, restaurants, box offices. She fended off the importunate. She came to know who was who, and where they stood in the hierarchy of those seeking access. She sent flowers to hostesses, and bought birthday presents for nephews and nieces. She acquired a telephone manner, a voice that she hardly recognized: "I'm calling from Mr. Portland's office . . ." Once, she looked up in the midst of such a conversation and saw him watching her from the door. She was a month into the job. When she had put the phone down she said, "Am I doing it right?"

He inclined his head. "As to the manner born. You have assumed a new persona. But mind you keep the old one intact."

She was now looking into a world of which she had known nothing. It was a world in which very large bills were paid at once and without a tremor (she knew this because one of her tasks was to present checks to James Portland for signature), in which there were cocktail parties and private views and charity dinners, in which men smelled of cigars and women each had an individual perfumed aura. These were the people who often arrived at the house in the early evening, as she was leaving, and were shown into the drawing room by Carlo, from whence would come gusts of talk and laughter. Often she knew the names of these people; she had fielded their phone calls, relayed messages to them, thanked them for the delightful party with a bunch of red roses.

James Portland was married, she learned. But Mrs. Portland—Eleanor—lived elsewhere. An amicable separation, this appeared to be, and indeed from time to time an elegant figure would appear on one of the cocktail evenings, and stand for a moment before the big mirror in the hall, tucking strands of dark hair into a chignon, adjusting a slim black dress. "Is wife," Maria would hiss to Molly. "Is wife not living here. Marriage is not like good marriage."

When her desk was temporarily clear, Molly would attend to the library, which was housed partly in the first-floor drawing room and partly in a big room above, which doubled as James's study. He was James now, at his request, rather than Mr. Portland; at first she had found this form of address inhibiting, but it was beginning to slip off the tongue quite easily. The books were indeed disordered, and she was enjoying the process of rearrangement and the compilation of a card index. There was also the interest of the titles themselves—a varied collection reflecting James's own taste for art and architecture, for travel, for history, and with a considerable assemblage of fiction, plenty of poetry, and an entire case of collectors' editions. It was while she was going through these that she found the Heron Press *Lamb's Tales* with her father's engravings. Delighted, she took it down to her office for closer inspection, and there James saw it lying on the desk when he came in with some letters.

He picked it up. "Ah. Yes—I remember this. Nice production."

"The illustrator was my father."

James opened the book and was silent for a while, turning the pages. "Matt Faraday. Of course." He looked at her. "Wasn't he killed in the war?"

"Yes."

"What a wicked loss. He was outstanding. And for you . . . do you remember him at all?"

"Pictures in the head," she said.

He nodded. "Good." He put the book down. "I'd be happy to give this to you."

"It's very kind," she said. "But Lucas has a copy or two left, I know. Lucas is . . ." She explained Lucas. And her mother. And Simon.

He listened attentively. "Now I understand the spirit of independence. You have had to be self-sufficient. See to things for yourself."

Embarrassed, Molly shuffled papers.

"The radicalism is another matter. But I can see why you and the Lit. and Phil. were not an easy fit. They're a bunch of old stick-in-the-muds, for the most part. I try without success to promote change. I must say, though, the Lady Chatterley proposal wouldn't have occurred to me." He chuckled.

Molly felt a rich blush creep from neck to hairline. "You knew about that?"

"Of course. I was hugely entertained. The outrage . . . Miss Clarence has never recovered, by all accounts. The Chairman blames the current educational climate—the universities have a lot to answer for."

"They produce people like me?"

"Exactly."

"Well," said Molly. "I don't care for pop music and I haven't got a black leather jacket."

"Ah, but you speak your mind. And the Chairman finds your mind perplexing—indeed, downright disturbing."

"Oh dear."

"I shouldn't worry. He's a nice old chap but set fast in whenever it was that he was young—if he ever was."

Molly said, "I hope I'm not going to be labeled 1960 for ever."

"If it comes to that, I am the 1940s—a wartime youth. Do you catch the whiff of austerity and deprivation?"

"Actually, no," said Molly.

"There you are. Some of us manage to rise above it. No doubt you'll kick free of the 1960s, in due course." He put the pile of papers down on her desk. "These by this evening, if you can. And a sycophantic box of chocolates to my sister, please—I forgot to go to dinner with her last night."

Molly tells Lucas, "Rich people are different. Well-off people. Like another species."

"So it's said. Personally, I've never known any. Except a few customers, in the glory days of the Press, and then they were just orders and checks, so to speak, not people. Do you find them congenial?"

"They don't notice me. I'm a telephone voice, or the girl in the office upstairs. An essential furnishing, that's all."

"How obtuse. What about your employer? I hope you are not just furniture to him."

"I think James notices me."

At James Portland's big house on the square, people come and go: deliveries from Harrods, from the dry cleaner's, from the wine merchant, the man who winds the grandfather clock (eighteenth-century longcase), the lady who does the flowers (roses out of season, gladioli for parties), friends, rivals, lovers (perhaps).

"Is pity no senora," says Maria. "Man should have wife."

"Bambini might be nice too," says Molly. "Why doesn't Mrs. Portland live here?"

Maria snorts. "Is lady who like her own way." She rolls her eyes. "Have other man, I think."

"Tut, tut," says Molly.

She has not identified any lovers in particular, but one has to assume that they are a possibility. This worldly view is new to her; that's what comes of rubbing shoulders with the metropolitan set, she thinks. I have lost my innocence.

I am in the Victorian governess role, she thinks—largely ignored, invisible, neither servant nor gentry. Watching.

She watches the people on the stairs: the polished men, the women in silk. She catches little gusts of conversation: James is buying a Paul Klee, he is selling his Brancusi, so-and-so has made a killing, someone else got their fingers burned.

"It's all white for this evening," says the flower arrangement lady. "Peonies and regale lilies. I do hope Mr. Portland will like it—he has such perfect taste. I love your new haircut, Molly."

"Some person throw up in downstairs toilet," says Carlo. "Have too much to drink. Pig."

There is a raffish fringe to James Portland's acquaintance. A handful of people who are not polished or silken, but wear leather-patched corduroy jackets and polo neck sweaters. These are the writers published by his firm—those who cash in on an arduous trip to a rain forest, or pull off a novel that gets adulatory reviews in the Sunday papers. Molly perceives that such people occupy an ambivalent position—they are not friends, and they are certainly not colleagues, they are both cultivated by James and kept at arm's length. They have to be appeased, but not allowed to come too close. There is a middle-aged lady writer who telephones far too often and must be fobbed off by Molly; "I'm not taking her out to lunch again for at least a year," says James. "Last time I had to hear about her hysterectomy, in vibrant detail." There is a voluble Irishman who has found his way up to Molly's office, where he hung around, and eventually suggested that they should meet up for a drink, when she had finished work. James came into the room at this point, and bundled him away. Later, James returned.

"Did that fellow chat you up?"

"Yes," said Molly. "At least I think that was what he was doing."

"I'm not having that." James was patently furious; Molly had never seen him like that before. "Carlo will be told he is not to be let into the house again."

Molly wonders why this incident has so got up James's nose. On the face of it, she and the writers occupy the same social level—they are necessary appendages but not associates—so it would have seemed rather appropriate for the Irishman to strike up a friendship.

Once a year or so, Molly would visit her maternal grandparents at the house in Brunswick Gardens. She did not find these occasions comfortable; she felt alienated by the determined refinement of her grandmother's lifestyle, and by her grandfather's hearty imperviousness to anything outside his own experience. Sometimes a breezy uncle would be there, with a complacent wife, and some cold-eyed cousins who clearly liked Molly no better than she liked them. Reporting to Lucas, she said, "I think I have dropped out of the upper-middle class. I can't seem to fit there at all."

"I shouldn't worry," said Lucas. "It's called social mobility. Mind, it usually operates the other way—upward rather than downward."

The Faradays she felt easier with, when she went to the little market town on the Welsh borders, though the place seemed to her entirely stagnant, as though you had stepped back twenty years. Her grandparents welcomed her lovingly, and would try to digest her into their hallowed regime of constitutional walks and chapel on Sunday. She felt displaced here also, but differently so, with a shred of guilt at not being able to acclimatize. So where do I belong? she wondered. Is it perhaps not necessary to belong anywhere in particular?

"How did I manage without you?" says James.

They are in the upstairs library, his study. Molly is explaining to him the classification system that she is installing. He rests his hand for a moment on her shoulder. "Perfect," he says. "For the first time I shall be able to find the book that I am looking for. And now I am going to take you out to lunch. I want to inspect the new Greek place around the corner."

"Lovely dress," says Glenda. "With your figure, you can wear these narrow styles. I've got too much bust. You know, you've come on no end over this year. I wouldn't have called you sophisticated back when you moved in here."

"Is that what I am now?"

Glenda considers. "Not really. There's something more unusual than that about you. You're a bit too quirky to be seen as straightforward sophisticated. No offense meant, mind."

"None taken," says Molly.

Lucas and Simon have settled to Molly's absence, still complaining from time to time. The house in Fulham is now in a state of complete dishevelment, full of dirty washing-up, old newspapers, and discarded clothes. It reminds Molly of the most debased kind of student encampment, and whenever she drops by she is driven to do some frenetic tidying, while Lucas and Simon look on tolerantly. Simon is now fifteen; his voice swoops up and down the register, he is nearly as tall as Lucas and has acquired a bass guitar. When this instrument is in operation Lucas sits at the kitchen table with his hands over his ears.

"I had no idea fatherhood would be like this," he tells Molly.

"He'll probably grow out of it."

"You were tranquil, by comparison. And organized. Homework done, school uniform in place."

"Girls are different."

Lucas sighs. "Women will take over, eventually. Just as well. Men have been making a hash of it for years."

"That's a very up-to-the-minute view."

"Really? I'm not usually seen as up to the minute." Lucas surveys his battered cord trousers, his moth-eaten pullover, and then looks at Molly. "You, on the other hand, seem very—contemporary—these days. The sassy fringe. Pink fingernails. Is that what comes of mixing with high society?"

"There's not so much mixing. More, I oblige. I needed a haircut, that's all, and my nails have been pink for years, on and off. Are you being critical?"

"Perish the thought. I look on with admiration. Simon and I are like gawking peasants. After all, we remember you in a gym slip and knee socks."

"I'm twenty-three, Lucas," says Molly.

"I know, I know. And a working woman. Incidentally, I hope he appreciates you—this James what's-his-name. Does he?"

"I get the impression that he does."

If it is not necessary to belong anywhere in particular, thinks Molly, then the trick is to float free, but to keep a weather eye out for what's available, if only out of expediency. One may want to touch down somewhere at some point—throw out an anchor. So far, I've not covered much ground. I do know that the upper middle class is not for me, nor is provincial peace, and I didn't get very far with the *haute bourgeoisie*—if the Lit. and Phil. is to be seen as that. I was comfortable enough in Lucas's house, even if always driven to clean up, but Lucas's way of life is not widely representative. And now I do not feel myself to be exactly in accord with the intelligentsia, if the crowd that comes to James's place is that, and I'm not entirely sure that they are, judging by some of the chatter I hear on the stairs. Be that as it may, I have not seen much, as yet. Maybe I should sign up as an investigative journalist, or do a Ph.D. in social studies—a spot of anthropology.

James has taken to staying longer in Molly's office, when he arrives with a string of instructions, or letters to be typed. Sometimes he settles in the armchair by the window, lights a cigarette, and talks: about some exhibition he has seen, about a book they may publish, about anything. On these occasions, there is something in the air—a crackle, a charge—that Molly finds both stimulating and unsettling. When he is gone, the room feels flat.

"There's this man who has circumnavigated the British Isles in a coracle. That's a kind of floating bathtub made of leather. Would you want to read about that?"

"I suppose it might have an awful fascination. As a thing you wouldn't dream of doing yourself."

"Exactly. But what about the memoirs of a lapsed nun?"

"I think not."

"My sentiments entirely." He is considering her, through the blue swirl from his cigarette—that intense look first encountered at the Lit. and Phil. interview. "Incidentally, I like the way you've got your hair now."

"Oh, please," says Molly, cross. "Everyone keeps going on about my hair."

"Sorry, sorry." He spreads his hands. "Very un-nunlike, anyway. Perhaps that was my train of thought. You didn't go to a convent school, did you?"

"By no means. I went to the local grammar."

"Of course. Convents turn out hothouse flowers. Eleanor was at one."

His wife is seldom mentioned. Now, for an instant, she seems to stand in the room, a suave observing presence.

There is a silence. James stubs out his cigarette, sighs. "I'd better go. There's a boring meeting for which I shall be late, and then I have to give lunch to an egomaniac author. And I have offended you anyway by making intrusive personal remarks."

"I'm not offended. Just—a haircut seems unimportant."

"You are such a level-headed girl, if I may say so. Oh dear, I'm doing it again."

Molly picks up her notepad. "Do you want an early morning flight to Geneva next week?" she says crisply. "And have you remembered about the Sotheby's sale?"

"Yes and yes."

James is now at the door. He pauses. "Do you like dancing?"

"Dancing?" she stares at him.

"It's my birthday on Friday. I thought we might celebrate together at Quaglino's. Are you free?"

"Oh . . ." she says. "Well, yes, actually."

Molly inspects herself in the bathroom mirror. Trouble has been taken. Indeed, she has pulled out all the stops—Paint the Town Pink lipstick and nail polish, Frosted Ice Blue eye shadow, mascara, a dab of Mitsouko behind each ear and at the wrists. The strapless green taffeta dress, with the bolero jacket that can be taken off for dancing. This is three years old but her only evening wear, and will have to do. She is not winsomely fashionable, like the women who sail up the stairs to James's parties, but the mirror tells her that she has certain advantages. She has a good figure, she is . . . well, reasonably pretty. And she is aware above all of youth. She sees herself with momentary detachment, and notes rounded flesh, bright eyes, that glow—that indefinable quality that says, fresh this morning, just hatched, new-minted. In due course, she thinks, one will go brown at the edges, like everything else. So make the most of it, eh?

"Quaglino's?" says Glenda. "You jammy beggar!"

The diners' tables surround the dance floor. The lighting is dim. Candles flicker in little glass bowls. Waiters flit about. There is a bottle of champagne in a silver bucket. When first this was poured, Molly raised her glass: "Happy birthday!"

"It's not my birthday."

"But you said . . ."

"A foul deception. I thought you'd feel you couldn't refuse if I said that."

Molly laughs.

He does not talk of books or exhibitions but tells her about his wartime experiences as a liaison officer with the free French in London. "They needed fluent French speakers, and that was about the only skill I had, thanks to my French mamma. Not exactly front-line stuff. North Africa with de Gaulle was the nearest I got to a battlefield."

Molly tells him about her parents, the Somerset cottage, the house in Fulham. "What a rite of passage," he says. "I can't think why you're as normal as you are."

"What's normal?" says Molly.

"Good point." The band is now playing. He rises. "Would you like to dance?"

He is a good dancer. He holds her close, he moves decisively, taking her with him, but at once they are moving in the most pleasurable accord. Molly feels that she has never danced so well. A quickstep. A samba, which she had not realized that she could do; she responds to his steering hand, and lo! she is doing the samba. Then the music shifts again, and they are into a foxtrot. He is holding her very close now, pressed right up against him, they are cheek to cheek. He murmurs something. "Molly . . ." he is saying. "My dear Molly." She can feel his breath in her ear, the roughness of his skin against hers, the length of his body. He is holding her so close that she can feel something hard up against her groin. You know where you are when you dance with a person, she thinks; dancing is very explicit.

He leads her back to the table, refills their glasses, and begins to talk about his family—his father who died when he was twenty, his mother who lives in Brighton, and is querulous. Presently, they dance again. And again.

He drives her back to the flat. He walks up the flight of steps to the front door with her. She had wondered if he was going to ask to come in, or indeed if she should suggest it, but the matter does not arise. He simply takes her in his arms and kisses her—a full kiss, his tongue in her mouth, searching. Then he draws back, cups her face in his hands and says, "What a wonderful evening. Thank you, darling Molly." And he goes.

She climbs the three flights of stairs to the flat, knowing that when the point comes, and he asks her to sleep with him, she will not say no.

She has wondered how it will be, when they meet again on Monday morning, when he comes into her office with a fistful of papers, says, "Good morning, Molly." Things are different now, are they not? How will this difference be? How will he deal with it? How will she?

And in the event, when he comes, he does not say the usual good morning, but stands in the doorway, smiling—a different sort of smile. "Hello," he says.

They sort out Molly's tasks for the day. He stands by her chair and touches her neck. "I have meetings at the office this morning," he says. "And then I'm elsewhere this afternoon. I should be back about six. Could you stay on a bit, so that we can have a drink together?"

Many hours later, she is lying in his bed. He has gone into the bathroom next door; she hears the shower running. He comes out drying himself, and she thinks that when you see someone you know without their clothes, they are transformed—intimate, startling. He sits down on the bed, pulls back the sheet, looks at her. Perhaps he is thinking the same. He runs his hand down her body.

"All right?"

She says, "Is it always like this?"

"Actually, no. In fact, quite rarely."

There were now two levels to life in James's house. There was the daily routine in Molly's office on the top floor, which continued much as it ever had: she typed and made phone calls and went out to do errands, and in spare moments she attended to the library. And now there was the other, extracurricular life, in which she and James dined out, and went to the cinema and to the theater, drove into the country at weekends. And spent many hours in James's bedroom.

When they were out and about, they sometimes ran into people that James knew. He would introduce her, and she read their faces.

"Your friends are wondering," she told him.

"Then they will have to do so."

He now wanted her to join those evening drinks parties in the big room on the first floor. She did so with reluctance, but he would steer her toward someone reasonably congenial, and after a few occasions she found a certain confidence with the suits and the silken women, though without acquiring any taste for this company. Some ill-adjusted writer was usually the best bet. Poets stood in corners, holding out a glass for replenishment and filching cigarettes. Hoary travel writers complained to Molly about their meager advances. Occasionally, such people were curious about her own status.

"I'm the amanuensis," she would say. Sometimes, she met a look of skepticism, or even amusement.

"Am I your mistress?" says Molly.

"Hmn. What exactly is a mistress?"

"You tell me. I don't know about these things."

"I will tell you one thing," says James. "I am becoming unhappy with this situation."

"Me?"

"I'm concerned about your reputation."

"I think I'm too young to have one."

They are in the Greek restaurant near to the house, a favorite haunt. Indeed, the proprietor ushers them now to their special table. Later, they will go back to the house, and up to James's bedroom.

"Maria and Carlo probably know," says Molly. "But they are hardly going to spread the news, are they?"

He frowns. "We should have somewhere else to go. Not the house. In fact, I have a proposition. I should like to get a flat—take out a lease for you. A nice flat. Near here. A bolt-hole."

She considers this, over the moussaka, through the carafe of retsina. And the more she considers, the more a still, quiet voice tells her that it will not do. Oh yes, one's own front door would be nice, privacy would be nice. But. But, but, but. Once again, she finds herself skirting the word independence.

"It's very kind . . ." she begins.

"No, it's not," he says. "It is entirely self-interested. The idea becomes more appealing by the minute. Somewhere to which I could vanish—incommunicado. With you there. If it smacks of kept woman, I'll deduct five shillings a week from your salary as rent, to keep you happy."

She laughs.

"Well, then?"

"No."

"Why not?"

"Because . . . because . . ."

"Because you're a nice old-fashioned girl? But you're not, are you?"

"Because I'd be . . ."

"Yes?"

She is silent.

He scowls. "Because you're just contrary, some would say. Can't see a good thing when it's staring you in the face."

"Now you're cross."

He sighs. Reaches out and puts his hand on hers. "No, I haven't managed to get cross with you yet. Though that may come. Oh Molly, whatever blew you my way?"

"Someone in the tube," she says, remembering. "Who left their paper on the seat."

The restaurant owner removes their plates, notes the enfolded hands, beams benignly.

"He very pleased since you here," purrs Maria. She has brought up a mid-morning cup of coffee for Molly, and lingers to chat.

Molly inclines her head. Any comment would be precarious. Both of them are well aware of Maria's subtext, but Molly is not going to acknowledge that.

Maria's dark eyes glitter. "Is busy man, have many friend, but is good have special friend."

This is a step too far. Molly says crisply, "Thank you, Maria." She slaps a sheet of paper into the Smith Corona, and starts to type.

Maria, at the door, does a kind of obeisance. Her expression marries complicity with deference, quite an achievement.

Carlo is avuncular. He treats Molly as a favored niece who is doing exceptionally well in some challenging occupation. "Va bene, Miss Molly," he says, on the stairs, exuding admiration. "Bellissima today, Miss Molly!"

"Paris?" says Glenda. "Well, it's all right for some!" She eyes Molly. "Love the little skirt. Green suits you."

She knows of course. She has observed the car, dropping Molly off at night. She has taken phone calls from him: "Molly . . . It's—um—your friend." She has put two and two together, and two and two have added up to James Portland. It is apparent that she is both impressed and a touch disapproving. This sort of thing is a far cry from a two-year engagement and the deposit on a semi in Bromley. Molly can hear her thinking: where does this go?

When Molly thought about the future, she saw a sort of murky calendar—the century unfolding ahead, with her written into it but in mysterious circumstances. Certain aspects were easy to anticipate, of course—one would get older, and cease to look as one did now, but what other metamorphoses might there be, what else was entered in the calendar? Whatever—there was nothing to be done about it except, surely, to be alert to all that arose, whether in order to avoid disaster or to make the most of an opportunity.

In that case, what exactly was she doing at the moment?

They went to Paris for a weekend, where James needed to look at a Dufy he thought of buying. In the summer, Molly accompanied him to Rome and Milan for a week; sometimes, he had business meetings, and she would wander off on her own, in a state of astonishment. Foreign travel, hitherto, had been a school geography trip to Holland when she was seventeen and a student cycling tour of Brittany. Lucas's idea of a holiday had been an excursion to Brighton or Hampton Court. Now, in Italy, she felt as though she were reincarnated, adrift in a new universe of color and noise and splendor—past and present rolled into one sensational panorama. She plunged into churches and galleries, museums and markets; when she returned to James, she was still heady with what she had seen. He was amused: "I've forgotten what it's like, coming new to it."

Molly was nettled. "That sounds . . . patronizing. I can't help being the age I am—and as untraveled as I am."

"Dear girl—if you haven't realized by now that that's what I *like* about you." He paused, looked thoughtfully at her over the café table. "And do *I* seem unspeakably old?"

She searched for an answer. "Not old. Different. Like a book with more pages. Ones that I haven't read—and can't read."

"Ah. Neatly put."

"And anyway you're not old. Older than me, that's all."

"True. A mere matter of relativity."

"The thing is," she said, high on sunshine and Campari, "that surely as you get older you shed skins, rather like a snake, and each time you end up slightly different. You leave your other selves behind. So you are also various people I have never known."

"You are making me feel unstable. Drink that up—I thought we were heading for the Sistine Chapel?"

Back in London, she began to feel as though she had lived for many years this fractured life, in which sometimes she played one role, and at others a different, private one. Her days would depend upon James's diary: if he had no essential engagements he wanted her to be available in the evening. When, on occasion, she made some arrangement with a friend, he would be piqued. She would be made aware of displeasure. He would stand at the door of the room, his face suddenly dark: "As you wish . . ." She became aware of a volatility in him that could be unnerving—a moodiness that would suddenly engulf him, the pitch into cold unexpected irritation. She liked to be with him, but she knew that she must also be without him. How do people manage to be with one another all the time? she wondered.

Did she love him? I don't know, she thought, because I am not sure how to recognize love. I like going to bed with him—love it, indeed. But is that love?

They drive out of town, one Sunday, and walk in Epping Forest. It is autumn; the place is a glowing tapestry, the leaves a brilliant quilt underfoot. Molly is exuberant, but James is somber. He has been silent in the car, driving rather too fast. Now, he stops suddenly and leans on a gate, staring out over fields.

"I need to talk to you."

She feels a lurch of dismay. It occurs to her that he is going to end things—the idea dropping into her mind from nowhere. Hence the silence, the sobriety. And almost at once that thought is chased by another: I don't want to, I'll be wretched at first, but nothing is forever, and one will recover. Job-hunting again—oh, dear. She joins him at the gate, and contemplates the field, the impervious herd of grazing cows.

He does not look at her, but says, "Molly, I am in love with you."

"Oh . . ."

Now he turns to her. "It wasn't meant to be like this."

"How was it meant to be?" she says, after a moment.

"Like most such things. And it turns out that this is not. For me, at any rate." He waits, watching her.

She has to reply, somehow. She says, "I haven't your experience. I haven't had many—such things. Indeed, any." After a moment, she adds, "Is it my fault?"

"No. It's mine. I should have known better. This is retribution—for seducing a minor."

"I'm not a minor," exclaims Molly indignantly.

"In my terms you are. I should have stuck with my shop-soiled contemporaries."

"Is it because of—bed?"

"No. At least, that comes into it, of course. Unfortunately it's something entirely uncontrollable, even for someone as controlled as myself."

There is silence. Cows chomp. She knows what she is supposed to be saying, and knows also that she cannot say it, because now she understands, she sees that this thing she has yet to recognize, has not arrived, not now, not with him.

He takes her arm. "We'd better be getting back." He shepherds her through the trees, the late rich October afternoon, talking about a play they saw last night.

He says nothing more for a week. He is calm, considerate, all is as it ever was. When he does speak, it is at the house, in his study.

"Not now," he says, "I am not asking you to marry me now, immediately, tomorrow. Obviously not—I already am married. But there is going to be a divorce. Eleanor wants it, so do I. It was high time. I am asking you now, for then, so that it can be the light on the horizon. At least, that is what I very much hope."

She has known that this might come, she has sensed it, and she has dreaded it. All through the week, she has felt herself drawing apart from him; for her, all has not been as it ever was, a fault line has sprung, she has been edgy, resistant. And now, craven, she is silent. They look at one another, in the quiet, book-filled, clock-ticking room.

Eventually, he speaks again. "Don't say anything now, if you'd rather not. You look like a rabbit in the headlights. I'm sorry—is this such a shock?"

"I can't marry you," she says. "I can't marry anyone. I'm not ready. And . . . and I can't live like you do. It has nothing to do with you being older. Just—I couldn't live here, like this." She spreads her hands—summoning up Carlo and Maria, the waiting chauffeur, the parties, the suits, and the smart women. "I'd be no good at it. In time, you'd get fed up with me."

"If I thought there was any chance of that I wouldn't be asking you. I have already made one marriage mistake."

"I'm sorry," she says, hopelessly, staring at the floor. She feels sick. She has felt sick all day, and the day before. It is because of being in such a state about this, she thinks. It must be. She looks at him. "I'll leave. Right away is best, I expect."

"You'll do no such thing." James gets up, puts his hands on her shoulders. "Molly, I don't understand you—but possibly I never have. All right—forget marriage. For the moment, anyway. Carry on as a scarlet woman, if that's the way you want it."

A week late. Ten days. She comes out of the bathroom, ashen-faced, and there is Glenda, silently proffering a cup of tea. They sit side-by-side at the kitchen table.

Glenda says, "I've got a phone number, if you want. A friend of mine was in some trouble, last year."

The Greek restaurant is now the seventh circle of hell. She had said that she didn't really want to go that evening, but he would have none of it. She stares at the plate of moussaka, takes a mouthful, puts down her knife and fork. Tries again, and cannot. Nausea surges.

James says, "Is something wrong? You like moussaka."

She pushes back her chair, flees for the toilet.

When she returns, her plate has been removed. James is concerned. "Are you ill?"

She shakes her head. Then she nods. "Must be," she says.

He is looking intently at her, and then, all of a sudden, he has understood. "No. It's something else, isn't it?" He is on his feet. "Come on, Molly, we're going back to the house." He pushes a note at the proprietor, seizes their coats, bundles her out of the restaurant and along the road.

He sits her down. He fetches a glass of water, and puts it into her hand.

"You're pregnant, aren't you?"

She nods.

"How long?"

"A few weeks."

"Have you seen a doctor?"

"Yes."

He gets up, walks around the room, comes back, puts a hand on her shoulder, walks around again. Sits down.

"This changes everything, doesn't it?"

She whispers, "No."

"What?"

She shakes her head.

"What do you want to do, Molly? Do you want—an abortion? That would not be my choice, but it is up to you."

She takes a deep breath. "I'm going to have it."

"In that case, *we* are going to have it."

"I still can't get married," she says. "I'm sorry, James. I'm so sorry."

"Molly, are you crazy?"

She is silent.

"No," he says, after a moment. "Just—unbelievably cussed. Listen—Molly, darling Molly—are you seriously proposing to go off, on your own, and have a baby? How do you think you are going to manage?"

"Somehow," she murmurs.

He sighs. "We'll talk again tomorrow," he says. "And thereafter. But, for now, I'm going to drive you back to the flat. You need to go to bed, and sleep."

Years after, she would think that you do not so much make decisions, as stumble in a certain direction because something tells you that that is the way you must go. You are impelled, by some confusion of instinct, will, and blind faith. Reason does not much come into it. If reason ruled, you would not leave home in the morning, lest you stepped under a bus; you would not try, for fear of failure; you would not love, in case it hurt.

Years later, that time has lost all chronology; it is a handful of scenes that replay from time to time.

She is with James Portland, in the big house that is still vivid to her.

"I give up, Molly," he says. "I despair. But if this is the way it's going to be, then I am going to make the following arrangements . . ."

Simon drops his school bag on the kitchen floor in Fulham. "Crikey!" he says. "I've just realized—I'll be an uncle."

She lies in a hospital bed; in the crib alongside is a dark-haired bundle at which she gazes with amazement, with love, with apprehension.

Part 5

THEY PICKED THEIR WAY along the dark street past great cliffs of rubbish sacks. Here and there these had given way, releasing a black gleaming glacier onto the pavement, so that you had to step over and around. Some sacks had burst open, spewing out empty tins, nappies, chicken bones, pizza boxes. A cold January wind had everything rustling and flapping.

"Did you see the rat?" said Simon. "Socking great brute."

Ruth screamed.

"Apparently they're everywhere. According to the *Standard,* one sauntered across the dining room at Claridge's."

They arrived at the front door of the house in Fulham, climbed the steps, rang the bell. Molly was carrying an Oddbins bag with two bottles of wine, and a grip containing a casserole swathed in a blanket.

Lucas opened the door, holding a candle, which guttered and almost went out. He had carpet slippers on his feet and a moth-eaten plaid rug around his shoulders.

"Oh, good," he said. "Here's the Red Cross." He took the bags from Molly. "I'm afraid you've hit our power cut slot. We alternate with the next street. It should come on again before too long."

They went into the kitchen, where more candles flickered. "The casserole is nice and hot," said Molly. "We must eat right away." She began to take knives and forks from the drawer in the dresser. Everything was as it ever had been, here; about the only place things are, she thought.

Simon filled glasses. "Well—happy seventy-fourth, Dad."

"You'll have to shout, all of you," said Lucas. "I am getting interestingly deaf. Interesting because the process seems to have a selective facility. I hear things I don't want to hear, like my French girl lodger prancing up the stairs at midnight, but miss choice passages of a Mozart concerto on the radio. I heard seventy-fourth quite clearly, unfortunately. Is it really that?"

Molly ladled casserole. "Eat, everyone."

Ruth said, "I'm freezing." She wore jeans and a skimpy cheesecloth shirt. She sat hugging herself.

"If you won't wear a vest, like any sensible person would in January," Molly told her, "Then that's your lookout."

"And this is the very winter of our discontent," said Lucas. "Or so we're told. Mind, for some of us it is just rather nostalgic. Shades of the 1940s—eh, Molly?" He looked kindly at Ruth. "Your mother and I have lived thus before, in this very room."

Ruth sniffed. "That was the dark ages, wasn't it? This is 1979, for heaven's sake!"

Simon was shoveling down bœuf bourguignon. "Great nosh, Moll. So what are you going to do, Ruth? Join the picket lines—help bring down the government?"

Ruth gave him a stern look. "I simply want to get on with my A level work, and how can I do that in darkness, with rats everywhere?"

Simon sighed. "We look to your generation. You should be manning the barricades. Sorry—womanning."

"Leave the child alone," said Lucas. "And anyway, if she brings down the government, there'll just be another one, won't there? I have long since lost interest in governments. You can't tell t'other from which. In fact, it's surprising how easily one gets used to this blackout—though I dare say it helps to be a veteran. Did I tell you I have a new lodger?"

Actually, this is a rather inviting scene, thought Molly. The light on people's faces, like in a Rembrandt; the candle flicker dancing in the surface of a pewter jug; the way the corners of the room fall away into darkness. We are some group from the past, she thought, a domestic scene from another century, locked away in the benign light of a lost age. Wipe out our modern gear, and we'd fit nicely—Ruth as the archetypal young girl, Lucas and Simon so evidently father and son, with those beaky faces and the specs, and me—well, I'm the hausfrau, I suppose, with my good peasant stew on the table. I need a kerchief and an apron.

"He's a Nigerian student," Lucas was saying. "Only been here a couple of weeks and today I realized that he thought this state of affairs was the norm. I explained that we are suffering a spot of industrial unrest and he was quite surprised. The poor fellow does feel the cold, though. He has borrowed the long johns I used to wear when on duty on blitz nights and is most appreciative."

There was a constantly changing population of lodgers at the house in Fulham, and had been for many a year—an economic necessity for Lucas but also, as he pointed out, a challenge: "At the very least I get a parade of contemporary types—it prevents a moribund view of the world." Molly and Simon, who conferred about Lucas, behind his back, would point out that the flotsam of the bedsit scene are not really representative of society in general. "Just as well," retorted Lucas. "I am spared solicitors and estate agents and stockbrokers. I get fringe figures—like myself."

"What happened to the clairvoyant?" enquired Molly.

"Oh, poor old dear. She went to live with her sister in Enfield. Business had got worse and worse. I suspect she was clairvoyancing all the wrong things—out of touch with the times."

"She told me I was going to marry into the aristocracy," said Ruth.

"There you are. Couldn't spot a nice egalitarian girl."

"One day," said Simon, "you'll get some real nutter. And we shall have to come to the rescue."

"I'm sure you'll do it with great zest," said Lucas comfortably. "Is there any more of this delicious dish, Molly?"

There are so many shadows in this room, she thought. Candlelight creates a further dimension. No wonder people used to believe so fervently in ghosts. Space seems suggestive, packed with possibility. It's Caravaggio as opposed to David Hockney. The Fulham kitchen had become a glowing cavern, its mundane furnishings muted, turned into vague murky shapes. The light picked out faces, hands, the red intensity of wine, the white cascade of wax from candles. Everyone had acquired a new presence; Lucas and Simon were craggy Hogarthian characters, Ruth was romantically pretty. When you can't see things clearly, thought Molly, they are open to interpretation. What is that shape in the corner? The small dark blob on the dresser shelf? What elegant hands Lucas has.

"So, Moll—what are you up to these days?"

"I'm lining poets up for a poetry festival in the summer. Next month, I shepherd three writers around the north country. Arts admin lies low in the winter, gearing up for activity. How's the bookshop?"

"Doing pretty well," said Simon, "considering that we are not much more than a broom cupboard. The thing is to specialize, I think. I'm into travel and topography."

Lucas beamed. "I'm full of admiration. He can talk stuff about turnover and profit margins."

"How's Paul?" inquired Molly.

There is a fractional pause. "Actually, I'm not seeing so much of Paul."

Ruth said, "Doesn't *anyone* in this family ever do anything that isn't arty in some way?" She flung out her hands—histrionic, half serious—stood up to reach for the bread on the dresser, and became for a moment the center of attention, each of the others seeing a different girl. Molly saw the person with whom she had spent much of her life—the *people,* the infant, the child, the children, stage by stage, subsumed into this almost-woman. Lucas thought: dear me, the child is half a head taller than her mother, and Molly is taller then Lorna ever was. Do women grow, generation by generation? Simon saw a flicker of Molly in Ruth's face, caught in the candlelight and remembered—hazily—the schoolgirl Molly, a bustling presence. This girl is different, he thought—quieter, less charged. Not Molly's fire and dash, but there's something else there. Something positive, firm. Got her own views. Good-looking, too—I suppose the boys are sniffing around by now. Help! A grown-up niece.

"We're looking to you to make the break," Simon told her. "Marine biology? Econometrics? And I'm a businessman, I'll have you know."

In fact, thought Molly, we are a conversation piece from another era. Goodness knows what we are, or do. We are a scene at which people stare in an art gallery, wondering about that woman's smile, and what the man is saying, and who spilled the wine.

The overhead light snapped on. Everything in the room leaped into sharp focus. The shape in the corner was the rubbish bin. The blob on the dresser shelf was a roll of insulating tape. There were cereal packets on the side table, and a pile of old newspapers on the floor. The candle flames became faint and foolish. Everyone looked a little seedy. Lucas needed a shave. Ruth had more blue stuff on one eyelid than the other.

"Eureka!" said Simon. "Thank you, Mr. Edison." He blew out the candles and reached for the wine bottle. "Where's your glass, Dad?"

"Now we all look overexposed," said Molly. "Too definite. I liked us better before. And the room."

Simon emptied the bottle and started to open another. "Yearning for a simpler life? That doesn't sound much like you. Actually, come to think of it, this kitchen has caught up with contemporary style—or rather, was always ahead. Dad has had a pine dresser for forty years."

Lucas was peering at the label on the wine bottle. "Good heavens—Australia! I had no idea wine could come from there. Maybe you have some atavistic memory of the Somerset cottage, Molly. That was the simple life all right."

"I remember hens," she said. "And going to the loo outside."

"Outside!" cried Ruth. "Yuck!"

"In a shed, silly. It was rather cozy. There was a bench with a big hole for the grown-ups and a little one for children."

"This is turning into a search for lost innocence," said Simon. "Personally, I'm up for any modern device that's going. I am splurging on the latest in hi-fi systems."

Lucas spoke with complacency. "Well, it's obvious where I stand on this issue, as one of the last operators of Gutenberg-era technology."

"And look what's happened to it," said Simon. "More's the pity."

"Oh, I know, I know. A museum piece, now—the dear old press. I give each new lodger a conducted tour. Responses are various. The French girl was much entertained—she apparently had no idea such primitive techniques ever existed."

"I loved the press when I was little," said Ruth. "You used to let me arrange letters in sticks, to make words."

Ah yes, thought Molly. Goodness! . . . unto the second generation. She saw the press suddenly through her own nine-year-old eyes—larger, mysterious, arcane. "We'll make a printer of you yet," Lucas had said. She saw a younger incarnation of Lucas, not so very different.

"They're collectors' items now," said Simon.

Lucas lit a cigarette. "Really? Maybe I should give it to one of these craft archives, where it can outlive us all."

"Not just yet." Molly rose, and began to clear plates. "You're not going to dismantle this place. It's the one constant element. By the way, did I tell you we're moving next month? I've found a small house in Tufnell Park that's just right."

"Footloose as ever," said Lucas. "I don't know where you find the energy. Or the time."

Ruth yawned. "She gets bored easily. She *likes* packing cases and removal vans. She always thinks somewhere else will be fabulously different."

"Actually," said Simon. "It is the sensible thing to do. It's called trading up."

Molly glared at him, outraged. "I am not sensible and I am profoundly uninterested in property values. Footloose is probably right. Call it some basic insecurity. We've got fruit and cheese and biscuits now—Okay? Bath Olivers, Lucas—your favorites. We'll have to be off before too long. Ruth has school in the morning."

Over the years, there had been the flat in Notting Hill and the one in Earls Court and the maisonette in Primrose Hill and the cottage in Highgate and the house in Kentish Town. They had migrated around London, with Ruth a size bigger each time, and with equipment that leaped from Lego and furry animals to stereo systems and posters of rock groups. There was little that was sensible about the removals, and Molly knew that, but knew also that she would forever have an ambivalent relationship with the places in which she lived, and there was nothing to be done about it, except to get rid of the current one from time to time. James Portland had bought the original flat in Notting Hill, overriding all objections. The first move onward and upward had been a deliberate strategy that would enable her to take out a small mortgage, now that she was working again: an act of bravado that she knew well was defiant rather than expedient. She was not short of money; James's child maintenance arrangement was generous. From time to time they bickered about this: "We don't *need* any more . . ." "She is getting older, and therefore more expensive. You turn self-denial into some kind of perversity." "It's not self-denial, it's just that we don't live . . ." "Like I do? Oh, Molly, you don't change, do you?"

And thus she had jumped from postcode to postcode, from flat to house, and could not fail to note that there had been financial gain in the process, which provoked contemptuous irritation. That was never the idea. Initially, she had wanted simply to be paying something herself for the place in which they lived, and after that it had become somehow a necessity to kick off and move on every few years. But each time she was startled and annoyed to find that bricks and mortar had a new accretion of expense, that the figures in estate agents' windows were larger: smugly and defiantly larger. It was as though the London stock bricks of which most of the houses in which she lived were built had turned into some substance that had intrinsic value. And if you wanted to look out of a different set of windows from time to time you had no choice but to hitch up with this inexorable process, however much it offended you. When once she told Lucas what the Fulham house would now sell for, he was aghast. "But it simply isn't worth that. I paid less than a thousand for it, in 1930."

"It's money that has got out of hand, not the house."

"Fickle stuff," said Lucas. "I never did have much faith in it."

Molly and James spoke quite often: arrangements for Ruth to visit him or be taken for a holiday to his house in France, quarrels over Molly's resistance to subsidy. In the early years, there had been an edge to these exchanges. He would be stiff, polite, reserved. She sensed that he was wounded, angry, and wanted to distance himself. And then, over time, there was a shift toward an accord that found an echo of the camaraderie they had once enjoyed; she even felt a nostalgia. He would arrive to fetch Ruth himself, rather than sending Maria and the chauffeur, and would sometimes come in for a while, looking around intently. On one of these occasions he said, "I suppose I see now what you meant."

"Meant when?"

He waved a hand at the heartland of the maisonette in Primrose Hill or the cottage in Highgate, with the beanbags and cheap rugs, the wicker chairs, the clutter. "When you rejected my way of living."

"That wasn't about furnishings."

"I know that. But there's a superficial symbolism. Well, you were probably right." He paused. "I still miss you, you know."

"I . . ."

"Go on. Go for broke. Say it."

"All right. So do I, in a way. Miss you."

"In a way? Never mind, that'll do. And there is Ruth, as a precious legacy. Who has started to look like me, people are saying."

"Yes. She does."

Around this time, James got married. Molly never saw or learned much of Claudia, and supposed her to be one of the stylish women who had frequented those evening parties. Ruth was not forthcoming about her: "She got a headache when we went to Whipsnade and Dad said we won't take her another time."

James was an attentive father—increasingly so as Ruth grew up. In babyhood, he had been at a loss; he was not a man to push a pram in the park. But as she advanced into articulacy and high spirits he became entranced. He said to Molly "I had no idea children could be so entertaining." Ruth, for her part, clearly enjoyed these sorties into a more extravagant milieu, where there were patisseries from Harrods for tea, and outings to the ballet. And she was evidently attached to James, who must have loomed all her life as a sort of benevolent patron on the fringes of everyday existence.

Occasionally Molly reflected upon the nuclear family and wondered how far they had lost out. Oh, there were advantages, obviously: mutual support, a shared bed, a man to carry the shopping and be handy with a screwdriver. On the whole, society still expected people to step out in pairs, nicely bonded in perpetuity, but increasingly that was not quite what happened. She observed marital fission on all sides; her friends and acquaintances seemed to be particularly prone to it. Sometimes, she would find herself briefly involved with the free-floating man of one such breakdown, as her kindly solace was negotiated by him into something more fulfilling, and anyway she needed sex from time to time herself. But it was always she who slammed shut the door, in due course.

She worked as soon as it became feasible to make child-care arrangements for Ruth, experiencing the statutory guilt but knowing also that, whatever the circumstances, she could not have done otherwise. There was too much out there that was inviting, challenging. She managed a small independent bookshop until there came a falling-out with the proprietor. Then there was a stint with a feminist publishing house. And then she discovered a talent for entrepreneurial activity, and flung herself into the world of arts administration. It was exhilarating to conjure up a music festival in a market town that had not even realized it needed one, to persuade bemused local businessmen that their reputations would founder if they had not been seen to contribute, to negotiate with fixers and performers. The purveying of culture had become a public good; state subsidy was on offer, so you could dip into that pot also. Between the Arts Council and the intimidated members of Rotary Clubs and Round Tables you could drum up enough to dispatch artists to places that had never before been confronted with a performance poet or an exhibition of avant-garde sculpture. In the process, you came across an assortment of frequently capricious people, some of whom you would willingly clobber, but professional integrity required a permanent smile and steely tolerance. Sometimes the wearily obliging Rotarians, writing out another check, seemed preferable to some egomaniacal performer, demanding hothouse nurture for a fragile talent. There is much abuse of the term art, Molly decided—but never mind, the real thing is also around.

She knew that she herself was not a frustrated artist, despite the occasional insinuations of disaffected practitioners, who tended to resent the hand that steered them. You had to put up with that, in this role of manager, patron, and chaperone. She had not the least desire to be any of these people whom she dispatched around the country, though some of them she admired and respected; rather, she enjoyed the idea of making something happen, the creativity in pulling off an event, the venture of exposing provocative wares. Success and failure ran in tandem; you could find yourself with a platform of three writers and an audience of five in a church hall in Carlisle, or an exhibition in Ipswich would suddenly become the talk of the day. Either way, you moved on; some other project filled the horizon. There was no place either for chagrin or for routine, but a constant onward thrust that satisfied Molly's need for change. A different rush of ideas; new faces, new places.

But what had happened to youth? She was forty-three—not old, oh dear me no, not even edging into middle age, but she had forged beyond that invisible, undefined barrier. No longer young. Youth had whisked by while she sold books and made books and changed nappies and wheeled Ruth in a pushchair on the last leg of an Aldermarston march and wore miniskirts and took the pill, which had arrived just too late to scupper Ruth's conception, thank God. From time to time, looking at Ruth, the thought would come: you so easily might not have been. And then Ruth's emphatic presence seemed to make nonsense of chance, of happenstance.

Ruth shared her father's dark good looks, and was a vigorous, outgoing child, but had also a conflicting tendency to lapse into abstraction—sudden withdrawals into some private reverie. When small, she would commune with herself for hours, quietly crooning nonsense narratives; as she grew she did well enough at school but teachers uttered warnings about lack of concentration, daydreaming. "What do you think about?" Molly would ask, looking for clues, and Ruth would stare: "It isn't really thinking. It's going somewhere else."

Occasionally, Molly had contemplated being with a man. A young woman on her own with a child was in an ambivalent situation—both available and yet conspicuously fettered. To go out in the evening, she would require a precarious infrastructure of babysitters; a lover who stayed overnight must run the gauntlet of toys strewn about the place, and Ruth's assessing gaze in the morning. Any man who survived this test of character was to be taken seriously. There was a divorced publisher, with a son of Ruth's age, who looked for a while to be a real option. Some time later, a sculptor whose work she had promoted seemed to be becoming a fixture, until she realized to what extent she was starting also to support him. A professional commitment to art did not mean that one had also to subsidize it out of one's own pocket, which was not so very deep. Besides, and most importantly, she knew that her feelings for him, though fond, were not much more than that.

You do not want to admit that you have never been in love, at forty-three. That the most compelling experience going has somehow passed you by, that you are a kind of emotional virgin, that when you read great literature, one of its central themes is mysterious to you. When Ruth was born, Molly had had an instant and awesome clap of understanding: she knew now what it was that drove the world, what it was that people felt for children. But, at the same time, she remained significantly ignorant. All right, she thought, so be it—I am disqualified, for some reason.

Youth was gone, then, which was occasionally dismaying but a truth that could be confronted, and faced down. More provocative was the erratic process whereby you went in one direction rather than another, did this, not that, lived here, not there, found yourself with this person and not someone else quite unknown, quite inconceivable. How did this come about? Oh, you made choices, but in a way that was sometimes almost subliminal, at others so confused that, in recollection, the area of choice is obscured entirely: what was it that was not chosen? And, sometimes, choice is not an option.

The television sits menacingly in the corner of the room. She does not want to switch it on, but she must; one o'clock, six o'clock, nine o'clock—each news bulletin. There come the pulsating concentric rings that announce the BBC news, and each time she watches them, she goes cold again. She holds Ruth, and the rings give way to the newsreader, to aerial photographs of the Soviet missile sites in Cuba, to the faces of Kennedy and Khrushchev, to film of the Soviet ships forging toward Cuba. If she opens a newspaper, she reads of families who have fled to the west of Ireland, to the depths of Wales or Scotland.

Each day creeps onward, subsumed into what is happening. The world is intense; the autumn leaves are fiery, children's voices in the school playground are so loud and clear, London buses are brilliant, paint-box red. Molly pushes Ruth through all this in her pram and thinks: she may never be a child, a person.

Ruth has been to France with James and Claudia. There is this converted mill, with a swimming pool. She is rather quiet, on her return. Has she not enjoyed herself?

"Yeah. It was fine. Mum?"

"Yes?"

"Why didn't you marry Dad?"

Ah. This was bound to come. Molly flounders. "Because . . ." She searches for what might be acceptable.

"He says you didn't want to live like he does."

So it has been discussed. Molly nods, overtaken. "That was . . . well, that certainly came into it."

Ruth's long straggly dark hair curtains her face. She is staring into it. What is she thinking? I might have had a swimming pool. I might have gone to a posh school. I might have a wardrobe full of trendy gear.

Ruth peers out of her hair. "Did you sort of toss a coin, or what?"

Eh? "Certainly not. I thought about it very carefully . . ."*—did I?—*

"We talked it over . . ."—is that what we did?—"It was a question of what would be best for everyone in the long run." Was it?

Ruth sighs. She is squinting at a piece of hair. "You know—I *do* have split ends." She looks at Molly. "I don't *mind* that you didn't marry him. If you didn't want to."

Molly stands in a rank of women outside the school gates, waiting for Ruth. She thinks: I am older than my mother was when she died. I am older than my mother ever was. For most people, the mother that they remember is middle aged, or old. That is a mother figure. For me, a mother is a person younger than myself.

She has hardly any photographs of her parents. There is a snap that Lucas had taken of Matt outside the Fulham house: a young man—a very young man—in rather baggy trousers and an open-necked shirt, squinting into the sun. Thick, darkish hair that fell forward over his forehead, strong features. Handsome. And there was one of Matt and Lorna together, sitting on a pebbly beach, also taken by Lucas; Matt is laughing, Lorna looks more serious, she has an apple in her hand and was perhaps about to take a bite, she looks up at the camera—at Lucas—a small face framed in short, dark hair. It is not Molly's face. Molly used to study this photo with detachment and think: she was prettier than I am, much prettier. I am not bad, but there is a more solid look to me—I have his features, and perhaps they are less suited to a girl.

No wedding photographs. Nothing of the commemorative cargo carried by most couples. There is Matt's portrait of Lorna, which Molly now has: she looks straight at you—at him, as he painted—rather serious, that face, the dark straight hair, a blue dress, and her hands folded on her lap. And there is just one more snap of Lorna, now with a toddler, Molly, on her lap—Lucas again, no doubt. Small Molly is looking to one side, distracted by something; Lorna is smiling, her hair is rather longer, she looks—well, she looks, quite simply, happy. This is 1938. Before everything.

The sculptor's studio is a section of a disused warehouse in Rotherhithe. At first glance, you would think workshop rather than studio, since the sculptor's raw materials are wire netting, sheets of aluminium, lengths of iron pipe, chunks of scrap metal. There is an anvil and a blast furnace. Molly's relationship with the sculptor has now gone beyond professional contact, but she has not yet allowed him into her bed.

The sculptor stands in the light of a grimy window, showing her a drawing. He is a skinny man—it seems surprising that he can move all this metal around. He is explaining a new project to her. It involves old railway sleepers and chain-link fencing, in a way that she does not quite follow, and is making a statement about freedom. The Vietnam War is in full swing, and this work has some connection with that but is more a general celebration of (or comment on, or meditation about) the human spirit and its triumph over circumstances.

The sculptor is holding forth rather, and perhaps at this very moment their eventual parting is heralded, before ever they have come together, the end implied at the start, as Molly listens and feels some instinctive resistance to what seems to be a paean of self-determination. In the last resort, he is saying, we all do what we are going to do, come what may, whatever cards are dealt, whichever way the cookie crumbles. We are free souls.

"No," says Molly.

The sculptor looks at her, quizzically.

"Unless you're talking religion," she says. "Life after death. That sort of thing."

The sculptor shrugs. He is an atheist, it seems.

Molly stares at the chain-link fencing, the tangled metal. This is one of those moments when art loses its appeal—temporarily, one trusts. She does not as yet know the sculptor all that well, but well enough to protest.

"Don't tell me that people direct their own lives. My father was killed in 1941—not at his direction. My mother died having a baby. She wanted the baby—she didn't plan to die."

The sculptor seems to find this outburst sympathetic. He places a placatory arm around her shoulder. "You'll come around to it—you'll see. You'll get what I'm at when the piece is further along the road."

"Actually," says Ruth. "I don't *mind* having a peculiar family. I mean, I suppose it's just that I'm used to it, but actually Lucas is rather fantastic, as a sort of grandfather person. And Simon's okay, too."

Molly eyes her. Such truths come out, from time to time, and can be reassuring, like this one. "All the same, you have been somewhat short-changed where relatives are concerned. A bit thin on the ground."

"There's Aunt Bryony."

"There is indeed."

They reflect on Bryony, who is a headmistress, and occasionally visits when she is in London, attending some professional gathering.

Ruth giggles. "I always feel as though she might be going to give me a conduct mark."

"Don't worry—she's retiring next year. She wouldn't be able to then."

In fact, Bryony is amiable enough, but her calling is manifest. And there is little common ground—none of the "Do you remember . . . ?" and "How is . . . ?" with which relatives paper over an awkward session. Just that mystic blood link; the communal genes. And the shadow of a person whom neither Molly nor Bryony knew for very long.

Bryony's parents have died. As for the Bradleys . . .

"Did I ever see your other grandparents?" says Ruth.

"Oh, you did, you did. It wasn't a huge success."

Marian Bradley has elegantly waved and silvered hair. Gerald is large, genial, compressed into immaculate tailoring. Molly has not been to Brunswick Gardens for several years. Contact was always tenuous; the occasional card from Marian suggesting lunch or tea, a little gift at Christmas. Ruth appears awed by her surroundings, and sits tranquily on Molly's lap.

"And here is Ruth," says Molly.

Marian's smile is effusive. "Well, this is such a surprise. We didn't even know about your marriage. You should have *told* us."

"I am not married," says Molly.

The Bradleys go quite still. Gerald ceases to tamp his pipe and stares over Molly's head, no longer genial. Marian smiles no more. At last she speaks: "Oh, my dear . . ." She looks away, then toward her husband. "How most unfortunate," she murmurs.

"You were considered unfortunate," says Molly. "Not a term I cared for. So that was that."

The winter of discontent gave way to the spring and summer of A levels, cultural endeavor and Mrs. Thatcher. Ruth worried about Wordsworth, the Tudors and Stuarts, and the roll of puppy fat around her midriff; Molly fielded a touring opera company in Orkney and the Shetlands, and a craft exhibition in Manchester, and fine-tuned the arrangements for the poetry festival. In the background, a woman with an iron coiffeur and awesome insistence began her long dominion of the nation's affairs.

Molly voted Labour, naturally. Always; regardless. So did everyone she knew. It seemed surprising that there could be Conservative electoral victories when you yourself had barely ever heard of anyone voting Tory, and even more so in that, when you thought about it, you realized that there must be millions of working-class people who voted Tory, which seemed somehow like shooting yourself in the foot. Why ever did they do it? And now, just when you should be rejoicing at the first woman Prime Minister, she came in the form of this dogmatic harridan with her handbags and her pussy-cat bows.

But if you looked beyond these shores, complaint seemed churlish. In the course of work, Molly had come across artists exiled from their homelands—people who had fled, or whose parents had fled, because circumstances were beyond tolerance, smoked out of Russia or Hungary or Czechoslovakia or wherever. Beside such histories, some local carping about the power of the trade unions or Mrs. Thatcher's bossy persona became positively obscene. No secret policemen would be stalking the writers Molly dispatched around the country, there would be no midnight knock on the door for strident playwrights or political satirists. You could blaspheme Mrs. Thatcher around the globe, if you so wished, and there would be no tap on the shoulder when you arrived back at Heathrow. Those who live out their lives in a politically stable country, in peacetime, have not had history snapping at their heels.

Except that I have, thought Molly. My father. And who knows what is in store. But in the meantime, the only sensible and expedient thing was to get on with private life, while governments came and went, a cacophonous backdrop to the real business of existence.

The organization of the poetry festival had taxed her to the limits. The chosen venue was a market town and former spa, satellite to a university, which should serve up audiences both of the young and the culturally minded middle aged who were inclined to sample the unfamiliar and might even buy a book or two. There were historic inns on hand, and elegant eighteenth-century pump rooms in which the poetic events could be held. It had not been easy to drum up sponsorship. Molly had spent many hours cajoling skeptical supermarket managers and garage proprietors. It had been an altogether simpler matter to line up the poets.

This was to be a weekend in which a range of literary talents would be on display, a sample of today's state of the art, which would include one distinguished name that even some of those who never read poetry might recognize, alongside a swath of others—known, obscure, fecund, costive, impenetrable, accessible, good, bad, indifferent. Molly was even handed, keen to give exposure to those who needed it as much as to those who could be relied upon to keep an audience nicely engaged for an hour, and who might even persuade a few doubters that they could from time to time get hold of a collection of poetry and enjoy it. Poets are as assorted as any other occupational group—indeed, probably rather more so than most. They come in many forms—combative, reticent, responsible family men; feisty single mothers, stylish, uncouth, occasionally inaudible. Never mind, this was literature, or at least some of it was, and the discerning public had a right to inspection of what the nation had to offer, right now. So Molly had studied her reference list, blackballed a few names (he who brought seven friends and family on another occasion and put them on expenses; she who forgot the date; they who got pissed out of their minds, trashed the White Hart, and lost her a major sponsor) and had selected a lineup that should be both eclectic and representative. Poets seldom said no, unless they were paranoically retiring, or of such eminence that neither exposure nor adulation were of any interest to them. Your standard poet—if there was such a thing—was only too happy with a free outing and the chance to socialize (or quarrel) with his or her peers. Forget the hackneyed image—soulful, solitary, unworldly—the twentieth-century poet was a social animal, often nicely disguised in some alternative occupation and emerging in true colors when it suited. This is what Molly had learned over time: never take them at face value, feed and water them well, make sure they've got their train ticket and are bringing one spouse or lover and one only.

The welcome party in the pump rooms on Friday evening: poets, sponsors, festival staff, and volunteers. These elements are not mixing very well; poet tends to cleave unto poet (they all know each other anyway), while the sponsors group together, trying to look at ease in this company, and the staff make much of the local volunteers, who are an essential component—they tout programs, provide transport, and, in some cases, hospitality. Molly is trying to stir all these people up. She tows over to the sponsors a poet whom she knows to be amiably gregarious, and serves him up to the manager of Barclays Bank and the owner of the high street wine bar. She selects an engaging young woman poet for the proprietor of the local garden center. She greets and thanks all of the volunteers. She checks over the poets; she has already had dealings with most of them, but there are a few strange faces. She moves from group to group, making sure to identify those she does not know.

"Great to have you here . . ."

"How *are* you?"

"Hello, Molly."

"Hi, Molly."

"I'm Sam Priest." Large man. Beard. She liked his last collection, she remembers.

"Terrific you could come . . ."

A thin, nervy looking girl. "Dawn Bracewell? You're on in the morning, aren't you? I'm so looking forward to hearing you."

They have all shown up. There are no unexpected appendages. The sponsors are thawing, putting back (sponsored) drinks and making inroads into the canapés and the literati. No volunteer has thrown in the towel. So far, so good.

He doesn't do festivals that often. You drink too much, sell six books if you're lucky, waste a weekend. He needs weekends—the only uninterrupted days of think time, writing time. So festival proposals are binned, usually. But this one is sited not far from where his mother lives, and could be tied in with a visit to her, and a good friend is going to be there—so why not, for once?

Now that he is here, he has misgivings. This clutch of colleagues looks suddenly oppressive, and he is being given hospitality by a couple whose home is so neat, scrubbed, prinked, and polished that he is afraid he will leave footprints in the deep pile carpets or disarrange the fragrant guest room. And he can't scarper early because he has a second event at the far end of Sunday.

Have to sit it out now. Nothing for it but to have a drink and get stuck in. Hello . . . Hello . . . Good to see you. Hi, there. And here's the Molly someone who has been blasting off letters and instructions.

"Terrific you could come . . ."

Molly what? He's got all the bumf in his bag—must look at it again. He feels an uplift, for some reason. Maybe it won't be so bad after all.

Molly has been known to fall asleep at a poetry reading. Well, she has attended very many, and you always go to bed late, at festivals. She puts herself in the back row, in case.

There are readings and readings. There are poets who do not only read well but embed their reading, who talk around each poem, who show you how a poem arises, who enlighten and intrigue. There are the performance poets, who stomp and shout a lot. And there are also those who mutter, who declaim, who have done no preparation, who simply forge ahead, eyes grimly on the page. So she sits at the back, fingers crossed, and if the going is rough she concentrates on remaining alert to any problems with the mikes or the ventilation. Once an event is under way it is an unstoppable process, or should be, short of the collapse of the performer.

Today Dawn Bracewell reads. She is young and unconfident, you can see her hands shaking as she turns the page. At one point she loses her place, and Molly goes tense in empathetic anxiety. Phew!—she found it. Dawn gets through her half hour, sits down, to applause from the audience at this first event (embarrassingly thin—oh dear) and hands over to her companion on the platform, a veteran of the circuit who will have no problems.

The reading concludes. Everyone drifts out into the central foyer of the pump rooms, where refreshments are on offer. Molly does some troubleshooting: a complaint about acoustics in the hall, the bookseller does not have enough display space, a poet has toothache—does the town run to an emergency dental service? She is hither and thither—listening, instructing, phoning.

Someone is putting a cup of coffee into her hand. It is Sam Priest. Oh.

"Here . . . Restore the blood sugar level. You look slightly frazzled."

"Thanks. Thanks, Sam."

Oh . . .

He's forgotten what an ordeal a reading can be. That poor girl who got her knickers in a twist—one was on edge for her. And sometimes you're bored and other times you're critical, and then you wonder what you sound like yourself. He'll take this afternoon off, before his own session this evening, and look around the town.

Such a smile she has—saying thanks for that cup of coffee.

Three down, four to go. Events, that is. The audience have plumped up, as the day wore on. There is a very healthy turnout for the big man, who parachuted in for his own session and no other, and left immediately afterward. No sociable evening with hoi polloi for him.

Molly feels able to relax. The thing has its own momentum now, it is proceeding as it should, her careful preparatory spadework has paid off, and so far there are no serious glitches. The poets are behaving, if not like lambs, and you wouldn't actually want that, at least like compliant racehorses, showing off their paces. She has picked up a number of appreciative comments from the punters.

At moments like this she experiences what is apparently called job satisfaction. She created this weekend, she brought together these people, opened up a dialogue, a discourse, enabled words to fly off the page and into people's heads. Now there is just one more reading to go today.

There is something . . . reassuring . . . about a man with a beard.

In a back street of this rather self-satisfied town—sparkling Regency terraces, exquisitely groomed parks and gardens—he comes across a gem of an old-fashioned hardware shop, with a range of tools that you don't often find. He buys a self-adjusting, self-grip wrench—he's heard about these but has failed so far to get his hands on one—and a Black & Decker drill guide, top quality. He walks back to the pump rooms with this satisfying parcel tucked under his arm. There is nothing so pleasing as a good tool—the heft of it, the thought behind its design.

Now if only there were tools for making a poem. Something with which you shaved off a syllable, spliced a rhyme, filed down a stanza here, screwed in an end-stop there. He imagines the kit on his desk—small stuff, it would be, perfectly fitted to the hand, little elegant specialized pieces that you would lay out before you got down to work.

He feels all set up for his event now. And then there will be the usual convivial festival evening.

He wonders about the evening.

Very nearly, she had not invited him. It had been a toss-up between him and another name, when she was sorting out the program.

She does not sit at the back, this time. It seems suddenly rather . . . offhand. She puts herself at the end of the second row, where she can still hop up if anything goes awry.

Well, thank goodness she *did* ask him. He is good, he is very good, he embeds, he expands, he enlarges. And the poetry is muscular, intricate, it crackles with surprises. The one about servicing a motor bike is extraordinary—that would not spring to mind, as poetic subject matter. The love poem is unsettling; for some reason she wishes she had not heard that.

She listens and watches, feeling off duty, as though she were simply here out of choice and out of interest, like the rest of the audience. Two or three times he looks directly at her.

When it is over, she goes up, as she always does, and says the sort of things that she usually says, even when there is some glaring reason not to (the performance has been dire, the audience cool).

Sam Priest inclines his head, grins. "Thank you. Thanks."

And then Molly finds herself completely tongue-tied. What is the matter? This does not happen to her. For God's sake! And so, apparently, is he. They simply stand there, she and Sam Priest, staring at one another. Until at last she manages: "They've got the book-signing table set up in the foyer."

"Ah," says Sam Priest. "Right."

Bugger it! Why had he not said: "Maybe we could have a drink together before dinner?" Before the buffet meal thing that is laid on for everyone later, when all and sundry will be milling around and there'll be damned all chance to have a chat with her. Instead of which he had stood there like a bloody zombie, let the moment pass, and now here he is stuck behind this table while not very many people buy a book, and there she is disappearing through the door.

You do not need to do much hostess stuff, with poets. They are self-sufficient. They are mostly delighted to see one another (bar the odd feud that may surface), hive off into garrulous groups, and don't need encouragement when it comes to the food and the drink. There are one or two people on whom an eye should be kept: Dawn Bracewell seems not to know many people, but one of the older women poets has taken her under her wing, and old Gareth Powell is famously taciturn and can spend an entire evening sitting alone, but even he seems to have melded with a group and is *talking*.

Sam Priest is over there.

Molly is hailed by a familiar figure, drawn into a party in the corner. She has many acquaintances here, and one or two who are on the cusp of friendship. The room is crowded now—the staff and helpers are here, too, and some of the sponsors—the buffet is in full swing, it is noisy, hot, you could even call it festive.

She eats, she drinks a glass of wine. She is called away to sort out a problem over book supplies, and another to do with a poet who must leave earlier than scheduled and needs a lift to the station. When she comes back the food is cleared away, some people have drifted off, it is drinks at the bar time for those who wish to continue, and plenty will.

And now Sam Priest is alongside.

There is an alcove off the main bar; miraculously, it is empty, and here they sit.

"This is a good town," says Sam. "It has a quality hardware shop. Look at these." He unwraps the wrench and the drill guide.

Molly inspects the tools. "I'm afraid I've never got further than a screwdriver myself. But I understand about the motorcycle poem better now, which I liked a lot. You enjoy . . . tinkering."

"Tinkering be blowed. I'm a mechanic."

Molly stares.

"I'm a mechanic by trade. That's how I earn a living."

"Gosh," says Molly.

"I do cars, bikes. Lawnmowers, as a favor. I'm at home three days, freelance, and I do two at the local garage."

Molly is entranced by this originality. Forget school teaching, editing, the life of ease in some library.

"Since when? Always?"

"Since about age twenty-five. When I'd finished my Ph.D. on Marvell and knew that I wanted to be a poet and not an academic. And I'd always been handy with a spanner."

There is a brief pause, as Molly digests all this. "I enjoyed the reading. Very much indeed."

"You've already said that, Molly."

"That was wearing festival organizer hat. Now I'm saying it as me."

"Ah. Excellent. So I'm having a drink with you rather than with a festival organizer?"

"Well, yes. But then—am I having a drink with a poet or a mechanic?"

"Good point. At this moment, neither. Just a man glad to be off-duty. And in good company."

"Me too," says Molly.

They beam at one another. The alcove has become suddenly a fine and private place.

Sam Priest lives on the outskirts of a Devon market town. "I've been there," says Molly. "Nice. We had a walking holiday on Dartmoor a few years ago."

"Large family?" Sam's tone is offhand; he takes a swig of wine, watching her.

"Just me and my daughter. I'm on my own. She was ten then."

Sam brightens. "I've got a boy. At college. Lives mainly with his mother, but he spends time with me."

They contemplate this symmetry for a moment. And then suddenly talk comes rushing—views, thoughts, opinions, circumstances, his taste for archaeology, her love of long walks, the son, the daughter, signals from the past that pepper what is said, that require pursuit. They exchange credentials: Molly's parents, Lucas and Simon, the birth of Ruth, jobs, the flitting from one part of London to another; Sam's youth in Manchester, son of a headmaster, his three brothers, the marriage that ended, the stint in a French village, the year in America, the writing, and the financing of the writing. In retrospect, the exchange would seem more like one of people who had lost sight of each other and needed to catch up than that of those who had never met before.

"*Three* brothers," says Molly. "I can't imagine that. I was just me. And Simon a long way after."

"Mayhem. Daily carnage. My mother's voice never fell below a shout."

"Where are they now?"

"Dispersed. One teaching in Canada. A local government officer in Sheffield. A doctor in Derbyshire. Good solid citizens, you note. I was always the rogue element."

"Not at all. 'Poets are the unacknowledged legislators of the world'—tomorrow evening's panel discussion—remember?"

Sam groans. "Oh, help—do I really have to do that?"

"You do," says Molly sternly. "You're down on the program."

"I thought I wasn't having a drink with a festival organizer?"

"Sorry, sorry . . ."

"I shall forgive you." His hand covers hers, then is quickly removed. They have company. Someone looms in front of the alcove.

"*There* you are, Sam. I'll join you, may I?"

Sam glares. Beat it. Scarper, would you? I am having a conversation with Ms. Faraday. He looks at his watch. "Not worth it. It's gone ten and I'm pushing off in a minute."

"Oh, come on—one more."

"No way," says Sam. "See you tomorrow."

The intruder is routed.

"Well, good night," says Molly.

"Don't be daft."

She laughs. "Is he a friend?"

"Not at that moment, he wasn't."

"I should really be seeing if I'm needed for anything."

"You are. You're needed here."

Molly savors this. She savors the moment, this succession of moments, these hours. What is going on here? Why am I feeling so . . . happy?

"As a rule," says Sam Priest, "I pass where poetry festivals are concerned."

"I know. You turned me down once."

"Did I? Thank God I saw the light this time. It's not that I'm against two or three poets gathered together—it's just that I grudge a weekend."

"Sorry."

"That's the second time you've said that."

"I know. The first time we were interrupted."

"Oh . . ." He grins; his hand comes out, and this time remains rather longer on hers. "As it happens, this is turning out to be the best weekend I've had in a long time."

Molly is briefly silent. Then: "When were you happiest? Ever?"

He reflects. "Probably in a field in France, when I was about twenty-one, on a camping holiday with a girl I thought I was in love with."

"Thought?"

"A flash in the pan, as it turned out. But it left one of those indelible moments. And you?"

"Hmn. I think probably when Ruth was born. Lying looking at her. There's always another person involved, isn't there?"

"Too true. The catalyst. But there can also be those transcendent experiences—solitary ones."

"Religion?"

Sam is shocked. "Good grief—no. Nor getting stoned neither. I tried that a few times and found it demeaning rather than uplifting. Happiness is the real world—the physical world, often."

"The splendor in the grass—that sort of thing?"

"That sort of thing. Sheer relish for what's on offer. An animal sort of feeling. Kicking up the heels."

Molly nods. "Sunshine. Stars. A flower. A color."

"I hate to tell you," says Sam. "But I can get it from a satisfactory repair job. Getting something to work that wasn't."

"Would that apply to a poem as well?"

"Oh, yes. A more abstract pleasure, though—lacking that gratifying tactile effect."

"Which I've missed out on entirely," says Molly. "A well-scrubbed floor is the nearest I've got."

"And is this happiness or satisfaction? And what about ecstasy, which suggests the flight of reason? Hence my queasiness about the claims of religion."

"Children can seem to know ecstasy."

"Exactly, and are not rational. Grown-ups settle for happiness. Gracious, Molly, what have you started, with that question? I'm going to find us another drink, before this discussion gets quite out of hand."

The alcove, like the rest of the pump rooms, is sternly in period; it is striped from head to toe, its lights pretend to be candles, it is adorned with prints of Regency bucks and belles. It is a far from likely habitat for either Sam or Molly, but has become now a home, a precious retreat; both know that they will never forget it. Sam takes a while to return, and Molly sits there feeling most strangely bereft, deprived. When he arrives, both are aglow—it is a reunion.

"I got nobbled," he says. "Had to be thoroughly rude in the end. I thought you'd give up on me and go."

He puts the drinks on the table. "Whew . . . I was thinking about your father, while I was waiting for these. Where could I see his work?"

"Well," says Molly "I've got some engravings in London. Lucas has more. The book illustrations . . . you find Heron Press editions and the other fine presses in antiquarian bookshops, sometimes, and they cost a bomb."

"I knew a wood engraver once. Marvelous stuff. If I could have been an artist, that's what I would have wanted to do. Using tools."

"My mother kept my father's. Lucas still has them."

"I'm occasionally in London," says Sam Priest. "Maybe at some point I could . . ."

Both glimpse some unthinkable future, and look away, lest this is tempting providence. Don't rush it, thinks Sam, don't bugger the thing up by going full pelt, you're not an eighteen-year-old, for Christ's sake.

Don't feel like this, thinks Molly, you've spent a couple of hours with him, that's all, don't start fantasizing.

By eleven-thirty both have learned more, much more. Each begins to anticipate the other's views, responses, reactions, a stranger is turning into someone else, a person partially known, tantalizingly known, about whom more yet must be exposed. Sam learns Molly's twitch of the eyebrows when she is surprised, the way in which she may shoot off at a conversational tangent, that brown mole on her left cheek. Molly discovers his views on various other poets, his advocacy of vegetable growing and indeed of a particular kind of potato, his sudden explosive laugh, the fan of lines at the outer corner of each eye.

It is closing time in the pump rooms, ejection time, shutters are being slammed down in the bar, others are already going out of the doors and down the steps. The alcove is no longer home.

"What about a walk?" says Sam. "Quite a long one?"

She has occasionally wondered what it would be like to be kissed by a man with a beard. At one o'clock in the morning on the doorstep of the people with whom she is staying, she finds out: a little scratchy, but otherwise the experience as known, except that it is not because this is better than any previous kiss, it is brand new, arousing, unnerving, it is the one she has always hoped for, it is . . .

Oh my God, she thinks, I believe this may be it.

Sleepless, she lay staring at an unfamiliar ceiling. She heard Sam Priest's voice, she saw him; again and again he returned to the alcove with a glass in each hand, and it was as though they had been apart for hours, days. He said certain things over and over; she felt his touch.

I'm going to be wiped out tomorrow, she thought. Must *sleep.* And at some point she tipped into a benevolent black pit, from which she awoke in daylight, gazing once more at the evening that was gone. How would it be when they saw each other again? Would there be embarrassment, and avoidance? What had happened? Had anything happened?

She was at the pump room, checking on ticket sales before the first event, when he came through the doors. He walked straight over, and stood in front of her.

"Good morning, Molly."

And she knew then that it was all right. The way he spoke; the way he looked. It was true; whatever had happened, had happened: she had stepped overnight into some new dimension of being, she was floating, she could focus on nothing else, she had knocked onto the floor the cash till on the box office desk, one of the volunteers was scrabbling to recover the contents, and there Molly stood, impervious.

Sam said, "Comfortable night?"

Molly smiled happily. "Frankly, no. Didn't sleep well."

"Funny you should say that, neither did I."

The volunteer finished retrieval of the cash box and its contents, restored it to the desk, and withdrew.

Sam said, "When and where do I see you?"

She spread her hands: the press of people around them, the impending event, the program that reached through the rest of the day.

"I know, I know. We'll have to sort something out. Meanwhile . . ."

Meanwhile . . . she thought. Meanwhile, all I want is to continue in this state of . . . grace, to stay in this new world.

"Meanwhile," said Sam Priest "I'll have to make do with getting you a coffee in an hour or two."

All through the day he is there. She glimpses him across the room, they are in the same group at lunch, they sit next to one another during the afternoon event. They are never alone, and yet entirely alone; they are surrounded by other people, but no one else signifies. When they manage to speak to one another, what is said is inconsequential, but they are in tacit alliance, they are a secret unit.

All day, Molly is busy. She is talking to people, she is troubleshooting, she is smiling and greeting and thanking, she is in the thick of it, but she is also cruising in her own stratosphere on autopilot.

And suddenly, somehow, the evening has arrived, and the last event, the panel discussion. She meets Sam at the door of the hall, shortly before.

"I warn you," he says. "I'm going to let you down. I'm not going to be able to get my head around this. I'm brain dead today."

"I don't know whether to be at the back or the front."

"The front. Where I can see you. Where you can be inspirational."

There are three poets on the platform, and a chairman, who invites each to comment on the proposition before they embark on a general discussion. The first speaker flails around somewhat, wondering at too great length what is implied by the term "legislators," it is apparent that he has not considered Shelley's essay and is winging it. The second is an impassioned woman who is also distracted by terminology, and seems to be saying that poets—all artists, indeed—are a unique category and should not be concerned with the banalities of social organization. It is left to Sam to refer the quotation to its historical context, to cite Shelley's unease with utilitarianism, to talk about the apposition of reason and imagination, to consider imaginative perception as a force for moral good. Shelley was incensed with the downgrading of poetry as significant comment, he says—Shelley thought poets were more crucial than political theorists. I'm not certain I buy that, says Sam, I'm not sure what sort of a fist we'd make of the blueprint for a perfect world, but I take Shelley's point about poetic antennae; maybe what we can do is point things out, whether it's a matter of moral choices or simply the perception and celebration of the world.

Molly is rapt. She basks. She basks in Sam's eloquence, his good sense, the way in which the audience pricks up its ears while he speaks.

She is . . . oh, dear, she is *proud* of him. Stop it, she tells herself, stop it—you have no right.

When the discussion is opened up, it is clear that lay members of the audience—the non-poets—have warmed to Sam's level-headed interpretation of the proposition in hand, and are mostly picking up on points that he has made. Someone comments that reason enables people to behave in a sensible and prudent way, but only imagination allows them to anticipate how others may behave—anyone concerned with legislation required both capacities. Nobody quarrels with this, but a few exotic kites are flown: why not have a small quota of parliamentary seats for poets and the like, representing a kind of virtual reality intellectual constituency? One or two commentators fly off at a tangent in pursuit of the idea of the artist as having a special status, a concept which evidently does not find much support. We are all in it together, seems to be the general view, but maybe some are favored with particular insights, in which case we would do well to appreciate what they have to say. A girl—student, probably—asks Sam if all this has anything to do with Keats and truth and beauty and all that. Sam, who is looking a little battered by now, replies that he has a nasty feeling that it may do, but that the Romantics' train of thought can be quite difficult to follow, from the viewpoint of today.

The chairman winds things up. The audience comes down to earth and heads for the bar, as does Molly. When she catches up with Sam, who has been buttonholed by one or two people keen to continue the debate, it is she who has a glass in each hand.

"You must be needing this."

"Too right I am. Bless you."

"You were . . . terrific."

He shakes his head. "We got by, just about."

"More than that. Thanks to you. I was . . ." She almost says it—pulls herself up.

"Proud of me?" He cocks an eyebrow. "Go on, that's what I'd like to hear."

In the weeks that followed, Molly walked into another life. There was then, and there was now. Her entire past was then, and her past self seemed like someone else, a person who had been fine, who had been content enough, but also quite ignorant, who did not know. Now, she was the person who knew, who knew how it was to be one of two, half of a partnership of delight, who knew the exquisite pleasure of anticipating the phone call, the arrival, the uprush of joy when you saw him coming down the street, or stepping off a train, or looking at you from the bed.

Sam came to London. Molly went to Devon. Ruth considered Sam and appeared to be graciously tolerant of the situation. Once in a while, Molly would catch her eyeing them with an expression of vague bemusement, as though she were observing the behavior of some unfamiliar species. Sam's son, David, visited, and, after an initial stiffness all around, seemed to join Ruth in a conspiracy of kindly sanction. It was A level time; Ruth moved in a miasma of revision schedules from which she peered out only at the distant sunlit prospect of a summer hitchhiking venture in France with friends. Her mother's euphoria was a side issue, of interest but peripheral.

Once, Molly said to Sam, "Is it always like this?" Even as she spoke, she heard an echo; she had used these words once before, but now she was talking not of sex—which went without saying—but of love.

"I wouldn't know," said Sam. "Not in my experience. Not like this."

Sam met Lucas, the Fulham house, the press, and came away richly approving of all three. "The place is a time capsule. Step back into the 1930s. I want to live like that."

"Not with me you won't. I once did, remember?"

"All right. Some discreet mod cons, if you insist. And your stepfather—I've never met anyone so untethered to the present. It's magnificent."

"It's been called unworldly, by some."

"Defiant, in my book."

"He liked you."

Sam looked complacent. "There's talk we might do a little edition of one of my collections. Give the press some exercise, is what he said."

"Oh dear," said Molly, "I hope this isn't going to be a full-scale retreat into an Arcadian past. Nothing Arcadian about Fulham in the 1940s, believe me."

"You're talking to a man who grew up in a schoolmaster's household. Cold baths and early morning PT. The point about the past is selectivity. You home in on the virtues, like that press, and Lucas's old trade—kicked aside by technology."

Simon rang Molly the night after he had met Sam. "This one's for real, isn't he?"

"What do you mean—*this one?* You make me sound like some kind of floozie."

"Not the intention. I was just recognizing a sea change. It stuck out a mile. He is, isn't he?"

"Well . . . yes," said Molly.

"High time too. Good on yer. Incidentally, I asked him to suss out Exeter for me, as a possible new home for the bookshop. See what the competition might be—that sort of thing."

"You're going to get *married?*" says Ruth. "You're going to *marry* him?"

"Do you . . . mind?" This is not what Molly meant to say at all. The words fell out, somehow—nicely identifying her worries.

"I don't mind. Actually, I like him. It just seems so odd to get *married,* when you've been not married forever."

"Should I meet Ruth's father?" says Sam.

"It'll probably just happen at some point. Better not to make a big deal of it."

"I have to say that half of me resents him and the other half thinks—poor bloke."

"Poor?"

"You wouldn't have him."

"It was a long time ago," says Molly.

Molly and Sam stand before the Registrar in Finsbury Town Hall. Register offices have done well out of my family, thinks Molly. She remembers her mother and Lucas; she casts back to her young parents, that legendary occasion. This time around, there is quite a crowd on the seats behind: Ruth, David, Lucas, Simon, various friends. Afterward, they all go back to the house in Fulham, at Lucas's insistence: "I am after all giving the bride away." Molly has arranged for caterers to supply the wedding lunch, which goes on for some while. Eventually she and Sam extricate themselves, to get into Sam's Wolseley and head off to Devon, and what is scheduled as a honeymoon but is in fact the first stage in Molly's move west. She is exhilarated at the prospect. No more fidgety shifts from one London postcode to another, just one big departure.

Ruth is aghast. "You're going to live in Devon? In the *country? We're* going to live in Devon? But we live in London. Everyone lives in London. And what about your *job?*"

Molly says that arts administration goes on in the far west too. She already has a couple of irons in the fire, an interview lined up.

Ruth's indignation diminishes when it is pointed out that she will soon be elsewhere anyway, for much of the time, at university, and that when London-deprivation becomes too great she can always hang out for a few days at the house in Fulham—Lucas will be only too pleased.

The road signs tell them that they are now in Somerset. This was meant to be, thinks Molly, I was meant to come back to these parts. This is where I began, and this is . . . not where I am going to end, but where I am going to be in one place, and happy—perhaps forever.

On a whim, she says to Sam, "Could we do a quick detour? Could we go to the cottage? My parents' cottage? I'd like just to peek at it."

They leave the main road and plunge down lanes. "Left here," says Molly. "Oh . . . maybe not. Sorry—have to turn around, I'm afraid." She stares at the map, at hedges, at signposts. "I know it's *near* here." And at last she gives a cry of recognition. "This is it!"

They pull off the road onto a track alongside the cottage, and get out of the car. Molly feels disoriented; she could not have described the place, but now that she sees it, it is entirely familiar: the squat lime-washed building, the presiding oak tree, the high hedge around the garden, the wide five-barred iron gate.

She says to Sam, "I used to swing on that gate. It was much, much higher then. Huge."

"Of course."

They stand there, her arm through his. It is late September; the field alongside is rich red plough, the hedge is dark with blackberries, somewhere above a buzzard calls.

Molly says, "You could hear the train, down that way. The whistle . . . I used to tell my mother—There's the train! And once my father came off it, in soldier's uniform."

"It'll be gone now. Axed. Branch line."

Children are playing in the cottage garden, invisible. There is an elderly car parked outside the cottage. A shirt-sleeved man comes out, a farm laborer perhaps, and glances at them.

Sam says, "Do you want to—introduce yourself?"

Molly shakes her head, suddenly awkward. "No, no. We'd better go. He'll think we're snooping."

"We are," says Sam. "But with good reason. I'm glad I've seen it. Is it the same?"

"The same, and not the same at all. I feel like Rip van Winkle."

"Rip van Winkle had been overtaken by time—asleep for twenty years. Everyone else had moved on."

"The cottage has moved on, somehow. The oak tree has grown, and the gate."

"But so have you. More like parallel universes than Rip van Winkle."

They get into the car. "Take me away," says Molly. "It's made me feel a touch unsettled. That it is still here—the same, but different."

Part 6

EVERYONE HAD GONE. There was just the family left: Molly, Simon, Ruth, Sam, Tim. The house in Fulham could never have seen such a gathering. The kitchen had been full, and the sitting room, and the room that was once the Heron Press office—packed with all those who had come on from the crematorium: associates of Lucas's from the thirties and forties—old men and women now—along with such neighbors as had held out against the eighties influx of wealthy young couples, a handful of former tenants who had never quite lost touch, and assorted people of whom Molly and Simon had barely heard, but for whom Lucas was evidently an iconic figure.

All these had crowded into the rooms; they had been given a glass of wine and something to eat, they had reminisced, and now they had dispersed, and the five others were left sitting around the kitchen table. Molly was exhausted, and angry with herself for being thus. How can you be exhausted when you neither walk nor stand? In the chapel, the wheelchair had had to be in the aisle; she had felt hideously conspicuous, stuck there in front of everyone, even if Sam was right by her. She had stared straight ahead at the coffin, at the sheaf of white lilies from herself and Simon, at Ruth's wreath of white roses. She had listened to Simon's tribute, to Ruth reading Lucas's favorite poetry, to the address from an old printing colleague. A cellist she knew had been invited to play. The coffin had slid away, almost without you being aware, and eventually all was done.

Around the kitchen table, without the cohort of unfamiliar faces, they were able to relax, to subside. Molly thought: it's over, we've done what had to be done, now for a world in which there is no Lucas. Simon thought: I am miserable and elated, both at once—it is obscene. Can I tell Moll? What are we going to do about the house? The press?

Simon's partner, Tim, began to stack plates, to assemble dirty glasses. Molly said, "Don't bother, Tim. The caterers are going to see to all that, later." Sam put his hand on her shoulder. "Are you whacked? Do you want to go?" She shook her head: "Not yet. I'm all right."

Ruth said, "The last time I saw him—a month or so ago—we had this weird conversation about whether life is a switchback or a maze. I said switchback—hurtling from a down to an up. He said no, no, it's a maze—there's a secret correct route, but one always picks the dead ends."

Molly stared. "Why?"

"Why what?"

"Whatever prompted this?"

"Oh, just—I was telling him I had to decide about something . . ." Ruth shrugged.

"Decide what?"

"Just something . . ."

What's all this about? Better shut up, thought Molly. She never did like interrogation. But she'd have these chats with Lucas. Well, we all did. So what's she deciding? New work? New hairstyle? Whatever—don't pry. You'll hear, all in good time.

Simon said, "As far as I'm concerned life is a matter of negotiation."

"Negotiation with whom?" inquired Sam.

"With what more often than with whom. Currently I am negotiating with economic circumstance. I'm not sure who is winning, so far."

Molly said, "And how do you negotiate with a war? Or childbirth? Or a man who drives with defective brakes?"

Simon grimaced. "Point taken."

"That's why some take cover with religion," said Sam. "Insurance policy. My parents weren't great churchgoers, but my mother had us all christened—saw it as a sort of premium payment, I think."

Simon turned to Molly. "I wasn't christened, was I?"

"What do you think? Lucas never set foot in a church, unless it was to admire the stained glass or the fan vaulting."

"Dad didn't negotiate, either," said Simon. "He bypassed negotiation. Just did his own thing."

There was a silence. Molly's eyes were shiny. She fished a tissue out of her sleeve, wiped them, blew her nose, muttered, "Shit . . ."

Sam got up. "I'm going to have a last fond look at the press. I suppose it's destined for some museum."

Tim and Ruth followed him out of the room.

Simon said, "Moll, I want to tell you something. We've had ourselves tested. And we're clear, both of us. It's—it's like coming out into the sunshine."

"I hadn't realized you were . . . worried."

"Christ, Moll, we've all been worried, for years now. Knowing it can lie doggo. You can be positive and have no idea. Eventually we screwed ourselves up to find out."

"But you haven't been . . ."

"Promiscuous?" said Simon primly. "No, of course not. Not since Tim. Not for years. Nor has he. But past follies can catch up with you."

"Well, thank God they haven't."

"The relief—I can't tell you. It's as though a sort of gray mist had been suddenly whisked away. I used to every now and then. Wake up in the morning and suddenly think about it. Now I just wake up and think—oh, it's all okay."

"Why did you wait so long?"

"Terror," said Simon. "Sheer terror. Thinking—if we are, or one of us, it's maybe better not to know."

"Well, thanks be. I suppose I'd have had to wonder, if Sam hadn't come along just before it all began."

"Fidelity is paradise."

They both smiled.

"But it's so confusing," Simon went on. "To be glad about this when one's also wretched about Dad."

Molly nodded. "Incompatible feelings aren't unusual."

The others returned from the basement, looking somber.

"I can't bear it," said Ruth. "I loved the press. And the house. It was like Lucas—refusing to conform."

Lucas's house was conspicuous and had been for many a year. The stucco was peeling, the railings rusty, the steps cracked. It was an anachronism, amid the vistas of sparkling fresh white paint, the bright front doors with brass furnishings and carriage lamps alongside. It was a shabby poor relation, a reminder that this area had not always been the haunt of the high-salaried young, or those blessed with expansive family trust funds. It was a fossil, a survivor of the early part of the century, when different folk lived here—respectable but not prosperous, office workers, salesmen, and that now-extinct species, the housewife. When an impecunious young printer could afford to buy a house in these parts.

"I suppose Lucas was always gentry," said Molly, "but when gentrification came he failed to behave like gentry are supposed to do."

Now the house would move on. It would be hauled into modern times; there would be ripping out and stripping down, it would be wired and plumbed and polished and painted and at last reborn with central heating, spotlights, alarm system, and a bay tree in a pot on the doorstep. It would have been integrated, and would cease to be a source of faint disquiet to the neighbors, some of whom had enormous mortgages and must maintain an active interest in property values.

Sam sat down. "I'm afraid I need a glass of wine, after that."

Ruth said, "I've got something to tell."

They stared at her.

"Peter and I have decided to get married."

So that's it, thought Molly. He's to be a fixture. Seems a nice enough guy, one doesn't really know him, more . . . intense . . . than she is, good thing maybe, highflier by the sound of it, career person, which she isn't, so much, bread-and-butter work, she calls it. "That's wonderful," she said. "Where? When?"

The occasion was to be low key, Ruth stated. The Town Hall in a month's time. Lunch for a few people at a local restaurant afterward. "By the way, he was sorry not to be here today. He had a deadline."

Peter was a journalist, like Ruth. They had been living together for a year or so now. Is there something a bit . . . flat . . . about this? Molly wondered. A bit perfunctory? Is she pregnant? No—she'd have told me.

"Well, that's great," said Sam. Tim asked if wedding presents were permitted. And then, somehow, no one could think of anything much more to say, and Ruth had evidently imparted all that she intended to impart. That was it: a late twentieth-century marriage, a formality about which not too much fuss was to be made, which would only superficially affect the relationship concerned. Plenty of people did not bother nowadays. We did, thought Molly, Sam and me. Because it seemed so amazing to have found each other at all that something emphatic had to be done about it. And my parents did—out of defiance, I suppose. And Lucas asked my mother to marry him, not just to live with him. Today it is a cursory matter, unless you are a movie star or the aristocracy or someone set on making a splash. Ruth and Peter will get married, and carry on living much as they did before.

Sam was looking at her. "I think it's time we were off. You're looking knackered."

Molly nodded.

Simon said, "Shall I get going on winding up the house, Moll?"

"Please. I wish I could do more to help."

"Not to worry. Tell me what you want to keep."

They trooped out, down the steps, into the road. As Sam helped her into the car, Molly looked back—just once.

That's it. An ending. The years there. Lucas. The evidence wiped out when the house is sold. All of it stashed away in one's head now, and nowhere else.

Molly cannot remember the accident. It is a black hole, it has been removed from her memory bank, perhaps was never there. She knows that she was driving along a familiar road, a few miles from home, on her way to Exeter and a meeting about an exhibition. And then everything stops: there is just a single fragment in which she is lying somewhere, and all is gray and fogged, but she knows that it is real, this is not a dream scene, something awful has happened. Nothing more—until she surfaces again, and for good, in a hospital bed, and Sam is there.

A man driving a car that was virtually without brakes—a person who could not be doing with MOT tests or insurance had come out of a side road straight into her path. Maybe he had tried to brake, maybe not. She had done so, apparently, but to no avail. The man has some minor injuries; Molly's are not minor.

In the ensuing months, she thought much about the way in which a stranger can finger your life: this man, who knows nothing of her, nor she of him, until both arrive at the fatal grid reference, which has always lain in wait. And now the man is gone, back to his own life, and she into hers, which will be different.

She will walk again. Eventually. When they have finished pinning and fixing, when the physiotherapists can get their hands on her. She will go home, and learn how to manage, first from the wheelchair, and, in the fullness of time, on her feet again. There are certain things she won't be doing, the specialist says cheerfully; she won't be running marathons, or joining the local women's football team, or going rock climbing. Molly smiles obediently, and says that it is fortunate that she never went in for any of these things. She understands that she will be whole again, but not entirely so. Her knee will never be quite right, nor her shoulder; she will hurt, the battery of painkillers will go home with her.

People say, "It could have been worse." That is always said of accidents—an automatic response. A strange one; equally, it might not have happened at all. Indeed, the odds must be heavily weighted against it happening; the sufferer has picked the shortest straw. "Why me?" we say. Why, indeed? Molly said this, to herself, for weeks, months, until eventually this event had become a part of the fabric of her life. This had come about, just as everything else had come about—the good, the bad, the insignificant. There was before, when she was able-bodied, and there was after, when her body dictated. She had seen the X-rays; she saw in her mind's eye now that shattered invisible infrastructure beneath the skin—the fractures, the shadows, the pins.

Once, back when she and Sam were first together, he had found a little white scar on her leg: "What's that?" "I fell on a rusty gate, when I was about five. The district nurse had to stitch it up. I can just remember—the blood, the affront, the shock-horror." Sam ran his finger over it:

"Our bodies keep the record, bear witness. Whatever we forget, they do not."

The half-inch of silvery flesh was merely decorative beside what has now happened. And then, a few months into Molly's convalescence, there came Lucas's brief illness, and his death.

"My mother has had this bad accident."

The paper's cafeteria. He sits down beside her—that Peter something from the Business pages, to whom she has spoken before—and he looks closely at her and says "Are you okay?"

So she says that, tells this man. And he is concerned, he asks sensible questions, is positive, rational. "Sounds as though she's going to be all right. It'll take time, that's all."

Ruth is angry with herself. She is not someone who pours out her woes to any old acquaintance. "I suppose," she says. She blinks—seeing again the hospital, Molly's ravaged form.

"You need another cup of coffee." He goes to the counter—decisive, brisk—returns with two coffees.

"I should be going," she says. "Deadline."

"You'll get there. We all do. Therapeutic break is what you need, right now."

She starts to notice him, properly. He is wiry, muscular, sprung with energy, you feel. An intense, dark look. A man who does not much sit still—he has a pile of papers beside him which he shuffles, and slides into a briefcase.

"What's the deadline?"

"Someone's glossy home." Ruth does not want to discuss her piece, which would no doubt seem arcane, frivolous indeed, to someone whose concerns are mergers, takeovers, and the intricacies of the market. She has graduated from roundups of lamp shades and cutlery to the occasional interview or profile. She likes working for this paper.

"Go for it," he says cheerfully. "Send it up."

She smiles. "As if. But it's tempting."

She is an accidental journalist, she sometimes feels, drifting into it from a dogsbody job on a magazine when first she left college, writing the occasional piece of copy, an article or two, eventually regular fee-earning journalism. It still surprises her, that this is what she does, this is how she can earn a living.

This man is different. He is a pro—you sense the narrowed eyes of purpose, of focus and commitment. I should read the back pages more, she thinks. She takes a gulp of coffee.

He is watching her. "Feel a bit better?"

She does. Perhaps this vigor is infectious. She homes in again on her mother. Molly has never been beaten by circumstance.

"Good."

They talk for a while longer, then he pushes back his chair. "Well—see you around. Though not for much longer." And he tells her that he is leaving the paper, moving elsewhere.

Pity, she thinks, later. Oh, well.

She is twenty-nine. Birthdays have begun to challenge. She sees thirty ahead, like some menacing shoal in the water. But things are fine, there is plenty of time. Time still to be young, to work, to enjoy, to find the right man, maybe, at some point, in due course.

She sees him across a heaving room, at the exact same moment that he catches sight of her. And at once he is waving his glass, detaching himself from a group.

"You again! Ruth. Peter Stern—remember?"

They shout at one another, amiably, above the racket. After a while he says, "This is a god-awful party. Do you fancy getting out of it?"

He steers her through the mob, helps her to find her coat, leads her to a nearby Turkish restaurant. "I know this place—it's fine." The talk is easy, casual, as though they knew each other better than they do.

"How's life at the paper?" he asks. "How are the glossy homes?" For an instant Ruth is on guard. Is he being patronizing? No, he is not, she decides. This is just his way. She tells him that she has left the paper, she is freelancing now: more scope, more variety. 'Issues,' she tells him, "when

I get the chance. You know—whatever the current argument is about. Right now I'm the ultimate authority on the dangers of cosmetic surgery."

"I don't have one," he says thoughtfully, eyeing her. "Do you?"

"What?"

"A home. Glossy or otherwise. Rented flat, is all."

"Me too."

"One should move on. I am thirty-four. Rented flats are juvenile."

Ruth laughs. "Juvenile?"

"And don't make economic sense. My job is to spot economic folly."

"Ah, mortgages," says Ruth, sagely. "The housing ladder." Dear me, she thinks, we're not going to talk about mortgages, are we? I was enjoying myself.

But they are not, it seems. He swerves off, questions her about her family—how is her mother?—talks rather cursorily of his own. Proposes, suddenly, a date next week, whipping a diary from his pocket. Business-like. Ruth is amused, confused. Where is this going, for heaven's sake?

Peter's courtship is vigorous, applied. It moves from stage to stage as though according to some manual. Further meetings—a film, a walk on Hampstead Heath. First kiss. A weekend in the country: first sex. Regular evenings and weekends together—in her flat, in his.

"This won't do," he says, looking around. "We need a place."

And Ruth finds that they are now a couple, they are looking in estate agents' windows, he is doing quick calculations on the back of envelopes. Does she love him? Does he love her? She is not quite sure, either way. She enjoys his company, his drive, his range of interest, his darting attention to anything that comes along. She would be put out if he suddenly departed. Love? I don't know, she thinks. Perhaps I don't know it if I see it.

"The blue one," says Peter.

They are buying a sofa.

"I rather prefer this." She sits down again, bounces, puts her feet up. "And it's cheaper."

"The blue. I thought I was paying, anyway?"

"Ooh!" says Ruth. "Is this a stand off?" She lies back on the sofa, eyed by other customers. She looks up at him, grinning.

"A deal, more like. The blue sofa and I'll throw in one of those halogen lamps you fancy."

"I've gone off them. Come and sit down. There, isn't it comfortable?"

"You are an obstinate woman," he says. "But I am not going to the wall over a piece of furniture. This one, then."

They sit, side by side. We have a sofa, thinks Ruth. And a sound system, and a Le Creuset cooking pot, and a kelim rug. We are now underpinned, in some peculiar way. We are doing what is required. When the time seems ripe. She looks around the store. People, in pairs, are buying sofas and coffee tables and lamps and magazine racks. It is a sober process; there is assessment and discussion and occasional dispute but not much merriment, except where children have happened, and now run amok. Ruth watches with appreciation, as a small girl assaults a pile of cushions.

"Eleven months," says Peter. "Give or take a few days."

The small girl is whisked away by a parent. Ruth beams the child a complicit look. Children? How is it, to have children?

"What? Eleven months what?"

"Eleven months since we moved into the flat."

"I suppose it is. Goodness."

"I've been wondering about June."

"June?" says Ruth.

He is in purpose mode, full steam ahead mode, that application to a matter in hand that she has come to know well.

"I'm thinking we should get married in June."

Ruth stares at him. "Peter," she says "We've never actually talked about getting married before."

"We've thought about it. Haven't we? Well, I have. So what do you say?"

This is a proposal, she thinks. Conventionally made over a candlelit dinner, not on a display sofa in a department store. Oddly enough, I do not seem to be going to take offense.

She finds herself on the edge of laughter. She puts a hand on his knee. "Go on."

His turn to stare.

"You should kiss me."

He does so, after a quick glance around. No one pays them much attention.

"We're all set, then?" he says. "June."

They leave the store hand in hand. So that's it, thinks Ruth. So it goes. We get married. And why not, indeed? Lots of people do it.

Peter is talking marriage arrangements, and of a holiday.

"Honeymoon," she says.

"Honeymoon, of course. How about Crete?"

There is a moment's silence. "Actually, not Crete, if you don't mind. Maybe . . . Sicily."

"Fine, then. Sicily."

Marriage carries its own impetus, Ruth found. It is a loaded situation, weighed down with requirements. It demands a move from a flat to a small house. It brings a bigger mortgage and larger bills and companionable silence and squabbles and the deep peace of the marriage bed, which is sometimes that and at other times is not.

It brings children.

When Ruth found that she was pregnant, Peter said: "Oh God, are you sure?"

It was not the response that she had anticipated. She replied that she was quite sure. "I thought we'd been assuming we'd have a baby sooner or later?"

"One was thinking later rather than sooner, I suppose."

For a brief and disquieting moment they stared at one another across some treacherous divide. Then Peter gathered himself and suggested a glass of champagne to celebrate. The champagne made Ruth feel even more queasy than she already was; he drank too much and later that evening they had an argument about the installation of a shower unit. The fact of an impending baby seemed to have been tacitly shelved, to be addressed at some other point.

Ruth tells the ceiling of the hospital delivery room that she is not doing this again, no way. She tells the ceiling and the midwife and Peter but she tells in yelps and grunts so no one takes any notice and when eventually someone puts Jess into her arms, this warm damp creature, this *person,* she forgets all that, she sheds the last few hours; with a single bound she is into a new world, a different world, one in which you understand something you never knew existed.

"What's for supper?"

Peter is City Editor now. His pay packet has prospered, his working hours have stretched. The Editor comes home hungry.

Ruth tells him that she hasn't a clue what there is for supper. The kitchen drain is blocked, she was half the morning on the phone about that, she had a piece to write, the child-minder only has Jess for three hours, may she remind him. Plus, she has news, but she decides to set that aside for now.

Peter is focused, as always. He ransacks the fridge and the cupboards and finds the wherewithal to knock up a pasta. Upstairs, Jess is refusing to settle. Her howls raise the temperature. Ruth goes up, comes down, goes up again. She reminds herself that all over the country there are households in this state of ferment. All over the world, indeed: Greenland, Sudan, Peru.

They eat. Jess subsides, eventually. Ruth feels like a simmering kettle; she judders a little, all over. Peter is reading the City pages of the *Standard,* plucked from his briefcase. He is back with boardroom machinations and share price predictions. Life as husband and as father suits him well enough, that Ruth knows, but he is able to float free, at will, when he wishes. She watches him reading, and it seems a sudden surprise that he is in her life, at the center of her life, that he arrived and made everything different.

He made Jess, of course, for which he is to be forever blessed.

Peter looks at her over the boardrooms and the takeovers—a kindly look. "Everything okay now?"

She tells him that everything is fine. As indeed it is. Blocked drains and a work crisis are superficial complications, above which a strong woman rises. She thinks of her mother, who waved such things aside.

"Jess seems to have packed it in at last," he says.

"How many children under two are there in the world?"

"How on earth would I know?"

"You're so handy with statistics. I thought you might. Anyway—scads of them. And presumably at any one moment about half are yelling. A kind of global uproar. It puts things in perspective—one's small local contribution."

Peter refolds his paper. "That's one way of looking at it. I can't say it helps much."

Definitely not the moment to give him her news. "Maybe there's an article here," she wonders. "Bedtime performance—the cultural divide. French toddlers dining out in restaurants. Is there bedtime in Zambia, say?" Write out of your own concerns, she has been telling herself. Motherhood is opportunity; half the nation was raising young, and professionally interested.

"Have fun," says Peter. "Coffee?"

She gives him a slightly sour look. Detachment is one thing, within a partnership, but sometimes Peter steps aside rather too swiftly.

"No, thank you. I am going to see what Google has to offer on the subject."

Simon arrived with two Sainsbury carrier bags which he dumped on Ruth's kitchen table. "Here it is—the family silver. A portfolio of your grandfather's engravings, and some of his tools, and some of his blocks. I've been meaning to bring them ever since I finished clearing out the Fulham house. I found them in a cupboard in the basement."

They spread the engravings out on the table. Jess reached up, trying to grab. Ruth provided a biscuit as distraction. In another room, the baby was grizzling. Simon thought: heavens, she's not a girl any more, suddenly. He saw ten-year-old Ruth, seventeen-year-old Ruth—overlaid by this harassed woman with bags under her eyes and a stained T-shirt.

"Wow!" said Ruth. "Some of these I've never seen. Mum's got the farmyard with geese. And that one—the church. Look at this—blackberries and spiderwebs—amazing. He was very good, wasn't he?"

"Very. One of the best."

Simon waved toward the carrier bags. "The tools are wrapped up. Maybe they should go to some young practitioner? And the blocks are in bubble wrap. I have a feeling they need some fancy conservation box. Lucas was never into that sort of thing, needless to say."

"I'll take them all to Mum. We're going down there next week. Do you know—there are only a couple of photographs of him. And he looks so *young*."

"He was."

"Younger than I am now. Not how you think of a grandfather."

Simon said, "What is known about how he died?"

"Not a lot. Mum's got a letter her mother had from someone in his unit. Just that he was shot in an action near—Heraklion, I think it was."

"I've never been to Crete. We thought of a holiday there once—then didn't go."

"Nor me." Ruth stared down at the engravings. Jess was tugging at her hand, vocal and imperious. The baby was now in full spate. Ruth sighed. "Hang on a minute—I'll have to get him." She came back with Tom propped over her shoulder, Jess clutching her leg. "He's their great-grandfather," she said. "That seems even more unlikely."

"Please remember that you have made me a great-uncle."

"Sorry—it wasn't deliberate."

"I am keeping quiet—it does my street credit no good at all."

Ruth sat down. She gave Jess a drink of juice, flipped up her T-shirt and began to feed the baby. "Could you put the kettle on—we need a cup of coffee." She was gazing again at the engravings. "It's so strange—that these are all that's left of him. A person gone entirely—but what he saw still there, and how he saw it." She looked at Simon. "I want to go to Crete, one day—where he was. Is, I suppose—there's a war cemetery, isn't there?"

Whenever Ruth saw Simon, Lucas hovered. There was his beaky nose—a little less pronounced—and the thick glasses, and that gawky stance. Later, she would look in the mirror, seeking her parents, and find at first nothing but her own familiar features, and then all of a sudden Molly would signal—something about the line of a nostril, the set of the mouth—and then she would see an echo of James Portland's intent look, those large brown eyes, and his sleek dark hair. The codes are eloquent, if you can read them. She would inspect Jess and Tom—their volatile infant faces, which in time would refer to herself, and to Peter, and to uncles and aunts and grandparents. The ineradicable genetic inheritance. We are ourselves, but we remember everyone else.

In the world that was without Lucas, Simon had found himself untethered. There was Tim, and there were the satisfactions of domesticity—the little Victorian terrace house, their pleasure in kitting it out; there was the bookshop in the prosperous London suburb, and its demanding routine. But he felt as though he had walked into strange territory, with crucial landscapes out of sight. He remembered doing just that as a child—getting lost in streets not far from home and searching in panic for some familiar reference point. He talked a lot to Molly, on the phone, in those first weeks and months. "I'm sorry—I'm making an awful fuss about being orphaned at forty-six."

"I'd like you less if you didn't."

He knew that Molly, too, was bereft, and had the additional burden of the struggle toward recovery from the accident. Her pain and frustration rang out, as she reported small advances. She had walked to the garden gate—"A ten-mile hike, in my terms"; she could do a few kitchen tasks—"Peeling a potato has never been so enthralling." Hearing her, he felt further disoriented; all his life, she had been the busy, feisty, vigorous presence. He could not bear this diminishment, this endurance.

He said to Tim, "It's not fair, is it? Nothing's fair."

"Of course not. One knew that at the age of five. And said so."

Tim was ten years older than Simon, an editor in a fine art publishing firm. He had been greatly admiring of Lucas, with a professional appreciation of his past achievements, and indeed had set about making a collection of Heron Press editions, trawling the catalogs of specialist dealers. For Simon, Tim had arrived in his life at a point when he was in discontented solitude after several short-term relationships, and he relished this stability, the unexpected haven that Tim provided, his solid presence, their shared concerns. The bumpy passage of his earlier years was a slightly distasteful memory; now, there were the holidays in Italian hill-towns, the visits to friends in the country, the considered acquisition of a CD, a new picture, something choice to cook at the weekend. "I feel middle-aged," he told Molly. "And I love it."

To the garden gate. Soon after, fifty yards along the lane. Then, a visit to the supermarket. Molly edged back into mobility, into a semblance of life before the accident. She could work again, but had to cut back and take a less demanding job; driving any distance was a strain, she could not walk far or stand for long. This is how it would be, now.

Sam had told her that in the weeks after the accident he came close to seeking out the man with defective brakes: "To clobber him from here to kingdom come, you understand. For the first time I knew blood lust."

"It would have been satisfying," said Molly. "Unfortunately you'd have gone to prison."

"Exactly. I have never before regretted the rule of law."

Molly, too, had known bouts of vindictive rage, in the early weeks. Now, she saw the man more dispassionately, as just one of those malign interventions, on a par with the cancer cell.

James Portland had come to visit her in hospital, bearing an armful of roses, and glancing around the ward with ill-concealed alarm. Molly said, "You won't often have come eyeball to eyeball with the NHS."

"I'm afraid not. Molly, if there's anything at all I can do. Somewhere more private . . . I'd be happy to . . ."

"No, thank you. I'm fine here. Or as fine as it is possible to be under the circumstances."

He sat down. Beyond a drifting curtain, a family party was loudly installed beside the neighboring bed. Molly shrugged. "It's all right, James—distractions can be therapeutic."

He shook his head. "I can't come to terms with this. You—of all people."

"Why not me?"

"Just that you have always seemed to lead some sort of charmed life. Ever since you so resolutely turned me down. You decide where you are going, and get there."

"Well, not this time." After a moment, Molly went on, "Actually, I thought something similar of you. You seemed to move with such certainty."

"It hasn't always felt like that," he said. "Or, indeed, worked out thus."

His hair was gray now; he had lowered himself a little stiffly into the chair. Molly had not seen him for some years, and was startled; he must be in his mid-seventies. She wondered about his marriage: over the years, oblique remarks from Ruth had hinted that perhaps all was not entirely well. The suggestion was that of an arrangement that was convenient rather than one that flourished.

James said, "Ruth will keep me informed about how things go with you." He paused. "Do you think this chap of hers is a fixture?"

"It is looking rather like it."

"She brought him to the house. Positive in his views, was the impression I got."

"In other words, you had an argument."

James smiled. "If you like. There was some talk about the publishing world. No doubt he saw me as a relict, where the trade is concerned. Which I suppose I am."

"What did Ruth do?"

"Sat there. Detached."

Molly laughed, then winced and closed her eyes for a moment.

"Look—I'm tiring you," he said.

"It's all right. Diversion is good for me."

He sighed. "Molly, once again . . . if at any point there is anything . . ."

"I know," she said. "I know. And thank you."

When Ruth became a mother she had the universal, unexceptional, hackneyed revelation—she perceived her own mother differently. She also stared backward and saw that almost mythical figure, her grandmother. This experience of her own had been theirs, but it had been otherwise, because springing from different circumstances. She thought of her grandmother, a girl alone in wartime, and of Molly, another girl—alone for another reason. She looked at herself—older than they had been, and with a husband who returned each evening to the Edwardian semi in which machines hummed and bleeped, where wars were pictures on a screen of somewhere far away, where children were a shared concern, and one that drove out most others—a source of delight, anxiety, and exponential expense. It occurred to her that children had assumed power, over the century. Once, they were to some extent expendable; you had lots, in order to end up with a few. Today, they arrived to a safety net of state provision and a status of near sanctity. They had rights and agencies and an elaborate infrastructure of support and protection. As a parent, you enjoyed some of the fallout; you had vicarious status, conferred on you by the children. So long as you performed as was required, you too were privileged citizens, with dispensations and handouts. Until you abused your position, when the guardians would come knocking at your door.

Jess and Tom had appeared to be well aware of their strength, and dictated from day one. Had the children of the past been less assertive, more propitiating, with survival itself in question? This seemed unlikely, given the nature of the beast; presumably their wails were merely background noise, casually ignored, instead of the deciding factor of daily life. Ruth danced attendance when on duty, and worried about the children's welfare when the child-minder took over so that she could work. The children howled at will, then smiled, and had Ruth at their mercy. Even Peter, whose involvement was less entire, found himself in servitude, early married life now an unimaginable nirvana. He made no complaints, and was briskly competent with the impedimenta of a family excursion, adept with buggies and car seats and travel cots. Once, he said, "It's amazing, the power they have."

"I know."

"An economic phenomenon. Incredible levels of consumption."

Ruth said, "I was thinking more of the emotional clout."

"Oh, that too." Peter was examining the new double buggy. "How much are these?"

"I can't remember exactly. Expensive."

"I'm going to do a big piece on nursery products marketing. Mothercare will be hearing from me."

He was a man who sniffed the breeze, as a matter of routine—an automatic opportunism that made him a successful journalist. Children had happened to him, but could also be put to good use.

Jess is threading beads. She works with intense concentration, small fingers steering the stiff thread into the hole, biting her lower lip. Red bead, then blue, then green.

Ruth observes. "That's a nice pattern."

"It's a necklace for you. To go to parties in."

Ruth glows. "Can I have some yellow beads too?"

"No," says Jess. "This necklace doesn't have yellow beads."

"Right," says Ruth. "Fine. It's lovely as it is."

Tom is in rapt communion with his police car, lying on his stomach, pushing it round and round, making nee-naw noises. This is one of those halcyon moments when everyone is content, fulfilled. The three of them. Let me stay here forever, thinks Ruth—in this hour, in this afternoon. This is as good as it gets, surely? And then, immediately . . . no, what a crass idea. No future? No anticipation, no expectations?

What does she anticipate? Expect? She looks at Jess and tries to multiply her by three, shoot her up to fifteen, sixteen, seventeen. She projects an adult Tom, driving a police car, maybe—nee-naw, nee-naw.

Jess is five. She lives by the day; past and future are murky areas, which she does not much visit. That is the difference, thinks Ruth: to be grown-up is always to be then as well as now. Most disconcerting.

Somewhere on the rim of memory there flickers an image of a pond toward which she leans, and topples. And then she is on the grass, and Molly is pulling off her legs great strands of slimy green stuff, and she is shrieking. Five? Six? Whatever, it is ineradicable.

She tells Jess, "When I was five I fell in a pond."

Jess is mildly interested. "Were you drowned?"

"Not quite. In fact, not nearly. I was silly to lean over the pond like that," Ruth adds, mindful of example.

Jess drops a bead. She drops a bead, tries to recover it, and then lets fall the string of threaded beads, which slide off, the necklace is disintegrating, Jess is distraught, this halcyon moment is shattered, like the still surface of water . . . like the surface of that pond, which Ruth now sees again, rising toward her as she falls. She gathers up the beads, she soothes. "Look," she says. "We can put it together again. Now—how did it go? Red, blue, green?"

The Twentieth-Century British Wood Engraving exhibition is crowded. This is the opening view, to which Molly has received an invitation, as surviving family of one of the principle artists featured. But Molly is down with one of these bouts of bronchitis that she gets so often these days, and has passed on the invitation to Ruth. And Peter, who announced at the last moment that he'd come along, too.

Ruth moves around the room. She spends a long time with Matt's work, so familiar, but looking somehow different here, alongside so much else that is beautiful, arresting, provocative—and holding up well, she notes with pride, with pleasure. He is not just good, he is one of the very best.

Peter is elsewhere. Occasionally she catches sight of him, peering at a label, making a note on that pad he carries always with him. Once, she is alongside him when he is quizzing the curator of the exhibition, who is politely concealing a certain impatience: no, he does not know the current value of a Gertrude Hermes. For that, he suggests, it might be better for Peter to address himself to one of the specialist galleries, or an auction house.

As they leave, Ruth says, "Why were you so interested in prices?"

"A piece on art as investment," Peter replies, rather shortly. He has appropriated the catalog and is making some notes on the back.

"Art is not just a commodity."

He gives her a slightly weary glance. "No one said it was *just* a commodity. But it is one."

Ruth experiences irritation like some physical affliction; it prickles down her spine, it makes her teeth tingle. She says nothing.

Peter scribbles another note and shoves the catalog into his briefcase. "Like any other commodity, it has a shifting value. There are some intriguing comparisons to be made with other investment areas."

"If you say so." Ruth's tone is icy. She holds out her hand. "Could I have that? I want to keep it."

"What?"

"The catalog."

"I'll need it for the editor. We'll use a print to illustrate."

They stare at each other. Peter gives a little grunt of exasperation. "I shall return it in due course, Ruth."

"Don't bother," snaps Ruth. "I'll get my own." She turns to go back into the gallery. "No need to wait—I've got some shopping to do. Oh—and don't under any circumstances use one of my grandfather's engravings to illustrate your piece."

There are apparently people who suffer from this thing called low self-esteem. The condition is spoken of as though it were some kind of debilitating illness. And it is a bad thing to have; those who suffer from it will be quickly spotted, they are losers, they will be passed over for advancement; plus, they make awkward friends and partners. To flourish in the climate of the day, you need to think well of yourself, to walk tall, to put yourself forward, to brandish an emphatic CV.

Ruth knew that she fell short of these requirements. She had never been good at self-advancement, and she did not much care for those who were. But equally, she did not see herself as suffering from low self-esteem. She thought that she was reasonably good looking, competent enough, and she did not lack friends. In a different age, or a different society, she might have been perceived as an exemplary person: unassuming, modest, without pretensions. A Jane Austen heroine, then? Dear me, no—put like that, Ruth sees her persona at once as perfectly modern, of its day, but a variant. She does not conform with contemporary icons. She is not a shrinking violet; just, she is no rampant Russian vine.

Is Peter a Russian vine? Certainly, he has tendrils out all over the media. He identifies a space, picks up the phone, sends out a shoot. His CV would paper a room. All of which is just as well, because it means that he is earning a good deal of money, so it matters less that Ruth is not. So why does Peter's flair for self-promotion (or his resourcefulness? his endeavor?) bug her the way it does? Why does she find it so unlikeable? When first she knew him, she admired his energy, his drive. Now, that quality has somehow gone belly-up, and is no longer attractive, but has become the aspect of him that she finds most tiresome.

Is she jealous? Well, no, because she does not want to be like that herself. Not in the least. Does she resent his long working hours, his absences? Not really, because his presence can be dismaying: the household is disrupted, the children become unruly, there are suddenly issues about some implement that has gone missing, or a repair that is overdue. He moves impatiently from room to room, he is constantly on the phone, the fax goes into overdrive. No, she does not resent Peter's absences, because then everything subsides once more, the pace slows up, things calm down.

What, then, is her problem with Peter and his careerism? She knows plenty of others like him who do not have the same effect on her—though she does not necessarily admire them; but of course she does not share bed and breakfast with them, negotiate with them on a daily basis, know everything about them from their taste for pickled herrings to the wart on their left testicle. Could it be that her problem is with Peter, rather than with Peter's approach to life? That she and

Peter are at odds, that Peter no longer looks the way he did when first they were together, that sometimes she wonders why they *are* together?

Could it be that she is in a dysfunctional marriage?

Ruth first heard this term on the lips of a friend—casually delivered, as you might talk of a recalcitrant child, or a rogue element. A cliché, then, but one that had slid so surreptitiously into the language that you had never noticed. Or did someone simply coin the phrase one day, to fill a vacuum, there being a lot of this problem around? As T. H. Huxley allegedly came up with the term agnostic in the late nineteenth century, by which time it was much needed. This arcane piece of information swims into Ruth's head, grace of her A level English teacher, talking years ago about the evolution of language. Agnosticism arrives when a lot of people find it impossible to concede the existence of a deity; you get dysfunctional marriage when . . . well, when many couples are in an uneasy alliance. But surely that has been the case since Adam and Eve? So what was it called before? And what was low self-esteem before it became a contemporary malaise?

When Ruth was a teenager she had been successively, and briefly, a vegetarian, a Buddhist, a supporter of Queens Park Rangers, and an environmental campaigner. The environmental campaigning had consisted of sitting with a gang of friends around the base of a tree that was about to be felled by the council on the grounds that it was unsafe; Ruth and her friends had hoped for arrest and public martyrdom, but in the event the tree fellers struck during school hours, when they could not attend, and the deed was done in their absence.

Molly had been cheerfully supportive of all these enthusiasms: "Why not, if that's how you feel."

Ruth and her friend Julia discuss love. Julia has been in love three times, she says. In lust—about three, again. The current love, she confides, is qualitatively different.

Ruth lifts an eyebrow.

"Daisy," says Julia.

Daisy is her two-month-old baby.

"Oh, well, yes," says Ruth. "But does that count?"

They decide that it does, as an eruption of feeling that is unanticipated, that is mysterious until you experience it.

Ruth finds herself diffident about her own record. She offers a *coup de foudre* when she was a student. No—two. She admits to a couple of lust episodes. "And Peter," she adds, gamely.

Julia has been sleepless, night after night, she has been unable to eat—starved, she has contemplated suicide.

Ruth remembers hanging about outside his hall of residence. She remembers watching a silent phone.

Julia scoffs. Beginner stuff. Pathetic. "And no way," she says, "Do I ever want to go there again."

They laugh.

Once, when eighteen, Julia told a boyfriend that she was sorry but it was over, and he threw up. Just like that. She had been impressed: "I hadn't realised they could suffer too."

"So you took him back?"

"Certainly not."

Ruth's recollection of a rejected suitor is less telling: righteous offense is what she remembers—as though you had trodden violently on his toe.

"Whatever," says Julia comfortably. "We're through with all that, thank God. It's Daisy now, for me."

Julia is in happy partnership with Alec, so far as Ruth knows. But what does one know of other people's lives? What does Julia know of hers?

"Suppose it didn't happen?" Ruth wonders. She is now picking at the subject in general. Love. Being in love. "Suppose we just mated, like animals. Sensible genetic behavior."

Julia reckons that we can't know what animals feel. A dog fox was killed on the road, near them, and the vixen howled at night for a week.

"If it didn't happen," says Ruth. "Poets and novelists would be more or less out of business. Maybe that's where it comes from—we get the idea from them."

Julia observes that many people never read anything, but still go in for love.

"Okay." says Ruth. "Point taken. But what is it, then? How does it happen?"

"Disease. Eventually they'll find a vaccine, for those who wish to be spared."

"And why do we fix on *that* particular person?"

Julia proposes pheromones. "You know, like animals—a chemical secretion that says, here I am, come and find me."

"How unromantic can you get?" cries Ruth.

Julia says that a scientific explanation is perfectly compatible with a romantic effect. "You can still go weak at the knees—it doesn't matter *why.*"

"Hmn. Maybe. But why does it end? You fall out of love, too."

"Not always. It can mutate." Julia sounds complacent, perhaps. Is this her experience? "Just as well," she adds. "No one could spend their life in that condition."

Ruth wonders if possibly some people do. She thinks of the way in which Molly and Sam can look at one another.

"It's surely the one great thing," she decides. "Isn't it? Disease or pheromone or whatever. Would we want to have missed out?"

Julia yawns. Sleepless nights, again. "Oh, no. You have to join the club. Sign up. But that's it, for me. I've signed off, now."

It is seven-thirty; the children are in bed. Ruth moves around the kitchen with practiced efficiency, as though she were dealing with the engine-room of a ship. She shoves dirty clothes into the washing machine, she turns on the oven. She takes a carton of soup from the fridge, and a quiche and the wherewithal for a salad. She whips up toys from the floor and stows them in various containers. She goes through into the adjoining room, which serves as her office; she checks her e-mail, she reads a fax, she listens to messages on the answerphone. She hears Peter's key in the door, returns to the kitchen, tips soup into a pan.

Peter opens a bottle of wine. They sit at the table. Peter is flicking through newspapers; Ruth has some household bills and her check book.

"Jess got a gold star for reading," she says. "Perhaps we have an achiever on our hands."

Peter turns a page. "Oil Price Rise Forecast," Ruth reads, and "World Bank Chief to Quit."

"And I am a multitasker, I learn. It's the new definition. Do you want to hear about a day in the life of a multitasker?"

Silence.

"No. Probably not," says Ruth. "How were things at the coal-face today?" She rises, goes to the cooker, starts to heat soup. Peter takes a pad from his shirt pocket, makes a quick note, folds the newspaper. "I shall be going to New York for a couple of days next week," he tells her.

Ruth does not ask why. The answer would be to do with something obstruse and economic. And she does not think that Peter has a mistress in New York, or indeed anywhere.

She serves soup, and ciabatta bread. Peter pours wine—a Chilean merlot. Machines churn, hum, beep, wink green eyes. Off-stage, a phone rings: a fax grinds. This is a heartland of the late twentieth century, abreast of everything, and its own obsolescence ordained, its tastes and technologies doomed. Ruth is thirty-six, which sometimes seems rather old, and at other times nothing much at all. She has always been aware of the long view—perhaps uncomfortably so. Other people seem to live in the here and now; she is forever conscious of then, and when.

She says, "Have you ever heard my mum talking about that Somerset place where she was a small child."

"On occasion," says Peter.

The neutrality of this is an irritant. Veiled criticism? Indifference? But Ruth is now in pursuit of her own reflections. "No amenities. But a sort of paradise. Or is that just how we see childhood? Will Jess and Tom see this place like that, I wonder?"

Peter shrugs. He is not a man given to abstract consideration, unless for professional purposes. "The dear old Zanussi fridge? Of course it might be a collectible by then."

"Aha!" says Ruth. "Potential investment. Maybe we should be laying down a few."

Under the table, Peter's foot has come across something. He bends down, finds a small plastic dinosaur and sets it alongside his place. "Some of these might be a better bet. Dinky Toys have gone through the ceiling."

"What are Dinky Toys?"

"Miniature cars, buses, fire engines . . . Correct in every detail. Rubber tires that came off. They were still around in our day, just."

"I was a girl," says Ruth. "They didn't reach me."

Peter is examining the dinosaur. "Where did this come from?"

"I have no idea. Toys simply appear. Self-propagation, I sometimes think. My mum used to make her own when she was a child—clothes-peg dolls."

"China by origin, would be my guess." Peter has got up, and is now rummaging in one of the toy bins.

"And stuff out of the hedges. She used to show me how—poppy heads and dandelion clocks and seed pods. I loved it."

Peter now has an ichthyosaurus and a tyrannosaurus rex. He returns to the table, lines them up with the stegosaurus. "The global market. Kids have the same gear right around the world."

"You can make a whistle out of a thick hollow stem. You cut a notch—no, two, I think . . ."

Peter has brought the toy bin over to the table. He extracts a Barbie doll. "I wonder if these are kitted out with regional variations. Burkas for the Saudi consumer?"

"Acorn cups for dolls' tea parties," Ruth is remembering. "And conkers, of course."

Peter returns the Barbie and examines a small robot. "The thing would be to look at demand and supply. Does the manufacturer determine fashion, or do buyers lead the manufacturers?" He puts the robot into his briefcase, finishes his soup and pours wine for them both.

"You can't take that," says Ruth. "Tom will go spare."

"A few hollow stems should keep him happy."

Ruth shoots a cool glance, before clearing plates, placing quiche and salad on the table. They resume eating.

Ruth says, "Tom is going to be a man who drives a rubbish truck when he's grown up, he tells me. What were you going to be when you were four?"

"Governor of the Bank of England."

"That's not true, is it?" It occurs to Ruth suddenly that perhaps Peter never was four, that he arrived fully fledged, with a calculator in his hand, at about twenty-five. His parents have seldom referred to his childhood, she realizes; they are a reticent couple who live in Amersham and seldom visit, finding London unsettling.

"No." He fills his glass, waves the bottle in her direction.

She shakes her head. "Is there anything you'd like to be?"

"What's all this about?"

"Nothing," says Ruth. "Just wondered."

Peter frowns. "Am I measured and found wanting?"

"Dear me, no. Idle speculation, that's all."

"Not something I much go in for," says Peter.

"I know. Very wise. Coffee?"

Summer in Devon. High summer. Bucket and spade time; combine harvester time; picnic and wasp time; traffic jam time. The motorway has discharged rivers of metal into the resorts, the caravan sites, the bed and breakfasts—cars piled high with cases, rucksacks, body boards, bikes, buggies, complaining children. These spill out over the landscape, homing in on some chosen target. Peter and Ruth, with Jess and Tom, are in the red Datsun, homing upon a farmhouse tucked away up a lane that you can't find unless you have done so before, where Molly and Sam await them for a weekend of extended family life.

Up and down the land, thousands of such weekends are being spent. Intergenerational weekends. Parents and children and parents-in-law and children-in-law and grandparents and grandchildren. Step-parents and step-children. Step-grandparents such as Sam. Molly and

Sam, Ruth and Peter, Jess and Tom. It is Jess and Tom who will be principal beneficiaries of these days, since most of the time is dedicated to their entertainment. There will be a trip to the beach, another to a Farm Center, they will be exquisitely fed, they will be played with and listened to. Since they know that this is their due, they will accept everything as such, and make further demands when any spring to mind.

Molly thinks: Ruth has got thinner; so much *stuff* they've brought; will the children eat cassoulet? Is it still fish fingers and chicken nuggets? I should have got some videos.

Ruth thinks: she looks older, suddenly; did I bring any Calpol? I must make notes for the *Observer* piece; will the mobiles work here?

Sam listens to the engine of their car, as they come down the lane, and does not like what he hears. Not firing right. He'll have a shufti under the bonnet at some point, if that's okay with Peter.

Peter unloads his children, the bags, a box of wine. He would prefer to be elsewhere. Nothing personal, no criticism—just, this is not his scene.

On the beach, the children bale out a rock-pool with buckets. They scamper back and forth. Sam builds a sand castle, with great artistry; it is the Taj Mahal of sand castles. Molly's leg is hurting; she has walked too far. She watches Ruth, who sits staring at the sea. Peter is reading newspapers. He bought an armful on the way here and reads, apparently, every page of each.

Tom stumbles into the sand castle, the Taj Mahal, which collapses.

Molly and Ruth sit in the garden, watching the children, who are appreciating the swing that Sam has fixed to a branch of the apple tree. Sam is out in the lane, tinkering with the Datsun. Peter is indoors, with his laptop.

Ruth says, "I've got this plan. I want to go to Crete."

"To see . . . ?"

"Yes. To see where it happened. Where Matt . . ." She always thinks of him as Matt. You cannot call someone of twenty-nine grandpa.

"Was killed." Molly pronounces, where Ruth stood back. "I've thought of doing that. I was too craven, I think. There's a cemetery. So when is this to be?"

"I don't know. It's just something in the pipeline. I suppose you wouldn't . . . ?"

Molly shakes her head. "My bloody leg. I don't do flights anymore. And I'd be a drag. Can't walk far."

Ruth scowls. Her—a drag? That it should come to this. "I know. Okay."

"That letter," says Molly. "The one his friend wrote to my mum. You've seen that."

"I was going to ask—can I have another look?"

"Take it back with you."

There is a small commotion; the children are squabbling on the swing. Ruth gets up, arbitrates, returns. "Sibling stuff," she says. "Neither you nor I know about that. One has been everything else—mother, partner, etc. Daughter."

"Grandmother," says Molly thoughtfully. "That's a turn-up for the books, let me tell you."

"Sorry."

"Your day will come. Oh dear—she's hitting him again."

There is further arbitration. Molly stumps to the kitchen and returns with biscuits. The children subside.

"I saw your piece on in vitro fertilization. Interesting."

"Ah."

"And the one on surrogate pregnancy. You seem to have escaped from lamp shades and cutlery."

"Sometimes," says Ruth "I think of jumping ship."

Molly stares, alarmed. "You what?"

"Doing something quite different. Chucking this in. Becoming a . . . oh, anything. A beekeeper. An upholsterer. A person who runs a farm shop."

"I don't know about upholstery," says Molly. "You were never much good with a needle."

Ruth shrugs. "Anyway . . . all that is also in the pipeline, merely." She pauses. "One should always consider change, no?" She looks intently at Molly.

From down the garden there comes a wail. Jess is in outrage. "M-u-u-m! He's *looking* at me!"

Molly says to Sam, "They never touch each other, she and Peter. They don't *say* much to each other."

Ruth and Peter pack up the car, the children. A practiced process—she does this, he does that. It requires little or no communication. Presumably.

Molly and Sam stand waving.

Sam says, "I cleaned his spark plugs for him. Filthy."

Molly sighs. "*I* don't know."

"What don't you know, my love?"

"I don't know about other people. I don't know about my own daughter."

One day, Ruth knew that she did not love her husband any more. Much of the time, she did not even like him. They had become two people who lived in the same house, had shared responsibilities and interests in the form of Jess and Tom, but who no longer much cared for each other's company. Because they were a man and a woman, they had sex; they had always done so, it was expected, it would have been odd not to do so. Each time, both strove for satisfaction, and found little.

Eventually, Ruth said it. "Shall we not bother?"

Peter shrugged. He was sitting on the edge of the bed, naked. He reached under the pillow for his pajamas, put them on, took his spectacles and his book from the bedside table, and left the room. Ruth heard the spare room door close.

The next day, she confronted the absence of love, or anything resembling love. In another age, this unexceptional marital situation would simply have been a grim reality; you would have lived with it as best you could till death you did part. In the late twentieth century, that was not really an option; the system supposed otherwise. There was every provision for the ending of a marriage. You sat down and talked about it, or you fought about it, the wheels were set in motion, the law got busy, and in due course the situation was resolved. There was no need for two people whose passion had frozen to remain under the same roof.

Ruth thought about change. Nothing is forever; possibly nothing should be forever. But change is a slippery concept. Some change just happens; children grow, become different people, friendships slacken or intensify. Above all, the world turns; the backdrop is a moving screen—an impervious chain of events, something new shouted from the newspapers, the television, different faces, different places. There is no saying, "Hold it! Let's keep things the way they are"—nor would you want to, given the circumstances. Perhaps change is the triumph of hope over expectation. Whatever, it colors the days, the months, the years. We go with its flow.

But then there is willed change. There is that moment of fervent choice: no more of this car, this house, this job, these people.

This husband, possibly.

The thing is to arrive at that moment, thought Ruth. To recognize it, to look it in the eye, to meet it head on. To see it as opportunity, not threat. To say, "Well now, let me consider the options." To have a strategy, several strategies, a whole quiverful of strategies.

I am young, she thought. Reasonably young. So far, most of my life has simply ploughed ahead—stage 1, phase B, this work, that work, this marriage, these children. Decisions—oh, yes—but muted decisions, more a sort of acquiescence: okay—fine, this'll do if that's what's on offer, let's not be difficult, all's for the best. No bravado, she thinks. No challenge.

So go for it, Ruth.

Part 7

RUTH E-MAILED PETER: "Jess has piano lesson after school so please see that she takes her music with her. Tom's eczema is back—on left leg. Use the cream night and morning. I am going to Crete for long weekend on 22nd, so would appreciate it if you have them Friday and Monday."

Their two flats were in adjoining streets. The children could thus live with Ruth but spend periods with Peter, as agreed. Ruth's flat was the ground floor of a large Edwardian semi; an Indian family pattered about in the maisonette above. Peter had the top floor of a similar building. Once, turn-of-the-century bourgeoisie had raised their broods here; today, the houses were chopped and spliced, accommodating flat-share girls, gay couples, and the fallout of failed marriages. Ruth had never been into Peter's flat; the children reported an accumulation of laundry, an enormous television, and claimed that he had tried to make toast in the microwave. From time to time Ruth gave them kitchen offerings to take to him—a batch of frozen soup, a serving of stew, some fruit salad. Like Red Riding Hood, they trotted away with a basket shrouded in a cloth; Ruth diagnosed her own guilt, compunction, a need to propitiate. She and Peter did not often meet; he would deliver or collect the children with a brisk wave; negotiation was mainly by e-mail.

It was the year 2000. She could never quite get used to that string of noughts, to the fact that you had arrived in that mythic future, another century. Jess had said, on January first, "Why is everything just the same?," which seemed a fair comment. They had talked about the arbitrary nature of the calendar, about the ancient need to harness time.

"Actually," said Ruth. "There are just days—daytime and nighttime. All the rest is like . . . like names on a map. The place would be exactly the same if it had no names. Do you see?" This concept of time and space pleased her. She had considered it, as she served the children's breakfast, and the new century rolled in. How appropriate, she had thought, that it should coincide with her own new beginning. She did not care at all that the flat was half the size of their old house, and that she had to keep a sharp eye on expenditure. She worried about the children, but for herself felt only a sense of anticipation, a kind of unchanneled energy.

The e-mail to Peter was followed up by others: proposals to editors, a completed piece, inquiries in the service of ongoing work. To Simon, she wrote: "Hi! How's the book trade? How about I interview you as basis for an article on the stranglehold of high street chains and demise of the independent? Jess says huge thanks for Laura Ingalls Wilder set and will write shortly. We are immersed—what good taste in children's lit you have. Mum has to see new specialist but no cause for alarm, it's thought." To her father, she said: "Lunch on Friday would be great. Sorry to hear about the hip op.—but they work, don't they? Thanks a lot for the birthday check—so *much!*" James Portland's periodic largesse made her feel obscurely uncomfortable. She had always enjoyed dipping into his prodigal way of life, but had never wanted to have it for herself. "My fatal puritanism," Molly had said. "Sheer perversity. What we've missed."

Nevertheless, that check would come in handy. There could be a new sound system—Peter had the old one—and bikes for the children and maybe a winter coat for herself. And the car was due for a service and the washing machine was on the brink of expiry. She had no complaints about Peter's financial contribution, but somehow there was often a shortfall. Undoubtedly, he would step up his payments if asked, but she did not wish for this. Their relationship was equable but distant; sometimes she thought that it was not so very different from that of their married years. Once, she caught sight of Peter in the local shopping center with a woman she did not recognize; what she experienced was hard to identify—not jealousy, exactly, but a startled sense of deprivation, as though you saw someone else walking around in a familiar garment of your own. She no longer wanted to be with him, but he was a part of the narrative of her life: with him excised, it was as though an aspect of the story were missing. Ruth supposed that this effect would fade, and anyway he was still there, off-stage, and forever would be. She did not know much about his own new life; he had been matter-of-fact and surprisingly compliant over the whole separation process. "I refuse to rack up massive legal bills," he had said at an early stage. "We are both reasonable people—we can sort this out." And they had done so, dealing out the household furnishings without dispute, agreeing on arrangements for the children, on who should pay for what in future.

When she looked around, Ruth saw that her own new circumstances seemed to be reflected on all sides. Most of her contemporaries moved on, or away, or aside, with airy ease; they shifted jobs, departed suddenly for America or Australia, found new partners, sold their London house and set up a consultancy in Yorkshire, converted an Umbrian farmhouse into an arts center. A few had made so much money from a handful of years in the City that they retired at forty, all set presumably for several decades of restless under-occupation. Was such fluidity the hallmark of the new century? What had happened to careers, to long service anywhere—in work, in a house, in a marriage? At a job interview, people were asked what they saw themselves doing in five years time; volatility was the expectation. She had discussed this with Molly and Sam, on one of her visits with the children.

"Don't look at me," said Sam. "I'm doing exactly what I've been doing for thirty years—fixing machinery and writing poetry." He turned to Molly. "You faffed around a fair bit—at least before we met. You were ahead of your day, it seems."

"Unemployable, more like. Until I discovered how to boss poets around."

Ruth was dismissive. "The likes of you don't count. The artistic set have always lived hand to mouth. Now everybody's doing it."

"There's a man in the village used to be a carpet importer," said Molly. "He's bought the Old Manor and they're doing B and B. Luxury B and B, mind."

Ruth nodded. "There you are. It's a kind of universal bohemianism. Or instability."

Molly said, "Does it matter?"

"I'm not saying it matters. Just that it's interesting. People living differently. Expecting differently."

"If you're middle class," said Sam, "You expect to earn better and better throughout life. If you're working class, you don't. That's the only sociological truism I know. I suppose it's a question of . . ."

Ruth broke in. "And that's what's changed. No more jobs for life, climbing up the ladder. Short-term contracts. You're better off as a plumber."

Sam grinned. "Those of us in a skilled trade have always known that."

"Which skilled trade are you talking about?" asked Molly. "Poetry?"

"Ha ha! But what's with this forensic study of society, Ruth? Some work project?"

"Actually, no. Just noticing. And thinking. Since Peter and I split up."

Molly sighed. "How are things going? Did you sort out that problem with the mortgage?"

"More or less. My flat has changed hands four times in the last ten years, I discovered. That seems to say something, too."

"Not about the flat, I hope?"

"No, it's a perfectly good flat. Just that people don't stay put, in any sense. And now I'm joining the movement. Up-to-date, at last."

"So enjoy Crete," says Peter, taking the children's bags.

"It's not a holiday." Ruth is a touch defensive. "I'm doing a travel piece."

Peter cocks an eyebrow, smiles slightly. "So enjoy anyway." Then, apparently, he remembers. "And of course there's the family connection."

"Exactly."

The travel piece will fund the trip. She has had to solicit. The editor in question was surprised: "I thought you didn't do travel, Ruth? On account of the kids."

She was not prepared to expand. "There can be the occasional exception."

"Okay, then. I could use something with a historical/archaeological slant. For the discerning visitor. Some off-the-beaten-track sites. We can put you in touch with a local guide."

So Ruth has a rucksack filled with books—stuff on the Minoans and on monasteries and on the Venetian period. She also has books on the 1941 battle for Crete, which she has read and re-read. She sits in the departure lounge at Gatwick looking again at the crucial chapter, while the screens flick up Palma and Rhodes and Corfu and Heraklion and the holidaying masses eddy around her. All travel is casual now, but this is travel at its most mundane, its most banal. The departure screens cite the globe, an eloquent litany of names, but the concerns here are shopping opportunities, delays, foreign currency, and which way are the toilets? Many people are yawning; some are sprawled, asleep. The atmosphere is not one of anticipation but of lethargical endurance. The only fix is to spend money: a coffee, a beer, some perfume, T-shirts, cameras, watches . . . anything to gobble up a few minutes of time, to distract, to amuse. Ruth calls Sam. She is concerned about Molly, who is ill again—another vicious chest infection—but there is no reply. She returns to her book.

Ruth reads of destroyers forging their way across the Mediterranean. She reads of the ships that evacuated Allied troops from Greece, the hazardous crossing to Crete. Periodically, she looks up, returns to the present; departures come up on the screens—Gate This, Gate That, Boarding, Delayed. Each time she surfaces from the page, she is startled by the gaudiness of it all; the vivid clothes that are worn—that pink sweater, the purple jacket, someone's emerald pants—the fluorescent sign above a shop. The world of which she is reading—the German parachute drop, the ten-day battle, the men dug into vineyards, pinned down on hillsides, hanging dead in trees—is somehow all in black and white, or rather, shades of gray. This may be an effect of the grainy contemporary photographs in the books, but it seems also to be some distancing requirement, as though that other time can only be known in a different dimension. She cannot see the blood, though that is there in the text, time and again, nor the palette of the landscape, nor the flowers that sometimes appear as furnishings, nor the blues of the Mediterranean and the sky. Only the departure lounge at Gatwick is allowed full-frontal color.

Her flight is boarding. She puts the book away, for now, and joins the stream of people that is funneled down ramps, along travellators, processed into the correct slot. She arrives in her seat in the plane, an aisle seat alongside a couple who are complaining about the non-provision of movies on short-haul flights. "Perfectly possible," says the man. "They could do short features." The woman agrees: "They're just cutting corners, aren't they?" The couple spend the flight in disgruntled boredom, riffling through magazines, eating and drinking everything on offer.

Ruth reads. She knows the campaign inside out by now—the parachute drops, the Stuka attacks, the disposition of the Allied forces, the engagements, the defeats, the ebb and flow of it, the place names—Canea, Rethymnon, Suda Bay, Galatas, Maleme airfield. And Heraklion, for which this plane is headed. When they touch down, she looks in surprise at the runways, the airport building, the waiting coaches, the ranks of taxis. Where are the bomb craters, the disabled aircraft? And where is the battered city, from which the inhabitants fled?

Ruth is disgorged into the airport, along with the packaged masses—the children and the buggies and the straw hats and the beach towels. She trundles through immigration and customs and achieves the exit, where she finds herself named: a smiling driver is holding up a sign that says Faraday. He is to take her to the hotel near Rethymnon booked by the travel editor. With relief, she sinks into the back of the car.

They drive through mountains, and then along a fast coastal road. Full color now—that grainy gray world of the books is extinguished. Tawny hillsides criss-crossed with silvery rows of olives, scoops of blue sea, brilliant white houses covered in purple bougainvillea and the cerulean blue of morning glory. Outside, the temperature is in the nineties but the car is air-conditioned. A tactful bottle of water sits in the pocket of the door beside her.

Back then, very young men were killing each other all along here. Lying in the vineyards and the olive groves—waiting, watching, desperate with heat and thirst, while out of the blue sky the Stukas came screaming down, and then the Junkers troop-carriers, black shapes that shed their flower trail of white, red, green, yellow parachutes that floated slowly down—hundred upon hundred. And if you were on the end of one of those parachutes, one of those other very young men, clutching your machine gun, you fell into a place with its fangs bared, where the bayonet waited, and the grenade, the pistol.

The car draws up at the hotel, which is not so much a building as a post-Minoan fantasy, a complex sprawled over several acres, with the sort of social zoning system that is usually built up over centuries—villas for the bourgeoisie, bungalows with little gardens for the less affluent, and suites in the main building for the nobs.

Ruth has a bungalow with a tamarisk in its garden, two reclining chairs and a parasol, from which she wanders down to the beach. All around her, German is spoken, and the beach itself is dense with mature mahogany northern European flesh. The car had passed similar beaches; in the mind's eye, this island wears a fringe of sunburned bodies, laid out like kippers on the coastal sand. Ruth considers having a swim and returns to the bungalow for her costume, where a flashing light on the telephone tells her that she has a message.

"I am Manolo," says a male voice. "I am your guide for tomorrow. For Phaistos and Gortyn, right? I shall come with the car at nine-thirty, if that is all right. Here is my number if you have any problems."

Ruth puts on her swimming costume, takes a towel and walks back to the sea, where she bobs around for a while in lukewarm water and thinks about the children. Will Peter see that Jess does her homework? Will he remember to get in apple juice, and put his foot down about bedtime?

She returns to the bungalow, has a shower, reads up about Phaistos and Gortyn, and goes over to the restaurant for dinner. The menu outside offers apfelstrudel and goulash. "*Guten abend!*" says the waiter, whisking open her napkin with a flourish. It is a long time since 1941. "Good evening," says Ruth firmly.

The next morning, she is outside the main building of the hotel at nine-thirty, and stands looking around. A young man is waiting. He steps forward: "Miss Faraday?"

"Yes. Ruth. You must be Manolo."

Manolo has the face of a Greek icon—dark brown, almond-shaped eyes, aquiline nose. He ushers Ruth into the car, talking hard. His English is immaculate. Within minutes it emerges that he is not a professional guide at all but an unemployed archaeologist who does this sort of thing in order to earn a bit of cash. He studied in both England and the United States, which accounts for his English. "And now we are too many. An excess of Cretan archaeologists. And fewer and fewer excavations."

"Has most of it been dug up by now?"

Manolo's hands fly from the wheel in a gesture of rejection—alarmingly. "You're joking! There is much, much more. Anywhere you put in a spade. Minoan, Greek, Roman. All still out there. You will see. I shall show you."

They are speeding along the coast road, back to Heraklion. Manolo has outlined his proposed itinerary. "You say you want the not-so-much-visited places—so, right, we just glance only at Knossos, and the museum. Then we go to Phaistos and to Gortyn and if time we do one of the monasteries. You have three days, yes?"

"That's right," says Ruth. "But there's somewhere else I need to go as well, apart from the historic sites."

"Fine, fine. You just tell me what you want. But first—how much do you know about the past of Crete?"

"Not a lot," says Ruth cautiously. "I mean, I've done some background reading, but apart from that . . ." She passes over her intimacy with 1941, which is irrelevant. Manolo has been hired to guide and brief her so that she will be able to write an informed piece for the Sunday newspaper reader who wishes to see more of Crete than the destinations of the tour buses. She will have to fit in her own crucial itinerary as best she can, later.

"Ah. So . . ." Manolo goes into over-drive. He whisks her through Knossos, ignoring the crowds, and thence into the museum, where he spins her from one choice exhibit to another, talking all the time. He talks with such verve, such panache, that Ruth becomes as absorbed in listening as in looking. He is a born narrator, he is telling a story—a succession of stories. He unfurls a verbal banner, a series of blazing pictures of these other times. His eyes flash. "Now imagine this . . ." he says. "Now this is how it would have been . . ." He conjures up entire societies, whole cultures—everything volatile, vulnerable, evanescent, time sweeping one lot aside, another surging up. The Minoans fade away—the palaces, the bulls, the dolphin frescos, the dancing girls—and the Greeks are here, putting up temples, doing things differently. The centuries roll on. "Wait," says Ruth. "I'm losing track. What date are we now?"

They are in the car again, heading for Phaistos, which is Minoan—that at least she has grasped. Phaistos is the Minoan site that escaped the ministrations of Sir Arthur Evans and remains an unreconstructed ruin. So we are back with 2000 B.C. or thereabouts.

These enormities of time are having a curious effect on Ruth. There is something both soothing and sobering in contemplating these immense reaches. It puts you in your place. She says as much to Manolo, who again takes his hands off the wheel, and bangs the dashboard in agreement. "Yes, yes! Just that!"

There is a good road from Heraklion to Phaistos. "Not far at all," says Manolo. "Sixty kilometers—from north to south of the island." Ruth looks out of the window as the landscape flies past—golden hillsides patched with gray-green scrub, the spring green of vineyards, the silver of olive groves, mountain ranges that are pink-tinted as they vanish into the haze. She takes the map and examines the long thin shape of the island, the north coast with its string of towns, where everything happened in 1941, the mountain ranges in the middle, the mountainous south coast. Not a big place, not a big place at all. So now time and space seem to be in apposition—the thousands of years of activity, construction, birth and death, do not seem to fit into this small island. How can so much have happened to so many within the confines of this place? She looks at the map again, and out of the window. But of course she is seeing it with the eye of the twentieth century—no, the twenty-first, one keeps forgetting—which shrinks the place to its own assumptions, just as her BA flight reduced Europe to a few hours of cloud and sky. She sees Crete in the context of her known world. Back then, it *was* the world. Sixty kilometers was a different kind of distance.

She says as much to Manolo, who once more thumps the dashboard in his enthusiasm, and hastily swerves to avoid a lorry. Ruth decides not to pass on any further thoughts.

Phaistos is a great baffling expanse of low rubble walls, paved areas, flights of steps. Manolo leaps goat-like from wall to wall, expounding: "Now we are in the Central Court . . . Here now is the Propylon . . . Imagine here a row of workshops." The sun beats down. Ruth blinks from under her big straw hat. Just as she is starting to wilt Manolo cries, "Now we take a break!"

They sit at a little café with a majestic view of mountain ranges, drinking ice-cold Pepsi. Manolo talks about their next stop, Gortyn—a city that was first Greek, then Roman. "And what are its first origins?" says Manolo. "Imagine! Zeus himself! Taking the form of a bull, he brought the beautiful princess Europa here from Phoenicia and married her beneath a plane tree by a stream. And there the city sprang up."

Ruth frowns. "In all the paintings I've seen, it's a question of rape rather than marriage."

Manolo spreads his hands. "I was sparing your feelings."

"I've got reservations about the Greek gods, I must say. Jealous. Vindictive. Squabbling away among themselves up there. Appalling examples to the human race."

"Or else," says Manolo, "a reflection of ourselves?"

"Maybe. Either way, they're not much good as role models."

"Is the Christian God any better? An eye for an eye and a tooth for a tooth. Fire and brimstone. Dealing out punishment on all sides."

"Well, I'm not that keen on him either."

"Ruth is a Jewish name, isn't it? Are you Jewish?"

"I don't think so," says Ruth. "But who knows what they are, in the long view of things."

"I am possibly a bit Turkish. A Cretan prefers not to think that, but it cannot be avoided that there was some—mixing up—during the occupation period. So I have perhaps a Turkish foot, or hand."

"Could there be Cretans who are partly Minoan?"

"Why not? Peasant families sit still in the same place for centuries." And he tells her the story of a Minoan pithoi, in perfect condition, a great jar used as his oil store by a farmer in a remote village. Some archaeologists spotted the pithoi and begged to buy it for the museum. No way, said the farmer, he was attached to it, it had been in the family for some while (like three thousand years?) and anyway where would he keep his oil? In the end, he was persuaded to part with the pithoi in exchange for a custom-made new one.

Time to move on. But at the car park Manolo stops, glances around, and beckons Ruth toward an area of scrub and olive trees that lies beyond. Here, he moves around, eyes to the ground, and after a moment bends down. "There you are—Minoan."

Ruth holds the little sherd with reverence. "One should not really do this," says Manolo, with a shrug, "but one does. Anything significant I would take to the museum but all this is just . . . everyday stuff. You find pieces like this all over." Within five minutes they have more—a thin fragment of rim, a black painted piece of a cup base, a lump of wall plaster with red Minoan paint.

The next stop is a thousand-year-old Byzantine church, where Manolo sets about a demonstration of the theatrical highlights of the Greek Orthodox service. He stands before the altar, arms raised, eyes flashing, and declaims. Afterward, Ruth studies the eloquent array of thank-offerings of today—a miniature leg, a pair of eyes, an ear, a baby.

"The gods again," says Manolo. "Or God. Demanding payment."

Ruth examines a tiny torso, and a cow. "Claiming credit, I suppose. Though on the other hand, perhaps it helps people to have faith. I wouldn't know, never having had any." She glances at Manolo—has she gone too far? But he would not appear to be a man with beliefs.

"When I was taking my final school examinations," says Manolo, "my mother prayed for a month on end. Throughout each paper, and before and after. When my results came—which were excellent—she fell to her knees once more, in gratitude to God for steering my pen. Any religious inclinations I had went out of the window that day."

Ruth smiles.

They walk back to the car. There is a small village—a scatter of buildings and a café with a turquoise blue door, outside which two old men sit on wooden chairs, drinking coffee. A dog lies slumped in the dust. There is absolute silence, except for the rasp of cicadas, and the occasional low murmur from the café.

"This place was a battle," says Manolo. "In 1941. A big engagement."

Ruth looks sharply at him.

"My father remembers," he goes on. "He came up here after and saw bodies lying all round—German, British, Australian, New Zealanders, all of them. He was very young. It stayed with him always, seeing that."

"Well, it would," says Ruth. She takes a breath. "Actually—that is why I am here."

And so she tells him. About Matt. About her grandmother and her mother. Manolo listens attentively. When she has finished he says, "Now I see. You are here for your ancestor."

Ruth has not thought of Matt in quite those terms, but she nods.

Manolo's eyes are huge, brown and complicit. "This I understand. Of course. So I take you to the cemetery. Tomorrow?"

"No," says Ruth. "First I have to do the rest of the itinerary for the paper. On the last day."

"If you say."

It is early evening when Manolo drops Ruth back at the hotel. "So—tomorrow? Same time?"

"Yes, please," says Ruth. "And we'll have company. I should have told you. I'd entirely forgotten—there's a photographer arriving today. He's probably here by now. The paper booked him. He was going to fly in straight from some other job."

Manolo raises his eyebrows. "We have photographers in Crete."

"That's Sunday newspapers for you. It's got to be someone expensive with a name."

"Ah," Manolo reflects. "Then I hope that you too are expensive."

"I'm afraid not. And I don't have a name either. I'm just a hack. But there you go . . . Anyway—I'm looking forward to tomorrow."

Walking over to her bungalow, she thinks about how she has enjoyed the day, which was not really the idea. She is not here for enjoyment. She has been intrigued and stimulated by what she has seen, Manolo's company has been a delight. He is a very attractive person. All right—sexually attractive, if one is going to be candid. Possibly he is gay—Ruth is aware that she lacks good antenna when it comes to that sort of thing. Whatever, there is no question that either of them will behave other than impeccably. Anything else would be the equivalent of package holiday girls cavorting with Turkish waiters, and an insult to them both.

At the bungalow, there is a phone message. A laconic voice announces himself as Al, the photographer. He will be in the bar from seven-thirty, if she'd care to get together.

Ruth showers, changes, makes some hasty notes, and then calls Peter's number, to talk to the children.

"Are you all right?" she asks.

The children are unspecific. Jess has an issue over her best friend, who no longer is. Tom has a new reading book.

"Love you," says Ruth.

"Love you back," say the children vaguely. They have pressing concerns right now, to do with a lost pencil case, and whether or not Peter will let them watch *The Simpsons.*

Ruth finds the photographer sitting beside the ambitious fountain in the hotel's central courtyard, drinking whiskey and reading the *International Herald Tribune.* He is a laid-back Canadian, and has come from an assignment in Somalia. "Bit different from this." He waves a hand at the surroundings: the fellow guests, fresh fried from the beach and decked out for the evening, the darting waiters, the three-piece band just tuning up. "Amazing outfit, this. They have twelve hundred beds, I've read. And four hundred staff. The shops sells mink jackets at fifteen hundred pounds a throw. Custom was not brisk, I noticed." He chuckles. "So what've you got lined up, Ruth?"

Ruth describes where she has been today, and outlines the plans for tomorrow. He will probably need to go to Phaistos himself at some point, and the monastery, she tells him.

"I'll hire a car. No prob. Or your guy can run me there. What about some dinner?"

They move through to the dining room. Ruth notes with irritation that the waiter treats her with greater deference now that she is with a man. Al talks easily; a person used to chance encounters, she thinks, accustomed to get along with whoever comes to hand. He zips around the world on demand, it seems, a hired gun for whoever needs prime quality photography of whatever. He has tales of disastrous shoots, of risky shoots, of shoots in places where shoots are not supposed to take place. He has fallen into the Amazon, along with most of his equipment, he has been sniped at by Afghan tribesmen, he has confronted a bear in the Rockies. A long, rangy man, he has a long, wedge-shaped face, and a cool assessing stare; nothing much would faze him, you feel. Ruth senses that she is measured up as he talks. Occasionally, his face breaks into a grin, and she finds herself grinning back. He'll do, she thinks, he'll do as someone to be stuck with for a couple of days. Him and Manolo—I've struck lucky.

"So—how's it with you, Ruth? Where d'you hang out when you're not on an assignment?"

Ruth explains that she seldom is on an assignment of this kind. She says she is a Londoner but does not refer to her personal circumstances. "Where do you live?"

Al is trying to get the waiter's attention. "Nowhere, really. There's a pad in London when I need it, and one in New York. Hey! Another of these, please." He points to the nearly empty wine bottle.

"Oh, gosh—I'm not sure I . . . It's going to be quite a long day tomorrow."

"Nonsense." He fills her glass. "We need to keep our strength up. Oh gawd—here comes the entertainment."

The band has moved to one side, to make way for the floor show. The lights are dimmed, and two over-worked but indomitable girls struggle into one set of sequins after another, shimmy around, and belt out songs in German, English, and Greek. "Christ!" says Al. "We certainly need to fortify ourselves against this." He tops up their glasses. His running commentary makes Ruth laugh. When eventually the show ends and the band strikes up again she is quite light-headed.

The floor has been cleared for dancing. Leather-skinned middle-aged couples are shuffling around, cheek to cheek. Al gets up and holds out his hand. "C'mon."

Ruth has not danced in years. Possibly she has not danced since she was at college. Peter did not dance, and anyway they never found themselves in dancing situations. How does one do it? Al holds her quite firm and close—he has that warm, toasty, male smell—it is far from disagreeable, in fact it is entirely to be commended, all you do is move. "That's the girl," he says, his hand in the small of her back. "D'you come here often?" Ruth giggles. The band changes tempo. "Tango," says Al. "Now this I can do. I had a South American girlfriend once. Let's roll . . ." He swoops her around the floor. The German couples fall aside. Dear me, thinks Ruth, I am getting a taste for this.

It is quite late when they leave. Al escorts her back to the bungalow. "That was great, Ruth. Take care. See you in the morning." And he is gone, loping off between the hibiscus and the tamarisks.

The next morning, Manolo is already waiting when Ruth arrives outside the main building. Within a minute Al appears, slung about with photographic equipment. He is brisk and professional; the off-duty persona of last night has been laid aside. "Hi, there. Hi, Manolo—good to meet you. Can we get this gear in the back? What's the program?"

They drive up into the mountains. Manolo has proposed a visit to Arkadi, the monastery that is the Cretan Masada, where a thousand inhabitants blew themselves up with gunpowder rather than submit to the besieging Turks. After that, they will tour some mountain villages to give Ruth material for her piece and to provide Al with photo opportunities.

Arkadi is tranquil, scenic—the mountains all around, the battered honey-colored monastic buildings, monolithic cypresses, a desultory café selling cold drinks and postcards. The place is not unvisited; there is a cluster of the fuchsia pink scooters and the scarlet or powder blue jeeps hired by the more adventurous tourist. Al is immediately drawn to these, and spends much time angling the right shots, with the monastery as background. It is easy to see why: the incongruity, the apposition, the colors.

Manolo gives his account of that fearful day in 1866, his voice hushed, in the ruined central room where the walls are still blackened. The defiant leadership of the chief monk. The cries of the surrounding Turkish hordes, the anguished decision. "Jesus!" says Al. "What a place. And you say these priests—monks—had been fighting alongside everyone else?"

"Of course. The same in 1941. In Crete a priest is a Cretan first, a priest second." Manolo is as enthusiastic and assiduous as ever now that his seminar has swollen to two people, but is perhaps concealing a certain impatience with the lengthy photographic sessions. He and Ruth sit outside the café while Al prowls around in search of a final shot.

"So tomorrow . . ." he says. "Tomorrow I take you to the cemetery. And Al also?"

"No. Al will need to go to Phaistos, and that church."

Manolo nods. "And it is better you are there alone, perhaps?"

"Mmn." Ruth is not at her best today. She drank too much last night; her mouth is dry, she has a headache. And the evening mood of gaiety has evaporated; indeed, she feels guilty about it. She is not here for gaiety, for enjoyment, that is as inappropriate to the matter in hand as are the sun-baked masses, the warbling girls of the floor show, the tour buses that pound along the coast road. So today she is in a state of self-disgust, and she feels somber.

Manolo takes them to picturesque mountain villages—small remote places that often appear to be totally abandoned, until a woman flings open a shutter, some children peer around the corner of a house. Al selects the choicest village for a lengthy shoot; it has a small central square, turquoise doors and window shutters, a café whose proprietor sports an impressive handlebar moustache and wears traditional costume of jodhpur-type trousers and knee-high boots. Neither he nor his clientele of three old men appear to have anything more urgent to do than take part in a lengthy photo session, with many pithy asides in Greek. Al hefts his tripod around, stands straddled peering into the camera, his jacket draped over his head to keep out the blazing sunlight, shoots roll after roll of film. Much coffee is drunk—and beer, and coke, and rakia. Chunks of feta cheese appear, and walnuts. Al rearranges the café's frontage of flower pots to greater effect, an obliging owner removes the only car parked in the square. At one point, a gravel lorry proposing to pass through the village stops to wait patiently till Al has finished his film; the driver gets out and accepts coffee and a brandy.

Ruth and Manolo sit in the shade and watch. "Words or pictures?" says Manolo. "Which tell the story?"

"Both, I suppose. I can describe this place, but the photos will give the color of the doors. That moustache. His boots. The cat sitting on the wall."

"For Minoan times we have only pictures, pretty well. You have seen—in the museum. The wall friezes, the vases. Plenty of pictures. What everyone wanted was the words—the language."

"Linear B," says Ruth. "I know. You explained."

"And then when at last the tablets are deciphered they are lists of sheep and oxen. Or records of wheat and oil stores, and an order for bathtubs." Manolo laughs. "No poetry. No pre-Greek plays."

"I suppose most of our words are about sheep and oxen, and bathtub deliveries, or the equivalent. Records and communication."

"Of course. That is how language began. Poetry and plays are luxuries. And history needs to know about the sheep and oxen and the bathtubs." Manolo turns those Byzantine eyes upon her. Ruth feels less somber.

Al is through. "Good shoot. Now I need some big scenery—mountain stuff. Hold on while I buy these guys a bottle of brandy."

There are heartfelt farewells all round. The café proprietor presents Ruth with a bouquet of plumbago, with a flourish. They get back into the car.

"Okay," says Manolo. "So I find scenery for you." There is a sense of diminished enthusiasm but even so he succeeds in extracting drama from every twisting road, each vista of olive-strewn valleys and majestic mountain ranges. Scenery may be inert, but it is also the backdrop to human activity. Manolo stops the car at a small, ancient church on a bend: "Here was before a Roman temple, and see, here in the wall are stones from the temple, with even an inscription." He points out an olive tree that has grown up around a Greek column, the gray trunk twined about the white stone. Al sets up the camera and snatches the image.

"And here . . ." Manolo has picked a new stopping point and is indicating a road which wavers through a valley ahead and marks the route taken by the Allied forces after the defeat, when they began to make their way through and over the mountains to Sphakion on the north coast, where the navy would take them off the island. He conjures up the straggling columns of men, exhausted after days in action, sleepless, desperate with thirst and hunger. "Up into the mountains," says Manolo. "Higher and higher. Not knowing how far they had to go, or what awaited them. Without equipment, some without boots, even. Imagine."

Ruth, who has already imagined, is silent. She thinks of Matt's fellow officer, John Marsh, who wrote that letter to her grandmother. He must have been one of those men.

Al is studying the map. "Christ—they had a hell of a way to go, didn't they. How many of them?"

Manolo shakes his head. "Very many."

"Around ten thousand," says Ruth.

Both men look at her.

"You've been boning up on world war two?" says Al.

Ruth finds that she does not want to explain about Matt at this moment. She has had little direct contact with Al all day; all conversation has been about what shots would best complement her article. He has been absorbed in the job. Once, when she refused a glass of rakia pressed on her by the café proprietor, he gave a complicit grin, and also declined.

Manolo looks as though he is about to say something, and then perhaps notes Ruth's reticence. He talks of how Cretan villagers helped the retreating soldiers with food and shelter, he talks of the resistance, the partisan fighters, the battle of attrition waged from the mountain hold-outs.

The light is fading. Al says he will pack it in for the day. There is discussion about plans for tomorrow. Manolo turns to Ruth: "I take you to Suda Bay, okay? I can fix a hire car for Al to go to Phaistos."

"You're not coming, Ruth?" says Al.

"No. There's somewhere else I need to go."

"Too bad. I'll miss you." As they get into the car, he puts his hand for a moment on her shoulder. "It's been a great day, anyway. I'll be in the bar later if you want to unwind."

Ruth gets into the back of the car and sits there silent throughout the drive to the hotel. She is disturbed by Al, and exasperated with herself for feeling this way. When they arrive, she gets quickly out of the car, confirms tomorrow's arrangements with Manolo, waves to Al, and walks away to her bungalow. She will not go to the bar.

Two hours later, Ruth is in her bungalow. She has her books in a pile beside her and revisits, yet again, the narrative of the 1941 campaign, this story that is now buried half a century deep, set fast, unchanging, over and done with. Churchill sent Allied forces to Greece from Egypt, in anticipation of a German advance across the Greek frontier. The Allied and Greek forces were driven back by the Germans, and Allied troops were evacuated by sea to Crete. Less than four weeks later German paratroopers landed in Crete. After ten days of fierce fighting the Allied commander, General Freyberg, considered that his position was untenable. The surviving Allied troops were ordered to make their way to Sphakion, in the mountainous south of the island, for evacuation by the navy. Over six thousand remained, as prisoners or hiding out, assisted by Cretan partisans. A total of over twelve thousand Allied prisoners were taken; 1,751 were killed or missing, including Matt Faraday.

This is what happened, it is history—but it is not over and done with, Ruth sees, because these writings are a cauldron of dissent. Why did this happen? What caused that? Decisions, actions, consequences. Was Churchill ill-advised to intervene in Greece? Would he not have done better to reserve his forces for the Libyan campaign? Should he have sent Ruth's grandfather to the desert, rather than to Crete and thus, finally, to a ditch on a hillside above Heraklion? And did General Freyberg underestimate the effect of massed parachute landings, obsessed by his expectation of a seaborne invasion? Did he make a series of seminal mistakes? Was he over-optimistic? Or did he, on the other hand, decide to pull out too soon? Did his errors commit Matt Faraday to his death on that hillside?

People know now what happened when, and where, and—up to a point—why. Historians look down with Olympian hindsight, and make judgments. The *Sturm und Drang* of the moment is raided for evidence—a snatch of eyewitness testimony—but that is all that it is. Those hours, days, are stashed away now, like reels of film, to be replayed at will.

Just as Ruth replays John Marsh's letter. She takes this out now—the copy that she has made to save further wear on the flimsy original—and reads it yet again, although she knows it almost by heart.

Dear Mrs. Faraday,

I should like to tell you as much as I can of what happened on May 20th 1941. Matt was a fellow officer, and a friend; I mourn him with you.

We were based at Heraklion. A seaborne landing was anticipated, or parachute drops, and we had been on full alert since our arrival. There was bombing of the airport and the surrounding area, where we were dug in, along with frequent Stuka attacks. Losses had not been great, but the conditions were difficult—great heat, and we were concealed in olive and bamboo groves where the slightest movement would bring the aircraft down on us. On the morning of the 20th all was quiet. The skies were clear and we were stood down. It was thought a good idea for some of us officers to do a recce of the surrounding countryside—we were only recently arrived from Egypt and not sufficiently familiar with the layout of the place. Matt and I set off and were a couple of miles above the town, in the afternoon, when a wave of bombers arrived, followed by Messerschmitts and Stukas. We had no choice but to hunker down and wait till it was over, concerned now about being away from our unit. As soon as the attack was done, we began to hurry back down, only to hear the bugle sounding the general alarm—signal for a parachute attack.

The troop-carriers came in wave after wave, and you saw the parachutes spilling out—the sky was full of them. We kept on heading down the way we'd come, to get back to the unit, until we realized that there was a drop coming down all around us. We got into a ditch beside an olive grove, and from there we did what we could. I got one German who had fallen into a tree, and Matt had another. But there were several more around, looking for their weapons canisters, and a couple of them came straight toward us. We got one of them, but the other opened up with his submachine gun.

Matt was hit. The German ran on—I think he thought he'd got us both. I made Matt as comfortable as possible, but he couldn't move, so I had to get to our nearest position, which was half a mile or so down the road, and fetch help for him.

I won't drag this out. What happened was that I ran into a nest of them on the way down and got a flesh wound myself, so it took longer than it should have done. When the stretcher party got up to Matt he was dead.

He was a fine officer and a fine person. I want to send you and your little girl all my sympathy. Matt and I were together in the Delta, before Crete. Whenever he could he was sketching, he had that pad always in his pocket, and I realized he was a jolly fine artist too.

Yours sincerely,
John Marsh

Ruth has scrutinized this letter many times for its omissions and its silences, she has searched beyond and behind its stilted language for what really went on that day. ". . . to tell you as much as I can." By what was he constricted, John Marsh? The attentions of the censor? A degree of inarticulacy? A wish to spare Lorna? For how long did Matt lie dying in that ditch? What exactly happened to John Marsh himself? Above all, the language of the letter excludes all she now knows from her reading—it excludes blood, shock, pain, horror, fear. Matt and John "get" German paratroopers; Matt is "hit."

John Marsh could of course have written a different letter. He could have written a letter simply recording that he was a fellow officer who was with Matt on May 20th 1941, when Matt received a fatal wound, and that he wishes to convey his sympathy. But he preferred this partial account, this awkward expression of dismay and regret.

Dear Mrs. Faraday, he wrote, not knowing that he was writing to the future, that he was writing evidence of a kind, that he was writing a letter to Matt's granddaughter. He thought he was writing to Lorna, to his friend Matt's widow. He was writing the decent, tempered, conventional account to the bereaved. Doctored, bleached.

So that is how it was, thinks Ruth—thinks the future. So that—up to a point—is how it was, when *then* was *now.* But this evening, as she stares yet again at that careful handwriting—the writing perhaps of a man for whom language did not flow too easily—today *then* takes on a different complexion. She knows so much that John Marsh could not know. He is trapped within the slide of the present, his present. Ruth, in her own way, knows what will become of his—that the war will end, but not for a while, that Nazism will be routed, that a complicated new world order will emerge, with new nightmares, new Armageddons.

As she reads—the letter, the books—time is collapsed. Past and present seem to run concurrently: what happened, what is thought to have happened.

The next morning, Manolo is subdued—in deference, Ruth realizes, to their objective. On the way to the cemetery, he says, "How old was he—your grandfather?"

"Twenty-nine."

Manolo sighs. "Younger than I am. Or you—excuse me." He glances sideways at her.

"Yes. I often think of that."

"Archaeologists become very used to young death. Most bones are young. Old people are for modern times. In antiquity, you did not get old. And always, it is the young who are sent to war."

"Yes."

"When we are there, I shall leave you. I have a friend in Canea—I shall go and make a visit. And then I will come back to fetch you. Two hours, perhaps?"

"Thank you," says Ruth.

They reach the cemetery through olive groves, which serve also as the car park, though the only car there is that of the custodian. Manolo points out the little reception building, where you can find out how to locate any particular grave. Then he goes.

Ruth walks through the olives, and there ahead is a great expanse of bright flower beds, and rank upon rank of brilliant white headstones that stretch right away down to the blue curve of the sea. So many. They make orderly patterns as she stands looking—diagonals and lines ahead and lines to right and left. There are gravel paths between the rows, and beds of flowers in front of each—geraniums, petunias, canna lilies, hibiscus, and rosemary bushes. Everything is groomed, immaculate. This is order, and control. It is the antithesis of everything that went on here back then—the confusion, the carnage. It is very quiet, there are no other visitors. Just blue butterflies dancing above the flowers, swallows zipping overhead, the gentle rasp of cicadas.

The custodian smiles in welcome, and shows Ruth the book in which she can find Matt's name, with a grid reference for his grave.

She does not hurry. She walks very slowly past line after line of headstones, stopping to look and read. Many say simply: A soldier of the 1939-45 war. Known unto God. Others are precise: Flying Officer G. S. Hall. Age 23. Gunner P. B. Graham. Age 20. Private W. G. Orme. Age 21. Trooper W. A. Willcocks. Age 22.

Boys, she thinks. Boys.

By the time she reaches the grave she is dazed. She feels numb. She has read name after name, stared at the impersonal, white headstones, each of which makes its simple statement. This was a person. A boy. A man. They conjure up nothing; she does not allow them to do so. Everything that she has read is pushed far away, where she can neither see nor hear it. She sees only the stones, and the blue butterflies, and the silver-green of the olive grove back there, and the sparkling sea beyond the graves. The names are silent, but also eloquent. Those many anonymous graves are differently eloquent; at each, she stands for a moment.

Here it is at last. Lieutenant M. J. Faraday. Age 29. The letters of his name stand out with urgent intimacy. This one. Him. Matt. Her grandfather. For a moment there floats before her eyes that photograph of him—one of the only ones. A young man in shirt and trousers, hair that flops over his forehead, his eyes screwed up against the sun, somehow nailed to another age by the cut of his clothes, the deck chair beside which he stands, the unfocused snapshot. But this crisp white headstone is very much here and now; it is tangible, present, evidence—and suddenly he is more real for Ruth than he has ever been. He was here, once, or not far from here. He too saw olive groves, and that sea, felt this hot sun. And he is still here—gone but not-gone, a mute, impersonal reminder, along with a thousand others.

She stays in front of the headstone for a long time. She has no thoughts, she simply stands there. Then she walks away down to the seaward end of the cemetery, past the long white ranks, and sits on a bench.

There, tears come to her eyes. For him. For all of it.

Back at the hotel, she and Manolo say good-bye. Her flight is tomorrow morning. Then she goes to the bungalow and speaks to the children, reminding them that she will shortly be home. They sound quite surprised, which she takes as a good sign; they cannot have been too disturbed by her absence.

She considers going for a swim, but the thought of that complacent crowd on the beach is off-putting. It is early evening now, but there will still be people clinging to the last of the sunshine. She is deciding to order room service dinner when her phone rings.

"Hi, there!" says Al. "How was your day?"

"Fine." This is an automatic response, and an inaccurate one, but she does not propose to go any further.

"Good. Me too. I got some good pictures. Listen—I'm tired of this dump. How about going some place else for a meal? I have this hire car. We could go along the coast."

Ruth dithers. No, she thinks. Then—why sit here?

"Ruth?" says Al.

"Yes. Yes . . . I . . . Well—Okay, then."

"Half an hour," says Al. "Meet you at the entrance."

They drive into Rethymnon. There are restaurants on the waterfront. "Great!" says Al. "Seafood. I could use a lobster. Shall we try this one?"

Al orders lobsters and white wine. They share a platter of calamari. He is relaxed, talkative, neutral. He is not making a pass, Ruth decides. Which is just as well because—well, because she does not quite know what she would do if he were.

Al talks about Phaistos. "Amazing place. Not that I could make much sense of it, but the shoot'll come out just as good." He laughs.

"You should have had Manolo with you."

"He's a great guy, our professor, but tell the truth I cover more ground on my own."

"Where do you go from here?"

"Berlin. A shoot for a German magazine. Then it's New York."

"I couldn't live like that," says Ruth.

"Not many could." He grins. "And I can't stay put for long. So . . . have you got your piece all sewn up?"

"Plenty of notes. It's just a question of writing it when I get back."

"And what's next for you?"

Jess's dentist appointment, she thinks. Tom needs new shoes. Fix for the boiler engineer to come. "Oh—routine sort of things. An article about the Child Support Agency."

"What the hell's that?"

"You really don't want to know," says Ruth. "It pursues deficient fathers."

"Not guilty, I'm glad to say. I've never fathered anyone, far as I'm aware."

The lobsters have arrived. Dismemberment is both messy and convivial. "Here," says Al. "You're making a real hash of those claws. Let me . . ."

It is dark now. The restaurant overlooks the harbor, its light flooding onto the water, where shoals of small fish flit to and fro. Ruth discovers that if you throw down pieces of bread a football scrum ensues, a silver melee of darting fish.

She says, "Tom would love that. My son. He's six. And Jess is eight."

"I guessed you had kids."

"Oh. What's such a giveaway?"

"You looked at kids a lot when we were in those villages. A sort of professional look."

Ruth laughs. Then she adds, "Their father's not with us. We're separated." She always prefers to get this out into the open; no good reason to make an exception now.

"Ah. Too bad."

The lobsters have been demolished. "Pretty good," says Al. "Ever eaten crocodile?"

"I have not."

"Don't bother. I met that once in India. Curried. You do global food, in this job—take what's on offer. Sometimes I'd kill for a Big Mac."

"Are you sure it was crocodile? I've simply never heard of them being eaten."

"Are you questioning my integrity, ma'am?"

"Handbags, yes. And shoes. But eaten?"

"Well, that was what we understood, from the gestures. Something long, with teeth. Mind, China's the worst. There it's dog. And owls. And fried cat."

"I've always thought oysters were going too far," says Ruth. "Let alone snails. I'm conservative, gastronomically."

"But you'll allow a lobster?"

"That's where I go a bit radical. They're so delicious." Ruth smiles wryly.

"In fact," says Al, "I can't get up a big interest in food. Gourmet stuff, I mean. Basically, it's just essential fuel, isn't it? Cookery shoots I will not do. Food and fashion—no thanks." He eyes her. "Hope I'm not treading on toes. You're not in that line, are you?"

"No," says Ruth "I've got out into . . . issues. The deficient fathers, and suchlike."

"And this sort of thing?" Al waves vaguely at the light-strewn harbor, the gleaming water.

"This was a one-off, really. I don't do travel."

"Very wise." Al describes various occupational disasters: a hurricane in Cuba, a dodgy aircraft in Mozambique. She looks at him across the table—the long rangy body, the maleness of him. She is disturbed once more. Damn, she thinks. Shit. She focuses deliberately on the backdrop: the floodlit Venetian ramparts, a line of bobbing fishing boats—and now the afternoon comes back, the geometric patterns of the white headstones, the cavalcade of names. And I'm sitting here, she thinks, drinking wine and talking, as though all that never happened, sixty years ago, as though I didn't know what I now know about it. But that's what you do, isn't it? It's what people do—move on. That's all that can be done. What must be done.

"Hey!" says Al. "I've lost you. Where've you gone?"

"Sorry. I'm a bit distracted. By where I've been today."

"More of Manolo's ruins?"

"No, no." And, without having intended to, she is telling him. About Matt. About all of it.

He listens carefully. He asks the occasional question. What's a wood engraving? How old did you say he was? What happened to his wife?

Eventually he says, "Now I understand why you seemed to know so much about world war two. It was personal."

"Sort of. Though how can it be, when I never knew him?"

"That's not the point. It's that he's—well, all those other guys who died are anonymous, as it were. He's real."

"Yes," says Ruth. "That's what it is, I suppose. It takes on a different dimension. And you start to feel—guilty, in some awful way."

"About being here, like this?"

She nods.

"Ruth," says Al, "you have to ditch that, right? Okay—I understand the sentiment, but it doesn't get anybody anywhere. Least of all your grandfather. If he's looking down from up there he'll be saying—go for it, girl. Live."

Ruth smiles wryly.

"So think positive, okay? This is now. Then was then—all we can do is respect it, and you've been doing that, today." And he pats her arm—a warm, friendly pat from a large sunburned hand. It seems to seer Ruth's skin.

Oh no, she thinks, you had better not do that. Kindly do not do that.

"So what I'm thinking," says Al, "Is that we should have some more wine, and perhaps a dessert, and when we're done here what about a stroll through the town?"

And so it goes—more food and drink, and then the lit-up populous narrow streets where shops apparently never close, and the beautiful youth of Rethymnon parade, eyeing up the competition. Al shepherds Ruth through the crowds, she buys T-shirts for the children. They stop off for a coffee at a pavement bar.

Ruth observes to Al that there is more left of this town than she would have expected, given the pounding it took in 1941. There are ancient houses, Venetian doors and windows, stone fountains.

"Of course," says Al. "Nothing gets wiped in this place—friend Manolo's history lesson. Nothing ever gets wiped—period."

"*People* wipe things. In their heads, I mean."

"That's shrink stuff. I don't go near those guys."

"Nor me," says Ruth. "I mean all the times that just vanish. Who remembers being four, or six, or even sixteen?"

"Sixteen is easy. First time with a girl. No one forgets that."

"Well, yes. Dramatic survivals—equivalent of the Venetian doorway. But what about everything that goes down the plug?"

"Ruth, this is getting heavy. I thought I'd got you off this stuff? Relax."

She smiles. "You have. And I am. I'm enjoying myself, which isn't what I expected to do on this trip. It's not what I'm supposed to do."

"Nor me," says Al. "But you never do know what will turn up in the course of work." And he gives her that large, quizzical, assessing grin.

They walk slowly back to the car. They pause to watch the long ribbons of light on the water of the harbor; they discuss whether that black ripple could possibly be a dolphin. "Probably not," says Al. "They're all but done for, the fishermen net them."

"I insist that it is," says Ruth—"another survival."

"Then specially for you, ma'am," says Al. "That is a dolphin. Something to tell your kids—they'll want to know about this trip."

"Some of it," says Ruth.

"They miss you?"

"Hard to tell," says Ruth. "They have their own agenda. And three days isn't long."

Except that it is, she thinks. These three days have had their own dimension—time out, time suspended, time confused.

They reach the car, get in. The coast road, once more. Not much is said. Al is humming the Greek song that had been played in the restaurant. Ruth glances sideways at him. This is a man who cruises through life with his hands in his pockets. How do you get like that?

Back at the hotel, he parks the car in the forecourt and they walk past the main building to the hinterland of bungalows. They are going to arrive first at Al's, Ruth realizes. I knew this would happen, she thinks. I knew it.

He stops, and stands looking at her. "Well," he says. "I guess we're home." And then he lays the back of his hand against her cheek for a moment. "So . . . How about it, Ruth?"

She cannot move. Or speak.

He takes her arm, guides her gently to the door, and then inside. He switches lights on, pulls down the blinds, and then, somehow, they are in the bedroom.

He sets about undressing her—kindly, efficiently, unzipping her skirt so that it slides down her legs, lifting her T-shirt (and she raises her arms obediently, like a child), undoing her bra.

"That's the girl," he says. Then he draws back for a moment, frowning. "So long as you're sure you want this?"

She stands there, in her pants—helpless, hopeless. "I'm afraid I do," she says.

"Who's to be afraid? This'll be good."

And it is. She is astonished. She has never before had sex with a man she knows she will not see again. She is amazed at how easy it is, in the event, how—well, how unembarrassing, how inevitable. The process is familiar—oh dear me, yes—but is also radically different. His stranger's body; her own unanticipated responses. At one point, she thinks fleetingly of Peter; it is like remembering some old home when you are in foreign territory. Al's love-making is in tune with the rest of him—companionable, frank, purposeful. The idea is satisfaction all round, and that is achieved. But afterwards, lying there beside him, Ruth thinks: what's missing? Something crucial, but it doesn't have a name. Not love—that would be too obvious.

It is past one when she makes her way back to her own bungalow. "Stay," Al had said, but she declined. She must leave for the airport at eight. "Okay—makes sense," he says. At the door, he gives her a hug. "You're a great girl, Ruth. Keep in touch. Take care."

She opens her door, and sees at once the red light flashing on the phone. She picks it up. Please come to the hotel reception—there is an urgent fax for her.

She runs, her heart thumping. Something has happened. Something has happened to one of the children.

And, indeed, something has happened. But not to the children. It is Molly.

Part 8

JESS HAS HAD HER EARS PIERCED. Without permission. She has taken herself off to Oxford Street, with her savings and two friends, and there the three of them have done the deed. She stands now in front of Ruth with pink ears, little gold studs, and an expression of distressed defiance: "You said I could when I'm fourteen. So what's the difference?"

"Ten months' difference," says Ruth. "And you should have *asked.*"

Tom is looking at the ears with interest. "They're all puffed up. Can I see the holes?"

Jess bursts into tears.

Ten minutes later, emotional order has been restored. Jess is texting an outer circle of friends to report on her rite of passage; Tom, bored with the fuss, has withdrawn to engage with his Game Boy; Ruth has conceded tacitly that there is not much point in trying to counter the tide of peer pressure. She reminds Jess that they have company for supper, shortly. Sam is in town for some poetic commitment, and she has invited Simon and Tim to join them.

"Be thankful it wasn't her belly button," says Simon. The children have gone to watch television; the four adults sit around Ruth's kitchen table. Throughout the evening, as always now, there has been a void in their midst, that keen abiding absence; they are broken-backed, but carry on. This, now, is the family.

"Or a tattoo," suggests Tim.

Ruth sighs, then laughs. "To think this is just the *start* of adolescence. Was I like that?"

"Of course," Simon tells her. "I recall door slamming and funereal silences."

Ruth looks at Sam.

"By the time I came along you were a mellow seventeen. Entirely reasonable. Or nearly so."

Sam today, in this new age, is himself, yet at the same time he is someone different, as though loss had stripped him of some aspect of personality. He is more silent, more withdrawn; he is thinner, he has honed an interest in bird-watching, and goes on long solitary forays to uncomfortable places.

"The thing now," says Simon, "is that teenage is a status. It's a social category, and they are well aware of that. In my day—or Tim's—it was seen as an apprenticeship. We knew our place."

Tim recalls that his parents imposed an eight o'clock curfew, which rose to ten when you were eighteen.

"Interesting idea," says Ruth. "I can't see it catching on these days. Oh well—the next few years are going to be challenging, that's clear." She turns to Sam. "That envelope you forwarded . . ."

"Ah," says Sam. "'For Molly Faraday or other connection of artist Matt Faraday.' I hoped it wasn't some belated creditor."

"No way." Ruth gets up and goes to the dresser. "Look." She lays on the table some photographs and a letter.

Sam inspects the photographs. "It's . . . they're wood blocks, aren't they? For engraving?"

"Right."

Simon is reading the letter. "This chap thinks they are Matt's. And he lives in that cottage."

"He does and they are," says Ruth. "I asked Max and he said definitely. But I knew anyway. This Brian Clyde found them in a box in a shed. And there's some sort of maquette, apparently."

"However did he trace you? Or Moll, rather." asks Simon.

"He sent the photos to the Society of Wood Engravers, and they got someone to identify them. And then he seems to have done some clever detective work. He's suggesting I visit, so he can hand over the blocks and the other thing."

"You must."

"Oh, I shall. Though goodness knows when I'll fit it in."

"Business brisk in retail art?"

"Business is never *brisk* in a gallery. We're more genteel than that. One transaction a day is thought quite good going. I have suggested a summer sale, but Max considers this vulgar."

"Quite right too," says Simon. "Someone has to maintain standards. We independent bookshops try to do our bit. No three for twos, no promotions, and no doubt we shall all go to the wall in due course. You should have diversified into merchant banking, Ruth, or share trading—whatever it's called. Not some fossilized area of commerce."

"I doubt if that was ever an option, given my credentials."

"We must rest our hopes in Jess and Tom. Mind you keep them well away from any sort of creative activity."

Sam grins. "Make sure they learn a trade. Plumbing's the thing, I'd say."

"Tom might do well there. He's been digging up what passes for our garden to make a fish pond. With fountain. Anyone like more coffee?"

Simon and Tim leave. Sam, who is staying the night, helps Ruth to clear up. The children have gone to bed.

"I've forgotten why you're here," says Ruth. "Apart from to see us."

"A reading on the South Bank." Sam pulls a face. "Time I hung up my clogs, where that sort of thing is concerned."

"Nonsense. You'd fester. Nothing but cars and birds."

"Festering has its appeal."

"Mum would say . . ." Ruth begins.

"Oh, I know what she would say. She says it frequently. And I say—I hear you, my love. And sometimes I obey and sometimes I don't."

Ruth smiles and nods. "Me too." And they both listen to her voice, see her face, as they stand there in Ruth's kitchen amid the debris of the meal.

Sam shakes his head, and picks up the butter. "This go in the fridge?"

The present flat was somewhat larger than the old one, and had this garden of brickbats and cat shit on which Tom had designs. Peter, his wife, Marta, and their two-year-old daughter had moved to a house in a neighboring postcode, which involved some shunting to and fro, though the children now spent rather less time with their father.

Ruth also made postcode transits, but hers had a wider significance, when she moved twice a week from the upland suburbia of north London to the city thicket of South Kensington. It always seemed to her that she moved not only through space but through time, as she left Edwardian brick and arrived amid Georgian stucco with its sparkling white terraces and squares, while the traffic and the glossy shops reminded you that a city mutates, puts on new clothes, changes shape, adapts—year by year, decade by decade.

The gallery was in a street of boutiques and restaurants. Ruth had come upon it after a visit to a friend in the big hospital nearby. Feeling in need of a coffee, she wandered along the street, in search of a likely place, and stopped for a moment to look into an art shop, spotting from the door a wall of what seemed to be wood engravings. She went in, glanced around—lithographs, watercolors, assemblies of prints, and this display on one wall at which she looked more closely, and there, dead center, was one of Matt's.

The churchyard one, with tilted gravestones and a yew tree. She knew it well—Molly had a print, which was still with Sam, though he had pressed her to take it, along with others. There it was, with the little pencil mark below: 8/25. Where are the other twenty-three, she wondered. She moved along the wall, to examine its neighbors. Here was a Clare Leighton, and a Guy Malet, and a Rachel Reckitt. Heavens, though—look at the prices! She returned to Matt, and stood rapt, enjoying this sense of intimacy, as though a hand waved to you from a crowd of strangers.

There was someone alongside. The gallery proprietor, presumably, who had glanced up from behind a desk as she came in. An elderly man in a cord jacket; shock of white hair and spotted tie.

"Matt Faraday, that is," he said. "Artist of the thirties. Died in the war."

"I know. I've got some of his work."

"Hang onto it, then. Hard to come by."

After a moment, Ruth said, "He was my grandfather."

"Well, well. Any talent in that direction yourself?"

"None whatsoever."

"It's a dying art, anyway. An endangered species, engravers. Fifty years' time, nobody'll be doing it. Collectors' items, all this early twentieth-century stuff. Which Faradays have you got?"

Ruth cited the engravings that hung on her walls. "I had a *Cleeve Abbey* last year," said the man. "Or was it *Mushrooms*? Hang on—I'll just check the catalog."

She did not see exactly what happened. He turned and headed for the door that led to an office at the back of the gallery. She heard a crash, ran across, and he was lying on the floor, face down, out cold. Later, she realized that he must have tripped on the edge of a rug.

The ambulance arrived within five minutes, to her relief. The stretcher, the red blanket, the two burly matter-of-fact paramedics. "What's his name, love?" She had to say that she had no idea. Then—"Wait . . ." She rushed to the office, fumbled through a pile of letters, and deduced that he must be Max Gardner. "Thanks, love. We'll get going. Head injury. Clipped it on the corner of that desk, by the look of it." And they were gone.

You cannot, as a responsible person, walk out of a place full of valuable artwork, leaving it open and unattended, when its owner has involuntarily departed for an indefinite period. Ruth hunted for keys, to no avail. She went out and visited the bistro on one side and the smart dress shop on the other, where nobody could tell her anything about Max Gardner, and there was a distinct reluctance to become involved. She found the number of the local police station, and was advised to contact a friend or relative of Mr. Gardner's. "Look," she said, "I just walked in off the street, I have no idea . . ." The police station became tetchy, and seemed to suggest that she was being importunate; Ruth understood that in a London of gun crime and potential terrorism the police could not be expected to take an immediate interest in an unmanned art gallery. A person came in, spent some time inspecting prints in the racks, and asked if she ever had any Hockneys. Ruth said, "I don't actually work here, I'm afraid," and received a look of exasperation. The customer departed. The phone rang: someone wanted to know if their lithograph had come back from the framers yet. "I'm afraid I don't actually . . ." said Ruth. A courier arrived with a package, which she signed for, in desperation.

The phone rang again. "Max?" said a female voice, puzzled. Ruth explained. Consternation. Max Gardner's sister, in Salisbury, poured down the line a muddle of anxiety and suggestions: which hospital? what sort of head injury? keys, keys? keys almost certainly in his jacket pocket . . . oh dear, I'd better come up to town . . . train times . . . if you could *possibly* . . .

In the end, a girl from the dress shop was persuaded to mind the gallery while Ruth went to the hospital, located Max Gardner in A & E, found him conscious but too dazed to comment, collected the keys to the shop from his pocket and returned to lock up, thus retrieving the situation at least until the sister could get hold of a colleague of her brother's who, it was thought, would hold the fort, rally round, pick up the pieces . . . and thank you *so* much, Mrs . . . er? Ruth was obliged to give her name and address.

And so it all came about. A couple of weeks later, Max Gardner arrived on the doorstep one evening, behind an enormous florist's bouquet, bearing some rather nice wine. He was recovered—"A mere dent—I've got a tough nut"—but under doctor's orders to take things a bit easier. "Pursed lips and insulting references to one's age—you know these jumped-up boy consultants." Ruth opened the wine, Max Gardner commented with enthusiasm on Matt's work, touring the walls of the flat; he told the children their mother was a Good Samaritan, at which they looked baffled, and eventually stayed to supper. "Very kind—I won't say no. I live over the shop, and it's something from the deli in front of the TV, most nights." He tucked into sausages and mash, and talked voraciously, shooting a question at Ruth from time to time. "I'm a dinosaur in my trade," he told her. "They're all thirty-somethings in designer jeans and Armani suits these days, into BritArt. That's all right by me—I cater for the finer sensibility." He produced scurrilous stories, threw artistic judgments around. She liked this man.

On the doorstep, leaving, he thanked her with some formality. "And one final thing. I have a proposition. Would you consider a part-time job in a prestigious Kensington gallery?"

Ruth said, "Well . . . I don't know much about art."

"You'd pick it up in a trice. An air of confident superiority is all that's needed. I fear I must give in to the prissy boy in the hospital and put myself on a three-day week. Anyway, think about it."

Ruth thought. She contemplated what she was doing now, and asked herself if she wanted to do that all the time, forevermore. A few days later, she rang Max Gardner.

Ruth worked two days a week at the gallery; the rest of the time, she continued with her usual commissions. She enjoyed this apposition of activities. The gallery rapidly became a known territory, and while Max's airy dismissal of the need for experience seemed a touch optimistic, she found that by looking and learning she was soon reasonably proficient, at least in basic knowledge. And, if up against the wall, she could always put in a quick call to Max, who was usually in the flat leafing idly through saleroom catalogs or irritably getting on with what he called "the pernicious paperwork that takes the joy out of being a connoisseur."

When Ruth's father visited the gallery, he bought a Patrick Proktor lithograph.

"You really don't have to feel you must buy something," she told him.

"I don't. I needed a birthday present for Claudia, and that solves the problem." James Portland walked with a stick now; his thick dark hair had turned silver. He seemed amused at Ruth's career move. "You've kept very quiet about this artistic expertise."

"There isn't any," said Ruth. "As you well know. I bluff my way along."

"Well, you look the part. Gallery ladies are always slim, beautiful, and dressed in black. You could perhaps be a bit more intimidating. The idea is usually to make anyone who comes in feel as awkward as possible."

"I can't do the hard sell. Fortunately that's not Max's line, either. This is a user-friendly outlet."

"Evidently. You don't often find a chair available." James had sat himself down, wincing as he did so. He was in his mid-eighties, and though he did not look his age, there was a sense of diminishment, of ebbing vitality. Ruth found this hard to grasp; each time she saw him she expected still the vigorous figure of her childhood and adolescence. The stick, the stoop, the hair, seemed a mockery.

"At least he has some decent stuff." James waved a hand at the gallery walls. "I'm too old for what's come out of the art schools over the last ten years."

"So am I, apparently," said Ruth. "And it's my generation."

"All the best people feel out of tune with their times. You were always a bit maverick. Like your mother, but differently so."

"Really?" Ruth was interested.

"She was defiant maverick. You were—are, presumably—introspective maverick, if there is such a thing."

Ruth could not recall her father ever before offering such personal comments, and was startled. As if in response, he went on, "I'm so old I can say things like that. Probably should—before it's too late. I miss her like anything, even though I hardly ever saw her. At least I knew she was out there."

"Yes," said Ruth, nervous now. This might be going a mite too far.

"She was the love of my life. I won't say she broke my heart—it was probably too weathered for that—but she made anything else seem second fiddle."

Ruth thought fleetingly of her stepmother, with something akin to sympathy.

"Well, there it is. No doubt she was right—we weren't entirely compatible." James got up, grimacing again. "Bloody knee, now." He stood looking at her. "At least there's you."

"A sort of memento?" she said, with a wry smile.

He patted her arm. "I'd put it rather more strongly than that."

Every conception is fortuitous, every birth. That said, Ruth always saw her own existence as perhaps peculiarly accidental, spun from the odd conjunction of two people whose meeting was an unlikely chance. But the same could be said of her grandparents: a park bench . . . Isn't it always like that? Well, no; she and Peter had been cogs in the same machine, almost bound to mesh at some point. Molly and Sam inhabited the same world; they might well have missed one another, but the odds were in their favor. When she was young, Ruth had never questioned her circumstances; she moved from Molly to her father, from disheveled flat or house to the French château or the Belgravia mansion, merely accepting this polarization as the way things were, and how could they be otherwise? Only now, in mid-life—for that was where she was, after all—did she see this background, and her very presence, as a distinctly precarious event. This put you in your place, somehow.

Mid-life, she found, was not a bad time. She felt more positive than ever she had in youth, more deliberate, as though she had found a more satisfactory personality and settled into it. Sometimes she felt infused with Molly's drive, a hidden legacy. She had had to manage children, work, the flat, a regular cash flow, and it had all been possible. Life might be accidental, but she could feel that she had met its challenges. She was without a partner, and that was flying in the face of social expectation, and maybe of nature, but she was coming to accept this. So be it. One or two skirmishes had come to nothing; nowadays, she seldom eyed a man for his potential. Outside of work, she was immersed in the children's dizzying development, the way in which they mutated month by month, year by year, became new versions of themselves—taller, smarter, saying and doing different things, bewildering, challenging.

She felt as though the flat were filled with the ghostly sloughed skins of last year's Jess, the Tom of two years ago—gone, extinguished, surviving only in her mind's eye. In her dreams, they were babies again, and then she woke to the pierced ears, the muddy football strip.

She found herself valuing more and more those who underpinned her life, those who had always been there—her father, Simon, Sam. When you are short on relatives, those that you have become essential tethers. Her friends had brothers and sisters, cousins, a full complement of parents. She had just this trio, who had no connection with one another. Somewhere, there must be people from the same genetic pond—her grandparents had had siblings, after all—but they were of no interest to her. A relation is a person whose face and traits you have always known, someone alongside whom you have grown, and while Sam did not quite fit, he was close enough and he was Molly's, and anyway she loved him. She spoke to him frequently, and to Simon.

But when sometimes Ruth thought about her descent—eyeing the children in some unfocused moment—it did seem meager that this should be all that was left from those mythic figures, her grandparents. Matt and Lorna. When you have never known your grandparents, when they are just a young face in a snapshot, they hang differently in the mind.

"Listen," Ruth says to Sam. "Are you around next week? At home?"

"I'm always around."

"Peter's taking the children to Disneyland, and I've told Max I'd like some time off. I thought I'd come down—and on the way I could call in and see this guy who's got Matt's blocks, at that cottage."

"Good idea. Excellent. I, too, will take sick leave. As it is, fiddling around inside cars is slightly losing its appeal."

"You should retire," says Ruth sternly.

"The village would grind to a halt without me. And the dosh is rather welcome. Anyway, unrelieved think-work gets me down."

"Maybe that's why I find the gallery a relief. Not that my think-work compares at all with your think-work."

"Self-abasement will get you nowhere," says Sam. "Pack your boots. I shall take you for a good long walk on the moor."

"I remember route marches with you and Mum when I was at college. I thought it was an infringement of human rights."

"You're a grown woman now. You'll love it."

"Simon?"

"Ruth. Could you hang on one moment—I'm up a ladder. There. Firm ground. How are things?"

"Why are you up a ladder, and do you always have the phone in your pocket?"

"To measure the wall, and yes, otherwise I forget where it is. We are considering buying an eighteenth-century French tapestry. Great excitement. We can't really afford it and fear that this is *folie de grandeur,* but we can't resist."

"Goodness—it was that arts and crafts chair last year. You never used to have this lust for fine furnishings."

"I know. I think it's a delayed reaction to growing up in the Fulham Road house. Cracked lino and chairs with wonky legs, and that sofa with the springs sticking out."

"At least there was Matt on the walls."

"True. And books everywhere. High thinking and low living really—a perfectly respectable tradition. But it seems to have spawned this hankering for the occasional delicacy. Tim is just as bad, and in his home they had inherited mahogany and an ancestral mirror."

"So indulge yourselves," says Ruth. "Actually, walls is what I wanted to ask about. Can you remember Mum ever talking about frescos on the walls of that cottage in Somerset?"

"Frankly, no. But she was—what? five?—when she left it. Would she remember?"

"Probably not. I've just looked at that man's letter again, and he talks about frescos. I'm going to call in on him next week, on the way down to see Sam."

"Give him my love. Sam, I mean, not the man. While you're at it, you might take in a few Devon antique shops, and see if you spot any nice Lowestoft pieces. We're starting a collection."

"Simon," says Ruth. "I wouldn't know a nice Lowestoft piece if I saw one. And Sam doesn't do antique shops. It's going to be long tramps on the moor."

"You poor dear. You'll be back here in a flash."

She had Brian Clyde's letter, and the map that he has sent in response to her phone call: "This place is quite impossible to find." She had some wine for Sam. And her walking boots—all right, Sam. The children were already gone; she shut up the flat with a certain sense of release.

The M4. The M5. Comfort stops at teeming motorway service stations through which flowed the August crowds. The nation was on the move, and the west country was the place to which it moved. Ranks of cars without, and a horde of people within. Lines shuffling forward for a fix of burgers, pasties, coke, coffee. Ruth had some lunch. Later, she had tea and ten minutes with the paper. And then, following her instructions, she was flung off the motorway into Somerset. First, a main road through a town and some villages. Brown signs displaying the area's wares: a ruined abbey, a cider farm, a castle, a beach, Butlins—something for everyone. This was holiday time, and the place was in full swing, everyone bolstering the local economy. There was a scenic railway, apparently doing good business; as she went through one village, she saw it at the station, in its cream and brown livery, with faces at every window.

The fields were stubble—stripped, spent, dotted with giant straw cotton reels, and black plastic drums. From time to time the river of traffic slowed to a crawl behind a tractor with its trailer. Cars fidgeted impatiently behind such obstacles, edging out to overtake. At one point, an oncoming car, skipping past a tractor, sent a stone spurting up from the road; a little star of shattered glass appeared in the windscreen in front of her. An older economy was still in operation here; the land itself was busy, spewing forth corn as it ever did, and a few more fancy latter-day crops that Ruth could not put a name to. What was the curious black stuff on that hillside?

And now the directions sent her off sharply into the hinterland. You burrowed into this landscape, she saw. The motorways rushed through it, and the A this and the B that, but as soon as you abandoned those dictatorial highways you had slipped off into another sphere. You were in the lanes, you were in narrow tunnels between high hedge banks, routes that also knew quite well what they were about and where they were going but that was their own immemorial business, and you were now in their domain. You went where they went, and that was that.

Ruth thought this was the right way. According to the map it should be. She had turned off the A39—thank goodness—and was proceeding cautiously, aware of the frequency of bends, of the fact that two vehicles could not pass one another. She did meet one car, which shot obligingly backward—rather too fast for comfort, a local presumably—into a nearby gateway. She continued, up a hill, round another bend, with here and there a glimpse through a gate of blue and green distances, like the jewelled vistas in medieval painting. Trees arched suddenly over the lane, so that she was in the center of a leafy sphere, through which sunlight splashed down onto the road ahead. The trees ended; the hedges rose again. A straight bit. Another bend, uphill again, and now at the crest of the hill the lane was blocked. There was a challenge.

A huge tractor confronted her. It filled the lane entirely. From somewhere high above in the cab, the driver gazed down at her, impassive. She understood that the ball was in her court—it was for her to back up. She did so, craning over her shoulder, lurching at one point into the hedge bank. She heard a concealed rock scrape across the car's bodywork. She lurched out again, managed to straighten up, glanced ahead at the tractor, which was inching forward—politely, not putting on the pressure. She backed around the bend—what if there was something coming?—and found another straightish stretch without, apparently, a passing place. She weaved from side to side of the lane. At last she arrived at a gateway into which she could cram the car.

The tractor roared past.

From time to time, a signpost appeared, as other lanes diverged from this one—equally sure of themselves, equally enigmatic. Ruth had by now quite lost any sense of direction. The signposts pointed every which way, so far as she was concerned—Roadwater, Rodhuish, Withycombe, Luxborough. What is where? Where does which go? She had quite lost touch with the map now, and did not dare stop to try to work things out; what if another tractor came? Or something even larger? Once, a horse and rider appeared, a helmeted figure advancing at a spanking trot. Ruth squeezed the car into the hedge bank, stopped, lowered the window and started to call out, "Excuse me, I wonder if . . .", but the horse and rider had spanked on before she could finish.

She knew what she was looking for. She had a description. She was looking for an old cottage, with whitewashed walls and a slate roof, set back from the lane, approached by a short track, at a T-junction with another lane which plunged off downhill to a small hamlet. And, by her reckoning, she should have reached this point by now, but no such place had appeared. She went up, she went down, she went through a village, a hamlet, but the wrong one, it would seem—and then—oh horrors!—she was confronted once more by the A39, with its glittering conveyor belt of cars. She managed to turn round, she was absorbed once more into the lanes, she tried different signposts, she went down where before she had gone up, left instead of right and suddenly, there it was, there it must be, this surely was it. But she was well over an hour later than she had said she would be. She turned off the lane onto the track. A terracotta-colored metal five-barred gate stood open on to the graveled driveway of the cottage, and the scrunch of her tires brought Brian Clyde to the door.

A tall man. Lean, a touch round-shouldered—a person who sat much at a desk, maybe. Craggy features. Glasses. Fiftyish.

Ruth got out of the car. "Sorry to be late. I got a bit lost."

"Of course. Everyone does. Congratulations on getting here at all."

The cottage sat in a triangular garden, with high hedges all around. There was a shed to one side, beyond which Ruth could see a shaggy lawn and unkempt shrubbery, and then a little orchard of old apple trees.

They went inside. The front door opened into a large kitchen with a gray slate floor, elegantly equipped, with a big dresser to one side, a long table, with a bench built into another wall. A staircase at the back. A door leading to another room.

"Tea? Coffee?"

"Tea would be great. Could I use your bathroom?"

"Upstairs and turn right."

At the top of the stairs, Ruth glanced through the open door of what was evidently the main bedroom and saw through the window a sloping field, hills, a sliver of gray sea. There was another open door; she saw a desk with computer, and a couch. Alongside was a small bathroom, newly and neatly fitted out. The bathmat was on the floor. She sat looking at a damp, bare footprint, which seemed somehow oddly intimate. She washed, tidied her hair, went downstairs.

He had a mug of tea in each hand, and indicated the room off the kitchen. "It's more comfortable in here."

She followed him. "Oh!"

The frescos. Ducks, in a procession around the walls. Willow trees that wept in each corner of the room. Quivery lines of blue water.

"Oh . . ."

He was smiling. "When I saw these, I knew I had to have the cottage. They were in a far worse state then—plaster coming off, I've had restoration people in. Of course, I had no idea then who had painted them. The place had been a farm laborer's cottage for decades, but local people remembered there had been an artist who lived here, a young man who was killed in the war."

Ruth stared at the ducks, the tumbling willows, the rippling water. She looked for a park bench, but there was none.

"The farm had changed hands—the people from whom I bought the place. They came in the sixties and knew nothing. And then I found the blocks and the maquette, and set about some research and . . . you know the rest."

There was a sofa along one wall, facing the square window that framed another view of hills, and sky, and a golden field. A crammed bookcase, more books piled on the floor alongside. A small perfunctory television. A stack of newspapers. Pictures—carefully hung so as not to encroach upon the frescos.

They sat down. On the coffee table in front of the sofa were the blocks, and a little chunky figure carved out of rose-colored stone. Brian Clyde picked it up, and put it into Ruth's hands.

"I found this under a pile of leaves just outside the old shed. I suspect it had been used as a doorstop. It's pink alabaster from down on the beach at Blue Anchor. And I suppose your grandfather made it."

A female figure, seated, body and limbs all in one, the head without a face. Like, Like . . .

"Makes you think of those little prehistoric votive figures," he suggested. "Or, I suppose, Henry Moore."

She nodded.

"Anyway, there you are. Yours. And here are the blocks. They were at the bottom of a box in the shed, which had been used as a dump for discarded tools and stuff. Amazing they've survived. Evidently none of the folk who lived here over the years had been great on clearing out."

Ruth lifted each block, studied them. "I can see now more exactly which they are. I've got an engraving of this one—*Dandelion Clocks*. And these with the figures are from an edition of *Lamb's Tales* from Shakespeare that he did for a fine press—the Heron Press."

"What happened to all the rest?"

"Lucas had a lot. Lucas was the Heron Press. He married my grandmother after—after Matt was killed. I suppose she must have taken them when she went from here, but overlooked these."

"In a minute," he said, "I'm going to show you something else. But first you need to recover from that drive. Everyone arrives here in a frenzy—getting lost in the lanes is a rite of passage."

He told her that he had had the cottage for a year. "There was a lot of work to be done. The farm had modernized a bit over the years—agricultural workers require higher standards of comfort these days—but the bathroom and kitchen fell somewhat short. The wiring was ancient. And I wanted a study that would double as a guest bedroom, and central heating seemed in order. Then the local builder suggested the slate floor for the kitchen."

He talked with beguiling enthusiasm. He had known this area well for a long while. "I'd always dreamed of having a foothold here. And then there was a bit of money suddenly—my poor old dad died—and I started looking around. Of course I can't be here all the time. It's my bolt-hole." An academic at a northern university, he had to return for each term.

His trousers were stained here and there with pink earth, as though he had been doing something outside; fingernails a bit grubby, too. On top of the bookcase, a little carriage clock ticked, a mere whisper. Ruth read the titles of books: *The Travel Journals of Celia Fiennes, John Leland's Itinerary, The Mediterranean in the Ancient World.* There was an old map on the wall, framed. She was listening to him, but everything around seized her eye. To be in this room, where they must have been. And her mother. The window was open; there came birdsong, and then a melancholy whistle.

She said, "The train? I saw it at a station."

"That's right. Reinvented in the service of tourism and the local economy. More tea?"

"I'd love some."

He went through to the kitchen. She looked at the pictures on the walls while he was gone. An etching of Dunster Castle. An old Great Western Railway poster from the early twentieth century. A framed photograph of haymaking with haywain and shire horses.

He returned. "Did you stop off on the motorway?"

"Twice. If only to touch ground. Motorways are insane. It's like flying. They make a nonsense of real distance. You hurtle from county to county."

He laughed. "Not always. Not on a summer Saturday. Not going past Bristol at rush hour."

"But you know what I mean. It's time and space gone mad. You think in terms of hours, not miles. So many hours to Exeter, when really it's a great expanse of land—fields and woods and rivers and towns. I always think that. It's a distortion."

"Is it?"

"Well, yes. I mean—you think of the . . . the intensity of all those places, of the baggage they carry, of how they've been the *only* place, for thousands of people, and now you whisk past—they become scenery, and the last half-hour."

"How very odd," said Brian Clyde.

"Odd?" Ruth became a touch defensive.

"Odd because that is very much what interests me." He paused. "I'm writing a book about something rather similar."

"Oh?" And I am probably about to get out of my depth, she thought.

"I'm interested in . . . the way in which elsewhere—the other place—has been perceived, over time. Whether it is of no interest, or territory to be acquired, or just an area over which you move. Anyway—you don't need to hear about that."

I might, she thought. Definitely I might.

". . . and I just want to show you something else. Come."

He led the way upstairs. On the small landing he paused outside the open door of the bedroom. "Tidy, I think. Now look at this."

The walls. Dancing figures. Pink. Nude, but discretely so. Male and female. Who hold out their arms to one another, link arms, swirl around the walls of the room.

He said, "They had been covered with distemper. I never realized they were there until the decorator began work, and spotted something. I wasn't here. They rang up and said, you've got people on the walls of your bedroom, you may want to take a look. When I got here, and saw a leg, and an arm, I got busy tracking down the restoration people—and there you are."

Ruth was amazed, transfixed. It was as though the room were filled with life—a mysterious, silent celebratory life that danced on and on, had done so ever since . . . ever since they were here. Him and Her. Matt and Lorna. She felt a rush of happiness, a burst of joy, as though something flowed through time, from then to now, from them to herself. She turned to Brian with a great smile, and saw that he too was beaming; for a moment they seemed to be complicit, an alliance of delight.

He said, "Aren't they wonderful? Every morning, they remind me that life is to be enjoyed."

She said, "My mother was born in here."

"I feel an intruder."

"No way. You rescued the paintings. I wonder who covered them up."

"Some previous occupier? They'd have been seen as a bit . . . indelicate, maybe."

"Sort of Matisse-ish, aren't they?"

"Yes. Or Bloomsbury. Very much of their day. But *sui generis,* too. His style—crisp but also suggestive. The shapes, the depth he achieved—like the ducks downstairs."

"And large-scale wasn't really his thing. He was an engraver."

"Quite."

They stood in silence. The room danced.

Downstairs again, Brian said, "Come and have a look at my jungle garden. That is the next restoration project."

Outside, he paused beside her car, frowning, and pointed at the windscreen—the little star of shattered glass. "When did this happen?"

"Oh—not long before I got here. A stone flew up. Luckily it didn't do more damage."

"But you can't drive on with it like that, you know."

"Surely? It's just a chip."

"No. The glass is weakened. It could all go. And it's bang in front of you. Not safe."

"I didn't realize. Oh, goodness . . ."

"I'll get on the phone. We should be able to sort something out. Go and look at what will one day be the garden."

She wandered through the long grass, thought that perhaps the apple trees were here back then. Was that a quince?

Presently he joined her. "I've found the people who do windscreens around here, but the man was off on a job. He's going to call back in an hour or so."

"Look, I'm so sorry," said Ruth. "I've entirely taken over your afternoon."

"It was going nowhere in particular, anyway. Fighting the bracken was rather losing its appeal. Would you care to go for a walk? I've left the answerphone on."

The lanes were different now. They had become friendly and inviting. They offered sprays of yellow honeysuckle, twists of vetch, bright ferns. Walking between the high banks, Ruth and Brian were a part of the place, it had digested them, there was mutual purpose—the lane was going that way, and they would go with it. When they heard the sound of a car, they stood against the bank while it went by, and endured its passage with resentment.

Ruth said, "The scale changes when you're walking."

"Exactly. You have to get on equal terms with landscape, and that means like this. I live with an Ordnance Survey map in my pocket."

"What's that purple stuff called?"

"No idea, I'm afraid. I haven't got to the Teach Yourself Botany course yet."

They were at the top of the hill now, and had stopped at a gateway. The land fell away down to the sea, a few miles off: the long gray reach of the Bristol Channel with two perched islands and the far rim of the Welsh coastline.

"Flatholm and Steepholm," said Brian. "Margam roughly opposite. The steelworks."

"Elsewhere. What people here must have thought—across the sea, miles away."

"Exactly." He looked at her, with a slight smile. She felt complacent. For some reason, it was necessary that this man should approve.

He went on, "But what would you have wanted to do about it. Go there? Stay away?"

She considered. "It would depend on circumstances . . . on when it is."

"Ah. Just so."

"If I'm prehistoric, I think I'd want to make a raft or something and go and see if there's anything useful there. Later on . . . maybe I'd wonder if there's more work over there, better opportunities."

"Actually," he said, "in the nineteenth century it was the other way round. Welsh miners were coming over here to work in the iron ore mines up on the Brendons."

"Then maybe I'd marry one of them."

He laughed. "You undoubtedly did. Plenty of Welsh names around here. I say . . . you've quite latched onto this, haven't you?"

They turned into a lane that plunged steeply down, walked through a hamlet—scattered cottages, farm building—and stopped by a little whitewashed church that sat above the hedge bank. Brian looked at his watch. "I suppose we have to be getting back. That chap should be phoning soon."

They walked slowly. Ruth talked about Lorna and Matt, about what happened, about Lucas. He listened intently.

"I had no idea the cottage came with so much baggage. I feel a gate-crasher."

"You shouldn't. You found the paintings. And someone else might have junked the blocks, and the figure."

"I shall be the custodian, then." He shot her a glance. "And what about you? You mentioned you'd be on your way to Devon. Holiday?"

She explained Sam. She lightly sketched the children, the gallery, her work. No need to overload the man.

He spoke of his own work. A grown-up daughter was mentioned, studying in America. They were walking up the side of a field now, the roof of the cottage visible at the top of the rise.

Ruth went upstairs to the bathroom. When she came down, he was standing in the kitchen, the phone in his hand. "Message. There's a nuisance I'm afraid." His expression was not that of a man who is finding any great problem. "They can't get the right screen until tomorrow. I don't see any alternative but for you to stay here overnight."

"Oh, heavens . . ." she said. "Look, I can't do that. I've imposed on you quite enough as it is. There'll be some local B and B . . ."

"No way. I'm already considering the dinner options. I've got some lamb chops in the fridge. Or there's the Indian in Williton."

"Oh dear . . . I feel awful about this. Well—thank you."

She took her mobile outside to call Sam, and stood there in the late afternoon sunshine.

She found that she was not feeling particularly awful after all.

"Sam? I've had a bit of a hitch . . ."

She sat on the sofa in the sitting-room, looking through a local publication of old photographs of the area, at Brian's suggestion. "Nostalgia industry. But there are some that give you an idea of how it was in your grandparents' day."

Farm workers in shirtsleeves and open waistcoats. Flat caps everywhere. Horse-drawn farm vehicles. Many bicycles. Women's Institute members in flowery pinnies. Little boxy cars.

Ruth peered at this black and white world, which, of course, for them had not been black and white at all but rich color, and normal, expected, unexceptional—the world as it was, and how could it be otherwise? Very young Lorna wore a pinny, perhaps. Certainly they had bikes.

She could hear the creak of floorboards as Brian moved around overhead. He seemed to be doing a lot of moving. He had vanished upstairs a while ago on some unstated mission, leaving her with this booklet.

She looked around the room again. It was a comfortable room, and would be cosy in winter, with that big radiator under the window. On this summer evening, all the doors were open. In the kitchen, the table had been laid for supper, and there was wine in the fridge—Ruth had insisted on bringing some out from the box intended for Sam.

Molly had remembered little of this place—a few stored images that she would pull up and talk of occasionally. The hens that laid their eggs in the hedge, where they weren't supposed to. Ice on puddles. Those homemade toys. Blood on her leg after she had gashed it on a gate. This gate, here? Ruth set aside the photograph book and considered the ducks, the willows, the water. Molly never spoke of those; perhaps they were furnishings so mundane, so accepted, that they vanished from her memory. What kind of duck is that, and that?

Brian was clattering down the stairs. He appeared in the doorway, looking rather smug. "Some rejigging of the resources. I am sleeping on the couch in the study, and you are having my bedroom. I've changed the sheets. I want you to wake up in the morning and see the frescos."

"Oh—you shouldn't have done that. But it's a very kind thought—thank you."

"Now I need to pay some attention to our supper, or you'll regret the decision to eat here rather than have a jaunt to Williton."

He returned presently with glasses of wine. "All under control." He pointed at the book of photographs. "Yesteryear is big business. You'll have noted the brown signs on all sides—the place is made to earn its living, and a good slice of the living is what's over and done with."

"The steam train."

"That—and a good deal else. But transport is of much interest, here as anywhere. Vintage car rallies. Gatherings of old tractors."

"I wonder why. Vintage leaves me cold, I'm afraid."

"It's a man thing, on the whole. Not this man, either. Though transport as such is certainly grist to my mill. How people got where they did, and why. Perceptions of time and space. Early travelers. The movements of armies. Oh dear, I'm off again."

"Please keep going."

"You're being very tolerant. I get quite bottled up, on my own here, and become the Ancient Mariner when a visitor appears. Have you ever heard of the Harepath?" He described the west country track, still visible at points up on Exmoor, along which Saxon farmers moved when summoned to war—the army path. "Ninth-century motorway. Now *they* certainly saw space differently."

"So do children. The world shrinking as they grow. Maybe they experience the whole process—from crawling to staggering to running. And they *always* want to get to the other place—the elsewhere."

He laughed. "I'd not thought of that. I like it."

"Alice," said Ruth, "drinking from that bottle, and getting larger and larger. Her arm sticking out of the window. That's all about confusions over size and space."

"Of course. Thank you. I see a promising digression here."

"And what about fairy story? The seven-league boots. That's about somehow defeating space."

"Jack and the beanstalk. Quite so. *The Arabian Nights*—magic carpets. This is a rich seam."

"And time comes into it too. The Sleeping Beauty. Rip van Winkle. What's all that about?"

"Hmmn . . . Escaping time? Stepping aside. Resisting the dictation of."

From the kitchen there came an imperative ping. They both laughed.

Brian got up. "That is telling me the potatoes are nearly done. And I must put the chops on."

"What shall I do?"

"The salad, perhaps."

They ate with the door open onto the evening. Ruth thought: This was not supposed to happen. I am supposed to be in Devon now, not sitting here having a meal with someone I never met until a few hours ago. About to sleep in the room in which my mother was born. This is a kink in time—my personal time. Contingency moving in—twitching you off course. That passing car, the stone on the road, and me—all meeting up at that moment.

Brian pointed out that bats were flying past—a black flicker against the midnight blue sky. "Now the bat perception of space is something else, by all accounts. I think we won't go there. Shall we have coffee outside? Dark—but not particularly cold."

He guided her across the grass with a torch, to the seat he had put under one of the old apple trees. From there, the cottage was a shadowy outline; the lit window glowed, private and inviting. Crisp stars above. The bats.

"An owl has to hoot," said Ruth. "To make it pure film set."

"I'm afraid they do, occasionally."

"Lucas—Heron Press Lucas—remembered it being very primitive back then. A standpipe outside. And he never mentioned the frescos. I suppose he forgot them."

"Do you think I should have public open days?"

"And a brown sign?" She laughed. "I think not. Sacrilege. They'll be for a select few only."

"A Matt Faraday Society, perhaps? Annual conference on Blue Anchor beach."

"He does have his admirers. It's connoisseur stuff." She paused; behind this talk there lay the reality of the young man and woman who had been here, once. Beached, now, decades past, while the place strode on.

"I went to Crete once, a few years ago," she said. And told him about that time. Well, not quite all. And Brian, too, it seemed, knew it, had visited when in pursuit of ancient Mediterranean trade routes. For a while, that sunsoaked landscape hung against the Somerset night.

"Are you getting cold?" He stood up. "And we didn't finish that wine."

Back inside, she said, "What time is the windscreen man coming tomorrow?"

He looked vague. "Oh—I'm not too sure. I'll call them first thing. Do you have a deadline for getting to Devon?"

"Well, I told my stepfather I'd probably be there about lunchtime."

It was nearly midnight before Ruth got into bed. They had talked on. Generalities; particularities. Lying there, before she fell deeply asleep, she was aware of a continuous flow, rare with a stranger, in which one theme segued into another, without a break, in which his views on contemporary farming practices had somehow become Ruth's account of selling artworks. She had glimpsed a life: a marriage long expired, a flat in that northern city, students, colleagues, commitments. She knew that she too must be supplying clues, hints. They cleared up the kitchen together; later, there was a polite skirmish about who should use the bathroom first. As she washed, Ruth looked at the shaving stuff, his bits and pieces, and realized that it was years since she had shared a bathroom with a man. This is all very odd, she had thought. But odd is all it is. That's all.

When she woke, it was full morning. Eight o'clock, and the bird life in full cry. She got up, drew the curtains, and lay there looking. She counted the figures. Were they meant to be a sequence, a troop, or the same couple repeated all around. They had no features, they were just flying figures—arms, legs, breasts, buttocks. The woman was fuller, softer; he was more taut, more muscular. Were they Lorna and Matt?

She heard Brian go downstairs. Then he came up again, and there was a knock.

"Come in."

Gingerly, he stuck his head around the door. "Thought you might care for a cup of tea." He put it on the chest of drawers and was gone.

When she came down he was getting breakfast. "I've spoken to the man, and it seems he can't make it until after lunch. Is that going to be a problem for you?"

"Not for me. I can tell Sam. But I'm not going to take up any more of your time. I'll just sit around—or go for a walk—and you must get on with what you're doing."

He grinned. He seemed to be in high spirits, like someone about to go on holiday, about to break out. "I have a plan. Sit. Toast coming up. Marmalade or honey? Tea or coffee?"

She watched him as he reached for this and that, talked. A little clumsy—the bread knife got dropped; short-sighted—he had to peer at a label before tutting and throwing a jar into the bin. "No, no—use before *January.*" She was wanting to smile. Why? His mood was contagious. Outside, the morning sang on.

The plan involved a drive, a walk. "My mystery tour. Your introduction to these parts. Up over the moor for a bit, then down to the alabaster beach in honor of Matt's little figure."

Introduction? She thought. Am I coming back?

It was a day of flying sun and cloud, the light changing from moment to moment. The stubble field alongside the cottage was yellow as sunshine. Beyond, the hillside was brilliant—a complexity of fields, a copse, one single patch of rich red earth—all of it set against dark gray cloud, against which stood a rainbow.

They got into his car. He was cavalier with the lanes, whipping confidently ahead, bolting into gateways when something came. They climbed, they rose up into space, amid the great slack contours of the moor, that reached away, that folded down into green combes. They stopped, got out, and walked for a bit along a heathery path, sat for a while on a great stone by a gate. He waved a hand: "Dunkery Beacon. Highest point. We haven't got time to go up. Perhaps another . . ." He bit off the end of the sentence, looked away.

She concentrated on the view: the purple hillside, a flare of yellow gorse, a little knot of sheep in a gully. What did he . . . ? Is this what I think?

They got back into the car. He was talking fervently of some conservation issue, his eyes screwed up against the sun.

She found that she had said, "You need dark glasses." It was meant to be a thought. She told herself: don't be a fool. This is not happening. Calm down.

He said, "You're right. I think there are some in that pocket. Could you . . ."

She found the glasses. He fumbled in her hand for them, took a bend rather too fast, narrowly missed the rear end of a sheep grazing on the verge. "Sorry. Nearly got it. The local roadkill."

They came down from the moor, drove across a vale, skirted Minehead. He waved at sparkling white canopies in the distance: "Butlins. Temple of holidays. You get used to the architecture. I quite like it." They arrived at the coast, the sea. He pitched the car through a caravan site. "We park here. Bit of a scramble down the cliff." They got out, left the caravans behind and the playing children, lolloping dogs, and walked over short turf pocked with rabbit holes. Someone's kite had escaped, a ribbon of blue that undulated overhead. Gulls floated, banked, fell beyond the clifftop in front of them. They climbed up, and were on the edge: a gray pebbled beach below, rocks, an expanse of shining muddy sand. Far off, a frill of waves, the tide right out. Ruth stood, taking all this in. He was beside her, and when she turned to speak he was not looking ahead but at her, had been for moments, she sensed—an intent look, an intimate look, that hung on after she turned to him.

He said, "There's the path down. Mind how you go—it's sometimes slippery."

She forgot what she had been going to say, followed him down. His back, his outline, just ahead, seemed infinitely familiar: that green shirt, his gray-flecked hair, the slightly awkward action, as though he found his legs too long. How can a person you've not known for twenty-four hours become familiar?

They walked on the shingle. He pointed out the seams of alabaster in the cliff, gray and rose-colored. "Apparently the time to find good bits is after the winter, when there have been cliff falls." They picked up a couple of small chunks. As must Matt have done, thought Ruth. Brian found another, and another, pressing them into her hands. "What do I do with all this?" she protested, laughing. Her cotton sun hat was full of opaque, veined rocks.

"Goodness knows. Doorstops? Paperweights? *Objets d'art?*"

They sat on a slab of rock. A gull watched children fishing in a pool. Further off, a boy reeled out another kite. Thin cries all around—other children, a calling parent, other gulls.

"The tide seems to be . . ."

"When are you . . ."

Both speaking at once. Both now embarrassed.

"I was going to say," she said, "that the tide is coming in. Waves a bit nearer."

"Right. Time and tide, and all that. Wonderfully concentrates the mind. I am fifty-four."

"I am forty-four."

"I know. I mean, I didn't know—what nonsense. What I meant was . . . I'm getting to the point when there's a certain tendency to seize the day."

"This one," said Ruth, staring ahead, "is a particularly seizable one."

"What *I* had been about to say was—when are you likely to be this way again?"

He turned. She turned. And now they are looking at one another. In silence. She does not, for a moment—for moments—answer. She looks at him, and in his gaze she sees a possibility of something she has not yet known. It glimmers. In what she feels, in what she sees. A future floats in her head. I know, she thinks, and he knows, and we each know that the other knows. There is no need to say anything. Yet.

"Oh," she said, "I'm not sure. But I shall be. Definitely. Sooner or later."

"Sooner," he said, getting up. "Shall we meet the tide?"

They walked down to the waves. Ruth waded in a little way. The water coming in warm over the mud, your feet sinking in. They returned to the car, talking about anything, about nothing in particular, about everything—this sub-text hanging in there now, unspoken, understood. They stopped at a pub, ate sandwiches, wondered at the array of real ales, laughed over the pretensions of the menu. Brian sighed: "Gone are the days of scotch eggs and a ploughman's."

Back at the cottage, there was a van parked outside. "He's beaten us to it," said Brian.

Ruth's car had a new windscreen. The mechanic was sitting on the doorstep, making out an invoice. Brian went inside while Ruth wrote a check.

"Nice spot," said the man. "Been here long, have you?"

"Oh—I'm just a visitor. I'm leaving now."

"Have a good journey, then."

She went inside. Brian was sitting at the kitchen table, with the blocks and the alabaster figure in front of him. She said, "I'll just go up and get my things together."

Upstairs, she put her case on the bed, gathered up her brush and comb, toilet bag, nightdress, her other pair of shoes. She packed, then sat on the bed, looking around her, to check for anything forgotten. She was aware of the dancing figures; she was aware, too, of sounds beyond the window—those enraptured birds, the far-off train. It seemed as though she had been here, in this place, for a very long time, as though the last twenty-four hours had strung out like elastic, unrelated to an ordinary day. Someone else, not her, some other Ruth, had left home yesterday; today, she was this new person, who was staring at a possibility, at a probability, at—perhaps—a certainty.

She went down.

He said, "I'm going to come clean. The windscreen chap. I fixed for him to come in the afternoon. So there could be more time. He would have come at ten. Entirely underhand, I'm afraid."

"Yes, entirely." She was smiling.

He got up. "I suppose you're going to go now."

"Yes."

He picked up her bag. She took the blocks, and the figure. They went outside. The bags, the block, and the figure were put into the car.

"When?" he said.

"Soon."

"It had better be."

They stood there, face-to-face. He reached out, put his hands on either side of her shoulders, held her thus for a moment. Then he stepped aside.

Ruth got into the car. He watched her put the keys in the ignition, start up.

"Do you know where you're going?"

"Probably not," she said. "It won't matter."

She drove out of the gate. When she glanced in the mirror she saw him standing there, one hand raised. Then she turned into the lane—that would take her away, that would bring her back.